FAT MAN AND LITTLE BOY

FAT MAN AND LITTLE BOY

a novel

Mike Meginnis

Black Balloon Publishing

New York

Published by Black Balloon Publishing
blackballoonpublishing.com

Copyright © 2014 by Mike Meginnis
All rights reserved

ISBN: 978-1-936787-20-3

Black Balloon Publishing titles are distributed to the trade by
Consortium Book Sales and Distribution
Phone: 800-283-3572 / SAN 631-760X

Library of Congress Control Number: 2014936998

Designed and composed by Jonathan Yamakami
Printed in Canada

9 8 7 6 5 4 3 2 1

for Tracy, my first and best reader

Contents

PRELUDE

Two bombs over Japan. Two shells.

One called Little Boy, one called Fat Man. Three days apart. The one implicit in the other.

Brothers.

If a person were to film them falling, it would have to be from a great distance, through a veil of Japanese cities: old homes, new factories, idling cars, passing carts, and kites. Little Boy or Fat Man a black spot, center-screen. Encircled, in future broadcasts, by white light: an emphatic moon where otherwise they would be missed, descending as the gnat-speck plummets.

Until pika don—"flash boom."

Or one might film them from the plane above. Some enterprising journalist or rising military star would begin with the shell in profile, waiting in the plane's cold, clamorous womb. It would fill the screen.

Then the hatch would open underneath. Fat Man or Little Boy would drop out of sight. The camera would pan down to watch the bomb shrink until it was a pinprick. Until it could not be sorted from the landscape below—the factories, the homes, the tangle of power lines.

Until pika don.

The swell of light.

FAT MAN MEETS
HIS BROTHER

Two soldiers tall and short at the edge of what was their city. Their empty rifles at rest on their shoulders. These cast long, frail shadows across gray earth. The tall soldier has a bright bolt of silk bundled in his free hand, tucked up against his gut. The short soldier has been limping several days; his foot snags on an empty can. The tall soldier catches him by the elbow. A word of gratitude. The tall soldier slows his pace to ease his fellow's travel.

Two soldiers search for living things and dead. Search for useful things and not. To see what has become, and come, and comes, becoming. To visit. To crawl. To know. When they grow tired they will rest in beds of ash or on well-angled slabs of concrete. They will sleep or they will close their eyes and pretend. They will feel a mystery at work beneath their skins.

They come to what was once a home. One wall still stands, the rest suggested by foundations—it was two stories, narrow, built from white stone. The morning's low sun shines through an open second-story window, shutters skewed, glass blown out. Although through the window, or the window's absence, it seems perhaps a little dimmer, a little more gray, as if colored by memory of glass.

Beside what was a home, in the long shadow of the standing wall, a bomb shelter. Squat concrete box two-thirds submerged. Stairs fitted to a niche in the earth, eight of them, deep. The tall soldier goes down first. He aims his empty rifle at the door. The short soldier follows down and reaches around him to open the door, slowly, slowly, unlocking it first with the key that they found. He levels his rifle as well. They put the business ends of their weapons through the narrow opening. They lead with these, and cast new shadows on the far wall. The short soldier stays behind the tall so as to hide his limp.

Inside there is a fat man lying naked on his side, arms wrapped around himself, hands tucked beneath, knees pressed to gut. A candle flickers by his side. The flame leans toward him as if pulled. His hair is all burnt off, eyebrows too, and beard. His head is fuzzed with brown stubble. His body smooth and hairless like a baby's body. Pink and pale. Soft.

Fat Man opens his eyes. He asks the soldiers a question. It must be English. He asks another, plaintive. His whole body racked with shivering as the fresh, cold air comes in. His whole skin reared up in gooseflesh. He asks another question.

The tall one throws him the bright fabric bundle. Its falling unfurling reveals a robe, silk and purple, embroidered with a blue flower pattern. It falls over his body, across his hips. He asks another question. He touches the silk and rubs it between his fingers, face twitching with hints of surprise, pleasure, fear, need, want. He asks another question. The tall one tells him to be quiet, though Fat Man will not understand.

The day they brought him his robe they did not bring any-thing else, or ever come back, until the next day, when his feeding was resumed.

Fat Man can stand inside the bunker, barely. Sometimes he paces, stooped for fear of bumping his head. Sometimes he sits up, folds his legs beneath him, and commences waiting for his daily meal. Sometimes he thinks about what he has done. How it was to fall. To explode.

Now, the Japanese soldiers come once a day. They open the door enough to let in a long sliver of light, which is crossed in-termittently by the slanted shadows of their arms and legs, and which climbs the wall as tap water climbs a glass. They lead with the tips of their guns so he knows they can kill him if they want to do that. He wants to know why they don't want to do that. He asks but they do not say. He asks them if he is free yet. He asks them when he will be free or otherwise dealt with. He considers the possibility of escape. The odds look slim. He is not quick on his feet. He asks them what's happening outside. He asks them how bad has it gotten or if things are better. They slide in a bowl of sticky white rice and a black crust of bread. They slide in a bowl of water. They give him candles and matches. He thinks the matches may be useful, and so he saves them, using the candles to light one another, pressing them end to end as if they are kissing.

He can tell when night falls by the distant hum of crickets, certain bird calls, and the quality of the air. He lets his candle burn until it is a glossy little pool of burning wax, a circle of fire. The wax spreads beneath it, becoming a spider. The spider's body becomes a char circle, becomes an ashy mushroom cap on the floor. The fire goes out. Then it is time to lie in the dark and do his best to sleep. His arms curled up beneath his head to make a pillow, his knees against his keening gut, he shivers. He rolls a little back and forth to make warmth.

He remembers. Dreams and memory devour the night, mingled beyond recognition. Half-faces and crumpled hands, footprints, coral reef.

He pees in the corner. He tries sometimes to open the door in case they have forgotten to lock it. The door locks from the outside and the inside, but they have the key. They have not yet forgotten to lock it. He has considered blocking the door with his body so they cannot come in. He thinks they could not shoot him through the heavy door. But neither could they feed him.

He tries to tie his robe more tightly closed. There is too much give in the cloth. The sleeves are frayed and offer little warmth. The bunker grows hot at midday, after the soldiers come with his meal and before his hunger remembers itself. It grows cold in the night.

He sits at the center of the room, making shadow puppets in the light of his candle, pretending to be a tree. Pretending to sway in the wind. Watching his tree-shadow sway as he sways. He makes a hand-turtle come out of its shell, tremble at the world, and duck back in. Peering from inside, sniffing the air. He makes a hand-rabbit leap around the room until it falls and breaks its leg. It snuffles, waits to die.

He is given to uncontrollable fits of sobbing without apparent cause, or with causes too trivial for words: the way his walrus shadow climbs the wall so that his head looms on the ceiling like an astral body. The first and last sparks of certain candles. The way his water trickles back between his feet after it rolls down the wall.

On the fourth day he can't hold it in anymore. He shits on the floor. The smell is terrible, though his candles obscure it, and on the fifth day the soldiers come in to see what he's done. There are purple blotches all over their faces and necks but he doesn't know what it means. They curse at him, using the only English words they know, as one guards him with a ready rifle and the other scoops up his mess with a shoe. It leaves a long brown smear like a sunflower shadow. The smell fades.

He finds that he can light his candles merely by touching their wicks with a finger. Once lit, this flame burns bright and tall, blue and angry. Wherever he goes in the room, the flame follows, leaning toward him as if pointing him out in a lineup. These flames cannot be snuffed but must exhaust themselves in their own time.

He gives up checking the lock and tells himself he has forgotten checking, so there is one less thing to worry about.

He plays with his body until it becomes strange.

On the seventh day he dreams of eating one of the burnt bodies outside the bunker. Beneath the charred black crust of their skin he imagines a pink, soft meat like salmon steaks. On the eighth day the soldiers do not come. On the ninth day they do not come. He shits again, mostly water. It makes him feel even more empty. He is hungry all the time. He is always looking at the door, waiting for the door to open. For instance he will count down from a high number, thinking that surely they must come for him before he can count down from a thousand, from ten thousand, from a hundred thousand.

He tries closing his eyes as long as he can bear it. Tries sleeping but can't sleep. Tries singing but he doesn't know a song. Tries thinking about women. Tries counting again. Assures himself they're on their way. Finds it easier to sleep as the hunger progresses, as he has less and less energy with which to want and think and need.

He remembers how it was to explode.

It was everything coming out everywhere. Shit and puke and blood and scream.

It was being the world.

It was having no body.

It was screaming till his scream was all he could hear and finding there was air still in his lungs: that he could scream forever.

It was sitting perfectly still at the center of a concrete cube.

It was his candle's first flare.

It was standing in place and spreading his arms and spinning and spinning and spinning until he didn't know if he was falling or flying.

It was none of these things.

This is how it was to explode:

It was like being born.

On the tenth day there is a sound outside the door. When the sound comes he is pretending to be a tree with burning wood like a barrier reef inside it. He is pretending to burst at the seams by pulling his robe open, like a flasher, and pushing out his gut. The knob twists in clumsy hands. The Japanese soldiers never fumbled with the door. This is someone else.

Fat Man scoots back against the wall and ties his robe closed. The movement of the candle's flame makes the walls seem to bloat and collapse. The door opens a sliver. There are no machine gun nostrils in the light that climbs the wall. The door opens wide. The light spreads like wings. There is a slight, distended shadow at its center. It is a little boy. He could be as young as eight or as old as thirteen. He is gawky and thin, and his bones all protrude from his limbs like knobs on a young tree. His hair is so fair it looks white; it sticks out like soft straw from under the brim of his blue felt fedora. He wears a matching suit. He runs his fingers over the wide black suspenders beneath his blue jacket. Fat Man cannot read his expression—though the edges of the boy's body are lit and bright, the center is dark, nearly black. He can only see the outer corners of the boy's eyes, which are white. Between those corners, shadow.

There is recognition. There is shame at the smell of the shelter, the filth of his body.

Little Boy says, "So, you are my brother."

HOW BROTHERS
TRAVEL TOGETHER

Little Boy is urging his brother out of his hole. Fat Man says he is not afraid, yet he trembles at the threshold.

"Then why are you shaking?" says Little Boy.

"I'm cold," says Fat Man. "This robe is all I have."

"I'll keep you safe if you come out," says Little Boy.

"I'm weak with hunger," says Fat Man.

"I'll feed you once you're out of there."

That does it. Fat Man takes a step out of the doorway. The sun hits him full-on; squinting his bleary eyes against its light, he sways on his feet. He holds on to the doorframe, waiting for his dizzy spell to pass.

"Come on," says Little Boy. "Aren't you hungry?"

"Ravenous," growls the fat man. "Do you have the food or not?"

"Not on me, but we'll have it soon enough."

Sweating and starving, Fat Man heaves himself out of the

doorway. His knees shake and strain as he forces his feet up the stairs in heavy, leaden steps. He still hunches from habit, as if the bunker's low ceiling has followed him out. Little Boy leads him up, walking backward, coaxing, "Come on big fella. Come on."

They sit together at the top of the stairs, not quite touching. Little Boy looks at their feet—his leather shoes, the fat man's bare, dirty feet.

Fat Man is like a shaved bear wrapped in someone's expensive drapes. His lips are full, his toes and digits wide, his skin smooth and soft as cream. His neck quivers like a rodent's breast when he speaks. His fingernails are all bitten down, the toenails peeled. A week's growth mosses his head.

Fat Man says, "I don't believe you are my brother." But he can feel it, the same atomic pull. Their elbows touch.

Little Boy says, "But I'm so happy to meet you."

"Are you?" says Fat Man.

Little Boy revises his expression several times until he finds the one that feels right for this occasion. Eyebrows raised, mouth-corners rising, eyes wide with pleasure, cheeks shading pink by degree and degree. He says. "Can't you see how happy I am?"

"If that's what it looks like, I guess you must be." Fat Man mirrors Little Boy's expression to see how it feels. He tries variations. He touches his face. "Happiness," he says.

Little Boy insists he is happy, that this is what happiness looks like. He wiggles his feet—his shoes squeak on the cement step.

Fat Man says, "Then I guess I'm happy too, if this is how that feels."

Little Boy and Fat Man sit and wonder if they are really happy, if they look happy, if someone else would be able to tell them.

They keep their eyes low, glancing at each other's downcast profiles as briefly as they can, so as not to see the wastes of Nagasaki. There is nothing to see.

"If you are really my brother," says Fat Man, "then you will know how it was to explode."

The little boy frowns. He pats his left thigh, his right, stalling. "How do you mean?"

"Are you my brother, or aren't you?"

Little Boy sighs. "It was like being born."

Fat Man asks Little Boy did he like being born.

Little Boy says, "What's to like?"

"Let's find food."

"So am I your brother?"

"I can't think on an empty stomach."

Standing, they face the city's ruin. Fat Man asks Little Boy does he think there is food in the wastes. Little Boy says there must be. He says, "There are still people living in there."

"What are they doing alive?"

"Mostly they seem to be sleeping." Little Boy tells what he's seen so far: Bodies that from a distance seemed done with life, but, more closely observed, revealed themselves as dreaming, bleeding, faintly breathing, on a bed of any given thing, or dirt. Some also clutched knives, or bowls with jagged broken edges, or horseshoes, or broomsticks, or other improvised weapons. They warned him off. Some reached for him with shaking, open hands. When he offered his hand in return this was not what they wanted; they must have wanted food; his warmth stuck slightly to their cold skin as they tugged free.

One woman did not let him go. She pulled Little Boy close, so that he lay down beside her, huddled up into her core. Her legs were pinned beneath a heavy bookshelf. Her blood had soaked into the books. It tarred and clotted their pages, scabbed them over. She wrapped her working arm around him. Some time later that day, he couldn't say when, she died. He stayed a little while after he knew. Then he left her, taking nothing with him from her home, though there were canned goods piled in another room. He would regret this later, and regrets it now. He could have fed his brother. He does not know the way back.

Fat Man asks him how he came to open the door.

"It was unlocked," says Little Boy.

Fat Man tries on another expression—it seems to be surprise. He feels his face to know what he's made. By hand he adjusts certain features. Now he seems surprised and saddened. Now he shifts them again, this time without his hands. He looks afraid. "We should go," he says. "They could still come back."

Little Boy says, "How do you think two brothers travel?"

"In this country?"

"Anywhere. Do they hold hands?"

"They might hold hands."

"Do they go side by side, or does one lead the other?"

"Side by side, I would imagine," says Fat Man.

"Do they speak or are they quiet?"

"I should think it depends on their mood."

"May I walk by your side?" says Little Boy. "May I hold your hand? May we speak to each other?"

"I will not hold your hand yet," says Fat Man. "I am not sure you are my brother."

They walk side by side into the waste.

The sun is falling. The clouds are frayed like Fat Man's sleeves. A black bird settles on a lamppost knocked askew. Ash lifts on a breeze, lilts this way and that, returns to the earth. Every building's shadow is injured. They have holes in them, or walls are missing. Fat Man finds an empty can of food. Only a sweet brown smell remains. Little Boy finds three dry grains of rice.

They find two bodies knocked dead by impacts to their heads. Their faces are crushed beyond recognition. Their bodies slim and sexless. They lay side by side. One body's arm flung carelessly across the other body. One body's wearing sandals while the other's feet are bare, and curled inward, as if the toes are reaching for their matching heels. If these bodies are brothers then this is how brothers die together.

Little Boy crouches to study them more closely. From inside them maggots come up and out for air—white studs in their skin become stunted worms. First six, then a dozen, then many seething. They eat through the bodies' faces, they fall from their ears. Little Boy startles, cries out, jumps back. The maggots calm. Some lie still on the bodies like white cashews. Others die and shrivel. Others burrow back into the flesh.

There are no flies here.

The brothers leave those bodies. They leave that place. Little Boy imagines worms inside him. How it would be to see them bursting through his skin.

Fat Man asks him when they'll find food. Little Boy says he doesn't know. He says Fat Man needs to be calm. Fat Man says it's been days since he's eaten. He says, "If you were my brother you would feed me."

The sun goes down. Things turn blue, gray, black. The brothers find a shadow on a wall. An image of a painter on a folding ladder. He has a bucket of paint in one hand, and in his other hand a brush. He reaches for the wall to apply the paint. The folding ladder is angled sideways so that Little Boy can see the gaps between the ladder's steps like spokes in a wheel. The painter's posture is stiff. The painter's body is gone. The ladder is broken in half, there, on the ground.

Little Boy touches the shadow. Cold, like the rest of the wall. He can feel Fat Man's eyes on him. There is a surge of heat through his body. He tries to rub it away but it won't go away. He thinks how it would be to reach out with that brush but never touch the wall. He tries to rub it away but it won't go away. Fat Man says he should leave it alone.

"We need to leave this place," says Little Boy.

He means Japan.

They walk together side by side in the way that brothers might do.

Fat Man asks Little Boy how he was born. Little Boy says he will tell it.

HOW LITTLE BOY
WAS BORN

Little Boy woke alone, lying naked on his side, curled inward. It was quiet. The ground was hot. He was afraid. Pink and pale.

Soft.

He pushed himself up on his feet. Faltered. Tipped forward and back. There were no people there. He called out for help. The wind was gentle but he lost his voice in it. His throat felt dry. Inside his body, a strand of whisper that couldn't get out.

There were crooked trees in the distance, black and pulled apart. There were ruined buildings far away. Everything close was rubble and dust. There were bits of wood and glass, and concrete powder on the air.

There was no one to see him standing there. No mommy. No daddy. He held himself and shivered.

He stood on a bald white depression.

Dozens of small fires burned in the wreckage. He walked forward. He needed away.

There was a cart wheel, there was a yoke.

There was a leveled home. There was the floor of the home.

Thin black smoke rose like a solid climbing thing, gnarled as the trees.

As he walked past the ruined home, bits of glass and wood and rubble pierced his feet. He left red footprints in the ash. It hurt badly. He didn't know what to do. He was breathing ash. He was caked with ash. His lungs burned. There was no good air to breathe. A body burned black was on the ground. Its skin had all peeled off and lay in rags around it. Its sex was burnt away, leaving only a lump or a crease between the legs. The fingers were the same. They were nubs. Its teeth had all been shaken from its head. They were scattered in the dirt like seeds. He shivered. He held himself.

Stone walls spilled broken on the ground.

There was a woman in the dirt, shielded by the wall that crushed her head. He could see her through the cracks in the wall where it was broken, where it fell. Her blood ran downhill, the hill on which he stood. She gave more and more. He stumbled on through more bodies. He walked over a stone bridge, across a stream that was white from the dust. There was a baby smeared across the ground.

There were papers from a painter's home, torn and weighted down by rocks, lumber, and dirt.

He came to a sapling. Stripped and blackened like the rest, with several broken branches hanging from its bough. It stood at a sad, sloping angle, pointing at the sun. It looked like a hair. A loose branch fell to land among the roots.

Behind the tree a standing wall. Ten feet high, not one foot more.

Only a section, the rest fallen and scattered.

Its edges rough, uneven like an old saw.

The window blown out, the glass all gone, the drapes thrown forty feet away.

It was a square window, four feet up, two feet wide, two feet tall.

There was a thin tree shadow on the wall. A black silhouette. This was the sapling as it was before. There were seven long branches, seven delicate arms, seven reaching tendrils. They searched the wall. One shadow branch reached into the window. The leaves were small faint smudges of gray, the wall was flecked with them. He sat down beneath the tree to rest his legs and aching feet. He coughed dust and blood into his hands. He watched the shadow on the wall. The tree behind him moved, swayed slowly in the breeze, searching the sky like a finger. Its shadow was still.

"Now do you believe I am your brother?" asks Little Boy. They are resting up against a squat gray pedestal where a statue once stood. They are careful not to touch.

Fat Man says, "How long have you been born?"

"Only a few days before you."

"So you're supposed to be my big brother?"

"I'll try to take care of you."

Fat Man says he doesn't think he can be taken care of by someone who can't even find him any food. He says that maybe he should leave his older brother, that they should part ways. He stands and makes to leave.

"Wait," yells Little Boy, who struggles to his feet and looks up at him with wide, pleading eyes. Little Boy steps close to Fat Man and wraps his arms around his leg. He squeezes him through the silken robe, presses his forehead to Fat Man's rubbery hip. His little hands are warm, though also bony.

Fat Man feels how very small his new big brother is. He puts one hand on Little Boy's back and his other on the crown of his head, which soothes the boy and relaxes his body. "Okay," says Fat Man.

Little Boy's eyes close. "Thank you."

Fat Man asks his new big brother what they're going to do.

"We're going to take care of each other," says Little Boy. "We're going to find you something to eat. Then we're going to find a way out of here."

Fat Man says, "I don't like it here at all."

Nobody does.

THE SOLDIER'S BODY

It is not long before they find the shorter soldier's body face-down in the shattered fragments of a limestone statue. The dashed pieces suggest that the statue was a furry creature, perhaps with a mane and clawed feet. The shorter soldier's gun is gone. His left arm is folded under him. The right arm points outward, three o'clock. The purple blotches have expanded through his skin; they have multiplied. Fat Man squats for a closer look. Little Boy turns his back on the body.

The taller soldier is nowhere in sight.

Fat Man says, "He had a limp. He tried to hide it."

"Why hide a limp from you?" says Little Boy.

Fat Man says he doesn't know. He says he thinks the soldiers were afraid. He says, "They found me wandering and locked me up. They can't have known what I did. I think I was supposed to be a hostage, or a war criminal. They never answered my questions."

"They didn't speak English."

"They didn't even try," says Fat Man. He rocks on his heels, balancing with his hands on the ground. Chill air lifts the loose threads of his robe. "I kept asking and they didn't even try."

"What were you asking?"

Maggots come to the surface of the body. A spider crawls from its ear.

"I wanted to know where I was. Then I wanted to know why they were keeping me. Then I wanted to know how things had changed outside. I wanted to know if the fire was done, how many people died, how many survived. I wanted to know if they were ill. Why the short one was limping. I wanted to know their names. I wanted to know what they thought of me. What they were going to do with me. What they called me. Was I alone. Was there anyone who wanted to see me. I wanted to know if I could do something."

"Like what?" says Little Boy.

The maggots eat of the short soldier's neck, they sprout in his hands. They squirm barely perceived beneath the soldier's heavy jacket. Between the fingers, worms writhe. The spider crawls over the body.

"Like help," says Fat Man. "Like could I do some work for them, could I fix things, make them better. Could I do something to make them like me more."

The soldier's body begins to sag beneath its uniform. The skin is riddled with holes. The hungry things favor the purple blotches, eating them first.

Little Boy says they should leave the body. He says today is a bad day to be an American standing over a dead Japanese.

Fat Man says, "Soon there won't be a body."

Little Boy asks Fat Man what he means. Fat Man points and asks if it is normal for a body to decay so quickly. Another spider crawls from the ear, which so far the maggots and the worms have left intact. They have focused on the cheeks, what is visible

21

of the shoulder, and everything beneath the soldier's clothes—perhaps cartilage is difficult. More worms rise to the surface of the dirt. The uniform itself, now damp from inside with blood, begins to grow a cotton mold.

"Yes," says Little Boy, "this is normal."

"Are you sure?"

"We should go."

Instead Little Boy folds his legs beneath him. He scoots up close to watch. Fat Man feels a warmth rising from the body and the things that grow inside it. His legs begin to ache from squatting. His hands as well, from the weight he leans on them.

"The taller soldier might come back."

Little Boy says, "Then we should go."

They do not go. The body becomes bones. The maggots become flies. These land on the two brothers, skitter and buzz their wings, but do not fly, keeping to the skin.

Fat Man says, "They itch!"

"Swat them."

"Won't they fly away and land somewhere else?"

"They won't." Little Boy squashes several on his left hand with his right. They do not try to move away. They become black smears.

Fat Man falls back on his ass, sore feet briefly rising up into the air and then settling back in. He holds out his left palm. There are two flies walking a slow circuit from thumb tip to pinky finger. His right hand casts a shadow over the flies. They perhaps twitch or tremble, but otherwise stay where they are—become still, in fact, where before they were crawling. Like closing an alligator's jaws, he lowers his hand. What is left of the flies, he scrapes off on the ground, and proceeds to remove the others from his face and neck and calves, one by one, pinching them dead, flicking away their corpses.

"Good job," says Little Boy, encouraging his little brother as he kills his own flies too. "That's the way."

The bones stripped clean. The uniform a mold-fuzzed tatter. The worms creep toward the brother bombs, who stand up, step back. Little Boy puts his hand on Fat Man's stomach, pushes him back farther, to keep him safe.

Fat Man asks, "What are we?"

Little Boy says they are brothers. "Only brothers. Always brothers."

Now there are more flies.

A cloud of them looms over the brothers—the only brothers, the always brothers.

Little Boy says, "We should run."

Fat Man has already started. He can barely find the strength, but what's left is enough. The cloud of flies follows them, sending dizzy scouts, which the brothers swat, or fail to swat—they flail, the flies dive and buzz around their ears and eyes. As if to say, "Look at me!" As if to say, "Listen!" They need to be heard.

"Does this often happen also?" pants Fat Man.

Little Boy says, "Sometimes this happens." He is running with less speed than he could so as not to leave behind Fat Man, who is doing his best. He's panting and clutching at his chest.

Now Little Boy jogs backward, the better to see the swarm, which lilts as one fly lilts, now several feet lower, now several higher, now right, now left, some stragglers and some who go ahead, and here and there colliding—a tipsy weave. A seethe. Always angled so their eyes are on the brothers—compound eyes, like black jewels. Specks on specks.

Little Boy trips on something unseen, some piece of rubble, and tumbles. Fat Man stops to yank him up. The buzz of the flies is momentarily damped by a whistling gust of wind. Everything is quiet. The ground is covered in a fine gray powder, some smashed statue or wall. The powder, kicked up by the gust, enters their nostrils, burns in their throats.

Fat Man tries to catch his breath. Little Boy watches, helpless, as the swarm descends on his brother. They crowd his eyes and ears, his mouth—some seem to fly, quite intentionally, inside him—and crawl on his hands, his neck, under his collar, beneath his robe. He flaps his arms like useless wings.

"Brother!" calls Little Boy.

He picks up a road sign—something yellow, he doesn't know what it means—and uses it to crush the flies on Fat Man, flogging his brother. Fat Man might tell him to stop if he could speak through the flies. Now the flies remember Little Boy and crawl over him also. He can barely see his brother's shadow through the swarm. Reaches in, finds his brother's wrist, and yanks. "Run!" he screams, tasting a fly. Fat Man struggles out again.

The flies have gotten old. They're going gray. As the brothers flee, the swarm begins to fall. Landing in small puddles, in cups and bowls (some broken, some intact among the ruins of what were once homes), on cars with melted tires, on roads. Each fall punctuated by a sound, a small brittle dry snap, like the crackle of a fire: for every fly, the sound of one spark. Some pelt their backs and bounce away. Some land beneath their feet just as they're stepping.

They slow again as the flies die all around them.

They breathe.

Fat Man chews what they left in his cheeks without seeming to know that he chews. Little Boy ignores the crunching sound.

There were families here once. The brothers can tell from the books that lie here and there in the streets, like bodies.

They can tell from the bodies.

HOW FAT MAN
WAS BORN

They don't find anything. They can't. They try to sleep but Fat Man's rumbling keeps them up. They search the wastes. Fat Man takes a tube of flavorless toothpaste off the ground, rubs off ash with his fingers. The packaging is plain and white. The tube is half-empty, squeezed flat from bottom to middle. It curls in on itself like a rolled-up tongue. This is all that remains of somebody's home. Fat Man looks to Little Boy. He says, "Do you think it's safe?"

Little Boy says he's not sure. He says, "I don't think it's food."

Fat Man says he knows it isn't food. "What I'm asking," he says, "is whether I can eat it."

Little Boy says toothpaste can't be poison if you're supposed to put it in your mouth. It might, however, be very bad for you, and it can't taste good at all. Fat Man twists off the cap and drops it. He squeezes out the white paste along the length of his thumb. He sniffs the paste—smells nothing, nothing different from the taste of teeth and spit. He tips back his head and squeezes out the whole tube into his mouth. It fills his cheeks and throat, he nearly retches, but does not retch; he chokes it down. He drops the tube when it's all gone. He wipes his mouth.

"That's disgusting," says Little Boy.

"It's. Been. Days," Fat Man says, glaring down at Little Boy. "Wait. I see a cricket."

He runs away, kicking up ash and pebbles, heedless of his feet and the flapping of his robe. There is indeed a cricket poised perfectly still on the end of a curling iron pipe embedded in the dirt. He sinks to his knees and crawls toward the insect. He gets up close. It is still quite still. He opens his hands and prepares to clap, to clamp the little fiddler, which does not twitch, does not leap, sing, flutter. He squeals in triumph as he closes his fingers around this morsel and corks the cage with his thumbs.

The cricket does not struggle. Fat Man does not feel the expected frantic searching of his hands for exits. In fact he feels nothing. He opens his hands. The cricket stands unmoved at the curling pipe's end. He pinches the dead thing and drops it down his gullet.

Little Boy asks if there is anything Fat Man doesn't plan on eating tonight.

"You're lucky I don't eat you. I'm still hungry. I need *meat*."

"There isn't any meat," says Little Boy. Fat Man says of course there's meat. Little Boy says, "If you find it, that'll be the first I've seen. It's been rice and vegetables for me from the beginning."

Fat Man says, "I see a home."

The home he indicates is largely intact. It was sheltered by a stone structure, much of which stands, though the function of the building is unclear. It may have been a bank. The roof has been swept away. The home's walls are torn, but they stand. Fat Man and Little Boy pick their way through the surrounding wreckage.

Inside there is a man on his back studded with all manner of shrapnel. Not only shards of glass, but blades of grass, which were blasted through the walls and his flank. They hang long and brown from his body. A bamboo pen protrudes from his gut. Slivers of wood bristle in his back and chest. His legs look fine but they don't work. He looks like a father. If he is a father, his wife and children are dead, or he is abandoned. His mouth is white and scabbed from days of thirst. There is an empty flask by his side that let him live this long.

The man croaks. Fat Man is afraid.

"I don't understand you," says Little Boy.

"Maybe he's thirsty," says Fat Man. He paces the home, searching for water. There is an overturned pail in what might have been the kitchen. If there was ever water there, it is vaporized now. Fat Man goes back to the shrapnel man. Little Boy is trying to pull the grass from his arm. Instead, the blades break, and what threaded his flesh stays. The man watches Little Boy's hands working without alarm. Fat Man says there is no water.

The man on the floor says, "I don't know what happened."

They don't understand.

Little Boy asks him if there are any canned goods. Fat Man makes a motion like operating a can opener, pretends to lift the lid, mimes delight at the treats inside. Little Boy tells him not to be stupid.

The man says, "If you want, you can have my other clothing."

Fat Man ransacks the kitchen or a room like a kitchen. There is a wooden container like a tall bucket with a thick lid. This, like the pail, has been overturned by the blast, and the lid is knocked loose. There is not enough rice to spill from the mouth. Fat Man has to reach in with his whole arm to pull a dry white moon of clotted rice from the bottom, where it huddles up against the inner wall. He eats the rice in seven bites. Little Boy comes in time to see the sixth. "No fair," he shouts. "We're supposed to share."

Fat Man finishes the rice and licks his fingers. "You didn't want the toothpaste," he says, defiant, "or the cricket. How was I to know you'd want the rice?"

"Well," says Little Boy, reminding himself that he's supposed to be the big brother, "I guess you'll let me have what's in that bowl then." There are two ceramic bowls on the low, wide table, with lids of the same material. One of them is shattered. Little Boy opens the one that remains intact and finds the cold dregs of a dish left unfinished, a salty fish broth with transparent peels of skin at the bottom. Fat Man seizes the bowl. As Little Boy calls his brother selfish, Fat Man takes the bowl to their host. He cradles the dying man's head and presses the rim to his painful-dry lips. He thanks the fat man; Fat Man can tell. One of his eyes is more open than the other. He has long eyelashes. They move the way the cricket did not move. He drinks the broth.

From the dying man's perspective: the looming face of Fat Man, half-sorrowful, half-blank, as if he has forgotten to finish his face; coming over the behemoth's shoulder, Little Boy, outraged but also very tired, with eyes half-lidded—eyes that want sleep.

The dying man says, "You can take anything you find."

He dies a moment later, or ceases moving, pretending to die to make everything simple, to let the brothers do what they will. Fat Man feels the life leave his body or pretend to leave his body. They do not know they are permitted to search the home, but they search anyway. Fat Man finds a can of beans and works on it with a sharp rock for a while, first sucking the juices through the puncture and then levering it wider with what looks to be a metal drinking straw. Little Boy doesn't ask for what he likely wouldn't get. Instead he rifles through the household's clothes, finding nothing that might fit his tremendous little brother.

"You're going to be cold," says Little Boy. "You could wrap some of their pants around your waist."

Fat Man says they should leave. Little Boy says they should spend the night. There are mats to sleep on in the other room. Fat Man says they can't sleep here or anywhere nearby.

"Why not?" says Little Boy.

"The tall soldier," says Fat Man. "He might not be dead. He might blame me for his friend."

"He won't find us," says Little Boy. "You can hide under a blanket."

"Are you sure that'll work?"

Little Boy says no soldier has ever found him while he was sleeping.

Fat Man yawns and stretches. "First thing tomorrow we have to get far away, though. We have to find more food. We have to get meat."

Little Boy says they can do these things. He leads his brother to the mats and lays him down, covers him with a blanket, making a soft hillock, from which protrudes a pair of dirty feet. As he tucks in Fat Man, Little Boy sees what's wrong with his brother's palms.

"They're black," says Little Boy. He lays other blankets on his brother's body—it takes three more to cover him.

"I know they are," says Fat Man, the mound beneath the blankets.

"Not like mine," says Little Boy. "Mine are white."

"I know they are."

Little Boy crawls underneath the blankets with his brother. He says this is what big brothers do when their little brothers are cold or afraid, or when they need comfort. He snuggles up against his brother, nestles his head into the doughy vastness of his brother's side and breast.

Little Boy asks Fat Man how he was born.

* * *

Fat Man woke inflamed, and though his body caught he did not burn. The fire coated him like a gelatin. He was naked and alone. He was on his side, inward-curled. Soft. He felt himself, and felt his skin was hot, and felt the sweat seep. The sweat evaporated, it became steam. What a smell. He was a torch. He was a fat candle. With some effort, he stood. He was ankle-deep in the orange-white-black fuel of the fire—the city, the ruins. The heat an awful pressure. He could feel his eyes boiling in their sockets, his tongue becoming thick and dry like something dead. He began to walk. The coal that was a city crumbled beneath him, fell to ash and ember, sizzled his skin. He wandered through the fire, grasping with his steaming hands. What he wanted was a way out. What he wanted was a meal. He was already hungry.

There was a deafening wind converging on the center: on him. It made the blazes bow before the fat man: he saw the extent of the fire, squat buildings like toys, a library or cathedral with a dome's blasted skeleton, burnt trees and some still burning, an Oriental arch of stone, upright, rigid. A corpse's clutching, upward-reaching hand.

The roaring wind cooled and burnt his body, its crevices and extremities. His hair stood up from his head and danced and burned away. The wind became a vortex, then seemed to rise, and then was gone. The flames sprung up as tall as rearing bears. He tripped over his feet and rolled in the charcoal, screaming, though his throat was swollen shut. A sound like a kettle came out. He rolled down a hill. He hit his side on a black, burning tree stump. It collapsed, exposing bright orange coal, which hissed up against his back. Orange sparks like fireflies.

His insides pulsed and pressed against themselves. His lungs inflated like two blue balloons. His heart was like a dying dog curled up inside his chest. He struggled to his feet. There was a car, its wheels melted, lights blown out, roof destroyed, windshield broken, hood gone, mirrors gone, engine pieces melted. Seated inside, two bodies, cooked, perhaps a young couple, their heads forced to impossible angles, facing each other. Twisted this way, they seemed to look at one another. They seemed to watch. Their jaws broken, hanging loose inside their mouths like decorations.

He was coming to the edge of the fire, which crept over trails of shredded paper, wooden beams, and fallen trees like a tightrope walker. There was a man at the edge of the fire standing in what was left of his home, calling out. He was inaudible, his mouth was open. The walls were collapsed to knee-level heaps; there was a metal bowl fused to his chin. Other kitchen items littered the ground around him, and there was a table overturned. He wrung his hands in front of him, pleading. His skin fell off his body in sheets. It hung from his fingertips and swung like streamers as he moved his hands. There were other bodies in the waste, twisted by a cruel hand, riddled with grass and wood pieces. There was a dead cat at the foot of a lamp. There were two bicycles lying on their sides, dismantled, their tires pooled and steaming round the spokes. There were lead soldiers. There were ceramic dishes shattered. There was a spoon. There was half a public bench. There were someone's keys. Having eaten the walls of his home and traveled the wooden table, the fire found the man whose skin bloomed from his body. It licked his feet and ate his ankles. He sunk to his knees. He watched himself sinking, looked down on the fire and saw where he would lay his head. Hands and arms in the flame, and the rest of him following inexorably as if tugged by his collar to bed.

Fat Man walked a long time after that. Slowly, the fire burning on him died and he began to feel his body.

He came to a tree. It was a tall, black tree. He put his hands on it. There was a pulsing heat inside. The hands sung pain. He pulled them back blackened, still singing. The three remaining branches—strong, solid limbs, which seemed to pour from the trunk—were aflame. They offered fire in outstretched hands. The trunk was split. Was burst open. Inside the cleavage, orange, scaly charcoal pulsed with life. A glow cancer, a barrier reef—it looked almost soft, as if it wanted him inside.

It spit sparks.

It groaned and sighed.

The heat of the tree pulled him in even as he tried to think of other things. He needed to climb inside.

He felt his face glowing orange in the tree's light. His body calmed as he breathed as he breathed as he breathed. He ran his blackened hands over the bark, which pulsed white where it was thin—which flaked off, revealing the orange, the heat, inside.

"And before all that?" says Little Boy.

"I exploded," says Fat Man.

Little Boy asks him how it was to explode.

"Like staring up into the night sky, not at the stars, but at the space between them."

"It was," says Little Boy, "like rubbing your hands together to make them warm."

"It was like breathing in and in and in."

"It was like drowning."

"It was like my hunger."

"It was peaceful."

"It was deafening."

"It was blinding."

"It was being light."

"It was pushing on a home as if to move it."
"It was being a mountain."
"It was being a moon."
"It was coming back from the dead."
"It was forgetting."
"It was perfect, awful memory."
"It was like having no brother, and being nobody."

LITTLE BOY'S NURSE

Little Boy dreams of the nurse who found him beneath the wavering sapling. He did not know she was a nurse then but would find out about it later. She was dressed in Western clothing: a checkered black and white turtleneck sweater and a long blue skirt, both stained with blood. She had yellow slippers.

She wiped her puffy red nose with the back of her hand and sniffled to win his attention.

He looked up at her, opened his mouth as if to speak. There was nothing to say. She was talking Japanese. She talked to him like he was a baby. Bending forward slightly, pressing her knees together, resting her palms on her thighs. It made him feel safe and he didn't want her to stop. He reached up for her as if his legs were broken.

For a second she looked very tired, and he thought he must not be the first to reach for her this way. He grunted like a baby, he moved his lips as if to suckle. Her face smoothed. Something in her posture hardened. She stooped to lift. He wrapped his arms around her neck and sighed. Her turtleneck collar hung a little loose. There was a black mark on the pale soft skin of her neck like a big thumbprint.

She made her way, bouncing him on her hip and humming a song. They passed through wreckage. She walked around two bodies. He hid his face in her shoulder so he wouldn't have to see. They met a man, not a nurse, who seemed to know her. He wore an undershirt with orange-red blots down its middle. His nose was red and puffy too. He sneezed. He wiped it with the back of his hand.

He made an empty-handed gesture and talked an apology. Yet he had brought her shoes. He let them hang from his hand by their laces. She looked away and then nodded, agreeing. The man came close. He wrapped his arms around Little Boy's chest beneath his armpits. Little Boy dug in with his fingers, he scratched and pinched her skin, but he was not strong enough to keep his grip. The nurse pried his legs from her hips. He left a boy-shaped stain on her clothing. The man whispered something in Little Boy's ear. Little Boy wanted to know how to say, Give her back.

The man shifted his weight from heel to heel and watched the nurse. She knelt to take off her slippers and put on the shoes. They fit her well enough. She kissed the man on his cheek because these shoes were better than the slippers.

They walked together. The nurse's new shoes clomped with each step. She sneezed into her sleeve. She wiped the snot from her cheek. The man kept looking at her. The man, like Little Boy, was very thin. Their bones touched through their skins. They were joined by a middle-aged man leading an old blind woman by her arm. He spoke to her in a constant, calming whisper, maybe describing the scenery or telling where her feet should go. All her clothes had burnt away from her body and her skin had fallen off her back in long, narrow strips. Little Boy looked away from her before he could see too much.

Here was the school. The walls were fallen down. Here was an overturned vegetable cart and here were the vegetables, pulped. Here a dead man.

They were joined by two women carrying a boy on a stretcher. He was sleeping. He was naked, and his face and chest were all burned and looked like wet tree bark.

Little Boy was passed off again to the nurse. She bore him cheerfully as she could.

They came to an improvised clinic, a small concert hall or a playhouse. The main room was large and littered with wooden folding chairs. There were bodies all over the floor on thin mats and blankets, some of them moving, some of them still. An old man lay spooning his adult son and sung to him, quietly, while the young man bled on the floor. Everyone was quiet, except for a woman Little Boy couldn't see, who made an awful sort of braying, until she stopped, until she started up again. A little girl prodded her big sister, who would not respond. A man and his wife lay facing each other. They watched each other's eyes and touched their noses. They were burned all over. They had been rubbed with white cream. Little Boy floated over the scene in his nurse's arms. She bounced him on her hip, which made the world stutter.

A doctor knelt by a policeman and pulled glass from his leg. After each piece was removed, he daubed the wound with a cotton ball. When the cotton ball was used up he pulled another from a bag and held it, overturning a bottle of alcohol in his palm, soaking the ball. The policeman gritted his teeth. He thanked the doctor for each piece that was pulled.

The nurse called someone's name. An older woman came and took Little Boy away from the nurse. The old woman placed

Little Boy down on the floor beside the wounded policeman. The doctor was pulling three inches of glass from the policeman's calf; he was pulling the long, thin shard quick as he could without its breaking. Little Boy's nurse and the old woman left. The old woman came back with a pair of tweezers and a small tin pan. She made Little Boy lie down. She took his left foot by the ankle and lifted it until she could see what was inside. Thick, partly-clotted blood fell out of him. She put the tweezers to his skin. They were cold.

The policeman took Little Boy's hand and squeezed as if to say, Now squeeze me back.

The hidden woman brayed.

The old woman put the tweezers in his foot. She pulled something loose and set it in the pan, where it glistened wetly. She reached in—he squeezed the policeman's hand—and pulled something else free. It made a scraping sound as it left him, as if it didn't want to go. The policeman screamed.

They made Little Boy wait for clothes until they could find something Western. When they did it was a little gangster costume; a blue suit, cheaper than it looked, with matching fedora. They watched him dress. They asked him questions that he couldn't answer, so he didn't. He sulked until they left him alone. He laid around on the floor.

He thought about how it was to explode.

They brought a little boy to the empty space beside him. The boy was pulling out the hairs from his own head one at a time. He set them in a pile on the floor. He was burnt all over but did not seem to notice. Little Boy wanted to trace the weird patterns with his fingers. He wanted to reach under the other boy's skin and see what he could find.

He wanted his nurse.

She was busy among the bodies, checking temperatures with the back of her hand, finding pulses with her fingertips. She wouldn't look at Little Boy. When the father holding his bleeding adult son cried out, it was *his* nurse that came running. She watched his chest and touched his temple. He was dead. One of the other nurses found the energy to say something gentle, to touch the old man's head. They left. The father held his dead son as before and was quiet.

Little Boy went looking for his nurse. He searched outside, where young people shared the cigarettes they'd found and watched the sun set over those parts of the city still standing. She was not there. He searched the improvised operation rooms where surgeons sutured, disinfected, stanched gut wounds, and pruned dead skin. They shooed away Little Boy. She was not there.

Next, the empty stage, on which the policeman slept. Little Boy slipped behind the curtain. It was dark there. Hanging on the walls, grotesque masks, whether pale or demon-faced, all glaring and grinning and twisted, distressed. Shadow puppets dangled from hooks, limp and cheap-looking. Costumes were heaped and hung on trunks and racks. More suits in other sizes, and dresses, Western and Japanese. There was a long paper dragon with many, many bright streamers coiled in the dark corner.

At the dragon's tail end, behind a rack of clothes, Little Boy heard his nurse's coarse, husky whisper drift on the air. The young man, her friend from the search party, stood behind her. Little Boy could make out their shapes because of the light that spilled from the window, but it was a small window, it was faint light. The young man breathed in her neck.

No doubt, thought Little Boy, watching them through a gap

between the silken costumes hanging from the rack, the vivid colors flattened by the window's graying light, No doubt he takes great pleasure in her smells of scorched caramels and dried vanilla. The nurse's friend was speaking into her ear or he was licking it. She swayed in his arms like a dead tree in the wind.

She said something.

Her friend said something back.

She was shaking her head.

He was nodding and kissing her neck.

She was lifting her checkered turtleneck sweater.

He was running his hands over her abdomen.

From waist to neck her skin was marked.

Smudged, like ink fingerprints.

Like charcoal squares, in checkers.

Burnt in the pattern of her sweater.

The nurse's friend kneaded her breasts as she fumbled to hitch up her skirt in the back—as they twisted their heads to unnatural, perhaps painful angles, like graceless swans, so that their eyes could touch, so that their lips could meet.

The masks on the walls made faces at the couple. They floated like ghosts. They seemed to react to the scene. Some with horror, some with great sadness, and some with a fiendish delight. Little Boy's nurse whispered something, leaning into the man. He hushed her.

Little Boy felt himself between his legs. There was nothing, no response. They backed away from him, into deeper shadow, so that he could not see what he heard, or know.

He felt very alone.

The sun was set. Only a thin red line on the horizon. Only the sound of their love, the soft squelch, like sucking a pool of thick spit through his teeth and pushing it out into the reservoir of bottom lip, again, and again. He chewed his cheeks to pulp. It was quiet there.

When they were done he ran away. Some days later, on news of the second bomb, he began to search for what would be a brother.

WHAT THE
SHADOW LOST

When they wake the next day wind whistles through the holes in their overnight shelter; the edges of their piled blankets flutter; there is a one dollar bill blown up against the wall as if it is a picture hung there. The wind lets up and the bill floats down to the floor. The wind picks up again and the bill climbs back up where it was. This is the greenest thing they've seen in days.

Little Boy says, "Grab it!"

Fat Man lunges for the bill. Snags it. "Don't know what good this is going to do us," he says, spreading the dollar smooth in his upturned palm. It does feel good though, the slightly fuzzy grain of the paper.

"The Americans are coming," Little Boy says. "They'll be all over this place soon. People are going to want their money. *I* want their money."

"So do I," Fat Man says, handing over the bill. "How do we get it?"

Little Boy says they find where this one came from. He tucks it in his breast pocket.

"Can we leave before the soldiers get here?" says Fat Man.

"Probably not," says Little Boy. "We need time to plan. We'll hide."

They drape Fat Man in another robe, which he can't close. They wrap his waist in someone's pants. They put a blanket over his back like a cape, tie the corners around his neck. This will keep him warm. He knows it also makes him look a little crazy. He asks his brother if he has to wear it.

Little Boy says, "I don't want you catching cold."

Outside they find a small cloud of dollar bills drifting over the waste. Little Boy scurries, catching what he can and shoving them in his pockets. Fat Man teeters clumsily in pursuit, snags one here and there, keeps them balled up in his fists for lack of pockets. Anyway, he's too hungry for this. He asks Little Boy if this money will buy them food. Little Boy's too busy to answer. Fat Man trips on a bit of concrete from a building no longer there. Lands flat on his front.

Little Boy shouts, "Where are these coming from?"

Still lying on his face, Fat Man points in what seems to be the general direction. Little Boy demands that he get up. Fat Man struggles to his feet. The green trail laced across sharp bits of glass, cement crevices, and other broken things leads them into a place between two buildings, the one on their right collapsed almost completely, and leaning on the one to their left, which in turn leans on itself. Together they form a sort of arch, which, as the brothers follow deeper, collapses further, becoming deeper darkness, a wind tunnel. Here and there a stray dollar brushes Fat Man's ear, Little Boy's cheek. One strikes Fat Man where his heart would be if he wore it on a chain. Another bill strikes his eye. They catch as catch can. The wind whistles. The slope falls. They crouch to walk. There is a bright place ahead of them where the slope of the right wall ends—light in threads, motes of dust suspended on the threads, paint chips also, gray crumbs.

There comes a point Fat Man can't advance. Little Boy crawls through the small end of the tunnel and out into the light. Fat Man kneels to follow but he can't get through past his shoulders. The light blinds. All flares and clarifies. He sees the shadow on the wall.

From Fat Man's perspective the shadow seems to reach for him, though in fact it is after the money. Little Boy caresses the wall on which it was projected—the profile of a stumbled man, fallen nearly to his knees, reaching for something fallen to the ground. The open cash case. The case's hinges were dashed against the wall by the force of the blast, or by the case's fall from the gone man's hand. They came loose, the locks on the other side—gold, once—melted, and on the melted locks the case hinged, as in all the violence it opened on the wrong end, revealing its payload. The hinges came apart like teeth, the gold locks bent into a new shape.

"What luck," says Little Boy. "We can buy you a damn suit."

"And some food. We can get meat."

"We can leave. We can get out."

"How much?" says Fat Man.

"Let me worry about money," says Little Boy. "That's a big brother job."

The case will close if Fat Man puts his weight on it. The gold locks are still a little soft, so the brothers slide the rod back in one of the hinges and this serves as a lock. The other hinge's teeth are too crushed. The case is otherwise, it seems, invulnerable—the corners and edges protected by an iron exoskeleton, identical in color to the woven wires embroidering the leathery material that is its skin. The corners are especially tough, their shell thick and sharp, like a steel-toed boot.

Little Boy tells Fat Man to carry it. He passes it through the small end of the tunnel to Fat Man, who carries it out to meet Little Boy, who goes around the tunnel, around the collapsed building. The weight is less in Fat Man's hands than he thought it would be. The money shifts inside.

"Now we can have anything we want," says Fat Man to Little Boy.

"We can have a few things we want," says Little Boy. "If we can convince anybody to trade us."

This means finding people, which means leaving the city. At the far edges there is woodland, there are fields and farmers. They go toward the sun. Fat Man tears cloth from the pants they wrapped around his waist, wraps the strips around his feet for shoes. This offers some relief from the pain of travel. Little Boy holds Fat Man's free hand. Fat Man asks his brother if he wants to take a turn carrying the cash. Little Boy says no, he would not like that; he says it is too heavy.

As they go, they pass the car Fat Man saw. The lovers still twist their heads to see each other, angling for a kiss.

They pass the tree Fat Man touched. It is split, charcoal all over, but not destroyed. The pulsing warmth of the orange barrier reef inside has become the inert gray-black of pencil lead. The branches are fallen and cooked down to nothing. Fat Man thinks of his hands.

He asks his brother, "Do you think they are a symbol?"

"What's a symbol?"

"My hands. Do they suggest guilt?"

"Do you feel guilty?"

"I do."

Little Boy asks him what for. He says hands are not a symbol. He says there is nothing to feel bad about. They are not thieves. The money was just lying there. No one had a claim to it. The shadow was dead.

Fat Man says, "That's why I feel guilty."

Little Boy says, "Nothing you could have done."

Fat Man feels the tree is pulling him in again. He feels he wants to touch it. He lets go of Little Boy's hand. He goes to the cold tree and presses his palms to it.

Little Boy asks him what he is doing.

The cool of the tree as it stands does not cancel the heat that lived inside it before. It does however smudge his body dark in several places where skin touches smooth memory of bark. This smudge will come away—Little Boy comes to him and rubs it off with spit.

They go on together. They find a Western-style door thrown on its side, wooden, with heavy finish, dark grain, knob melted so it looks like a wilting brass flower. There was black lettering before that is now burnt away, leaving a streak of scorch.

"This is where the soldiers found me," says Fat Man. "I was crying."

"What for?" asks Little Boy.

"Am I a good brother?" says Fat Man.

"So far you're fine," says Little Boy. "Just do as I say."

They pass another man's shadow projected on a wall. He is reaching toward what killed him. The cinders that were the body remain face-down on the road.

"He looks like he wants our money," says Fat Man, fearful, squeezing Little Boy's hand.

Little Boy squeezes back. He does not deny the shadow wants. Stooped body, thin wrists. It would take what it could get.

By night they come to the outermost edge of the city, where the wilds begin to encroach and the crickets insist.

A BAG OF RICE

They find a home. It is a flimsy-seeming thing. Damp rags flutter yellowed on a line of cord stretched nearly taut between a pole and a tree branch. If there were a sun they would dry by its light. Little Boy looks up to his little brother. Fat Man wears a tired, bearlike expression, fists clenched, head seeping down into neck and chest like a mudslide.

"There must be food inside that home," Fat Man says, "but there are also living people."

"If I give you some money," says Little Boy, "can you go inside and get the food?"

"I thought you would get the food. You're supposed to be my big brother. You have to take care of me."

"I'm just a little boy. I'm scared to go inside."

"But I'm even younger than you," Fat Man pleads. "What if they know I left you out here? What if they come out here to get you because they know you're really in charge? What if they're angry because you sent your little brother?"

Little Boy strokes the fat man's gut. "You need to be brave and do as I say."

"I'll go in if you come with me. You don't want to be out here alone if the soldier comes, or the man who had our cash case before we did. He might not be dead. We never saw his body."

"I'll hide," says Little Boy.

"Come on," says Fat Man. "You're coming."

With a grip that hurts, he grabs Little Boy by the shoulder. They march to the home and knock on the door. It rattles. A woman cracks open the door, draped in purple robe and white sash. Her eyes take them in without comment. She has seen stranger things than white men in mismatched clothes. She does not move to welcome them.

Little Boy elbows his brother, whispering, "Go on. Food."

"I don't know Japanese," says Fat Man, as if this has just occurred to him.

"Mime it."

Fat Man looks down at Little Boy and back at the woman. Jagged white patches of her scalp shine through thinning hair. Fat Man brings his hand to his mouth as if cupping a handful of rice and eats from his palm. He nods to the Japanese woman, repeats the action. She does it back—and also, by way of an offer, pretends to drink a cup of water. Fat Man smiles and nods.

Little Boy fans out a small handful of bills. She snatches one from his hand; one of the white crescents of her long, dead nails nicks his skin. She peers into the face of Lincoln, perhaps imagining a name for the face (not Roosevelt, not Truman) before settling on the numbers in each corner. The rate of exchange is a mystery. What does the woman think the bill is worth? She secrets away the bill inside her robe and leads the brothers inside.

There is a shirtless man lying motionless on a bed mat; he glistens with sweat and his skin is blotched purple. At eye-level, he has a small potted tree with sweet green leaves like flower petals. One arm extends to touch the pot. The other's wrapped around his face, which is obscured from mustache to hairline. His lips part and whistle softly with each breath. A second man, a soldier, is propped up against the wall, his machine gun wrapped in both arms and framed by crossed ankles, like a strut supporting his body. A helmet falls over his eyes. He has a patchy beard, and his shoulders and chest are dusted with fallen hairs. His hands are bloody at their knuckles. He is also purple-blotched.

Fat Man squeezes too hard. Little Boy shrugs off his brother.

"That's him," whispers Fat Man.

The woman sets up a small stove, fills a pot with water.

"Your soldier?" says Little Boy.

"I think so." Fat Man folds his hands together and begins twiddling furiously. His stomach rumbles. The woman gives both of them a cup of water. Little Boy hands her another bill. They chug the water, wipe their mouths with the backs of their hands. The woman brings them more. This time Little Boy does not give her more money. If she wishes to protest she does not have the words.

"We should go," says Little Boy.

"But I'm hungry."

"We can get food somewhere else."

Fat Man whispers, harshly, "You already gave her the money."

"We have more."

The sitting soldier starts. The woman looks at him. She looks at the brothers, clamping her hand shut in front of her mouth.

"It means shut up," says Little Boy out the side of his mouth.

"I know what it means," says Fat Man.

They wait. The water comes to a boil. The woman pours in rice. Little Boy cranks his arm in circles, motioning for more. She glares, relents, adds more—and more water. Now she must bring it back to a boil. The brothers stand hapless at the door, swaying on their tired knees. There is a red radio in the corner with several batteries scattered beside it. They might be spent or waiting for their chance.

"Do you think they're loaded?" whispers Fat Man. "The guns?"

"Shut up," whispers Little Boy.

"I never actually saw them fire. All this time I've just been assuming."

"It's the safe assumption," says Little Boy. He pinches his brother's thigh. Fat Man grits his teeth, thumps Little Boy on the back of his head. The woman in the purple robe stares at them. A lock of gray-streaked hair falls from her scalp.

She empties the rice into a brown cloth sack. Fat Man takes the sack from her. She motions for them to leave. When they hesitate, she hoists an invisible rifle and fires off several rounds, heaving from the recoil of each shell. She mimes pushing a helmet up from over her eyes to better see her kills.

"I wanted meat," moans Fat Man. "All my life so far it's always been rice. I need something else. Something *filling*."

Little Boy rolls his eyes. He holds out the rice in one hand, demonstrative, and then his other hand, empty. He motions with it for something else, something more. He takes a ten-dollar bill from his pocket. The woman shakes her head, crosses her arms, waits for them to leave.

"Please," says Fat Man. He rubs his tummy. Speaks slowly, as if she'll better understand. "I am *so, hungry*."

"Shut up," says Little Boy. He pockets the bill, hands his brother the rice, and tugs him by the elbow. The sitting soldier snorts. His head lolls forward and his helmet drops off. It hits his kneecap and thuds on the ground. His eyes shoot open. He squeezes the gun with his whole body. He sees the white boy, the white man—his prisoner—and nearly falls on his face trying to lift the gun. He calls out. The man with the potted tree shudders awake. In his panic he knocks over the little tree.

There is a moment where the man with the potted tree looks merely startled. He wears the blankness of confusion. Then a malice enters his body. He looks on the brothers with hatred—knowing hatred, as if they are old enemies.

"Run!" screams Little Boy.

Fat Man knocks the sliding door crooked as he forces his way through.

The soldier and the shirtless man follow, both hollering weakly. Just outside the doorway, the soldier raises his gun and shoots. The bullets whistle past. Dirt bursts around their feet and then farther out.

Their pursuers stumble and bark at them. "Assholes," screams the soldier, demonstrating his obscene English. "Bastards." Another shot. The shirtless man falls to his knees and throws up.

The brother bombs plunge into the woods, Fat Man heaving like a panicked ape, Little Boy whipped by thin branches, loose roots, string trees. They run blind, surrounded by sinister rustling, leaves crunching underfoot. Soon rain begins to fall, making the whole forest seem to swarm with lives, with sick Japanese, with raging soldiers. Sometimes they hear a distant curse. They fall and scrape their knees. They stop to breathe when Fat Man says that he can't make it, he won't make it. A twig snaps. They're running again.

They come to an abandoned farm, now lousy with rotten gourds and collapsed melons. This could have happened many ways, but Little Boy chooses to believe the family collapsed when the men were called to fight the Yanks.

"I can't run anymore," heaves Fat Man. "I'm going to throw up. I'm so thirsty."

"One thing at a time," says Little Boy. "First we hide and hope they don't kill us." He surveys the land. There is a shelter, but someone may still live there, and the spot is too obvious. Little Boy spies a slightly raised patch of dirt, a very small hill, crowned with dead vegetables and wild grass. He leads his brother there. Fat Man hobbles, clutching at his lungs through his chest as if to arrest their labors.

"Lie down in the muck," says Little Boy.

Rain is pelting them loudly. Fat Man does as he is told—belly up like a dead tuna.

Little Boy kicks mud on his brother, and gourds and so on. "Lie very still," he says. He lies down as well, on his belly, head-to-toes with Fat Man, the rice bag clutched under his chest. He wallows. He watches the woods where they came from.

"Your suit," says Fat Man, horrified.

"It'll wash out, or I'll buy a new one."

Little Boy listens for gunfire. He waits for the soldier. His brother's breathing calms, and slows. Soon they are breathing together. Their bodies swelling and diminishing, touching and shy-ing away. The brother bombs take great care in their breathing.

The soldier and the husband all purple-blotched are search-ing the field, shooting anything that moves. The soldier has the gun. The husband serves as a spotter, his shouts followed by three rounds. The mud accepts the bullets. They are far off but not so far.

Little Boy tries to count the shots. He doesn't know how many bullets the soldier has. It can't be too many.

"Here!" calls the husband, very close to them. Not in Eng-lish, but they know. Three rounds into the dirt. Nothing. The soldier swears. The husband coughs. He sways into Fat Man's view, standing over the brothers, his dirty heels at eye level. The husband coughs.

A dry rustle—some bird or rodent. The husband points in its direction, coughing into the back of his hand. Three rounds into the dirt.

The husband has an awful coughing fit. Something wet comes out of him. The soldier stops shooting for a moment. He joins the husband and holds him like a brother. The husband vomits on the soldier. There was not much in him. Now, less. He collapses, his body landing with a great whumph only feet from the brothers. His hand, a pale claw between them, twitches once, and then is done but for the slightest pulse of blood beneath the skin. He is dying of what killed the short soldier, which is something in the air, a mystery. Rain shivers on his skin. Death calms the hand.

The soldier's legs are weak. He coughs as the husband coughed. He hacks.

He says, "This isn't how he dies." He shoots the husband through throat and face. Blood foams. "This is how he dies."

He says, "We will not wait for the Americans to do what we can do ourselves."

He says, "This is how I die."

He pushes the butt of his rifle into the mud. He kneels before it and slides the barrel past his teeth. Balancing on his left knee, he raises his bare right foot, presses his right knee to the rifle. He puts his toe on the trigger. One round. Flesh and chips of bone. The body falls.

Little Boy darts up on his feet. He runs away to throw up what's inside him. Fat Man wipes the rot and mud from his face and shoulders, chest and gut. Little Boy still has the food, but he will come back, and then they can eat. Rain drums on Fat Man as if he were a tarpaulin. Two bodies grow cold nearby. He feels at home here. He looks up at the clouds. He is like the bodies, he thinks, but he is also the home of a terrible hunger. That is the chief difference.

They hardly notice anymore the rot of the bodies. Busy little white worms tunneling the flesh, other bugs as well—spiders on their faces, flies on their extremities. This time the soft meat of their cheeks will be the first to go, and then their eyes. The skin between their thumbs and forefingers. The pink beneath their nails. The soles of their feet.

The brother bombs leave them like this. Eat rice from their bag with dirty hands. Open their mouths and tilt their heads back to drink rain.

Little Boy says, "What did you do to that soldier?"

Fat Man, incredulous: "What did *I* do? What did *we* do."

Little Boy, blank: "What did we do?"

Fat Man doesn't say. Doesn't know how. They walk together.

They will walk for days. They will huddle for warmth. They will say few words. They will be brothers.

OCCUPATION

Several weeks have passed. Fat Man kneels at the table. Little Boy sits with his legs outstretched beneath it, cash case in his lap. He carries the money now. He still refuses to count what's left. He eats fish and sticky rice. Fat Man sucks noodles from a black ceramic bowl. They eat quickly, almost frantically, for fear of what will happen to their food if they do not. During recent meals there have been growths inside their dishes: molds, scum, and other rot. They are discussing ways to leave Japan. Little Boy thinks they might steal a fighter plane. His ideas are more and more impractical. Fat Man maintains that they can take a boat. He says that would be easiest.

American soldiers drink sake and wave their dollars. They tease and pinch the woman who serves them their food. She tucks her chin into her neck and hides her face behind a veil of hair. Fat Man asks her for another bowl of noodles. He waves his dollar too. She takes it as she passes and tucks it in her sleeve. He gulps down the broth.

"However we get there, we should decide where we're going," says Little Boy. "What do you think of America?"

"Whatever you say," says Fat Man.

"Whatever I say?"

"If we go to America, we'll have to watch the parades."

"I like parades," says Little Boy. "Or, I think I do. Little boys like them."

"But what if they find us?" says Fat Man.

Little Boy asks what he means. Fat Man says he means Americans. He means what if they find out. "Bombs aren't supposed to *make* people," he whispers. The server sets a bowl of noodles in front of Fat Man and leaves without acknowledgment. The soldiers are calling her Charlene. They call her to their table; they want more. Fat Man continues, screening his mouth with his hand, "It's like sex. Little bullet gets shot at a uranium egg. Egg bursts open and all hell breaks loose. Something big comes out of something so little. It sounds like a baby."

Little Boy picks up the fish bit with his fingers and drops it down his gullet. "I do feel like a baby," he says.

"Babies can't speak at first. They can't eat solid foods. And they don't know what we know," says Fat Man.

When he was born Little Boy remembered it all. He knew what the scientists said to him as they stroked his shell, thinking no one could hear them. He remembered what it was to live as potential. Now he doesn't know. He only feels he used to. Here everything is strange. He can't absorb it. Japan is another kind of absence.

"Where can we go?" says Fat Man.

One of the soldiers, one with thin bristles of black hair and a forehead etched with many lines though he is young, calls Charlene to his side of the table. She comes. He's got a ten-dollar bill in his hand, ragged and half-torn down its middle, pale as new grass and leaf stems. He waves it underneath her nose as if scenting a bloodhound. The soldier presses the money to his cheek and smells it himself. He drags it down the side of his face, across his neck, over his collar bone, his uniform. He drags it over his left nipple, down his stomach, across his left hip, and down, to the center, between his legs. He hangs it from his open zipper, half exposed, half obscured. This looks like something he has practiced, a routine.

Charlene shakes her head slowly. She goes into the kitchen and does not come out until the soldiers have overturned the table and left. Little Boy leaves what he thinks the food was worth. No one here says what anything will cost.

Outside, after their meal, Fat Man begins to walk home, crunching fallen yellow leaves beneath his leather shoes; Little Boy stands still just beyond the closed door, bending in on himself and rubbing his knees forlornly, watching his brother's back. This is the third time this has happened today. The last two times, Fat Man has gone on walking and Little Boy has scurried belatedly to catch up. This time the boy shows more resolve. There are twenty feet between them now and he is still rubbing his knees. Twenty-five feet, then thirty.

Fat Man turns around and asks him what's wrong.

"My legs hurt," whines Little Boy. "My feet still hurt. They're still healing from the glass."

"What do you want me to do about it?"

Little Boy reaches up with open arms as if the fat man were close enough to touch. "Carry me?"

Fat Man says he doesn't want to carry Little Boy.

"This is what good little brothers do. They carry their big brothers when they hurt."

Fat Man relents. He takes his little older brother on his back and carries him down the paved road, which becomes a dirt road shaded by trees. Little Boy clings to him around his neck, sometimes strangling him to the point where Fat Man makes a coughing sound that means "loosen up," which Little Boy does, until his arms draw closed again. He breathes hot and loud on Fat Man's neck and ear, his legs dangling and kicking at the air and sometimes Fat Man.

"What do you think we're here for?" says Fat Man.

Little Boy doesn't answer. He is listening to the air. Crickets sing in the trees.

They come to a farm. Night is falling. There is a man in a pigpen tending to the grunting things. They are like tumors of the landscape, soft and gray and pink. They move but not often. Fat Man and Little Boy watch them. Fat Man says, "I feel for the pigs."

Little Boy says, "I feel for the one who cleans up after them."

A woman comes out of the home and leans against the pen's fence to speak to her husband. Her hair is a thick black strand. Her face is a slope; they cannot see her eyes. She's younger than she looks.

Little Boy says, "We'll spend the night on their land. Tomorrow they can feed us."

It is raining very lightly. It feels good. Little Boy is awake, watching the fabric weigh down and cling to his little brother's upturned back. They are sleeping or not sleeping across the road from the farm, under partial shelter of tall trees. They hid the cash case under piled leaves.

The woman comes out of the home and slides shut the door. She goes into the outhouse, which is beside the pigpen.

Little Boy creeps up to the outhouse. It's a shanty thing built from spare timber and irregular nails. He steps up close so that his bare toes touch the outhouse wall, finds a gap with his hands, bends to press his eye against the peephole. She is squatting on a platform raised on a box that stands over the hole. Her robe hangs from a hook on the door. There is no roof on the outhouse. Moonlight on her body, moonlight on her thighs, moonlight on her ribs. On high, hard breasts. Muscles underneath her skin, muscles that he didn't know existed. The pigs snort and snicker in their pen. He can hear her shit fall thickly. It runs down a chute at the bottom of the hole, out the back of the outhouse, and into the pigs' trough.

Moonlight on her body as the pigs crowd the trough, eating her night soil. They belch and squeal. She grunts back at them and squeezes more. They eat it all. Moonlight on the pigs hunched over their meal. Moonlight on the meal.

He can smell her, a green smell, a smell in the pit of his stomach.

She wipes herself with her hand. Little Boy grips himself between his legs, squeezes the softness. Nothing happens there. As she wraps herself in her robe, he rushes back to his resting place beside his brother, running under cover of pig ruckus. She goes back to the house. As she slides open the door she looks across the road and seems to see the brothers through the dark. "You don't see me," whispers Little Boy. The woman goes inside.

When Fat Man wakes there are two policemen standing over them. A tall one, a short one. Fat Man shakes Little Boy's arm.

The policemen wear the expression of hatred the dead soldiers wore for some days, the expression that the dead husband who slept with a potted tree wore for less than an hour.

Little Boy jumps to his feet. He is smeared all over with mud. Fat Man slept on his face: only his front is so dirty, his back side rinsed by the rainfall.

Little Boy says, "We haven't done anything."

The policemen's skin is purple-blotched like the soldiers' but it seems to be healing. They are very thin. The tall one has a beard and the short one has no beard. They may be brothers because they hold hands. They say nothing.

Fat Man tells Little Boy to ask them what they want.

"How am I supposed to do that?" says Little Boy.

The policemen look at the brothers.

"Are you brothers?" says Fat Man.

The policemen shake their heads. It isn't clear whether they mean to say they are not brothers or mean to say they disapprove of these two who are.

"Is this about the money?" says Fat Man.

"Don't talk about the money," hisses Little Boy. He flicks his brother's ear.

The policemen go on shaking their heads.

"We're leaving soon," says Fat Man. "We promise."

The short policeman says, in Japanese, "We are watching you." He says, "We know you are wrong."

The policemen leave them, hand in hand. The tall one has a limp.

"I don't know what he said," says Little Boy. "What did they say?"

"I think it was a threat."

Little Boy tells him not to worry. Little Boy says he'll take care of everything.

"How are your feet today?" says Fat Man. He does not want to carry his big brother today, as his own legs ache terribly. What he wants is to rest, to sleep under that family's roof. Not because it is difficult to sleep outside but because it is so easy—to sleep, and to sleep through whatever happens, such as the approach of two police who may be brothers or may not be, who may recognize them, who may suspect them of some crime.

"They hurt," says Little Boy. "I could barely sleep."

Little Boy says it's time for breakfast. The pigs watch them as they approach the home. A man is kneeling in the pen, examining a sow's corpse. The man does not know they are there, or knows but does not care. As Fat Man's gaze lingers on the sow's body a maggot surfaces between its teats. The man startles. He flicks away the little worm.

Little Boy lets them into the home. Inside mother and daughter eat rice with their fingers. They are quiet like dead things are quiet. When they see the brothers they do not startle or speak. They look at their food. The daughter tightly gathers the fabric that covers her breasts, the better to cover her skin.

Little Boy says, "Here." He offers the mother a dollar. She shakes her head and motions for her daughter to leave the table. Her daughter goes. Little Boy says, "Here." He says, "Food."

The mother looks to Fat Man as if for confirmation. Fat Man says, "Food." He mimes eating with his fingers.

The mother takes the bill. She gives Little Boy her daughter's bowl and Fat Man her own. She goes to make more rice. They sit at the table to eat. The daughter watches from the next room through a partly open door. She is still quiet like a dead thing.

They use their fingers, quickly eating the rice to keep it from molding. Spores form beneath their touch, giving the remaining grains a bitter, musky, gamey flavor. This is getting worse. Neither has spoken to the other of it yet. Fat Man knows it is not normal. They cannot cover their bowls with their hands, as this would make the growth worse. The mother boils water for more rice.

They are quiet a long time. When the new rice is done Little Boy puts another dollar on the mother's leg. His skin brushes her skin; Fat Man hears it happen. With some reluctance, she gives him the rice. She seems to consider boiling more water, decides against it. Leaves the kitchen, taking her daughter by the hand. They go to another place, to be together, quiet like dead things.

The quiet gets to be too much for Fat Man. "What about France?"

"Why France?" says Little Boy.

"They were barely in the war, and the food is supposed to be good."

"Does it always have to be food?"

"I think we were put here for a reason." He stuffs handfuls of rice into his face, sullen as a fish.

"Uh huh?"

"I think we're supposed to help rebuild, now that the war is done."

"Then we should go to Britain," Little Boy says, finishing his rice.

"I don't want to go there."

The father comes into the home, sees the brothers in his kitchen. He is shirtless, coated everywhere with pig muck, except for his feet and his hands, which he must have scraped clean in the grass outside. He is thinner than his wife, thinner than his daughter. He is a small man. He looks at the brothers a while.

It becomes clear they still will be sleeping outside. The father watches them until they go.

"Does it really have to be France?" says Little Boy, as the door closes behind them. They've grown accustomed to the idea no one understands them. English might as well be a code the way they use it.

"It doesn't have to be anywhere," says Fat Man. "I'm as scared of leaving as I am of staying."

"Take responsibility for yourself," says Little Boy. "I can't play nurse to you forever. You have to make some of your own choices. We're going to France. It's your decision, and you'll live with it."

"Then can we go by boat?" says Fat Man.

"No," says Little Boy. "We're still hijacking a plane." If he smirks it is a subtle smirk.

They bum around the farm for the rest of the day, planning their hijacking, contemplating the hogs. They pay for lunch and dinner inside the home—the father watches them eat as if they were livestock—and they find a place to sleep behind the farm, among trees, on a bed of leaves they press into the damp dirt with their shoes.

A PORTRAIT
OF BROTHERS

It takes them several weeks to find a forger. The way they do it is Little Boy talks to American soldiers about fake passports while behind him Fat Man watches silently. The soldiers assume Fat Man is using Little Boy to make himself look innocent. But Little Boy's thinking is that this looks the most natural. As the older brother, he should take charge. Fat Man wonders several times why they always seem to talk to him when ostensibly answering Little Boy's questions. Little Boy says it's because he's taller. "They don't have to crane their necks that way," he says, his voice thick with disdain: what lazy brutes, these soldiers.

There are also whole days where they talk to no one but each other, where they lie in the dirt and breathe. Fat Man tries to talk about the fire, about birth, about the tree. Little Boy doesn't want to hear it. He says that's all over. He says, "Little boys don't have to think about such things."

Some days the farmer's family feeds them salted pork. The farmer's family never speaks in their presence. The brother bombs whisper when they enter the home. Some days they do not visit the farm to buy food at all, which Fat Man takes to mean the money's running thin. Most days Fat Man wants to leave.

The police still wake them up sometimes, holding hands. They don't say anything. Only watch the brothers and after some time leave. They look thinner every day. Little Boy won't leave the farm, won't say why. The brothers find new sleeping spots around the property. The policemen find them. One time the brothers found the policemen sifting through the leaves where they had slept the night before. One of them found a small something—the brothers couldn't see what. He showed it to the other and put it in his breast pocket.

One day Little Boy talks to the right soldier. The soldier whispers into Fat Man's ear what to do, where to go, who to see.

Their forger is a GI who goes by Ralph. They meet him at his post outside a former munitions plant, which is being repurposed to make washing machines and refrigerators. He wears his helmet at a rakish angle. They know him by the red handkerchief tied around the end of his gun's barrel. He knows the brothers are coming. When he sees their tentative approach he closes the distance to offer his hand. "Hello," he laughs. "You the ones want the passports?"

They follow him back to his post, where he stands with another soldier who doesn't bother pretending to do anything but listen in.

Ralph says, "So?"

"We heard you could help," Little Boy says. He attempts a commanding tone. It comes out of his mouth slantwise, like it doesn't want to go. "What's it going to cost to get documentation that says we're two American brothers?"

"Not too much," says Ralph. "Got to wonder why you'd go with such a cockamamie story though."

"We don't look American to you?" says Little Boy. "How many Japanese you know his size?" He raps his brother on the gut.

"Looks like a sumo to me," says Ralph. "But you ought to go as whatever you really are. Father and son, uncle and nephew, two strangers passing in the night. Not that it matters for passport purposes. They don't exactly come in matching pairs you know."

Little Boy fumes. "He really is my little brother! Can't you see it?" He holds Fat Man's hand to show how close they are.

"I heard you were weird ones," says Ralph. He slaps his knee but doesn't laugh. "Listen, if you'll drop the routine for a minute I can help you, and not just with passports. I can get you American ID if you want it, cheap liquor, American food, Japanese hash." He puts his hand beside his mouth to shield it from Little Boy, mouths to Fat Man, "Women. Pussy."

"We only need the passports," says Little Boy.

Fat Man says, "We're going to France to start over with a clean slate and forget about everything."

Little Boy scowls. His brother didn't have to say that, not any of it.

"All right," says Ralph. "What we'll do, I'll take your picture. Then I'll give the film to my man and he'll put it together for us. You pay me half now, the rest while you're picking your jaw up off the floor from how good he is."

"You're not the forger?" says Fat Man.

"I'm the vendor. Forger's a little yellow craftsman I keep holed up at home all day."

"How much?" says Little Boy.

The vendor musses the little boy's hair. "Hundred-fifty each," he says to Fat Man.

"We don't have that much," says Little Boy.

The vendor twists up his mouth in the corner: You serious?

"We can do two hundred flat."

The vendor waits to see if the boy means it. When he's seen the boy means it, he laughs.

"Fine," says Fat Man. "One-fifty now, one-fifty when we see the job. Pay the man, Brother."

Little Boy glares up at him. Fat Man grabs him by his ear and tugs a little. He growls, "I said pay up."

Little Boy tears up. He thumbs the money bill by bill from his jacket pocket. Fat Man lets go of his ear. Little Boy rubs it, sullen. He curses beneath his breath.

"That's what I thought," says the vendor, counting the money. "Nobody goes to France without cash. Gotta buy some paintings, buy some cheese. Now there's one other thing. I'm gonna need your names. Of course they don't have to really be yours, so long as you can remember them when you're asked. If I could do it all again, I think I'd have them call me George. Like a king."

Little Boy ignores the question; he's still biting back tears.

"I'm John," says Fat Man. "This is Matthew. You were right. He's my little nephew."

"Course he is," says the vendor. "But I don't care." Later, when it occurs to him they never offered a last name, he will choose one for them. He will wonder why he failed to ask. The forger will provide their heights, the colors of their eyes and hair, their dates and places of birth, and Fat Man's profession.

"Now let's take your picture. Then you and the tyke come back and see me in two days."

The vendor assembles his camera and unfolds his tripod. He mounts the camera on the tripod, makes it spin, flashbulb and all. They've never seen a passport, they aren't sure how to be, so they pose there together, their backs to the trees. Fat Man stands behind Little Boy, places a meaty hand on his shoulder.

In his passport photograph Little Boy will stare at the camera while a soft, faceless behemoth in a blue suit towers behind him.

In his passport photograph, Fat Man will look down at Little Boy with something like warmth and affection. Fat Man's face will be partly hidden by the brim of his hat, which neither brother has thought to remove.

"Two days," says the vendor. "Come back then with the rest of my money."

Little Boy makes Fat Man carry him home. "Put me up on your shoulders," he insists. They go this way for a while in peace, Fat Man's knees and spine straining but willing; he feels bad about undermining his brother in front of the vendor. This is meant to be a peace offering.

"Go faster, *Uncle*," says Little Boy.

"No."

"Go faster," says Little Boy, using his heels as spurs.

They careen down an empty road. Fat Man's sides burn; he reaches back and slaps the boy's face. Little Boy grabs his brother's ears and pulls with both hands, hard. Fat Man roars, rears back. Now Little Boy hangs from Fat Man's ears, gripping tight to stay up. Fat Man thrashes. Slaps his brother on the back. Digs his fingers into the little boy's ribs. Hurls him off, so Little Boy falls to the ground, rolls onto his back. He groans. Fat Man stalks away, off the path into a forest of tall, thin trees. He squats among them, breathes deeply. The sullen slump of his back, the lump of his body, like a mushroom.

Little Boy sits up. To his brother's back he says, "We agreed I was in charge!"

He says, "We agreed I was your big brother!"

He says, "We never agreed on those names! You did that alone, without my permission!"

He stomps his foot. "You have to listen to me!"

He stomps his foot again. "Do you know how much money we've got? What you promised them means either we stow away on the boat or we stop eating immediately."

He stomps his foot again.

He says, "What do you have to say for yourself, *John*?"

Fat Man turns around like an outsize baby who just learned to sit up. He looks his brother dead on, sees the snot that runs from Little Boy's nose, and the narrow thread of blood therein.

"I'm sorry, Brother," he says. "Nobody believes it."

Little Boy asks him who anybody is to tell them who they are. Who that rat bastard GI fraud artist was. Who anyone is to tell them how they should be. "You were no one when I found you," he says. "You were a coward in a hole. I searched for you and I found you. I've taken care of you. Taken care of everything."

"I'm only saying nobody believes it," says Fat Man. "You know I've tried. But when people say big brother they don't seem to be thinking of age. They're talking about size. And anyway, I look older. Do you not like Matthew? We could call you something else. We could go back now and tell him your name is whatever you want it to be. You could be George, like he said."

"I can see I've been too easy on you," says Little Boy. Unsteadily, he climbs to his feet, and goes into the forest, where he pushes Fat Man by the shoulders. Fat Man, still sitting, rocks a little back, is otherwise unmoved.

"What are you doing?" Fat Man asks.

"Spanking you," says Little Boy.

Fat Man laughs.

"I'm spanking you," shrills Little Boy. "Bend over!"

Fat Man bends over. "Go ahead," he says. "If it makes you feel better you can wail on me all you want." Their positions suggest a father playing horsey with his son. Little Boy seems about to climb on. However, he inserts his knee beneath his brother's gut, kneeling a little to achieve the effect, as if he supports the lummox. Little Boy brings down his hand on Fat Man's left buttock. The sharp sound echoes in the trees. Fat Man feels nothing. Little Boy strikes him again.

Again.

Again.

Fat Man holds in his laughter the best he can.

Little Boy goes frantic. He wails on him with both hands. Each impact produces a satisfying but meaningless sound, no pain, no catharsis.

When he's done Little Boy says, "There."

He says, "I hope you've learned your lesson."

He says, "I don't like doing that. But it's for the best."

They walk home together. Fat Man expects Little Boy to demand another ride. But Little Boy knows better.

That night Fat Man counts the money. Makes a budget, accounting for the cost of their tickets to France. Tells Little Boy they've got enough money left for the passports, for their journey, for one meal a day.

Nothing more.

"When we get there," says Fat Man, "we'll need jobs."

Little Boy closes the cash case, snapping its ruined hinges into place. "You'll need a job," he says. "Little boys don't work."

They visit the squealing pigs.

They sleep in the mud.

THE PIG KNOTS

Little Boy wakes. He sees the farmer's daughter is stalking toward him and his snoring brother. He raises his hand in an awkward, fearful greeting. She grabs him by the scalp; she breathes words he cannot understand, words he can't answer. He can't see her eyes in the darkness. Only the long, sallow shadows cast by her brow, which creep into the gaunt valleys of her cheekbones. He can't see her teeth or her lips—only the divot underneath her nose like a teardrop, and the hole of her mouth.

He thinks she is asking him questions, that she's blaming him for something he's sure he didn't do, would never do. She holds him by the hair on the back of his head, pulling it harshly. She takes his hand in her hand. Her hateful grasp.

"How can this be?" she says, in Japanese. "I am a virgin."

She pushes his hand against her stomach as if she means to pull him inside. Their sticky skin is touching, her belly, his fingers. He didn't think she was naked. Perhaps her robe is open. She says, "What have you done to me? What has America done?"

Then the drums begin. Wild-thrashing in her gut. She holds his hand in place until the thing inside her makes him sore. He digs with hard, dirty nails into the cold, taut swell of her belly. He means to draw blood but the heat doesn't come. It doesn't come.

Morning now. Little Boy finds Fat Man standing with the mother at the edge of the pigpen, leaning over the fence, her hands on a post. The wind tugs at her hair. She leans over the fence and watches. The father and his daughter kneel in pig shit, it is smeared all over their bodies. The sows birth lumpy little piglets into father's and daughter's waiting hands. They rinse the piglets with well water from a bucket, straining blood and mucus through their fingers. They tuck the newborns in the blankets. They roll them up together; they pile baby pigs for warmth.

The piglets seem only half-formed, pale and fetal.

The father instructs his daughter as they work. He lifts sow tails and points to the swollen, painful things beneath. He whispers to her how to care for new mothers, how to pull free their young. The mother pigs look bloated in some places and in other places thin. Their bellies are distended, their ribs protrude. Their skin is shiny and wet, overstretched—nearly transparent. They lie on their sides in their filth and their blood, panting for air, squealing pitiably. Little Boy thinks what it would be like to toss them in the river. To make them drown. There is something loathsome about them. Something he can't name. For the first time, the father acknowledges Fat Man and Little Boy. He says a word of greeting, lowering his eyes demurely as if it were *his* body sprouting new things. Little Boy says nothing. Fat Man imitates his word.

Little Boy leans in for a closer look at the piglets. They are very still and very quiet.

The father sees his interest. He takes a piglet from the rest and rolls it side to side in his hands as if molding dough. Fat Man understands that this is meant to keep the small thing warm. When the father hands it to him he rolls it in his hands too. His hands shake from repulsion; he struggles not to drop this dumb, half-made thing. The father hands another piglet to Little Boy.

These newborns are bald all over. Their faces sag with exhausted agony; their eyes have not opened; their ears are so thin that you can see the veins inside them. They are weak children—this one can barely move its hoof, can barely move its head. Its piggy nostrils flare and shrink. This animal is too thin to live. The joints are blueish, and its mouth hangs slack as if unhinged.

Fat Man leans in close. The flesh is so doughy, so pliable—it molds itself to his fingers as he rolls it in his hands.

Little Boy's piglet opens its eyes and it tilts its head to look back into Little Boy's eyes. There is perhaps a spark of recognition, some brief lucidity, and the child begins to keen. To sing for his attention, like a whisper, like a plea. Little Boy realizes he is dropping the piglet.

Little Boy has dropped the piglet.

"Careful," shouts Fat Man.

It's on the ground, crumpled, barking for help. The father clucks to scold Little Boy; he shakes his head. He is whispering something about the right way to care for a piglet, and the wrong way. The dropped piglet stands up faltering, it sways on its knees and soft cloven hooves, it looks up at Little Boy.

Fat Man says, "He looks like you. He wants to be carried."

It barks again. The father and the daughter are busy with the sows, there are still more babies coming out of their hindquarters, some of them have died from giving so much birth.

The other piled piglets come to in their blankets. They wriggle out of their folds and traipse across the pigpen, halting, dipping their noses in muck and muck and muck, dragging their soft white bellies, leaving shallow furrows in the muck and muck. They sneak under the fence. They are a swarm. They are crying for something, for hunger, for love, for *anything*. They crowd the brothers. They gnaw toothlessly at their shoes and pant legs, tugging with slow, zombie strength, weak and implacable, urgent and breakable. The piglet swarm begs their attention. They put their fore-hooves up on their shoes. They soil themselves in anticipation, though they have not eaten; it comes out a gray milk that leaks from underneath their tails. Fat Man holds his hands up against himself like a tyrannosaur. He wants to kick them away. Little Boy leaps up on the fence. The father sets a newborn down and it too begins to cross the pen, to slip beneath the crossboards of the fence, to join the throng around Fat Man's ankles. It is a kind of worship. They look up and beg with their eyes for him to lift them, for him to hold them in his arms. They call for Little Boy to come down.

The mother and the daughter watch with the same pinched, illegible expression. From Little Boy's new height, the bulge of their stomachs is apparent. Little Boy remembers and it fills him with terror. He knows what it is to be born. How it hurts, then and after.

Fat Man calls to the farmer, the mother, their daughter, "Help me. Can you take them away?"

No one knows what he's saying. The piglets crowd and oink for his love. They call for Little Boy, who now balances atop the highest crossboard on the fence, feet and shaking hands, precarious. No one comes to help them or seems to understand their fear. The pigs exhaust themselves. Some go to sleep or collapse, squealing. Some of them may die. When the herd has thinned, Fat Man and Little Boy run for the house, pursued by several of the more robust piggies.

They stay for midday meal. The births have made them guests—the mother refuses their money. The farmer brings in a butchered sow from outside. Peeking through the doorway, Little Boy assures the still panicked and nearly tearful Fat Man that the piglets are all asleep or suckling with their mothers or those mothers still living.

Fat Man collapses against the wall. He heaves. He says, "The way they look at us."

"I saw it," says Little Boy.

"They know," says Fat Man.

"What can pigs know?"

"They *see* us. What we are."

"You can't be sure of that," says Little Boy. But he saw it too.

The mother cooks the pork. It smells the way a burning person does.

"Do you recognize that smell?" asks Fat Man, sweating through his shirt.

"No," lies Little Boy. "I don't."

The sun comes down low. The pigs raise a ruckus as if calling for a meal, though they have been fed today. The father, the mother, the daughter go outside. There are mutters thereafter but no discernible words, no sounds of swine.

Little Boy goes outside first. Fat Man reluctantly follows. The women's hands worry the timber. They scratch against the grain. It makes a sound like grinding teeth. Fat Man and Little Boy join them at the fence.

The father looks up from his sow. His hands are full of blood like oil. There's a gray-pink thing like a worm with knots on its sides half-submerged in the blood. He places the worm on a tumorous pile of like worms and wipes his hand in the muck among tens of other red streaks. Blood floats on muck surface like oil on water. The father puts his hand inside the pig. He pulls out another pink, knotty worm.

Fat Man says, "She's dead."

They are all dead or dying, all the sows and all the new babies. The newborn shoats have given up their suckling but do still nuzzle their mothers as if to urge them back to life. The hogs stand indifferent. They are still like gelatin is still. They stare into the middle-distance with puckered eyes and wait for someone to feed them, casting shadows in various of the cardinal directions. Some east, some west. As if the sun's come down close, has deigned to walk among them in the pen. The father hums a sad song. The women are crying. All their pigs are dead, or will be soon, except the hogs.

What good are hogs alone, Little Boy wonders.

He sees his brother's face in a hog's face. Neither of the brothers has ever looked directly into a mirror. Little Boy's face might be the same. Fat Man may not know his own resemblance to the hogs. Or he might guess.

The father's pulling red-tinged strings of mucus from between his fingers and flicking-flinging them away. He begins to pile the sows' corpses, dropping them one by one onto something like a wheelbarrow, a flat wooden platform perched on two tin legs and a tin wheel.

The daughter shrieks. There's a growing wet stain on the back of her blue robe. Briny water trickles from between her legs. The mother assaults her with questions while the daughter fights a swoon. Her water has broken.

The mother says, "Come inside, or you'll give the pigs a meal." She takes her daughter by the hand and rushes her into the house.

The piglets that live have begun to crowd the brother bombs, again oinking at their ankles.

"The pigs must think you are their fathers," says the father, laughing a sour laugh. The sound dies in his throat. A darkness passes over his face. He understands something that he did not before. The hog shadows grow longer; the animals themselves do not move. The piglets oink and squeal. The father turns away from the brothers. They don't know what he said. They don't know what he understands.

The father wheels the piled sow bodies to the home, where he takes them on his shoulders and carries them through the door. As the paper door slides closed Little Boy glimpses mother and daughter inside the home. Mother sets down a short, broad wooden bucket. The daughter watches her, shakes her head, and whispers painful secrets. She clutches her robe—gathered up in her fists so that her strong young thighs the color of moon are exposed—and presses it between her legs as if to staunch the flow. The mother comes to the door. She closes it, glaring at the brother bombs. The daughter is staring into the wooden bucket, and then she is bisected by the closing door, and then she is gone.

Little Boy looks at the pile of unfinished pigs in the muck and muck and muck of the pen. They are weird lumps of raw, misshapen meat, almost certainly inedible. He wonders, Do they have bones?

He says to Fat Man, "Carry me," and, before his brother can object, leaps into his arms. Fat Man stumbles back a little. He tries his best not to kick any babies as he walks them toward the house. The oinklings follow. The hogs lie down in the filth; several loll onto their sides.

The mother sits behind the daughter. The daughter, now naked, squats over the pail, her heels butting up against either side, her legs already trembling. Her breasts are painful-looking—sharp, high fistfuls that seem to be ever and constantly squeezed, even now, by the hands that made them. A thin red stream like razor wire falls between her legs, though it does not seem to fall but rather to hold fast, like a measure of yarn connecting her body to the water below. In the water the red is murk. Marbles clarity with unclarity.

The mother is massaging her daughter's abdomen. She pushes and prods with her fingers, and the flesh turns ivory white where she presses, and pink around the white, like burning film. The mother's legs splay out around the daughter. They can see the hard, cracked skin lined with dirt on the soles of her feet. They cannot see the mother's face.

They can hear the mother screaming at them. They do not know what she says.

They know exactly what she means. "GET OUT!" she is saying. "GET OUT!" They cannot see the father, but hear him in the room like a kitchen, butchering sow bodies.

The red yarn between the daughter's legs is cut. Droplets fall, then nothing.

Fat Man closes the door. The brother bombs sit down among adoring piglets.

They sit against the house. The piglets are curled up against them asleep, or they are sitting in their laps, or they are sniffing all about their shoes. There is one sitting on the cash case. If they are awake they are looking at the brother bombs, contemplating their vastness through puckered piggy eyes. Inside the home the daughter cries for mercy. It's been maybe an hour. Little Boy circles his finger in the dirt. He draws clouds.

"Do you think they knew she was pregnant?" says Little Boy.

"I'm not sure she knew," says Fat Man.

Little Boy holds his tongue. She knew *something*. He thinks of his hand on her stomach, her hand pressing his, the heat of her body, and the ruckus inside. He remembers the mother squatting on the toilet as her daughter squats now in what is like the living room. He remembers the frenzy of the pigs, their midnight meal, a feast of night soil. It all must be connected but the only connection he can find is that he saw all of these things. They listen to the rising symphony of crickets, to the farrowing daughter, the butchering father.

Fat Man lifts a baby pig to look in its eyes. "Do you think she'll be all right?"

Little Boy doesn't answer.

"Why do the little pigs know who we are and not the big ones?" says Fat Man. "And if they know us, then why do they love us?" He sets down his pig and looks at his black palms. "How can they love us?"

"This is love?" says Little Boy.

"Who knows what pigs feel?" What he means to say is, Yes.

The daughter weeps. The mother is crying now too. They hear one savage chop as the father embeds his knife in the block's corner and then nothing, footsteps, nothing, wailing, wailing.

The father comes out with a baby. It is a soft thing, unfinished like the pigs, and seems to have too little skin—the elbows won't straighten; the toes curl in, and express themselves mostly as lumps in footflesh; the chin tucks into the collarbone. The fingers flex and squeeze like hungry claws. The father puts the baby in Fat Man's hands. He says, "Somehow this is your fault." For a moment Fat Man thinks he might know what was said.

The baby grabs Fat Man by the lapels of his suit and pulls. It burbles stupidly, its throat raw from crying, too weak now for the life ahead. Spit bubbles in the corners of its mouth. Its eyes are like wet marbles.

Fat Man burbles at the baby. He gives it one of his fingers to clutch.

"It doesn't look quite right," says Little Boy.

"Maybe this is how Japanese babies look when they're fresh from the oven."

"It makes me think of the pigs."

"I can't think who would be the father," says Fat Man. "I haven't seen her with any men, other than her own father."

"And you," says Little Boy.

"I hardly count."

The father returns to the wailing house.

Little Boy pats the baby's tummy. There is something familiar in the child's dumb gaze.

The next time the father comes out, there's a second baby in his hands. This one is smaller, grayer, and still. He hands the body to Little Boy. The head falls back from the body, exposing what is like a neck. The eyes are closed, the mouth half open.

The father watches him hold the baby and waits, as if expecting Little Boy to say something. As if Little Boy will confess to the murder. Little Boy shrugs. So does Fat Man.

"Are the women all right?" asks Fat Man.

The father goes back into his home. The brother bombs are left to watch their babies.

Fat Man's child alive and Little Boy's dead.

Little Boy says, "I don't think mine is breathing." He concentrates on the face of the baby, watching for the slightest hint of motion. "Why'd he give me this one?"

Inside the home the family is quiet like dead things are quiet.

FAT MAN EXPLODES

Inside the home it is dark. There are the ripe smells of open bodies. The women must be in what is like the kitchen. They have left their pail, which brims with things that came from inside them. Fat Man sets his baby in a blanket. Little Boy is still trying to read the dead thing in his hands. The kitchen wall slides open. The father stands naked in shadow, half-butchered pigs piled on the table behind him, an iron cleaver in his hand. His bones show through his skin like actors behind curtains. His penis is long and thin like some sickly root. They cannot see his eyes.

"How did you do this?" he asks them.

Little Boy clutches the stillborn against his chest as if the father is a hungry thing. Fat Man might know what's being asked. He might recognize the words.

The father says, "Before you came, before the Americans, everything was fine. How did you put babies inside them?"

Fat Man says, "What?" He asks in Japanese.

The father advances on the brother bombs. "How did you do it to my pigs? How are you to blame?"

Fat Man understands "how." He understands "blame."

There is motion in the dark. The daughter cradles her mother's rubber body behind the table. The mother is breathing like she does not mean to do it.

Fat Man searches for a weapon. Little Boy trembles and crawls behind his brother. "Help me brother! Save me!"

The naked father lunges. He sinks the cleaver into Fat Man's shoulder. Blood sprays the wall. The father pulls the knife loose, and Fat Man is screaming, he lashes out at the air. The father wipes the blood from his eyes with the back of his hand—it smears, a sticky stripe. His left eye is stuck closed and the right is spiderwebbed with angry veins. They breathe into each other's noses and mouths, they taste the sour inside each other, they hear the rush of air. Fat Man is still screaming. He is squeezing his shoulder when he should be fighting back.

Little Boy has fallen to his side. The baby rolls like an empty jar. Little Boy knows what it's like to explode. It's like this. He is going to explode. He can feel the awful, acid heat inside him between icy bones and sizzling skin. He feels the vertigo of expansion—the giddy over-filling of a straining bright balloon.

He is a bomb again, he is a bomb again, he is a bomb exploding.

Fat Man falls on his back, the naked father is on him. The naked father cleaves the ground beside his ear.

"The baby," shouts Fat Man as he claws the father's face and peels of skin bunch up beneath his nails.

Little Boy puts his thumb in his mouth. It soothes him. The expanding inside does not expand, but pulsates, hot and cold, too much and too little, in and out, boy and bomb and boy and bomb. He sucks his thumb.

Fat Man hits the father with the cash case. The father carves a corner from his ear. His blows are wild. Fat Man hits him with the suitcase again, and again: flat, dull thuds. Until a golden corner finds the father's temple.

The body now is like the stillborn baby, but so heavy. Fat Man holds the suitcase in both hands and brings it down like a guillotine, smashing the father's head against his own breast. The skull gives. Warmth flows over his chest. Fat Man knows that he is screaming, has known from the start. He means to continue.

Little Boy is safe. He opens his eyes and unclamps his teeth from around his thumb. He has fouled himself. In this dark the stillborn's body looks like pink-blue sand dunes sloping toward oblivion. The limbs are all wrong, the head all crushed, like the father's now.

Fat Man pushes the father's body from his body. Their blood is everywhere and looks identical.

"What did you do to him?" says Little Boy.

"What did you do to *him*?" says Fat Man, indicating the stillborn.

"I nearly exploded," says Little Boy. "I was so scared."

Little Boy puts his blanket over the stillborn and takes the still-living baby from his brother's bed. The baby has been wailing; now it stops. To stare at Little Boy with moony, tired, porcine eyes.

"I did explode," says Fat Man.

The women are asleep in the kitchen. For the first time, the brother bombs see the sleeping mats the family hid beneath the table. Little Boy places the living baby down with the daughter, its mother. Fat Man goes through their food stores. He takes

83

their rice bag and their small portable stove. He takes their stores of pork and drops them in the rice sack.

Little Boy says, "I don't think we should do this. We just killed their father."

"You talk as if he didn't try to kill me first," growls Fat Man. "Besides, I'm starving. Every time I asked for seconds she just stared at me. As if she couldn't work out what this meant." Fat Man holds out two fingers insistently—two, two, two.

Little Boy rubs his eyes. The newborn watches them silently. It's trying to read them, as Little Boy tried to read its stillborn brother.

"Would you even care if I died?" says Fat Man. His brother answers with a glare. Fat Man clenches his hand. "You hid behind me. You were supposed to protect me and you hid behind me instead. How can you question me?" The gash in his shoulder sings like an old brass bell. "You stink," he says. "Take off those pants."

"I told you not to take their food!"

The daughter stirs. She sees the bloody giant standing over her with her family's rice, her family's stove. She asks them, "Where are you going?"

"God damn it," roars Fat Man, "I'm hungry! I'm hungry, and you're done telling me what to do." He rubs his palm over his face. He leaves the room and comes back with the blood-covered suitcase. The daughter understands what she is seeing. She shakes her mother hard. Fat Man opens the briefcase and hauls out great honking wads of cash. He hurls it at the women. The mother wakes. Some bills stick to them, sticky with blood. The rest fall around them like green confetti.

They harp and twitter with inscrutable questions, accusations, threats, pleadings. The newborn cries. There are open pigs on the table between them, all viscera and threads of fat. "Why did you kill him?" shouts the daughter. The mother fights to keep her eyes open. "Why did you kill him?" the daughter screams, again, again.

When the cash case is maybe too low and the women have been thoroughly feathered with dollars, Fat Man sets off running. Little Boy follows, still stinking in his soiled pants, and crying for the stillborn.

They sleep this night by the road, in the brush. They should leave the scene but they are too tired.

In the morning Fat Man makes all the rice the stove can hold and roasts pork over the flame. Little Boy takes a handful. Fat Man eats the rest.

Little Boy is wearing his other pair of undershorts, his dress shirt, his tie, and blue suit jacket. He left behind his hat. Fat Man slept in his bloodied clothes, now festooned with small green leaves, yellow weed blossoms, and a crushed spider's legs. Between handfuls of rice he progressively disrobes himself—drops the jacket, opens his shirt, shrugs it off, pulls off his pants over his shoes. Shiny white grains of rice stick to his hands and face as he wolfs down the food.

"Why did he do that?" says Little Boy.

"I never claimed to understand the Japanese mind," says Fat Man. He begins to dig at the dirt with his hands.

"Why was he naked?"

"Why am I naked?" says Fat Man. This is not strictly true— he still wears a too-small undershirt and a mostly-white pair of shorts, but so much of him spills out, and he is so pink, that the effect is very much that of a bare body. The shirt is red-stained on the shoulder, but not like the one he wore last night, which lies in the dirt, crusty and so red it's almost black. "Like us, he had very few clothes to his name. He didn't know who we were or who we knew—for all he could say, we had big, important friends with guns who would be coming by to check on us the next morning." He rolls his sodden clothes into a heap and puts them in the shallow hole that he's been digging. "Had he done otherwise, he would have ruined his clothes, and there would have been evidence. This way, had he killed us, he would only need to take a bath." A disquieting thought crosses his face like a crow's shadow. "And bury our bodies."

"What now?" says Little Boy.

Fat Man pushes dirt over his clothing and pats it down flat as he can. He sweeps loose brush over this, tears leaves from the nearest tree, and drops them on the mound.

"Now we go to town, we avoid soldiers, police, and Japanese in general. We buy some new clothes." He shakes the cash case. It makes a nearly empty sound. "Cheaper ones. We wait for our passports and plan our escape."

"They'll be looking for us," says Little Boy.

The two policemen, tall and short, limping and not limping, come out the front door of the farmer's home. They see Fat Man and Little Boy but do not dwell on them. They walk down the road, away, away.

"They're leaving?" says Little Boy. "Did you know they were in there?"

"You're full of questions this morning," says Fat Man. "You done being the big brother?"

"I don't understand what you're talking about," says Little Boy. "Did they not see the bodies? Did they not know it was us?"

"They don't care," says Fat Man. "You haven't figured it out? They don't care. They don't care, and you don't know anything." He wipes the sticky rice from his face; leaves dirt trails on his cheeks. "Get up on my lap, Matthew," he says. He pats his knee. He is kneeling.

"What?" says Little Boy.

"Come up here on my lap," says Fat Man. Pats his knee again. "Come on."

Little Boy climbs up. Fat Man grabs him by his scruff and forces him down on his belly, across his knee.

"You didn't protect me," Fat Man says. "You were supposed to be my big brother. But nobody buys it. I'm the big brother now. And when we are with people, I'm your uncle."

Fat Man begins to spank him. Little Boy feels each blow.

"Who is your big brother?"

"You are," says Little Boy, choking back a sob.

They buy new clothes. They sleep behind the home of a man who makes luxury cars. Every morning he sees them waking up in their new clothes and their white skins and thinks they must be customers. They walk away without a word.

Fat Man pawns their fancy suitcase, having cleaned off the blood as best he could. It fetches a very good price. He buys another suitcase: same size, same shape, only gray, simple. They live on the pawn money. They buy their tickets to France.

Fat Man eats constantly. He buys rice and cooks it on his stolen portable stove.

Little Boy doesn't mention how his brother's getting fatter. Little Boy eats too-small helpings and burns inside. He makes prolonged eye contact with strange girls on the street. They stare back at him blankly. He finds a black felt hat on the road and he wears it, though it does not match his clothes. He makes Fat Man piggy-back him wherever they go. Because he is the big brother now, and sometimes the uncle. Fat Man never complains.

Nor does he talk anymore when he eats.

WHAT EVIDENCE
THEY LEFT

Fat Man sits in a small Japanese home, an open suitcase on the floor before him. This is the cash case. It is still clean on the outside. It still opens from the wrong side—the broken hinges, bending at the soft lock. On the other side of the cash case are the two policemen, one short and one tall, both quite starved and deadly thin. They have shown their credentials. They showed their credentials and indicated that Fat Man and Little Boy should come with them. "He's a child," said Fat Man. He said this in Japanese. So they took Fat Man away from his brother. They left Little Boy alone.

Little Boy who asked Fat Man, "How do you know Japanese?"

Now the policemen are sitting on the floor on the other side of the open cash case. Its lock will only bend so far. They cannot see what's in the case, but they know. They put it there. There are inside perhaps a hundred dollars, clumped and clotted by dried blood. Some leaves the brothers may have laid on, now reduced to twiggy skeletons, also crushed. A small, gray mound of dirt or dust. The fat man's bloodied shirt. The father's knife. So surely they have seen the father, collected testimony from his wife, his daughter.

They do not ask the Fat Man any questions. Only look at him and wait for him to say what he will say.

They wait.

They only wait.

"My boat is going," he says, slowly, with some effort. The way he learns he's learned a word is he says that word. He says, "I need to go also."

"What did you do?" asks the tall policeman. "What are these?"

Fat Man shakes his head. He means to say he does not understand. He does not know what he understands until he answers. There is language. There is somewhere language. On the air or in him. Like a spider's web is snared somewhere on his body, but he can only see the trailing thread: there is language.

"We found the body," says the short one. "We found his knife."

"What did he do?" says the tall one.

Fat Man takes a twiggy leaf bone from the case and twists it between his fingers. He says, "No."

He says, "I need to go."

He lays the leaf's bone down in the cash case, now an evidence case. He looks at the knife. To see it makes his shoulder ache.

The policemen study his face. For signs of guilt? For feeling? They must want to arrest him. To put him in prison. Yet he is American. There are rumors of American soldiers who travel in rape gangs. It's said they cut the telephone lines on one city block and move from home to home, raping wives and sisters, mothers and daughters. Some of the women they kill, but mostly they can't be bothered. There are no trials. If these men cannot be tried, then how can Fat Man? The wife and her daughter, if they have given testimony, may well have told the truth, in which case it was self-defense. If the mother and her daughter lied, then Fat Man is still an American—a well-fed one. One who wears a suit. Though it is always the same suit. He may have connections. Perhaps he knows MacArthur. Or so they may think. Or it may be they are waiting for Fat Man to implicate himself. To break down sobbing. It is not precisely guilt he feels for what he did, though on other days it has been guilt. To what could he confess? Not the pigs. Not the babies. But neither the father: the father least of all. His palms are black. Do they think this normal? Do they see it as a sign of guilt?

It may be the language barrier protects him. They do not know how to interrogate a person with so little Japanese. Are confused by the fact that he has any in the first place. They cannot accuse who they cannot interrogate. Or they empathize, perhaps. They imagine him on the witness stand, if there is a witness stand, if in Japan they have such a thing. They imagine the prodding questions of the prosecutor if there is a prosecutor, or a judge if there is only a judge. They imagine Fat Man listening dumbly, waiting for a word he knows. His pidgin responses. Unresponsive, even inappropriate, puzzling and puzzled. He might think they didn't care about his guilt if not for the hardness in their faces, if not for their resemblance to the dead soldiers, one short and one tall.

It may be these sickly men could not arrest him if they wanted. These do not carry guns. They have only truncheons. They are perhaps too weak to wield the truncheons. He could maybe crush them, or they may think that he could crush them, that there is no arresting him without the aid of others. He has seen so few other policemen in this city on the coast. They are watching him. He is looking back at them. He is looking at the evidence case. Perhaps they mean it as a gift. He could close the case, slide its hinges into place, and go—a memento. The sound of a knife in a suitcase, the sound of scabbed money. Some dirt. Luggage, only luggage. Only what he carries.

The tall one closes the evidence case. The hinges click into place.

Or it may be there's no point. Even assuming the possibility of arrest, of conviction. There were these bombs. Not here, but nearby. There were these bodies. The bodies are gone. There is no good count of these bodies. There were other bodies? What's a hog farmer's body? What's a stillborn baby? What are two crying women? Compared to two cities and all the bodies therein, now gone?

They cannot know he was the thing exploded. Or can they know? They cannot know.

Still there are his hands.

"Are you sorry?" asks the tall one. But Fat Man does not understand.

"I need to go," says Fat Man. "The boat is going." He realizes he can say "without me." "Without me," he says. "The boat."

It occurs to him he can leave. The small Japanese home may be the home of the policemen. They do not seem at home here. But there are signs that someone lives here. Used dishes, an open book, a telephone in the corner, on the floor. A painting of mountains hanging on the wall. A sock, discarded. These things all could be theirs. This home is not a prison.

He stands. He leaves the small home. The policemen only watch. As he passes through the doorway, one of them—the tall or the short, he does not turn to see—reaches for his hand, and holds it. The policeman's skin is cold. His grip is tight. Not painful, but tight. Not a threat, but tight. Not angry, but tight. What the hand seems to say is, Wait. What the hand seems to say is, We can talk.

Fat Man pulls his hand loose. He goes.

Outside the home is Little Boy, who followed them here. He's been sitting on the ground, back propped against the home, waiting just beside the door. He might have heard it all or nothing. He says, "We need to get to the boat."

"They have the cash case, and other things."

"So we should go then," says Little Boy, taking Fat Man's hand. "Do you know Japanese now?"

"No," says Fat Man. What he means is that he only knows a little. What he means is that it was no use. What he means is he rejects the language. He rejects this country. He rejects the evidence case and everything within, not because it's wrong but because it's not enough.

They go to the dock. They wait in line to board their boat. They hold hands so as not to lose each other.

When they board the boat the Japanese policemen are there to watch them from the shore. Not to stop them or to wave. No goodbyes. Their faces are illegible from the deck. Their bones show through, but not their eyes. Their uniforms are clean and pressed. As the boat departs, the tall one collapses. The short one catches him in both arms, and for a long time they seem to kneel together. When it seems they will not, cannot stand, then they do stand, together, the short one hoisting the tall one up to his feet. When each is righted, they lace their fingers.

They too hold hands.

HOTEL GURS

WHAT FRANCINE KNOWS

Francine lies awake in bed, pretending to know where her husband is now. She pretends to know he is with another woman. She pretends to know they're sitting together outside an abandoned café, her husband and the other woman—a blonde—and that he brought them cheeses and melon chunks to share in the dark, seated on chairs he took off a tabletop and set down for them. He makes two flirtatious jokes before forgetting to charm the other woman, before resuming the comfort of his usual half-sullen silence, the silence that makes him pout so pretty. The one that makes his eyes seem to float in his skull like paper lanterns on the water. He pours wine for himself and neglects to offer her any. She has to pour it if she wants it. He's smoking between chews. It would be rude if it were anybody else.

She pretends her husband will not be home tonight. If she weren't sure of this, she would have to watch the door, or, more discreetly, the wall opposite the door, for changes of light. She would wait for a wedge of yellow to open, and his shadow.

Now she doesn't have to wait, because she is certain. Instead she clenches closed her eyes.

Her hard heart wavers. She is no longer certain. So she changes the story. Now he is sharing a hotel room with this other woman, who is a brunette, who is also married, whose husband is away on business—scrabbling for a piece of the new action, the foreign investors, large Americans. They are making raucous love to each other. He presses her face and breasts to the cool thick window, through the curtains, but he tells her to imagine he's drawn the curtains. And it's light out. And everyone can see her. They can see the way she moans, the way her nipples press flat against the glass, like veal medallions.

When she comes he comes too. He doesn't pull out, doesn't spray the brunette's back, doesn't watch it trickle down her thighs, but pushes deeper in her; damn the consequences; damn him, he's coming. He grits his teeth the way he does. They squeak, he's sucked them dry. Francine's sure of it, lying in bed.

She's sure of it. She reaches down between her legs, then stops, thinks better.

"It shouldn't bother me if he doesn't want to do it inside me," she says to herself, fortified by her confidence that even now her husband's clever sperm are striving for this other married woman's eggs.

Francine is thirsty. She climbs out of bed and puts her feet in their blue slippers. She goes to the kitchen for a glass of water. There's a faint chill on the air like an unwelcome secret. She tips back the glass, finishes the water in one gulp, and licks the dewy moisture from her lips. Her husband never believed in marriage, as he acknowledged on the night of his proposal. He asked her anyway, during all the excitement, when people did these things. But clearly children are out of the question.

She pours herself another glass of water and walks back to

bed. Should he come home early, Francine doesn't want to seem to have been waiting up. She isn't waiting for anybody. She only woke up thirsty.

Francine reflects that her husband would not leave her alone all night simply for sex. "He's more discreet than that," she whispers to her glass. She revises her confidence again. Her husband is still in a hotel, but now it's more expensive, and yet no one's having fun. He sits up in the bed, back to the headboard, married brunette head in his lap. He's just paid for her abortion, so he strokes her hair and twists the ends between his fingers. The brunette rubs her stomach very slowly and wonders how it would be to feel a kicking thing inside her. He whispers drowsily how everything will be all right, like drooling honey in her ear. He's drooling honey, that's his fault, but the brunette doesn't turn her head to block the flow. They'll spend the night together. He'll leave early in the morning while she pretends to sleep, buy them a sweet breakfast and chocolates, and carry the food back to the hotel in a small brown basket. This might be the end of their affair, or not.

Francine won't know about that until circumstances call again for certitude, for deciding for herself what she can't know and won't ask.

Francine has finished her water. She rolls a cigarette. She puts it between her lips and chews the paper without chewing hard enough to break it. That feels like breaking skin. When she can't wait anymore she strikes a match and lights it. She breathes deeply and blows smoke through her nose. She's never been like the leisure-soaked, cold-blooded women who can drag out a cigarette for nearly an hour, lace an evening, threading wisps of smoke through conversation. She huffs and puffs, Francine. She pauses only to cough. The taste still tickles her throat.

It must be a stranger knocking at her door. It must be a small stranger: the door makes a small sound. Francine finishes her cigarette and drops the stub in the trash before going to the door. On second thought, she brings a large knife with her. The small hand knocks again. *Put-pat.* She peeps through the peephole. There's the top of a dirty blond head in the hole and a thin white hand drawn back, waiting, shaking. It looks like a girl's hand, if the girl chewed her nails and her knuckles were knobby and pale. The hand moves as if to knock again and then falls out of sight, defeated. The dirty blond head turns away.

Francine opens the door. There is the blond boy sucking his thumbnail. He shivers pointedly. A fat man steps into view, a real behemoth. He shivers too. When he opens his fat mouth and hazards a greeting in clumsy, fat French, she knows he's American. He holds out his hands open-palmed, showing her they're empty, except for a charred blackness and a floppy blue hat that hangs from his fingers.

"Don't worry," she says, "I know some English. Come in, come in." She waves them in with her hands and steps back from the doorway, like guiding toddlers. She leaves the knife on the kitchen counter. They follow her inside. The little one rubs his hands on his pink cheeks. He sucks his thumbnail and bites at what spare rind is left.

She tells them to sit at the dinner table and they do. She asks them what they'd like to drink. They both say water. The fat one asks her does she have something they could eat—a crust of bread, or some old fruit perhaps. He says it's been a day since they've eaten. She says yes, there is bread. The man and the boy are looking at each other across the table as if it's been more than a day since they've done that as well, as if they're surprised to see what they see.

Both wear haggard formerly-blue suits, stained with mud and rain, threadbare at elbows and ankles. Their shirts are untucked and their tails hang with loose white threads. The shirts are yellow with sweat and filth. They set their tired hats on the table and the hats seem to sag beneath the weight of the air. The hats have been slept on many times, used for pillows, turned inside out by angry fists.

The fat man threatens to pour out of his chair at any second—his whole body slumps precipitously in every direction, folds overhanging folds, like a pudding trying to be still. He rests his elbows on the table, holding his face in his hands, sagging glum. The little boy is nervous. He runs a hand through his hair again and again, seeming to feel for fleas. He bounces his legs.

They are both very tired.

Francine butters two slices of bread for each and sets them on the bare table. "Thank you," says the little boy.

The fat man says, "Merci."

They eat the buttered bread. When they're finished the fat man brushes crumbs from the little boy's face. The gesture is both tender and brusque—he means well, but it looks like it hurts. They sip at their cups. When they're finished Francine pours more water. She waits for some explanation of who they are, how they came to be here, and what else they expect her to do for them. She feels—she doesn't know why—it would be rude to ask them. Yet what else can they discuss?

The fat one wipes moisture from his upper lip, where he is growing a regrettable mustache, probably not by choice. He says, "We've run out of money." The little boy nods: they have. "We're here from America." The little boy nods again: it's true. "His parents are dead." Here the fat man points at the boy, who confirms it. "His father was a GI. His mother killed herself when the news came."

"Terrible," says Francine.

"We came here to see where his father died, which we've done, and then to start over. I'm his uncle. I am a failure. I'm looking for work."

"Francine," she says, extending her hand to the boy first.

"Matthew." He takes her hand in both of his, shakes it three times, and doesn't let go. His skin is still cold.

"John," says the fat man, and he takes her other hand. The three of them are joined together. A portentous feeling passes through them. Francine notices the fat man is looking at her stomach with an expression of deep concern.

She slips out of their hands, which fall to the table among the crumbs of buttered bread. "Is something wrong?"

"Not at all," says John. "I was thinking how beautiful you are. I hope that's all right."

"Flattery," says Francine, lowering her eyes. "So you need somewhere to stay the night."

Matthew nods. "The floor will be fine," he says. "It's cold out."

"You can stay in the living room. Use the sofa if you like. If anyone comes into the house, don't worry. He's supposed to be here. I'll tell him the same about you."

She puts their cups in the sink, turning her back on her visitors. She runs the faucet a little. "Not that I think there will be anyone coming. You can tell me everything tomorrow. I'll try to help you find work."

"I don't want to sound ungrateful, but my curiosity overwhelms my better judgment. Why are you helping us?" says John. "I noticed you answered the door holding a knife."

She turns off the faucet. The three share her home's quiet. They commune with the still air and its faint chill.

"I'm lonely tonight," says Francine.

* * *

There's a white bust on the mantel in the living room. An old, bald white-skinned and white-haired man who looks like milk poured into a mold and frozen forever. His gaze is crisp, patient, brave, fogged, stern, shallow—lifeless. He wears a white mustache. It is smooth and featureless, not hair but a guard for his lip, a beetle shell on his face. Beside him on the mantel sits a dandy military cap.

"Who's that?" asks John. He has claimed the sofa. Matthew curls up in a worn chair. Francine takes down the bust, cradling the old man's head and shoulders against her breast. He stares blankly askance at the fat man.

"This is the marshal," she says. There is no spark of recognition in the fat man's eyes. "Pétain."

"How did you find yourself in possession of so fine a depiction?" says John. Francine wonders if he talks more the more tired he is—all the shiver has gone out of his pudding and now he seems so close to perfectly still, eternally slouched.

"Most people around here have one. They made quite a few. They were everywhere for a while. These days, most paint them, usually as a joke. Sometimes as another kind of statement. If you see someone who painted his Pétain realistically, it probably means he's a supporter, or at least a mourner." She puts the head back on the mantel. "Unless there's an emphasis on liver spots, wrinkles, or other deformities. Then it's hard to say."

"He's white," says Matthew. "You left him blank."

"I guess I don't know how to paint him," says Francine. She puts the dandy cap on his head. It casts a snug shadow over his face. "We like to put the hat on him for formal occasions. I guess that would be you."

The fat man adjusts his yellowed collar. "A formal occasion," he says, closing his eyes. "Me. Like a small dinner party, or a banquet. I like that."

The little boy laughs. "You'd be some banquet."

Francine lies in bed, knowing her husband will not be home until morning. She considers staying up, waiting—it's already nearly sunrise. She wants to suffer. She wants him to come home and see that she's suffered. She wants him to feel guilt, for once, or fear—fear of what she might do in her exhaustion, in her exhausted rage.

There are strange, hungry people downstairs. The marshal overlooks them, smart as a puffin in his cap and smooth mustache. His skin is colder than the air, colder than the windows.

She feels an urgent warmth against her belly. There is nothing there. There is a hot nothing, a wanting nothing, pleading nothing, thirsty nothing, loving, lonely, grasping nothing, nothing, urgent warmth against her belly. Like the visitors downstairs, it wants in.

WHAT GROWS
AROUND THEM

The brother bombs wake to the sounds of stairs straining beneath a man too tired for stealth. The staircase is behind them and they are afraid to sit up. Fat Man looks to the bust on the mantel as if its reaction could tell him what's coming. Pétain is calm, his eyes are blank as ever. The tired man makes the floorboards cry for help.

A pistol lowers itself from over the back of the couch. It dangles over Fat Man's cheek like a hanging tongue, though dry and cold. He feels around him in the blanket for help. It's wet. He understands he's had a wet dream. Under other circumstances he would like to take a moment to remember it—what he dreamed, or rather who—and savor the memory. Now, staring sideways up the barrel of a gun, he remembers the imagined feeling of a woman's hips melting in his iron grip. He chokes it down. He tells the first lie he learned to say in French. "We are not vagrants."

The gunman prods the fat man's cheek with his lethal probe.

He uses it to pull Fat Man's eye open wider. The gunman peers inside.

"Are you Francine's husband?" asks the fat man. The gunman nods. He is a handsome man with thick black hair, sharp wide eyes, and a nose like some ripe lovely root, with a pink, glowing tip. There are bags under his eyes and his hair is mussed—it stands on end in the front. The fat man smiles up at him, spreading his jowls like curtains. "I'm John," he says. "It's good to meet you."

The gun points down his open mouth.

"Albert," Francine shouts, running down the stairs. She vomits language—what must be French. People say it's a beautiful tongue. Sometimes, reflects Fat Man. Not always. Albert answers in low, measured sentence fragments, nodding or shaking his head, gun still trained on the fat man.

"I'm sorry my husband's an asshole," she says to the brothers. Then back to the fight. She pulls his gun arm up and away from the fat man. She wrenches the weapon from his hand. He doesn't fight back. She tries to empty the chambers, but they're already empty. She wrings the air as if it were his neck. He shrugs.

"It's safer that way," says Albert.

Fat Man is proud to understand him.

Albert says, "What if he knocked it out of my hand and turned it on me? Do you want me to die?"

"What's happening?" says groggy Little Boy, whose French is not coming along.

"Or what if I accidentally shot him?" asks Albert. He takes back the gun from his wife and tucks it in his belt like a bank robber.

Francine slaps her own forehead demonstratively. She says, perhaps believing John can't understand her, "Where were you all night?"

Albert answers in a whisper, perhaps out of shame, perhaps realizing the fat one understands them.

Fat Man motions to Little Boy that it's time to get up and go. The little boy wants to hide beneath his blanket. Instead he stands up, brushes grit off his clothing, and begins to dress. He pulls on his pants over his shorts, his discolored jacket over his ragged shirt the hue of an old smoker's teeth. The fat man is doing the same. He struggles with suspenders so tested they might give way any second. The jacket feels like it wants to strangle him—any thoughts of buttoning it closed are instantly forgotten.

Fat Man listens in as Francine whispers to her husband an explanation of the guests' presence. She offers something about being homeless, pathetic, without work. Something about how cute the child Matthew is, and something about how hungry they look. The husband laughs, probably thinking of the fat one's suspenders. Francine interrupts herself twice to smile at the fat man. He can see she likes to reassure people. The husband goes into the kitchen, gun still hanging from his belt, and lights a cigarette. He puts his feet on the table. Somehow it looks like they belong there.

Francine makes them breakfast while the brothers sit at the table listening to the English version of the conversation she and her husband just had. This time no one is pathetic or hungry. It's not clear how much her husband follows. He nods when she's not talking. He ashes his cigarette onto a scrap he tore from the newspaper he's reading. Little Boy draws small shapes on the table's surface with his own grease and sweat.

When she's done talking and the sizzle of eggs and sausages fills the air, John starts filling in the gaps. "We thought we brought enough money but we had to bribe several men to get through the border."

"You're lucky it wasn't more," says Francine, tending to the sausages in the pan.

"It's sleazy but I guess to be expected."

Albert chimes in, "Everything is chaos."

Little Boy Matthew turns his own collapsing hat in circles on top of his head.

Fat Man John continues, "We've found odd jobs here and there but it's hard. Of course as things return to normal, people want to give the jobs to Frenchmen. I understand that." He looks at the hard, slow curve of Francine's shoulders and the slope of her back. She wears a light yellow dress with a flower print. He says the thing that everybody wants to hear him say—the thing they wait to hear without knowing they wait. "I guess it was a mistake to come here, especially with him."

Little Boy pushes down his beaten hat until it covers the tops of his ears and his eyes.

"We've traveled much of the country, starting at the coast, moving south. It's so beautiful. I regret bringing little Matthew, I guess, though I'm all he's got. But I don't really regret coming." He reaches for his brother's hand. This time Little Boy remembers not to recoil. Their hands are hot when they touch. "I'd just like to find some simple work so we can establish ourselves. He's happy to work as well, until we can get him back into school."

Albert taps more ash onto the newspaper fragment. He turns a page. As he shifts his weight, his gun clicks against the chair where it hangs from his belt.

An empty thing can be so ominous.

Albert says something to Francine. She straightens her back and turns to look at them each. First her husband, then John. She says, "He wants to know what happened to your hands."

"How do you mean?" Of course he knows what she means.

"Your palms," she says.

He shows Albert the blackness of the soft parts of his hands, the heels and inner knuckles. "I burnt them," he says. "On a burning tree."

Francine translates. Albert smiles and gestures with his cigarette as if to say, All's well then.

Francine serves up breakfast. Fat Man takes his time. He doesn't ask for seconds. As he chews he thinks what it would be like to hit Albert, and though its chambers are empty he wonders how fast he would need to move to get the gun.

Albert goes to his office without the gun. He manages money—his own, the money of others, it's not clear, Fat Man doesn't ask. Francine brings the brothers to a restaurant that serves sandwiches, salads, and coffees spiked and sweetened with mint and fruit liquors. She knows the owner. She goes into the kitchen while Fat Man and Little Boy sit at a table inside and watch the handful of patrons—all of them half asleep, drinking from blue ceramic mugs and smiling lazily when the shift's only waiter walks past, tipping sugar into their cold coffee and stirring with brown-stained fingers. There are several women among them, all would-be Parisians compromising with practicalities of budget and scarcity in pursuit of the improvisational fashions from up north. Their skins, like the skins of most here, are damaged; plagued by boils and rashes that rose up in the hunger and deprivation under Nazis and Vichy. One is missing several teeth. Another has very thin hair. They do their best to simulate their former beauties. They are rowing upstream against time.

Fat Man estimates three days before these women start to show, and after that two weeks until they are bursting, until all their waters break and babies flow. Little Boy points out no one will know it was them, that no one possibly can. They could stay.

"I suppose you *enjoy* being subjected to the adoring stare of three dozen strange babies everywhere you go." Fat Man rubs his tired eyes. "How about when they get pregnant for a second time so soon, and they're birthing some half-formed thing a week later, some hideous child who would be better off dead, and they die in delivery because it's just too much? I guess you won't mind that either."

Little Boy shivers.

"No," says Fat Man. "You're right. We'll definitely stay for that."

"We'll leave in two weeks," says Little Boy, looking at the floor.

"You're damn right we will. No one asked you anyway." The waiter comes by with eyebrows raised—do they need assistance? Fat Man waves him away. Or perhaps the waiter swerves that way because he's come close enough to see the state of their clothing.

"I only wonder how long it'll last," says Little Boy.

"Maybe forever."

Francine comes out of the kitchen with the glow of good news on her face. Fat Man is drawn instead to the sight of her stomach. Perhaps it already bulges with some budding human fruit. It's hard to tell through the dress, which could slim an ox under the right circumstances. Francine shouts, "You've both got jobs." She seems to believe English is meant to be screamed. She throws her hands up in the air as if to summon a shaft of merciful light from the sky, through the ceiling, and onto the brothers. "John, you'll wash dishes, and Matthew will sweep the floors."

"Thank you," says Fat Man. "What's the pay?"

"Dreadful," declares Francine, her tone surrendering nothing to the word's meaning. "But it's something. You can stay with us until you've set yourselves right."

"Thank you," says Fat Man again. "Shall we get to work now?"

* * *

The large pile of dishes hidden in a humid closet of sorts behind the kitchen does not seem commensurate to the small number of customers. But then this must be why Fat Man was needed in the first place.

The owner is a thin man in a white shirt with a stiff, bent collar and both sleeves rolled up to just below the elbow. His name is Jacques. He doesn't know English and he doesn't know the fat man knows some French, so he points at the dishes and makes a scrubbing motion on an invisible plate. When the fat man doesn't respond he tries scrubbing harder. Fat Man nods, makes the OK sign, and gets to it.

Coffee stains are tough. There are sick sticky brown rings on all the plates and on saucers, and in the bottoms of the mugs. Tendrils of discolored gunk that overflowed the rims and dribbled down the sides are frozen there, seemingly forever, fixed in place by the things that cream and sugar do together. Worse though is what that coffee makes when it finds sugar. A deposit, a rich vein, like volcanic rock, like shale on a plate, brittle gunk. He scrapes it with butter knives and fork tines. He lets the water run over this, and the cake crumbs collected at its edges, and the pastry flakes, assembled bread bits, and lettuce leaves. He rubs some off with a washcloth, rinses, and then rubs some, but it won't come loose from the ceramics. Instead it becomes a kind of black-brown scab that runs with greasy water like a sore runs with human juices.

But the worst thing of all is the mold that springs up in the sink, sometimes faster than he can scrub it away and rinse it down the drain, sometimes so fast he can actually see it grow up from nothing into an inch-thick layer of white-green cotton yuck. It sprouts from everything he hasn't cleaned, all the leftover food and orange peels and cheese rinds. The mold grows to be near him. Where he touches the dishes, it rises to meet him, reaches out, or grows up, and reaching for him seems to seethe, and seething hums with energy he knows without knowing what it is.

Any meat he finds he picks up with a fork and hurls into a garbage bag before the hungry white worms come.

Fat Man asks the owner if they have to pay for meals. Jacques explains that he doesn't know English—explains it in French. Fat Man tries to ask him in French, then, but Jacques has already left the room. Several hours later he comes back with half a loaf of bread and a bit of roast beef for the fat man. "You looked hungry," he says, though not, of course, in English. The fat man nods. He is always hungry. He eats the beef first, and though he feels a faint tickle in his mouth on swallowing the last morsel, he assures himself no worms have grown. Next he eats the bread. There are two mold handprints in the crust when he's finished. It feels alive.

THE LANGUAGE

Little Boy knows little French. He likes it this way. He is sweeping the restaurant's floors. Conversation hangs shimmering over his head like thick, moonlit fog over a highway, or orbiting planets. He makes no effort to discern the meaning or mood of these exchanges, and because the restaurant grows busier as the day advances there is little risk of differentiating prattle from chatter, verb from adverb, idle talk from debate. There is only the continuous rattle, an eternal phoneme, spit-flecked.

If he should find himself sweeping next to some confiding, sweet-whispering old lady, her skin spotted with after-marks of hungry rations, her teeth patchy and many gone, her hair thin beneath the tightly tied emerald-green kerchief she wears like a disguise. If he should find himself sweeping beside her, and she should put some treat in his mouth, thumbing it past his lips and his own aching hungry teeth. If this should happen, then that's okay, and who cares why, or what she whispers in his ear, or how she calls him, or whether he is rude because he doesn't answer, or whether she expects an answer or does not.

About one in four people leave something behind when they leave a restaurant. One in three times it's only some food they meant to take home. One in three times it's an object of small value. One in three times it's a bit of cash, or something of real value: a good watch, a set of cufflinks, a gold chain, or some such. The first category can be eaten. The second and third can be pawned.

When someone leaves Little Boy does what he can. This means cleaning and thieving—what he can do is often both. If someone sees him they don't say a thing, and if they did say a thing he wouldn't know they said it, and so he could stare back at them blank and blameless as a tea light. What could they say?

He doesn't know what they could say.

If it's food he's taking from their table then it isn't really stealing, since the alternative is throwing it out. He brings it to Fat Man or he eats it himself. If it can be pawned, he puts it in his pocket, or brings it to Fat Man if it's too large. These are his brother's instructions.

A couple calls him to the table, or seems to call him. They wave at him. They're young and he's wearing an eye patch. She's always touching him with one hand or both. They're married or young lovers. They speak French like they are blowing smoke rings. Little Boy nods when they want him to nod. The girl musses Little Boy's hair. Her sleeves are ruffled, as is her dress. The girl tweaks his cheek. He giggles, perhaps coos. This must be what it's like for babies before adults make them learn to listen and speak. His own sounds are part of the language cloud apart from Little Boy himself; he can hardly feel them in his throat, can hardly hear them at all.

He feels happy like a baby. He feels simple and empty, like

Hiroshima without all the people and rubble. The young couple is looking away from him so he drifts away from them and sweeps a corner of the floor. To live without language is like living in the time before Fat Man, when nobody knew who he was, or what. If he wasn't happy then it wasn't the silence that made him that way. It was the environment and what destroyed it. No one could be happy in a place like that.

Here and now he is happy.

If in his happiness he should hum some tuneless tune, then what harm amidst insensible French? Which itself is not wholly unlike the sounds of scales played on a flute—the flutter of the air's escape, the soft, soft fingers fingering. He bobs his head. He sweeps the floor. His arms are numb.

He wants to piss himself he's so happy.

When the owner gives him bread he holds it through his yellowed cuffs so the mold will grow more slowly. He drinks the milk like shooting hard liquor, swallowing faster than it can spoil, tasting nothing but a hint of fat.

When the night is thick and the tables are full Albert comes, without Francine. Little Boy goes to him, nods while Albert speaks to him, and if Albert is cruel then Little Boy doesn't know or understand. Albert smokes and reads a novel. He kicks up his feet on the table. For a while he seems to talk to Little Boy about what he is reading, or not what he is reading, and then they are done talking.

Little Boy sweeps the floor. He sneaks a bite of cheese from an abandoned plate. He takes a crumpled bill forgotten at an empty table. He knows, as he knows whenever he steals, Fat Man will be pleased with him. Perhaps if they exchange more money they can exchange fewer words.

* * *

113

That night Fat Man counts out the cash and the pawnable items, passing them from one soft black palm to the other and then piling them in a cloth sack.

"What a good little thief you've become."

Little Boy shrugs. His cheeks throb like an oven's coil.

"It's circumstances. Are we supposed to go on wearing these clothes? People can barely look at us."

"They can look at me just fine," says Little Boy. "They think I'm cute."

"When Francine asks us where we got the money you can say it's from begging."

They lie together in the quiet. It's not quiet enough. Francine and her husband are arguing upstairs. Little Boy doesn't ask his brother if he understands. He curls up more tightly in his blanket. His tongue feels fat from speaking and he'd like to stop now.

As if to cover for something embarrassing, Fat Man pipes up again. "Have you learned any new words yet?"

Little Boy doesn't answer.

"Matthew," says Fat Man, "have you learned any new words?"

"No."

"How do we say that in our French?"

Little Boy shakes his head.

"It's *non*. Just no with another n. That one's easy."

Francine shouts something at her husband. Something about babies, thinks Little Boy. He doesn't want to know that word. He covers his head with a pillow.

"What about cheese?" says Fat Man. "How do we say cheese here?"

Little Boy says, "No."

"*Fromage*. It's fromage. We've been over this a thousand times. You'll never learn if you don't even try."

Little Boy pretends to snore.

"Some women would count themselves blessed to live child-less," growls Albert. The ceiling seems to sing along. "Some women would call it a curse to feed their mouths, to suckle them while they grow their sharp little teeth."

"Zzzz," says Little Boy, like an engine.

Francine makes them breakfast. When she leans over the table to serve up sausages Little Boy watches her stomach for any telltale bulges. He sees Fat Man is doing the same. They've also learned to watch the breasts for any growth, and legs and feet for swelling. They know about morning sickness and the things women eat.

Francine isn't showing. But she will. Fat Man says later what Little Boy is thinking now: she's going to be a big one, ripe and swollen like the best, most juicy pear. As for Albert, he suspects nothing. He sits with his bare feet on the table, reading the paper until breakfast is served. His nails have not been trimmed in weeks. If he still wears his gun, now he at least secrets it away somewhere. There is a bulge in his gray suit jacket this morning, which makes the cloth hang heavy from his thin, handsome body. He talks to Francine about something Little Boy wills himself not to understand. She is hunched over the stove. The words roll off her shoulders and down the long, hard curve of her back. She waves him away with a limp motion of her wrist.

"There's an Oriental spirit medium coming through town in two weeks," says Francine. "I hear she's quite lovely. Maybe we should see her when she comes."

There's a little blonde girl at the restaurant that day, there with her mother on holiday. Maybe her birthday. The girl eats cake and other sweet things. Her mother seems to be there to watch her eat. Little Boy sweeps a spiral around their table until he is sweeping beside them. Today the language is like a hundred balloons floating overhead and bobbing up against the ceiling. Little Boy smiles at the little girl. He's pulled his suit jacket closed and buttoned it to hide the yellow filth of his shirt. It doesn't fool her. She won't show her teeth. It occurs to him his teeth are all the wrong color.

There's a pile of dust and pocket lint and bits of crust and crumbs pushed together where he left them by the wall. He nudges newly collected debris—picking up a brass key that fell from someone's pocket, tucking it in his—and adds it all together. He sweeps up all of it in his dustpan and empties it out in the kitchen dustbin. He looks at the blonde girl with her mother in the dining room. She's babbling at her mother. Today all the language is like vomit sloshing ankle-deep on the floor.

Now Albert comes into the restaurant, a friend by his side. They sit at his usual table and light cigarettes. They tap out their ashes at the same time—it looks as if the orange lit ends are kissing in the blue ceramic tray. The friend is tall and wears a gray flannel suit with a blue tie. His cheeks are lousy with burst veins. His eyes bulge unpleasantly. He sees Little Boy staring and calls him over. He touches Little Boy on his shoulder, on his tummy, through the boy's threadbare suit. He musses his hair and tweaks his nose. There is laughter in his eyes, his mouth is partly open, Little Boy can see his bumpy tongue between his skewed white teeth, peeking out like an inmate. Albert is droning softly in his friend's ear, and Albert's friend nods slowly, accepting each word. His mouth is tight at the corners. His Adam's apple rises and falls like a hand-cranked elevator. He won't stop touching Little Boy's hair. Little Boy walks away, and if they object, if they don't like the way he leaves them to their own, then he cannot hear them say it, or does not know he hears.

Two French policemen, one short and one thin, come into the café. Little Boy pretends not to recognize them. They seem, for one glorious moment, not to recognize him either. They do not meet his eyes or say a word to him, do not acknowledge his familiar face. Maybe they have forgotten, or maybe these are other police who only look very similar; he is too afraid to study them openly, to confirm they are or are not who he thinks.

They go to Albert's table. They tell Albert something to the effect of he is under arrest. Or maybe they are only asking him to go with them: they do not cuff his hands. He seems to have known they would come for him. He may have told his friend, who does not seem to be distressed. As they are leaving, the short one—Mr. Bruce—turns to Little Boy and winks.

Little Boy goes to see Fat Man. He doesn't tell about the police because he doesn't want to make his brother mad. Fat Man will find out soon enough. They share a lunch of bread and cheese. The cheese grows a slow, strangely colored mold as they eat it. When they want another bite they scrape away this second skin.

Fat Man says, "It feels good to be working again." The sink is full with filth, and maggots squirm therein. "Would you like to see the Oriental spirit medium when she comes?"

Little Boy nods.

"Of course if she begins to look too authentic we shall have to leave. We've got a lot of ghosts to think about."

THE CRIME

"Albert won't be joining us this morning," says Francine.

What she means, thinks Fat Man, is that he'll be with the police. Again. "I wonder why they don't arrest him already. Or declare the matter concluded." They speak French together, as they have taken to doing since he inserted himself in a domestic dispute between mister and missus. Little Boy moves food around his plate.

"Her husband won't accept it was an accident," says Francine. She joins them at the table, as she never does when Albert's home. "Not that I blame him. And not that I think it excuses everything. But it was an accident, John."

"I know. Man won't even load his gun. Besides, those cops are twits." He puts his hand like a fat pancake over her small, cool hand, which trembles and jerks beneath his. Not from romantic fervor, he knows, but perhaps because he disgusts her. Why not? His tits are bigger than hers.

She extracts her hand to hold the fork. Not without a certain glancing piquant eye contact as her flesh withdraws from his, nor without embarrassment at the moist suction applied by his skin. But women think they have to be tender.

He excuses himself to the bathroom. The waste runs like crude oil. His body is like a tarp draped over the emptiness it leaves. He feels numb and tired, the way it feels to bleed.

He watches himself wash his hands. His reflection looms in the mirror, swollen and hunched like a caterpillar worrying a leaf. The soap froth slicks him. He rinses and dries on his new gray wool sweater, leaving greasy-looking streaks on the breast and gut. He had hoped that fresh clothes would make him feel better, new again, alive. The folds at the corners of his eyes droop; they threaten to fall away like flower petals.

He squeezes his tits and pushes them together. He claws his cheeks until they are marked with red streaks the way his sweater's streaked with damp.

"Not me," he says to the mirror. "It wasn't me."

He says it until he believes.

When he comes back to the kitchen he sees Little Boy's collar is askew. He straightens it and does the top button. Francine has left, her plate half-scraped into the garbage. It pains Fat Man to see such waste.

Everyone wants to know more about the Oriental spirit medium. She'll come tonight, she'll do a show, it will be at 7:30. This much is known. The rest is all rumor. She is said to wear many scarves and paper charms, but little else. She is said to be the most beautiful Oriental anyone has ever seen. She is said to be cursed or a genuine devil. They say during her last performance she made a table float several inches off the ground. They say she keeps a dead boy bound to her by his ankle, though no one can see or hear him. They say she talks to snakes. They say that everything talks to her—not only spirits, but rocks and trees, picture frames and pitchers, cookie jars and sugar bags.

Jacques relates all of this as he tells everything, as if it were a wild joke. He interrupts himself often to laugh. Fat Man smiles back at him—even when he tries, the boss doesn't give him an opening to speak. He still assumes that Fat Man has no French, yet he does speak to him (natters, really, at the speed of a rock slide) as though he'll understand. Jacques has taken to visiting him every day. Fat Man thinks it must be like visiting the zoo.

He is careful to work very hard when the owner comes calling. He uses his fingernails if he has to. They're black underneath.

Jacques leaves laughing. Fat Man opens up a pack of cigarettes he keeps on a shelf beside the sink and lights one. He watches the smoke rise, imagining it's a spirit, one that can talk to him.

He can't imagine what a spirit would say. What can they want? They have nothing. What can they need? They *are* nothing.

Jacques comes back to the dishwashing station. Fat Man twists his cigarette against a dinner roll and throws it away. There are two men behind Jacques. The two police, short and thin. Mr. Bruce, Mr. Rousseau.

"Will you come down and have a talk with us?" says the short one, in English. "It's in connection to your host, and the matter of a dead girl, among other things."

"We've got you this time," says the thin one.

They sit around a table in a room like a large closet. The walls are white bricks, and the white bricks pockmarked and cratered as if they've been nibbled. There is a bare, flickering light bulb hanging above them.

The short policeman, Mr. Bruce, has a coin-slot gap in his front teeth and glasses with thin, silver frames. Mr. Rousseau, the thin one, has long, greasy, clumpy sideburns like whiskers and a large pimple on the side of his nose. They examine Fat Man as if *he* were the bulging zit. They wear the faces worn by the soldiers and Japanese policemen tall and short.

"How are you doing, John?" asks the short one. "Are you well since last we met?"

This is his very subtle way of alluding to the fact they have met before, north of here, in another place, and perhaps implying he plans to develop their relationship; something like cowboys and Indians.

"Why are you here?" asks Fat Man. "Are you following me?"

"A pure coincidence," says Mr. Rousseau.

"The purest," says Mr. Bruce. "Of course we were interested to encounter you again, here, under such circumstances as these. So very much like the last time."

"We wonder," says Mr. Rousseau, stroking his left sideburn, "what you know about the murder."

"The alleged murder," says Mr. Bruce—an elaboration, not a correction. He merely enjoys the word.

"I understand the doctor made a mistake and the girl bled out. I guess she was a bleeder. I guess no one warned Albert, or the doctor, that she was."

"Abortionist," says Mr. Bruce. "We prefer to call him the abortionist, for the purposes of this case, since he was not practicing medicine at the time, but rather death."

"You've brought Francine a lot of suffering by clinging to this tragedy like it was a crime," says Fat Man. He wants his cigarettes. They are a new habit, but he can do nothing in half-measures. He wants a real big sandwich to eat while they talk at him, too, or a platter of cheeses. A tall, frosty mug.

"You know how they do an abortion?" says Mr. Rousseau. "They break the baby into chunks, and then the mother passes it out, usually into a toilet." He gestures as if jiggling a handle.

Mr. Bruce says, "Imagine a sweet baby's arm dangling from your bleeding snatch."

Fat Man says maybe they should arrest the abortionist then.

Mr. Bruce raises his hand as if to strike him. But the hand rises slowly, and then it returns to the table. "We'll deal with him. Why did you come here?"

"I wanted to start over," says Fat Man.

"We mean here, as in now, this city."

"I wanted work."

"It wasn't because of us?"

"Me and Mr. Rousseau," says Mr. Bruce, touching himself where he keeps his heart, "we hope you weren't fleeing any investigations."

"It's hard to get work with two cops following you everywhere you go."

"Do you remember Laurel," says Mr. Bruce, "from Paris?"

"This again?" says Fat Man.

"Do you remember Laurel?"

"I remember Laurel," says Fat Man.

They had worked together in a Parisian bakery. She died in labor because she was so small. The child died as well. The police, on seeing Fat Man and Little Boy, assumed the hard, hateful expression of the Japanese soldiers and policemen, and then somehow connected her death to Fat Man, terrorized Little Boy in an interrogation room very much like this one, but ultimately came away empty-handed.

"We didn't have you then," says Mr Bruce.

"We've got you now."

"How do you have me?"

"We've got a pattern here, developing, as we speak," says Mr. Bruce.

"What pattern?"

"Two sweet young girls bleeding to death out their cunts," says Mr. Rousseau. "Both times your fault."

"I never met Albert's girlfriend," says Fat Man. His hands become fists on the table. "What you have are two unrelated, however terrible, events, and a ghoulish outlook on life. The only ones that see a pattern here are you."

"The girlfriend's name is Marie," says Mr. Bruce. "Marie Blanc. She was someone's wife as well."

"I never met Mrs. Blanc."

"Did you or did you not begin lodging with Albert on the night of the murder?"

"I did. We arrived while he was out, probably at more or less the same time he was watching Mrs. Blanc bleed out on the abortionist's table. His wife Francine will confirm this. So you see it's impossible for me to have been there myself, and so I couldn't have participated in any murder, assuming there was one, which I very much doubt. He threatened me with an empty gun that night, which tells you first what sort of terms we're on and secondly his ratio of bark to bite."

"You said you needed work," says Mr. Bruce. "Maybe you found it. We understand you're lodging with Albert rent-free. He doesn't seem the giving sort to me, does he Mr. Rousseau."

"No he does not, Mr. Bruce."

"What did you do for him?"

"Nothing," says Fat Man. "His wife gave us the room."

"How did you buy your fine new clothes?" says Mr. Rousseau.

"I wash dishes at a café."

"You bought a new wardrobe on a week of dishwashing money?" says Mr. Bruce.

"Are you sure you weren't there when she died? Are you sure you didn't help?"

"I wasn't there, and I couldn't have helped. I am neither doctor nor abortionist."

"He means you helped to kill her," says Mr. Bruce.

"Based on what evidence?"

Though he knows he is innocent of the murder, and in fact believes that there has been no murder, his heart begins to burn as if the police are pouring in a boiling vegetable broth. He mops the sweat from his brow.

"The pattern," says Mr. Bruce. "The pattern."

"What do these two things have in common beyond vaginal bleeding?" thunders Fat Man, losing self control just long enough to regret it immediately.

"I'll tell you what they have in common," says Mr. Rousseau. He puts his hands on John's shoulders, as if about to begin a massage. He kneads the excess flesh. "Neither of these girls was supposed to be pregnant. You say Laurel didn't even know she was. Well *no one* knew. Her parents insist she was a virgin. She wasn't known to be involved with any men. We only know she was your friend."

"We didn't know each other long," says Fat Man. "It was only a couple months, and then she was dead. I do miss her."

"Did you fuck her?" says Mr. Bruce.

Mr. Rousseau sinks his fingers into Fat Man's shoulders.

Fat Man shakes his head. "She was lovely, sir, but young. Imagine me rolling over onto her small frame. Then I really would have killed her."

"Like you would be the first heavy man to prefer the woman on top," says Mr. Rousseau—a sexual position that had not yet occurred to Fat Man in his brief life. "We think you pricked her. We think you had a hand in her death, and so do her poor, mourning parents."

"Having murdered once," says Mr. Bruce, "perhaps you didn't

plan to do it again. That is, until you needed work. Needed room and board and clothes to keep you warm. You met Albert. He said you could have a place to stay and some money and he would find you a job if you would help him with Mrs. Blanc. You said, 'Shit, why not?' You got away with the last one, after all. So you did the girl and you worked with him and the abortionist to make it look like a mistake somehow, and now here we are, about to bring you in for good."

"Do you know if we have the death penalty in France, John?" asks Mr. Rousseau, spitting out the fat man's name as if it is uniquely harsh, stupid, American.

"I hadn't thought to ask," says Fat Man. "I don't suppose you'll tell me."

"We'd rather let you think about it on your own," says Mr. Bruce. "Reflect."

"You know the problem with your theory," says Fat Man, who is calming now, who is collecting himself, who sees his way out, "apart from the lack of any material evidence or witnesses, apart from the fact that it's very strictly a theory and so shall remain, is if he's got a cooperative doctor willing to help kill the girl and hide it, why in fuck does he need me?"

Mr. Bruce looks to Mr. Rousseau, and Rousseau to Bruce. They look back at Fat Man as if they hadn't thought to ask this question, or, perhaps more charitably, as if they thought he'd never ask it.

"We've got you now is the important thing," says Mr. Bruce.

"Got you in our sights," says Mr. Rousseau, squinting at Fat Man to drive home the point that they can see him.

"Is that all you've got for me today? I was hoping to see the spirit medium with my nephew."

THE ORIENTAL
SPIRIT MEDIUM SEES
THE BROTHERS

The show begins with a stage, empty but for a table draped with red velvet, gaudy jade pillars that look like stacked, scowling heads, and what seems to be a golden urn filled with bamboo stalks. Someone offstage plays a piano—tittering Orientalisms and angular, discordant cords. *Chi chi chi chi chi-chi, chi chi chong, chi chi chong, chong.* A gong gongs.

From both wings, men in black, red, and white kimonos run across the stage, crossing each other as they scamper. They wear wooden sandals and scowling white masks with thick black savage brushstroke eyebrows. *Chi chi chi, chi chong, chong, gong,* and the stage is empty.

They run across again, this time wielding katana-like clubs, waving them over their heads, screaming sounds that might be Japanese. They crouch as they run.

A careening glissando introduces a proud, tall man with a silken white rising sun on his black, billowing robes, stomping the stage as if he means to crack the wood, which creaks with each impact. He nods officiously at the audience, his actor's bright, blue eyes glancingly visible through the mask's eyeholes and their shadows. He pretends to twirl his painted mustache. His robes give the impression of a master of ceremonies.

He removes a bamboo stalk from the golden urn and holds it out to the audience between thumbs and forefingers, running his hands demonstratively over the length of it, as if to say, "This is all of one piece."

He shouts something from his gut and tosses the bamboo in the air. One of the samurai sprints across the stage, raises his sword to touch the falling bamboo, and then he is gone. The referee catches the bamboo—one half in each hand. He shows the audience the clean cut, then discards both measures, tossing them back into the golden urn. When he turns away from them the audience can see the red ribbons that tie the mask to his face, and the bald, crumpled skin of his head. Someone strikes the gong.

He takes two more stalks and throws them up. Two samurai run screaming across the stage. They slash at one another—one low, one high—and seem to miss. When neither can be seen, both bamboo stalks split in two, fall to the ground. The referee will not deign to bend and lift them. Someone strikes the gong.

Fat Man looks to Little Boy, and sees he is amazed, or feigning amazement. The child nearly shakes from pleasure. Beside him Francine touches her chin. Albert might be sleeping, his face is turned down.

Now the referee throws into the air stalk after stalk. A continuous parade of samurai runs across the stage, leaping to cut the bamboo, flipping over each other, sliding on their silk-sheathed knees, swords whispering past one another, never touching. They grunt and shout. The unseen piano player pumps his left hand like a bellows, his right hand like pistons. The keys shriek. Gong gongs.

Everyone is here. The policemen, Messieurs Bruce and Rousseau, sit toward the back of the auditorium, hands ready on their truncheons. They watch the stage as if they anticipate a crime, their chins upturned and eyes narrowed. Jacques is here, and so are his regulars, and so are the waiters. So is every woman Fat Man has dreamed about since they came to town—the brunette with her hair done up in a tight bundle, the teenage girl with a handkerchief holding her red curls in place, the blonde with eyelashes like hummingbird wings.

Having only seen Mr. Blanc in passing, and from a great distance, Fat Man can still discern him now. He recognizes Blanc by the pumpkin-like shape of his head, the way his eyes never fully open, owing to the prodigious fat of his cheeks; he recognizes Blanc by the quizzical weight of his brow, nearly one continuous arch, and by the way he sits with his hands at rest on his gut, all his fingertips touching their opposite palms. He recognizes Blanc by the slump of his widower's figure. If they were shaking hands, he is sure Blanc's face would be transformed by proximity, by unseen moles or lines or other features, such that he would not recognize Blanc, or suspect that they had ever known of one another.

In the time it takes for Fat Man's gaze to return to the stage, the samurai are gone and so is their bamboo. He missed the roar of applause that followed their finale. Now, the Oriental spirit medium approaches.

She is a tall, slender figure in robes shot through with brilliant color like thick veins of quartz. The robes trail her like the train of a wedding gown, though they are black and bright purple and jelly red and silver and gold and forest green and tiger orange and sun yellow. Her robes are open at the shoulders, revealing the kind slope of her collarbone, the fairness of her skin. There are no sleeves apart from knots tied just beneath those exposed shoulders. She wears a large silver necklace hung with obsidian and pearls. Her black hair is piled atop her head in a tight, thick knot. One long strand falls down her back, mingling with jade beads and bits of precious metal that dangle from a comb.

She walks to the velvet-draped table. She sets down a small, featureless wooden box—about eight inches long on each side. There is, on closer inspection, a wooden slat on the top of the box with which it could be pulled open. From the ease with which she carries it and the softness of its landing on the table, Fat Man thinks it must be very light—perhaps empty.

The medium bristles with peacock feathers. Or rather, they seem to be feathers but Fat Man sees that they are long, silver needles done up with plumes like peacock tails. There are needles in her arms and shoulders, which must puncture her perhaps an inch deep. They stand wholly erect. As she breathes, the needle-feathers flex and sway. There is one between her eyes and like a quail's headfeather it droops forward.

The medium folds her hands. She breathes through her nose and mouth together. Deep, deep.

The invisible piano player fingers a mystic mood.

The medium unfolds her arms and gestures violently offstage. She shouts—her voice resounding, deep as the afterlife, deep as a fortune-teller's should be—"I told you not to play that shit once I came out! I won't have it!"

Several men exchange words offstage. The piano player stops, though not without striking the keys one more time.

"Unlike everything you have just seen," says the medium, in perfect French, "unlike everything else on this stage, and unlike what they tell you in church services or funerals—unlike all of these things, I am real. What I *do* is real." She strokes the wooden box. Her nails are long, elegant, and speckled all the colors of her robes.

"Tonight I will speak to you of the dead, and the dead will speak to you through me. If you don't like what you hear, this is not my fault, and I don't wish to hear of it. If you do like what you hear, I am happy for you, but you cannot expect me to speak to you of them again—or to speak to you otherwise, for that matter. Is this understood?"

Fat Man nods. He feels and hears most of the audience do the same. His eyes are fixed on her. There is a prickling all over his skin, and inside it, an itch, like he too is hedgehogged with peacock needles.

The medium says, "Now I'm going to begin. I'm sorry I won't be able to help all of you. Time and my own limitations allowing, I'll do what I can."

She places one hand on the box and with the other points out at the audience, as if extending an antenna for the dead. All her feathers shiver. She says, "I've got something. You, there. The one who brought a dog."

An old woman in the back says, "Me?"

The medium nods and says, "Why do you bring that dog everywhere?"

"He reminds me of my husband," says the old woman. "Are dogs not allowed? No one told me."

"Do you believe the dog *is* your husband, madame?"

"The thought has occurred to me. He's always so attentive, as if he means to make up for some slight he has done me in the past. A past life, maybe. They share the same sad little eyes."

"The dog is not your husband. He tells me that he is your former grocer."

The old woman gasps. "Who?"

"He says you never learned his name, but describes himself for me now. He says he was a middle-aged man, and that when he was not at work he wore a white felt hat around town. His hair was red, and his mustache streaked with blond, and his shirts were always stained with the pulp of squashed fruits. He wants you to know he didn't choose to be your dog, but he did love you in life, and now he's happy to be yours."

There rises over the audience a heavy, steady panting—the dog. He yaps once.

"Well that doesn't make any sense," says the old woman. "Why should some infatuated grocer be my dog? Why should he look so much like my husband?"

The medium ignores her. "I have a message for Rosie Cummings, from your father. He says you should go back to America. Forget about your fool hotel. He says it's too soon for you to give up on children."

A tall American woman in a blue frock and curly red hair stands up several rows in front of Fat Man and company.

"Can you tell him I'm barren?" she says, in a flat, Midwestern accent that comes through her nose as much as her mouth.

"He says that's your imagination. He says the women in your family have always taken to childbirth very naturally."

"Forget him. Can you hear my husband? Does he have anything to say for himself?"

"No, ma'am. I can't hear him," says the medium.

"It figures," says the American, and she sits down.

"Now I—"

"Wait," interrupts Rosie, standing up again. "I'm sorry, but concerning America and my hotel and what my father said, is it your experience that the dead are, on the whole, more wise than the living?"

"Not at all," says the medium.

"Okay, thank you," says Rosie, and she sits down again. Her chair makes a sound like a hinge.

The medium stands and paces the front of the stage, eyeing

the audience. When her gaze passes over Fat Man the prickles in his skin intensify, and when she has moved on he sees that he is holding hands with Little Boy, who looks up at him in amazement, and some kind of guarded tenderness, which suggests to Fat Man that he's the one who reached for his brother.

"Barbara?" says the medium. She holds out open hands. The quills hang from her upturned arms as worms will hang from silk. "Barbara Trudeau, can you stand for me now?"

A stout woman with a kind face stands before the audience as she looks at the medium with something like love or acceptance.

"Your daughter wishes to speak to you."

"My daughters are with me," says Barbara. "Perhaps you mean someone else."

"Your other daughter," squeaks the medium. "The one you had before your marriage. The one you strangled."

Barbara squawks. It was meant to be laughter, but no one laughs like that. She looks around herself again, begging support against the madwoman on stage.

Now the medium watches her own hands rear up and wrap themselves around her neck. They squeeze and twist like opening a bottle. The dead girl's voice is not impeded by this grasping. It sounds as if it's coming from a bottle. She says, "I just wanted you to know that, in spite of your faith and your prayers, not all small girls are blessed," she drawls this last word—she drags it through the muck, "enough to live the hereafter in Heaven. It's different than what you think. I watch you comb the others' hair. Your new little girls, who are quiet and sweet."

Barbara Trudeau watches the medium throttle herself and makes her face hard like a cliff. Her bosoms climb her body and fall. Her girls look up to her on either side, the younger tugging at her skirt, their hair festooned with paste costume jewels. The medium falls to her knees and thrashes in her robes as her face like the moon turns red and throbbing, as she squeezes and wrings her own neck.

"Do you ever think how it would be to do it again?" says the voice from a bottle. "When you comb, or pluck the lice from their scalps, or when there was no food, do you, did you wonder what your husband would think? Every day I try to haunt you, but I can never work out how. Now," she says, and releases the medium's throat. She plucks a quill from her own borrowed body. A bead of blood forms on the arm it came from, and likewise on the needle's tip. The audience gasps as she wields it, stumbling forward on her knees and jabbing at the air.

The medium drops the quill on the stage and stands, and smooths her robes.

Barbara stands, hands made fists, squinting, grimacing, a bulwark against some coming wave. The younger girl tugs again at her skirt. Fat Man wonders, will she mount the stage?

"Sit down, madame," says the medium, and she sits down as well.

"It isn't true," says Barbara, such that everyone can hear. After the whispers have stopped, and only after this, she sits down. She hugs her girls in both arms.

The medium says, coolly, "Audience members compromised by my communions with the spirits should take comfort in the knowledge that modern courts do not admit as evidence the testimony of mediums, soothsayers, or shamans of any kind."

The medium holds her hand over the box as if to warm them. There is dead air in the auditorium. Little Boy digs his nails into his brother's fat black-burnt palm. "What?" whispers Fat Man. Little Boy only squeezes. Fat Man shakes his head, but he feels it rising in him too—like black moss climbing his spine, like his brain becoming broth, like exploding.

The medium's eyes open wide and her nostrils flare and the

things all tangled in her hair jangle; the quills in her skin all stand on end, including, especially, the quill feather quail thing pricked between her eyes, which seems even to twist in some brief violent updraft. She looks directly into Fat Man, and then Little Boy, and then, most alarming, their joined hands.

She doesn't say anything.

Waits.

She touches the box, and fingers the slot by which it might be opened, but does not open her box.

A man calls to the stage, "Can you hear my son?"

"Your son says to let him rest," hisses the medium, waving him away with a flick of her arm like a lizard's tongue. She points to another man in the audience. "Your father looks on you as a disappointment. He says your brother is the better man." She looks to another. "Your sister is the one who makes the tree move when there is no wind." Another: "It's your dead mother rocks the cradle when you think it is the dog."

She stands again and pushes back her chair so hard it falls, bouncing off the left jade pillar and clattering on the stage. She approaches the fore. Hands in fists. Quiver-chinned.

"Monsieur Blanc."

The grotesque is erected.

"Your wife married you for your money. Knowing that, she wonders if you might not waste it all on destroying better men."

He is a gargoyle trembling.

"That's quite enough," speaks Mr. Bruce.

"Leave a mourning husband be, you shrew," says Mr. Rousseau.

"Albert," says the Medium, her voice a bottled girl again, "I thought you would pay me more attention were I pregnant, and I convinced myself I was, but I wasn't. Now that I'm gone, you should treat your wife better. And get your fucking feet off of the table."

Handsome Albert grunts. Francine taps the ground with her heels.

The medium coughs into her hands. So much wet comes out of her mouth, hanging in strings and ribbons from her hands. She is shaking her hands, and some hits the audience, and some now are standing to leave, tripping over others' feet, excusing themselves, all harrumph-harrumphing.

Fat Man feels a fart like the sun inside him. He tries to hold himself shut.

The medium wipes the rest of the wet on her robes, leaving vertical streaks. She sniffs back more. "Mr. Bruce," she says, and both the thin one and the short one stand to show themselves. "Your father asks you to remember your prayers."

The medium settles on Fat Man and Little Boy as if at the end of a long journey. Goosebumps form thick as shingles on them. She kneels at the fore, offering a hand to the audience.

"Fat Man. Little Boy. Come here. Let me see you."

Fat Man looks to Little Boy.

"Don't be shy," says the medium.

Little Boy takes to his feet. He pulls up Fat Man by hand and elbow.

Francine bites her lip. "Don't go up there," she whispers, in English, so both the boys can understand. "She'll tell awful lies about you."

"It's just a show," says Fat Man.

"She'll say it either way," says Little Boy.

They walk the aisle. Fat Man hoists Little Boy onto the stage and pulls himself up after, huffing and puffing. He wipes his head dry with his sleeve. No one can see the manic way he clenches his fat sphincter to keep the gas giant inside.

"My name is Matthew," says Fat Man, in French.

"I'm John," says Little Boy, in English.

"Are you sure it's not the other way around?" asks the medium, who weaves between French and English now and for the rest of her time on the stage, assuming each accent with only the slightest slurring transition, then returning, so that everyone who cares to follow can do so. Little Boy and Fat Man look to each other and wonder if the medium is right—they wonder if they've switched.

"I mean he's John," says Fat Man.

"And he's Matthew."

"Oh well then that's different," says the medium. She prods the Fat Man's gut. "Women, guard your wombs. This man and this boy are haunted, haunted by tens of thousands. They killed them all, ladies." She stomps the stage. "Now those people and children follow them wherever they go, jostling for a chance to be born again near them, whether as infants or livestock or rot. Do you want a ghost in your belly?" She sculpts a gut like a dome in the air before her own gut to demonstrate the concept. "If not, then leave—their collected haunts worm their way up inside you even now, and will soon demand nutrition from your unknowing bodies, which will give and give, indiscriminate. You and your daughters. Lucky Rosie, lucky barren Rosie. I see them coax your flesh but they cannot. They all speak to me at once. A gibbering chorus. What do you have to say for yourselves?"

"It's not true," says Fat Man. He shifts on his feet, fighting back the gut-buster. "I don't know what you mean."

Little Boy stares out at the crowd, arms hanging from his sides like streamers.

"I told you she was a liar," shrills Barbara Trudeau, the daughter-killer.

The medium spits, "These readings are for entertainment purposes *only!*"

"Who the hell are you?" says Fat Man.

"Did they kill Marie Blanc?" shouts Mr. Bruce.

"Was the fat one in cahoots with her lover?" shouts Mr. Rousseau.

Mr. Bruce yells, "What about Laurel?"

The medium circles the brother bombs, sizing them up. Little Boy trembles, and scratches himself, and—unaware of what his hands do—pulls at the foreskin of his penis through his trousers with one restless hand, squirming, as young boys sometimes do. "Who am I?" says the medium. "Who are you? Do maggots form in the flesh of your victims with terrible speed? Do infants pour from every womb you see, unfinished, rushing to be near you? Does the food on your fork sprout mold before it reaches your lips? Do spiders crawl from inside dead bodies? Do you dream at night of mosquitoes devouring your flesh? Do you LIVE in SHAME and FEAR of EVERYTHING AROUND YOU?" She rears up, claws hoisted over her head. "Do you wake up sometimes *soaked* in your own mess and piss, flailing for something to break your fall, screeching like a goddamn harpy?"

Little Boy sobs—a snot bubble growing from his nose. "Yes," he cries, "yes I do."

"Shut up," says Fat Man, not to Little Boy, but to the audience, which is silent. He holds his arms out like wings, displaying his bloated body. He feels his entrails roil inside him like hot tar.

"I want to die every day and I'm not even sure why," says Little Boy.

"Does the guilt bring you pleasure," hisses the medium, who fairly gyrates on the stage. "Does it, to know what you've done to them, the lives you destroyed, you took for your own, and their fascination, and the way they suck and clutch your fingers?"

"I don't know."

"You are fat with them," she says, jabbing Fat Man's belly.

"I'm fat with food," says Fat Man. He squeezes his carriage

in his arms. The blood is rushing. His heart burns. He is sure to explode. "I eat too much."

"You hardly eat at all, most days," says the medium. "I know you eat what you can get, I know, but your fat comes from the children. They're lining your insides, like good soldiers throwing themselves on a grenade, *wave after wave*."

Fat Man looks down at his body. "They can't be."

Little Boy falls down on his ass for no obvious reason. The audience is mystified, but cannot speak, cannot look away. He wails like a newborn. "Leave us alone," he pleads. "Leave us alone. I am Matthew. I sweep the floors clean, and kill no one. Please ma'am, my brother is the killer."

"Not me," bawls Fat Man, rocking on his heels, stumbling back against the table. "It isn't so. Not me."

"Come clean," calls Mr. Bruce.

The table rattles beneath his fat, shaking hands.

"I'm going to explode. I'm going to explode." Fat Man's sphincter flutters, pulses. There is such a force inside him.

The medium pulls the feather needle from between her eyes. She holds the point up, gesturing at the ceiling, which is painted thickly with cherubim and other naked things. She wrenches the needle, once, twice, showing the audience. They murmur or remember to breathe.

She marches on Fat Man. He lurches around the table, collides with one jade pillar, upending it. The ugly stacked pillar faces put their ears to the ground, and sway forward and back, listening to the thrum of spirit medium and Fat Man, Little Boy's shoes scraping the boards of the stage.

Fat Man pants, and feels the cold, itching rivulets of saltwater running down his peaks and valleys. He holds out his black burnt palms. "I'll explode! You don't want to see! You don't want to be here! I'm sorry!"

He chokes down vomit.

The medium plunges the needle in between his eyes. It scrapes the bone. He raises up his hands as if to lift the ceiling.

The gas he's been holding explodes from his body, hot and sulfur, wet, like a failing machine, like a rhinoceros goring a hog. He screams. Deflates. His arms fall to his sides. He falls too, and lands on his ass. A simple, sad expression spreads like grape jelly over his face.

A bead of blood rolls down his nose.

He can hear Little Boy's piss trickling down his pant leg and onto the wooden stage.

"Are you ashamed of what you have done?" demands the Oriental spirit medium. Much of the audience is leaving. The short policeman and the thin one walk against the outflow, truncheons at hand.

"Yes I am ashamed," says Fat Man, hoarsely. "I am ashamed. Yes I am ashamed, yes I am ashamed."

"See what I see," says the medium. "Know what I know."

She's retrieved her box from the table. They are swimming in the eggy fumes of Fat Man's explosion—the air is hot, and seems to warp and bend around them.

"Touch the wooden box with me," she says. "Hold it as I hold it."

She proffers the box, kneeling beside him.

"Are you Japanese?" says Fat Man.

"I am."

"You survived," he says.

"I did."

Fat Man reaches for the box.

It's cold. The grain is smooth.

THE BROTHERS
GO HOME

Fat Man and Little Boy wake up on the stage, spent and alone. Fat Man has had another wet dream, as the stain crusting the front and inner thighs of his slacks testifies. Little Boy merely wet himself.

Fat Man, sitting up, finds a handwritten note at rest on his gut. It reads:

WE ARE SORRY FOR WHAT THE MEDIUM HAS DONE TO YOU, AND ANY SHAME IT BRINGS. WE TRIED TO WAKE YOU, BUT COULD NOT. INSTEAD WE THOUGHT IT BEST TO LET YOU REST. WE WILL CLEAN THE STAGE IN YOUR ABSENCE. PLEASE LEAVE THE BUILDING AT YOUR EARLIEST CONVENIENCE. FRANCINE SAYS SHE'LL BE WAITING FOR YOU WITH WARM SOUP.
SIGNED,
THE MANAGEMENT

Fat Man folds the note and puts it in his pocket.

"You smell awful," says Little Boy.

"Well you're a bed of fucking wildflowers," says Fat Man. "You're a goddamn spice rack. You're a basket of scented soaps and rare cosmetic treatments."

"I get it," says Little Boy, rubbing his arm where a bruise is forming—he doesn't know why there is a bruise.

"You're a goddamn Parisian perfume counter."

"I get it! At least I didn't fart on stage."

Fat Man goes backstage and Little Boy follows. The samurai costumes hang from a rack on wheels, on wire hangers. The robes are very light and cool to the touch. Their swords are sheathed and piled on the floor. The table and jade pillars like ugly stacked heads are behind the piano, an upright with yellowing keys and cigarette burns, and ash around its base. Someone left his hat on top of it.

They find the medium's dressing room, but she will not answer no matter how they knock. Fat Man shouts into the keyhole, then kneels and peers, cold in his come.

Little Boy leans against the wall and sucks his fingernail. He says, "She's not there or she's not answering. Knock down the door or let's go."

"I'll knock *you* down," says Fat Man.

They leave, holding hands.

In the lobby there is a table. The marshal's white stone head is balanced upside down, the bald top sanded flat so it can stand on what's left. He is painted in spatters, the colors of the flag. He seems panicked. He watches the brother bombs go.

It's night. Neither can say how late, but they can see the moon and the stars, and there are few people out. It's quiet. They hear the distant burble of some body of water, one they never heard before. Someone's horse wanders the street, alone, no saddle, shoes heavy and muffled with accumulated mud. Little Boy watches for the horse as they walk. He would like to see it. He would like to touch its mane.

"We have to leave town," says Fat Man. "I can't face Francine after that. She must hate me."

"Is she going to be okay?" says Little Boy.

"If she hasn't left Albert yet she never will."

"That wasn't what I meant."

"Then what did you mean?"

Little Boy says, "I worry about her. Do you think Albert hits her?"

Fat Man shakes his head. Albert has many failings. That isn't likely one.

"I'll give Jacques our week's notice tomorrow," he says.

Little Boy says, "I want to go home."

"What home?"

"America."

"You wouldn't like it there."

Little Boy hears the horse or he believes he does. It is distant now, and now more gone, drifting toward the dirt roads and disused lots at the city's outer edge. Little Boy will not be allowed to touch the horse's mane. He will not get to watch it breathe. The mud is shaking loose from its hooves. Its footsteps are more crisp and clear than ever, though they are very far away.

"We'll live out in the country," says Fat Man. "There are too many people here."

"Is there work for you in the country?"

"Should be something. If not, we'll eat squirrels."

Francine and Albert are fighting so loud Fat Man and Little Boy decide to wait outside the house. They sit beneath the window, legs folded, eyes closed.

Little Boy says, "What are they fighting about?" He rubs his ears to keep them warm.

Fat Man says, "He's angry she's pregnant."

"So he worked it out."

"He thinks it can't be his kid."

"Why not?"

"I think he uses something called the withdrawal method."

"What's that?"

"It's when you take it out before you finish. She's explaining that pre-ejaculate has sperm in it too."

"I don't know what that means," says Little Boy, looking up at the stars, breathing little chalk clouds.

"Then how do I know?"

"We're supposed to know all the same things?"

"I thought we did," says Fat Man. "We're brothers."

"Not anymore," says Little Boy. "I mean, not about being brothers, but about knowing. You know French now."

"You really don't?"

"Not so much. Some foods, mostly. Greetings, goodbyes. We're more different now than we used to be."

"Now she's asking him why he doesn't take her to get an abortion the way he does with everyone else," says Fat Man.

"Well why doesn't he?"

"Suppose she dies. How would that look?"

"That's not what he's saying, is it?"

"No. He says he doesn't want to put her through all that."

"So they'll have the babies?"

"One more reason to leave," says Fat Man.

"Imagine those eyes. Staring up at you as if you made the world and everything good," says Little Boy.

"When really you destroyed it."

ROSIE CUMMINGS
HAS A JOB

Rosie watches someone else's cigarette butt burn out orange then gray in the ashtray on her table. She is waiting for service. She is tired.

After Fat Man and Little Boy passed out on stage, the medium had stormed off, leaving the audience to fend for themselves. The hidden pianist played a few resounding chords as if to resolve the evening. An F, a C minor, a major C, and that was that. The crowd filtered out into the night like powdered sugar through a sifter, and Rosie went with them, jostled at every interval by strange men and beautiful women, the latter wearing stylish homemade dresses. As she walked through the streets, Rosie reflected on what the medium had told her. It was possible her father had spoken through the Oriental woman—she especially believed it after the medium's climactic histrionics, and the smells that fogged the theater when the show was over. In her hotel room, after the medium, she had prayed for guidance, and apologized for idolatry, if that was what she had done. So far, God was keeping mum, but that was his way. The Lord was not a talker.

In any case, her father was wrong. Her husband is dead, she will not marry again, she will not have babies, she cannot have babies.

A waiter bustles by. She consults her dog-eared phrasebook for a firm way of saying, "No one has helped me yet." There are no firm ways of saying anything in her phrasebook. The closest she can come is, "J'apprécie votre aide." She looks up from her phrasebook and the waiter is gone. She lights a cigarette. The smoke tickles her throat and makes her eyes feel dry. She flips through the phrasebook, searching for things she might need to say soon. "How are you with a broom?" for instance. Can you cook? Do you keep a clean home? How is your English?

She tallies her expenses. The cigarettes come first as they are very guilty things. Then the room she has rented, which she will quit tomorrow morning. Then the meals she has eaten—which were more expensive before someone told her, with unnecessary surliness, that in France one does not usually leave a tip—and meals she will eat. The hat she bought herself, which she has since lost. The apple she snacked on, the orange, the bread she took to her room, and the soft brie. Every day she thanks the Lord she has already bought the land. A spendthrift like her would otherwise be short of money long before she arrived, she is sure. The cigarette is half-done, and so there is half of one eighth, a sixteenth, then, of the money she spent on the pack, burnt away. It's all gone so quickly, and that's just like her, to waste. She needs to keep a certain amount. She is afraid to look in her hotel safe to see if she still has that amount; she always runs through money faster than she thinks, and then she feels cold inside, and skips meals to close the gap between expectation and fact.

The waiter comes by again. She is resolved to ignore him unless their eyes meet. Of course their eyes do. She says, "J'apprécie votre aide."

The waiter cocks his head. He asks her if she's been helped, but she doesn't understand.

She is not sure what this means. It doesn't matter. "Un sandwich au rosbif," she says, "et un café." This too from her phrasebook, pages 25 and 28. She mentally deducts the sum of this lunch from the diminishing heap of her savings. She thanks the waiter in English.

A boy sweeps in the corner, corralling dust and crumbs. He has the slow, steady rhythm of someone who knows he will be sweeping the same spot clean the next day and the day after that. He collects it in his dustpan, disappears, and comes back before her lunch. He lifts a chair, propping it up on its forelegs against the table, sweeps out from beneath it, and sets the chair back down.

That's him, she thinks, the boy from the night before. The one the medium called up. She hadn't realized, sitting in the audience, how thin he was. He hadn't looked so tired.

"Hello," she says. "Come sit at my table with me."

He startles at her flat, Midwestern English. His lips twitch.

He shrugs, saying, "No English," affecting a mealy French accent.

She pats the seat beside her. "That's a lie. Come on."

"I'm supposed to clean."

"I'm a respected hotelier. No one will punish you for doing what I say."

Little Boy does as she asks, setting his dustpan on the table, holding his broom erect in the crook of his elbow. When she asks his name he answers "Matthew," his voice a sullen croak. She snuffs her cigarette. He watches the last wisps of smoke, and then the tray. His bulging eyes are hesitant to meet her own. His hands fiddle in his lap.

Rosie asks, "Are you wondering if I recognize you from last night?"

"I was."

"Well," says Rosie. Her waiter approaches with sandwich and coffee. He leaves without acknowledging the boy. "See, I told you. The customer is always right. Is Matthew really your name?"

He nods.

"I shouldn't ask you what the medium was on about," says Rosie. "You're too young to be guilty of anything, aren't you?"

"I guess."

"What are you afraid of? Are you hungry?"

"Yes." He glances up.

She cuts her sandwich in imperfect halves and gives him the smaller portion. He keeps his broom upright as he takes his share.

"Do you drink coffee?"

"No."

"I think what she did to you was awful. Very rude. You paid for a ticket the same as anyone else."

"Yes ma'am."

"Is your brother here?"

"I misspoke, ma'am. John is my uncle."

"Of course. Is your uncle here? You are both American?"

"Yes. He washes dishes in the kitchen."

"That's perfect. But he speaks French?"

"Some." He finishes the roast beef, licks his finger, collects breadcrumbs from the table.

Rosie asks if she can speak to Matthew's uncle John. Matthew says no, John is washing dishes in the kitchen and he has to get back to sweeping. She asks him what about the sandwich half she gave him. He takes his dustpan from the table.

"I liked the half sandwich."

She asks him if he goes to school.

"It's mandatory."

She sighs. "Can I speak to your uncle?"

"He's doing dishes in the kitchen."

"My husband died freeing this country," says Rosie. "He was hanging by his parachute in a tree and they shot him full of holes. I came here to start an international hotel and learn four languages. If there were more international hotels and everyone knew four foreign languages my husband would still be alive today."

"I'm sorry," says Matthew.

Rosie is not convinced. The little boy goes back to his sweeping. She considers another cigarette but at that rate it would be four a day—two at lunch, one at six, one before bed—and though this inevitably will happen, and worse, she can't afford that kind of habit now. She would have to go without breakfast.

"Well I can go to the kitchen," she says.

Here is the fat man John at the sink. He attacks the dishes as if he means to grind them down to dust. He's humming unfamiliar tunes in his deep rumble as he struggles not to bite his cigarette in half.

Rosie offers her hand. "Rosie Cummings. Hotelier."

John's eyes are darkly, deeply ringed, one side of his face marbled with bruises from his fall. "Good to meet you, Rosie. As you can see I'm occupied."

She insists on her hand. He holds up his and says, "I'm filthy."

"My husband was killed by Nazis freeing this country," says Rosie. "He was hanging by his parachute in a tree and they shot him full of holes. I have come here to start an international hotel and learn four languages. If there were more international hotels and everyone knew four foreign languages my husband would still be alive today." She pauses. "John, please shake my hand."

He wipes a mitt on his apron, front and back, and again, and again. It's the wrong hand—she changes hers to accommodate him, and they shake. His grasp is as loose and soft and warm as half-baked dough. His eyes are deep set, dark and sweet like raisins.

"My name is Rosie Cummings. Please listen to me."

"Were you at last night's séance spectacular?"

"I was. I told your nephew Matthew how I thought the medium was very rude to you."

John shows her his hands again. This time she notes their blackness—apparently not a layer of grime, as she had assumed. "Well she accused that other woman of infanticide," he says. "I guess it's that kind of show."

"To say nothing of what she said to me. Of course, as she conceded, sometimes the dead are wrong. In my case they would have to be, so I'm sure they're wrong about you as well. You don't look like a guilty man."

He goes back to his dishes, scraping with his cloth and nails, turning up the water until steam rises in thick plumes. He takes the unlit cigarette into his mouth and pushes it back out, and chews. "Do you find yourself a good judge of character in general?" he says.

"You never know," says Rosie. She fingers the zipper on her purse.

"Then I won't take your word on it." He turns down his eyes. The conversation is over.

"There's a place called Gurs," says Rosie. "You need to see it with your own eyes. I think you're going to love it."

"Gurs," says John.

"It was a prison. But not the way you think of them—not like back home. More a lot of little huts, and this tiny fence you could jump if you wanted. You know, with razor wire and all that, not electrified, but I'm going to take that out. I'm going to make it a hotel."

"A hotel."

"Yes, my first international hotel in what will one day be a chain. If everyone learned four foreign languages, then my husband would still be alive. I want to make the prison into a hotel so people will be able to move past all the unpleasantness." She whispers, now. "That's where Vichy kept the Jews before they were shipped out."

"Jews?"

"Before they shipped them out to Germany."

"What happened to them? Were they hurt?"

"Well, they didn't come back."

Rosie explains that she has been eating at every reasonable restaurant and staying at every decent hotel she can find on her way south, where she is going to convert the prison into the first of many international hotels. She says there will be language classes, and everyone who stays there will learn four foreign languages, and then people won't lose their husbands with such awful regularity. She explains she has been eating and staying at so many places because she needs to find staff for her first hotel, good staff with a command of several languages. At least two. Maybe he would like to work for her, she says.

"Which languages?"

"Four foreign languages should be enough, in the long term, to prevent the most bloodshed."

"Which four?"

"For instance, we would need to learn Japanese, German, French, and Spanish."

"Not Italian?"

"I don't think we'll have to worry about them getting into any more trouble. But there is always Mexico to consider."

"Yes," says John, puzzled. "Always Mexico."

"So would you like to come work for me?" says Rosie. "I'm sure I can pay a little more than this café, and you would be able to do many interesting tasks, and not only wash dishes."

John says that he can't leave, that he has only just settled down, that he only knows one foreign language, not four. Rosie asks him is he sure he can't be persuaded. She says he can do the dishes at Hotel Gurs if he likes it so much.

"No, no," he says. "No, I'm sorry."

She turns to leave. He grabs her shoulder with his muck hand. His raisin eyes shine brightly. "Wait. Is it true you're barren?"

THE ROAD
TO GURS

Fat Man tells Francine the news over breakfast. "We'll leave to-night," he says. "This is an excellent opportunity, I'm sure you'll agree."

"Of course," says Francine. She bites through her buttered toast. Her hand reaches across the table and rests on his. Warmth passes between them. She touches her tummy and circles the swell. Fat Man can feel her pulse in the tips of her fingers. "If you need anything, you can send me a letter."

"And you can do the same."

Francine smiles and nods as if there is the slightest chance that she would want to see him again, that she would need his help, that he could ever do anything for her. He wants to tell her how beautiful she is. He wants to ask her to leave her husband, who is not in any case the father of her babies. He wants to grasp her by the shoulders and shout, "Those are my children inside you!" His, and his brother's.

Instead he asks her, "Should I say goodbye to your husband?" She forces a smile, shakes her head no. She has been gentle since the medium had him up on the stage. "Albert is very busy looking for money," she says, "under every rock, behind every door, in every seat cushion. Or so he tells me. Now that he's going to be a father he says it's time he really *provides*."

"A father?" says Fat Man, with all the cultivated mincing friendliness he despises in his fellow fat men. "Congratulations, Francine! May I?" He indicates her ballooning tummy. She agrees. As he lowers his head, he recognizes his mistake. As he presses his ear to the swell, regret bubbles inside. At first he hears nothing. Then the thrashing begins. Francine moans, pained.

"They like you," she says. "They like you a lot, I guess."

It sounds as if they will tear their way out if he stays. Fat Man reminds himself why he is leaving with barren Rosie Cummings. "Would you like some water?" he says. Francine raises two curled fingers and shakes them no while she swallows back some burning thing, covering her mouth with her other hand. He goes to the sink. "Twins," he says. "I hope they get along."

"Mmm," agrees Francine, nodding.

"A brother you can be really close with," says Fat Man. "That's special. That'll save your life." He fills his glass. The water smells a little strange out here, he's noticed. Water's different everywhere and no one ever wants to talk about it.

"Do you have any brothers?" says Francine.

"I guess I've got one." He says this in a way that means he'd rather not discuss it.

Little Boy comes down from the bathroom. He walks into the room slowly, hands tucked into his pockets like secrets.

"I think Matthew has something he'd like to say to you," says Fat Man. Little Boy nods.

"Well go on, Matthew," says Francine, "I'm listening." She rests her hands on her babies. Rubs them in slow, small soothing circles.

He removes folded paper from his right pocket, unfolds it, and grips it with both hands to pull the creases smooth. "Mademoiselle Francine. Merci d'avoir pris, soins de nous." He refolds the note and pushes it into her hand so she can think of them fondly later.

"How darling," says Francine. "Thank you for letting me hear your first words."

"He used to talk all the time," says Fat Man. "These days it's a battle."

Little Boy looks up at them and smiles vacantly as if he is forgetting all his English.

Rosie Cummings has bought them bicycles to match her own. They are solid brown metal like grasshoppers on wheels. They have bells with clear, sharp sounds and wide wheels with white sides. Their seats are long and wide in the back. Fat Man thanks Rosie. Little Boy forgets until his brother cuffs his ear.

They'll ride south. Rosie says there are men at work on her hotel, and it's okay if it takes them a little time to arrive—the men will still be working when they get there, tearing down fences and rebuilding the huts-cum-rooms. If they come to a large hill, they will walk their bikes to the summit and picnic when they get there, or they will ride around it in a slow circle. When they find a paved road kind to bicycles, they will ride on it even if it takes them out of their way.

Fat Man tells Little Boy how lucky they are to be on this trip, to see such a beautiful country, to spend time in the company of such a generous and charming widow. "Woman," he corrects himself. "Woman." Little Boy crosses his arms, bites his lip, and climbs atop his bicycle. It immediately falls over, in spite of the kickstand. He lands on the street, elbows scraped, eyes welling. Fat Man waits for Rosie to kneel and comfort the boy the way women do—to dry his tears with her blouse tails, to bandage him with things she's stowed in her purse. She looks at the child, watches him begin to cry. Fat Man sees that she will go on watching. He kneels over Little Boy. He smoothes his brother's hair and puts his hat back on. "You'll be okay," he says. "Come on. Dust yourself off."

Little Boy gets up on his feet and brushes grit and gravel from his elbows. He bitterly regards his new conveyance.

"He's never ridden on a bicycle before," says Fat Man.

"Never?"

Fat Man almost admits he's never ridden one either before realizing how strange that would sound.

"His parents were very poor, the same as me," he explains. "Here, Matthew. Try again." He props up the bike, holds it by the handlebar and the back end of the seat.

Little Boy hoists himself up cautiously.

"That's the way," says Rosie. "You look smart perched up there, Matthew."

Fat Man lets the other two get out ahead before he mounts his own bike, carefully observing Rosie's example—even Little Boy's—for clues. As they pedal out of town he sees two police walking the far side of the street. These are not their police: not Mr. Bruce, not Rousseau. So his escape is clean. He needn't shiver as they pass.

They ride like this: Little Boy goes first to set the pace because he is the slowest, then Rosie. Fat Man guards their rear. Here he is well-positioned to watch her pedal. The steady rise and fall of her ankles, the same of her hindquarters as wide and flat as the disc of the moon, the flag-like flicker of the loose ends of her copper hair drawn back and tied up tight.

When they come to a hotel the widow lets the staff think them a family so they can share a room. She sleeps on the bed. Little Boy sleeps on the floor until one night Fat Man suggests it might not be indecent for widow and child to share, and she agrees on the condition they lie in opposite directions. Fat Man therefore has the floor to himself, which makes him remember Japan. He swaddles himself in what sheets the bed can spare and rests his head on woolen towels. One night he comes back from using the bathroom, padding softly, and finds himself looking down on them in their bed like a rejected father. There is a little color on her wide, full lips. A little red. A little pink beneath her eyes, perhaps natural, perhaps applied and dithered by hand. Unfurled on her pillow, her hair is limp and slightly curled. There is a calm in her body. Fat Man contrasts his beating heart, his heaving acid tummy. Yet again, he is seized by the urge to thrash himself until his ribs break and his contents spill out on the floor.

He goes to his swaddling, his towel-pillow, and covers up as best he can.

Everywhere they are haunted by the marshal, Pétain, his bust, his white head—his smooth, featureless eyes. One farm has mounted his head on a pike, hanging red rags from his interrupted neck to suggest the severance to come. In a restaurant, a row of Pétains holds hats for customers.

They ride through a small town with a chocolate factory that makes everything smell wonderful when it rains. Fat Man wants to eat the town, the people, their things.

They see Camp Gurs far away, far across a rat-gray field of mud. Dozens of triangular huts, yards and yards of barbed wire fence—some stripped, most still threaded. There are signs of trucks and men at work. Tracks in the mud. No fires though, and no movement among the ramshackle.

FAT MAN WORKS
WITH HIS HANDS

There are about four hundred cabins divided into square clusters of thirty, each cabin's foundation occupying twenty-five square meters of ground. They are built from thin, cheap cardboard-like wood, which has been covered with variously colored fabrics and pasted with tar to seal out the constant rain. The tar does not work; rot develops, slowly eating the fabrics with heavy molds. The roofs leak. Three out of four cabins are knocked down easily with sledgehammers, leaving only the strongest, safest one hundred structures. Furthermore, they destroy the triangular support beams that lie on either side of the stronger structures, holding up the cabins with bits of scaffolding on the inside. Around these squalid cabins the men lay white and slate-blue bricks, and build them new wooden roofs over the old ones. They cut out windows and inlay the squares with glass so thick it looks like the ocean—glass so thick you can see waves in its surface, and ripples, and the grainy impurities suspended within. A single wooden beam is fitted to each wall inside, waist-high, and slid into grooves within the bricks, so that nothing collapses inside. They set down wood flooring, and thick green carpets over that. Each hut is given a stove to keep it warm. Otherwise the interiors remain untouched wherever possible. Rosie calls it restoration. Outside the new cabins are charming, oddly feature-less freestanding brick buildings the color of mountains. Inside they are historical artifacts: educations in the standard of living enjoyed by those in concentration camps. She says, "It is impor-tant that in building new history for ourselves we do not forget the old. We could do that anywhere. Here, we can also remem-ber, even as we rebuild."

"Yes," says Fat Man. "You've got to remember everything."

He remembers how it was to explode.

At first he tries to help the men. They are squat, broad beasts of burden, often shirtless, and their skin trembles with the shift-ing and straining of strange muscles. Their bodies are ridged with hair and layered with small pouting folds of fat. They have fierce, broken noses, cauliflower ears, gappy crooked teeth, and knotty, gnarled hands. They have a way of speaking all at once so he cannot really hear or understand them. Still he tries to earn his wage by their sides. He wields a sledgehammer, smashing cab-ins designated for destruction. It is blissful to destroy something, wonderful to knock out the support beams, to watch it collapse all around. They tell him he is too slow with the hammer, he is inefficient, he swings too wildly. He does not doubt them. So he gives up on destruction and he tries to lay bricks. He can't get them to rest straight atop each other. He spreads the mortar too thickly. His work looks childish and unsound beside theirs. The men tell him he is no mason. He agrees.

He gives up on bricks and tries to dig pits for the new out-houses. He cannot dig the pits as fast as the men can. He gets in their way. His shovel bumps into their shovels like a blind, nosing thing. He overturns their dirt back into the hole, and throws dirt on another man, who nearly pushes him into the pit. They say he cannot help them dig.

At night they warm themselves by the fires they build with broken cabin wood, drinking whiskey and cheap wine; they rub their chests and arms, mutter to each other under the crackling, and look askance at each other, at the fat man. They do this until the small hours and then they go separately to the large tents they share. Fat Man cannot share Rosie's cabin, the first to be completed, so he finds a place in the tents. Sometimes there's a blanket he can use. Sometimes there isn't.

He tries stripping barbed wire from those fences that remain. This requires tan work gloves and wire cutters, which he borrows. He cuts the spiny wire at the point equidistant between two posts. He spools the wire around his left hand until he comes to the post, where he cuts it again. He drops the ball in the mud—an iron tumbleweed. He wrenches the fence post forward and back like a lever until he can bend it to the ground and pull it free by the root. He's slow at this as well. The other men gather their measures of wire in smooth, careless motions as they walk—and yes, some bleed, but it's good and right to bleed. They uproot fence posts in three brute efforts: grunt, grunt, huhhn. They clear dozens of yards of fence in the time a single measure takes him. That night he starts a rumor that he isn't being paid as well as they are, so they will not resent him as the American's fat pet. Because of the rumor, it takes two more days of plodding work before Rosie comes to him, presumably at their request.

He is wrapping his glove in barbed wire. She puts her hand on his back. He is shirtless, having drenched his undershirt long ago. He turns to face her. His pants are streaked outside, swampy inside, and the sweat trickles down into his socks and fills his shoes. A grime of dust on his belly and arms, disrupted by the shape of his hands where he has rested them or tried to clear the dirt away. She is clean, wearing a new dress and smart canary-yellow hat, perhaps the barest hint of scent. She has a canary-yellow shawl to match the hat. "You've been working hard," she says.

He wheezes like a dying horse.

"That's very kind of you," says Rosie. "But I didn't hire you for this kind of labor. I have builders. I have masons and sledge-hammer men. You are more delicate than these brutes, John. You will work very hard for me, I know, but you can do something else. While they build, for instance, you can search the cabins." Rosie studies her palm, and the glowing film of Fat Man's sweat spread on it.

"Why search the cabins?" says Fat Man, hoarsely. "Squatters all the way out here? Wild animals?"

"You needn't go armed, if that's the question." She wipes her hand clean on her dress. The stain fades quickly, but it is a stain. "The conditions here were deplorable. However, the rules apparently were not so tight compared to those of many prisons. The poor prisoners were segregated by sex, as in other camps, but they were still allowed to make art, to socialize, even to put on plays. In fact, they had a playhouse." She points out a cabin several lots away, across standing fences and those still coming down, past half-naked working men the color of mud. "I want you to go in there and find anything that ought to be preserved, before the men get in and trample everything."

Fat Man wipes his brow and rubs his burning eyes. "What ought to be preserved?"

"I guess that's the question," says Rosie. "I'm trusting you to know the difference between prop cups and prison mugs, play-bills and toilet paper."

"Have you seen Matthew?"

"He's around here somewhere. I saw him at breakfast this

morning. Maybe he found another little boy to play with. How old is he anyway?"

The last time he was asked he said nine, and his brother didn't like that very much. "Thirteen years."

"Oh," says Rosie, vaguely. She tilts her head a little to the side. "You should feed him more. He's a bit stunted, isn't he?"

Fat Man does not remind her that she sets the rations now.

He washes himself at a stream before going into the playhouse. The dirt falls away from him in crusts and skeins. The water's cool and sweet. The puckers of his nipples rise all raspberry-bumped.

He goes in shirtless. The air is still. Motes of dust part like curtains around him, and curtains, and curtains. There, at the opposite end of the cabin, is the stage; planks of scavenged pine-wood propped up on crates filled with rocks and potato sacks stuffed with straw. There are coat racks crowding the corners, hung with costumes: hats, vests, boas, a poncho, a paper crown, hand-sewn skirts, a felt beard and mustache, a trench coat, a pith helmet, a jacket. Dozens of prop shoes stand in close pairs around the coat racks, in overlapping circles, like cowed onlook-ers: cowboy boots, ruined beggar shoes, high heels, many san-dals, children's booties. Prop swords and canes bundled like fire-wood behind them, spears and crude standards. Flat cardboard trumpets. Hand-crafted wooden whistles. A cardboard fire set in the notches of brittle, long-dry logs at the brink of crumbling. A broken guitar.

Fat Man walks through the scattered chairs where an audi-ence once sat. Some are aligned in rough rows, others clustered as if to confer, and others overturned. A sock balled up on one, a pamphlet on another. A boot's tongue, expelled. Several spoons.

Fat Man can hear the gathered prisoners, the actors, the singers. Their rattle and laughter, clatter and applause. They laugh until they cry. They make filthy jokes at the commandant's expense. Their voices reverberate in the cobwebs, in the deepest, most itching parts of his ears.

He examines the pamphlet. The first page declares it a description of "those provisional compensations allowed the cast." Leading male: 2 eggs, 2 bowls broth. Leading female: 2 eggs, 1 bowl milk, 1 bowl broth. Villain: 2 eggs, 1 loaf of bread. Director: 1 egg, 1 bowl milk, 1 bowl broth. Secondary characters: half a loaf of bread, 1 bowl of broth. Tertiary characters: 1 heel of bread. And so on.

He drops the pamphlet and climbs up on the stage. It groans. He tests each plank before giving it his full weight. There are fabric backdrops hanging from the wall, all pinned up together at their corners and middles. The one on top is painted like a sunset. He lifts its corner.

Behind that one a starry night.

Behind that one a clear June day.

Behind that one a forest.

Behind that one a castle wall.

Behind that one a blank white cloth, perhaps symbolizing a snowstorm, or the bleak perfection of paradise, or only an unfinished backdrop. He lets them fall back into place. The sun sets again.

He shouts. The dust shivers. He does it again.

He shivers too. It's cold here.

He goes to a coat rack and takes down a shirt from one of its many wooden bulbs. It is a simple cotton shirt, no collar, no buttons, no pockets. Only sleeves. It fits him nicely, which makes him suspect it was an element of a larger, more complicated costume; there was no one here stayed fat long enough to star in any play. He smells his sleeves, and the shirt's breast. First the smell of time, of stale air and busy microbes. Behind that a chalky smoke smell: skunk tobacco. Behind that, the cotton itself. Hints of the man or men who wore this before him. These were real people that lived here.

He takes an old black hat and smells inside it. Sharp sweat, hair clumped with filth. He fits it to his head. It shapes itself to serve his needs. It is creased and battered all over, as if it has been sat on many times.

He takes a black costume vest. It smells of corrupted skin, sores, and pus.

He takes a blue handkerchief in his fist and pushes his nose inside it. He breathes deeply. Of fresh history, of old Jew, of death, of abandonment, of hunger. He folds the cloth and puts it in his vest pocket. He tucks in a white fabric flower on the brim of his hat.

It's warm here.

Rosie is overseeing the beginnings of a trench to drain rainwater. Fat Man touches her elbow. He tells her, "It's all to be preserved."

"Everything?"

"The whole playhouse. We're keeping it just as it is. Everything stays."

"Now you see why I trust you? A sensitive, delicate man." She turns her back on him to watch the trench.

He wants to pull her elbow roughly. He wants to tell her there were people here before them and now they are dead. He wants her to mourn with him. He wants to make her smell the things he smelled. Of course she knows all about it. She knew before he did. He knows there is something terribly prurient about his

new, borrowed costume, and the interest he's taken in their absent corpses.

He has found something sacred. He plans to worship a while.

He walks away examining his black hands.

HOME LIFE; HARELIP

Fat Man and Little Boy don't speak for two weeks, until all the builders are gone and they've moved into their cabin. It's night and all their work is done. Fat Man has documented and preserved various artifacts in the playhouse-museum. Little Boy has swept a dozen cabins, cleaning away all traces of boot prints and masonry. They climb into bed together, each in his underwear. They share a bed because Rosie didn't give anyone a second. Little Boy hogs the covers. Fat Man is too warm anyway—he kicks away what's his.

Outside it is quiet. The fences are uprooted, the communal toilets smashed to bits and trucked away. The new outhouses stand like coffins wedged upright in the dirt, moon stencils casting moonlit crescents on their back walls. The trenches have been dug, draining into the stream nearby, their nadirs still an inch deep with rainwater. The destroyed cabins are burnt, and narrow stone paths conjoin those remaining. The abandoned foundations will erode and smooth in time, until they have become like the rest of the thinly-grassed muddy fields. The restored cabins are empty, except for theirs and the widow's, which are so massive they still *feel* empty—or haunted. Grass seeds have been planted. The brothers must be careful not to let Rosie notice the way the grass springs up beneath their feet wherever they walk. Their cabin is circumscribed by such blades, glittering like silverfish as they waver. The leaves and needles of tall trees sound like crashing waves. Crickets rub their wings together.

As warmth rises from the earth and leaves the brothers' bodies, they grow cold and colder.

"Little Boy?" says Fat Man.

"Yes?"

"Are you awake?"

"Yes," says Little Boy.

"You should know I told the widow you were thirteen." A tickle of hot breath whispers across the back of Little Boy's neck.

"She believed you?" He rolls onto his side, to face away from his brother. In the periphery of his vision, the square of fogged moonlight hovers around their window like a stench.

"That's about how old you look."

Little Boy sighs. Fat Man paws at his back. Little Boy shrugs off Fat Man violently.

"You didn't like it when I said you were nine. How old do you want to be?"

Little Boy rolls to face his brother, with the unfortunate consequence that they grow closer. They breathe each other's bitter breathing. "I'm supposed to be a baby. I'm only a few months old. I should be on my back in a crib, staring up at the ceiling and forgetting for the hundredth time how my toes taste. I should be wallowing in my own mess, and people should be feeding me."

Fat Man touches Little Boy's cheek. "I'm three days younger. You think I should be a baby too?"

Little Boy swats away his hand. "We agreed you would be the older brother now."

"I didn't know what I was in for." Fat Man grasps Little Boy by the thin blond hair projecting from his upturned right temple, squeezes. "I didn't know I was going to be dealing with a nasty little boy who disappears for weeks at a time when there's work to be done. I didn't know I was going to be your slave and permanent caretaker. As far as I can tell you're not getting any older. Are you going to be like this forever? I made an effort to be a good little brother when it was my turn." He pulls at Little Boy now with both arms, tries his best to force his brother closer. The boy thrashes, gnashes, claws.

"Fuck you," Little Boy wails.

"Quiet," rasps Fat Man, pinching together Little Boy's cheeks to keep him from speaking. "When will you be my good little brother? When will you listen to me? When will you do as I tell you? Not because you fear me but because you see the wisdom of my requests?"

He wraps one arm around his brother, still squeezing shut his mouth with the other hand. Little Boy is buffeted by the waves of his bigger brother's body—he is smothered, and he can feel all the oxygen leaving him in fits and starts, rushes and wheezes. Fat Man wraps the other arm around and squeezes him close. Little Boy smothers. He pulls his head out for air.

"Quiet," hisses Little Boy, through flesh and flesh and flesh. "The widow."

"The *widow*," growls Fat Man. He hugs his brother, smoothes his blond mess into place.

"You're the one said you would spank me if I didn't do as I was told."

"You're the one crying out for a beating, complaining about your age, claiming the right to wallow and drool. You are *thirteen* now, if I'm your elder brother. You are a teenage boy and growing if I'm a man."

Little Boy begins to bawl his best baby impression. Fat Man pushes him away. Little Boy kicks viciously in the leaving.

"Go on, cry it out. Get up tomorrow ready to work."

They look at each other across the wrinkled sheets. Fat Man wraps himself anew in the covers. Their warmth is still leaving their bodies, and they haven't any wood to start a fire. So as they drowse they creep nearer. Until the boy is in the man's hands again, and arms and arms and skin and skin and skin. Enough life between them to sweat—to drip, and kick the covers.

Little Boy beats the sun by an hour. He slips from the bed, gathers his clothing, and creeps through their cabin, stepping outside the door to change in the cold, dewy morning. Grass grows beneath his feet as he weaves between the new blue cabins. Sometimes weeds grow also: dandelions and clover.

He takes his bicycle from the utility cabin. There is a light fog on the air. His skin beads with moisture as he pedals through it. He rolls over mud and grass and pavement, past white busts of the marshal and shops not yet opened. Church bells sound. The sun's coming.

He jumps off the bike at a bakery. The bike clatters to its side, scraping his calf on its way to the street. He stands it back up and lowers the kickstand. The bakery's just opened. When he opens the door a burst of warm air, smell of flour and of jam, cheerful ring of eager little bell, a glass display, a man kneading dough at the counter. The display is piled with braided breads, flaky crescent rolls, split-top loaves, and pastries.

The bell rings a second time as the door closes and cold air dissipates. The baker sees Little Boy. He has a big neatly combed mustache and big red-ringed watery eyes that swim and shimmer. "Hello," says the baker, in French. "I don't think I know you, little boy."

Little Boy tilts his head and shows his teeth. He points at the · display.

"Hello? What is your name?" The baker reaches out his floury hand. "I am Mr. Girard. A pleasure to meet you."

"Hello," says Little Boy, ignoring the hand. He points at the display. He understands the baker reasonably well, though mostly from context.

"Do you want something to eat?"

Little Boy nods. He points at the display again, and then at his mouth. He smiles.

"Which ones do you want?"

Little Boy indicates a raspberry pastry and one filled with sweet cheese. The baker takes them from behind the glass and wraps them in wax paper. As he thumbs the creases creased, he tells the little boy how much they cost. Little Boy pretends incomprehension, trying to pass off paying half the price as a misunderstanding. The baker insists, counting out coins from his own pocket to show how it's done. Little Boy relents and follows his example. He glances out the window.

There is a girl passing by with strong, lean calves peeking out beneath her skirt. Her ankles are pretty knots of muscle and bone. Her dark hair bobs in the breeze.

Little Boy smiles for the baker, takes his pastries in their brown paper bag, and begins to leave.

"Wait," says the baker. "Are you mute or something? Where are you from?"

The question floats to the ceiling and settles there. Little Boy opens the door. The bell cheerfully retorts, and a second time behind him. The girl has already walked a fair distance. She is brisk

and graceful, though she does not bother with the feminine niceties of the schoolgirl's walk. Her ragged, yellow school books are
not held primly underneath her chin in folded hands, but slung
from her shoulder by one limp, swinging arm. Little Boy stuffs
the pastry bag in his coat's breast pocket and, running, mounts
his bike. He flails to raise the kickstand with his heel. How old
is she? He tries to count the years in her clothing, in the snappy
rise and fall of her buttocks. He is pedaling toward her, wheels
flecking mud on the pavement. He doesn't know what to say.
The only French that comes to mind is an apology. He wants to
know how to say goodbye as well. He wants to know how to say,
Are you finished with that? These are all the wrong words.

She hears the bike coming. Pauses, mid-step, twisting on the
toes of one foot and the heel of the other. He reaches into his
coat for the pastries, fumbling to offer her one. She begins to
greet him and then they are too close, and then his bike speckles
her hem with dirt. Her eyes, and the roses in her cheeks, and the
faint worry lines already framing her mouth. She is, he thinks,
thirteen. Just like him.

He passes her. Other children filter into the street, converging
on one habitual procession. They all have the same school books,
in various jackets and states of repair. He whips the bike into a
hard turn, loops back, stippling the other side of her dress as well,
and shouts his name: "John!"

Wait, that's not right.

He whips back again. He calls out, "Matthew!"

A fist meets his gut. He lets go the handlebars as if someone
asked him to do it. His feet slip from the pedals. The back of his
head meets the pavement, and the bike falls, and he swallows
back stomach acids. A circular peach shadow descends on him,
becomes an oval, becomes a head and shoulders. He focuses his
eyes. A harelipped boy in cap and red blazer grimaces down at

him, hiding all the teeth that he can hide. An ivory sliver and puffy red gums peek through his upper lip's division.

"Who are you?" he asks, leaning in to study Little Boy. "Why don't you leave her alone, Yankee Doodle?"

Other children gather around them laughing—smaller boys and girls, teenage youths. One of them is standing up his bike, no doubt to steal it. Little Boy scrambles to his feet, kicking the harelipped boy in the shoulder on his way. Walking feels like swimming. He makes for his bike, picking up the pastry bag as he wades. He wrenches his bike free. There, several dozen feet away, is the dark-haired girl with his mud on her skirt. She walks as if nothing has happened. Little Boy climbs up on the bike. He considers running her down. The harelipped boy, however, tugs on his jacket. He holds the bike in place with his left hand, by its back wheel. He coolly motions over his shoulder as if to say, Go back the way you came.

Little Boy spits on him and rides away bawling.

When he comes back to Hotel Gurs, Little Boy has eaten both his pastries. Raspberry and sweet cheese residues scab around the corners of his mouth. There is a harelipped boy set aflame in his heart, a weirdly handsome monster with tusks and massive fists. There is a harelipped boy, blond like him, but better: butter gold to Little Boy's corn-silk white, forever pushing him from his bike. Making him dirty his clothes. There is a harelipped boy with a sharp little chin and cheekbones like the split tops of the baker's bread. There is a harelipped boy, brutal and genuinely French— a harelipped boy who can see he is American just by looking, which isn't even fair because he's never even been to America, not really. There is a harelipped boy who would keep him from a dark-haired girl he only just met, whom he has never hurt.

He puts away his bicycle in the utility cabin.

Collapses sobbing against the blue brick wall. The sound becomes inarticulate, awful, like a baby bird begging, but lower, wetter. Fat Man follows it to him. He looms stupidly—another oval, another head-and-shoulders shadow. There is a harelipped boy.

"What's got you in a fit so early?"

Little Boy sticks out his tongue.

"Did you fall down somewhere?"

Little Boy shakes his head.

"What's that sugar doing on your mouth?"

Little Boy wipes his mouth.

"A pastry," says his brother, sniffing the little boy's breath. "*Two* pastries!"

The bawling continues.

"With whose money did you buy them? That was *our* money. You didn't even get me one. That's really unfair, Matthew."

Little Boy croaks, "Carry me?"

His brother raises his hand to slap him. Little Boy quiets himself, wipes the snot from underneath his nose, and ignores the tears still flowing down over his cheeks and ears.

"Please, brother. Carry me home?"

Fat Man sighs, hoisting his little brother. "All I'm saying is next time you have to share with me."

THE BABIES

Fat Man is watering the milk when their first guest comes to stay. Fat Man pours half the big glass jug into an empty. White threads split down the sides, weaving pooling liquid at the bottom. He pours a pail of water down its mouth and watches the milk multiply. He lowers the pail into the well and draws it back up; fills the other jug. It gleams a bluish white in the failing light, smooth and sweet as pearls.

"Water," rasps someone. At first, Fat Man thinks the well is speaking. He peers over the edge, expecting a disembodied claw to hang from the rim, attached to a wrist, dangling and all corroded to nothing by shadow. Instead he spies a crunchy mop of colorless hair on the well's opposite side, at rest against the stone. "Water," says the mop. It tilts a little to the side.

"Are you thirsty?" says Fat Man, stupidly. He caps the jugs and circles the well, hands out as if to approach a wild dog or a cornered raccoon.

"Been waiting," says the someone. After a long pause, "All day."

She is a heap of rag and bone, skin the color of dishwater, dirt mustache, eyes all crusted, limp arms she can't lift. She opens her mouth and shows him her tongue. Dry split down the middle, coarse as tree bark, half white. Her teeth rotting and soft, some of them misshapen. Gums receding like candle wax recedes.

"I'm sorry," says Fat Man. He lowers the pail and draws the water. He has no cup. He cups his hands and pours it down her throat. She sputters a little.

"Thank you," she says. "Very kind." The water pools in the hollows of her collar bone, stains her blouse-rags in a spreading circle. He pours another handful in her mouth. "Very kind, very kind."

There is mold forming on her chin. Fat Man yanks away his hands. It slows and stops. He thinks of the fog blotches that form on a window around the mouth and nostrils, growing out from the center and then retracting sharply when the breathing stops. The mold likewise shivers in, the weakest outcroppings falling away, dead chalk spores that float on the pools between her fine bones. Japanese souls, he thinks, claiming her body for their own.

"What's your name?"

She looks down at the sprawl of her legs, and seems to lose herself in the snarls and tangles of loose fabric, the spurs of her bare ankles, the leather wrappings on her long feet.

"I thought so," says Fat Man, taking a pen from his pocket and scraping the mold from her chin with the point. It falls like old snakeskin. "Bet you're cold out here, aren't you?"

He hoists her up on his shoulder. He is big but not strong. She weighs about as much as Little Boy, though she is not so warm.

"What doing?" she says. He takes the milk jugs underneath his arms. "Where?"

"There's a place I know you can sleep the night," says Fat Man. It should take about that long for her to die.

175

* * *

Fat Man hides her in the cabin where he keeps his Jewish things. The bed is clear, the sheets are mussed—sometimes he sleeps here. He lays her down, pulls up the blue blanket to her chin. The tramp makes a sticky sound in her throat. He thinks she's going to throw up.

"Do you want milk?" he asks her. "Milk? Num num?"

She nods.

"I'll get you some. Do you like it here?"

The tramp's eyes roll around the room, glancing at the collection. There is a dressmaker's dummy. There is a hat on that dummy, feathered, soft-brimmed. There are shoes hanging on the walls.

"I built this cabin," says Fat Man, bustling around, searching for a proper cup. "Not really, I guess. But I found these things and brought them here." There are no proper cups. They are small brass mugs, droopy cusps down-curled by the heat of hungry mouths, pinched and distended. It seems wrong for her to touch these artifacts, especially the ruined ones. He touches each one he examines, touches the toes of his shoes to the other shoes that litter the floor, as if a small crowd, scattered, facing in various directions, a careful, criss-crossed network of vision. He runs his hand through the crude wigs. Smells the shirts that hang on a rack. "What do you think the odds are you're Jewish?"

"Milk," she says.

"What is your name?"

He finds a squat white clay cup, brown inside, with thicker beads of paint dried hard to the surface. He pours the milk inside. It separates briefly in the pouring, not wholly—a pale swirl in a paler stream, becoming white again in the mug, though with a thin sheen layer on the surface, skim water.

"Here," he says, and he puts his hand beneath her pillow, lifting her head. He pours the milk into her mouth, careful not to touch her skin.

"Ahh," she sighs.

"You can sleep if you want to," says Fat Man. "I'll come back to see you tomorrow. I'll bring you food."

She further eyes the collection. He worries she will take the clothing for herself while he is gone, for warmth. He cannot bring himself to forbid it; he is doing the same.

"This is a sacred place," he says. "You should be safe. Don't worry if you hear anything strange. It happens sometimes."

"Thank you," she says. "Anne."

"You're welcome Anne," says Fat Man. He takes the watered-down milk. He stands a while in the doorway, framed by the dim walls and the sky another darker shade of blue, and then he goes.

Little Boy waits for his brother in their cabin. He is seated at their little table, an empty glass before him. Some time ago he indicated, by the tilt and quiver of his chin, the flaring of his nostrils, that he might like some milk. He has been asking for a lot of milk, frequently when it is too late, when there isn't any more. Thus the water in the milk, to thin it. Fat Man fills the glass and pours one for himself. If Little Boy sees the water in the swirl he doesn't say anything.

If he would like something to eat tonight with his milk he doesn't say anything.

If he has some grievance to air, some close-clutched anger, he doesn't share that either. Only sits across from Fat Man, arms folded on the wooden tabletop, lips curled, eyes opaque, milky as the water, watery as the milk. His hair uncombed, his fingernails filthy—black crescents at his fingertips. He sips his milk and scowls at the window.

177

Fat Man dines on bread and cheese, holding his food through a napkin to slow the growth of molds, scraping them where they still come. He drinks the water milk. He talks to Little Boy about his day, describing unloading the supplies that came—the friendly little napkins with "Hotel Gurs" printed on their corners, the silverware case, the new sheets, spare pillows, the sweets that they'll give away in the office, and the beginnings of an international library to be established beside the museum cabin, where borrowing books will be free, though anyone can purchase any volume they want. The inevitable marginal notes will, as Rosie sees it, add value—a reminder that readers are members of a community. There are Japanese books and German books and French, of course, and English, with illustrated dictionaries and several foreign-language encyclopedias.

"I've been thinking of learning Japanese," Fat Man says. "What do you think?"

Little Boy's eyes widen, take on a spark of life. Then he remembers to blank. Fat Man is only being provocative.

Fat Man finishes his meal. Sloshes what's left in his cup; even half-empty it nearly spills over. "Dogs are still circling the place, trying to catch a nose of our food I imagine. Rosie says loud noise will scare them off, so I holler and rattle my keys, but they always come back."

Little Boy lays his head down on the table. Sometimes he sleeps this way, drooling, until Fat Man can't take it anymore and tucks him into bed. Sometimes he lets his urine go, lets it pool on the seat and run down the legs, drippling on the floor for his brother to clean up.

"It was just a girl," says Fat Man. "Do you know what people put themselves through for girls? Do you want to be like them? You could starve to death this way. If I left you outside tonight— if I picked you up, opened the door, and dropped you off there, you would have to get up, or you could die of exposure. Or if I waited long enough to bring you back in, you would die from thirst. People do that for girls. They start fights, start wars, start books, go off to culinary school."

Little Boy begins to drool on the table.

"I know it's not just the girl. You won't say it but I can tell what's going on in your head, at least some of the time." He goes on, in his meant-to-be-educational household mixture of English and French, describing what he imagines his brother keeps balled up in his mind like a fist: the memory of the Japanese family, the babies, the piglets, the fires, their trees; the times they've run, the entropy or growth that touches everything they touch—the little fires that light on every wick they handle, hungry maggots; their poverty, their loneliness, each other; the way the fat man hits him; the bed they share and the chill that makes them hold each other underneath the blankets; Fat Man's secrets—his cabin hidey-hole, his run of the grounds.

There is also the matter of Little Boy's wage as a hotel employee, which he earns by small tasks and regular cleaning of the communal areas, their own cabin, and Rosie's. Outraged by his brother's squandering of money on candies and toys, Fat Man asked Rosie to entrust him with Little Boy's wage to save or spend on his behalf. With their earnings they can feed themselves if that's all they do, and put a little aside for illness and new shoes. Her argument is that since she lodges them they do not want. Little Boy does not indicate by any quiver or angle of his chin that he understands the budget. Sometimes he tries to wheedle sweets. So far no such luck.

The last straw was Fat Man's agreement, as his Uncle John, that Little Boy should go to school next year, where he will learn French and times tables, little gleanings of natural science, and they will train his handwriting.

Fat Man has grown increasingly concerned about what will happen if Little Boy goes to school. It has also occurred to him that girls of Little Boy's purported age can sometimes bear children, and that it would be wrong and dangerous to inflict this on them. He has tried to speak to Rosie of school again, but there is no reasonable explanation that he can share with her for why his brother shouldn't go. He has tried to tell her what a strange boy his nephew Matthew is, how little he speaks, how nervous he has become since his parents' death, but she refuses to draw the natural conclusion: school can wait.

School, then, for Little Boy, or they must go hungry again. Surely Rosie would not employ an uncle who neglects his nephew's education. As for the threat of pregnancy, that will need a solution.

"I know it's been rough," says Fat Man. "I know how hard you worked to find me. I know you get lonely, though I am still your brother, and though I am still here for you. But I need you to help me so we won't get in trouble. I need you to be a little boy, not a baby. I need you to help me make money, and save, so we can take care of ourselves. We need to get some guests for the hotel, or we're going to be in trouble. We won't be able to keep guests if you act like this. It's going to creep them out."

Little Boy drools on the table.

Fat Man says that's exactly what he means. He says, "I'm not going to tuck you in tonight," though they both know he will when it gets cold. They both know that before long he will undress Little Boy and put him in his pajamas. They both know that he will roll up Little Boy in the sheets and the blanket, and himself, and he will hold his brother.

CATHEDRAL

Little Boy is being a baby. This is his second time. The first time, he was in a shell. It was like an egg. They built him in New Mexico, built him special, and they were very careful, which is different from how most babies happen. Most of the time people make the baby and they don't know what it is—who the baby will be—for ten, maybe twenty years after. It wasn't like that with him. They knew what they were getting. The question was how much. There was the small chance—about two percent, they estimated—he would incinerate the atmosphere. Or would be a dud. But most likely there would be a terrible explosion, which could have different effects depending on where it happened, meaning civilian deaths or military deaths, infrastructure destroyed or machinery, factories or weapons, planes, etc. He would be defined in terms of what he exploded, and they could decide that too with some confidence. American bombers had a lot of practice. Little Boy, if asked by his brother, would say he does not remember this time. So would Fat Man, though with less vehemence.

So there he was in his shell, more or less defined, only waiting to come out and be. They liked to touch him. They moved him around. He didn't have any way of feeling or hearing any of this through his shell. But he unfelt them. He unheard them. The shadows of their touch, the negations of their voices. He didn't understand what they said, precisely, but there were many languages, soft voices, harsh voices. They laughed nervous laughs. They whispered.

He was clenched the whole time. Cold. Waiting to explode. Not wanting it, not precisely, only knowing or feeling, or unknowing and unfeeling, that he would, wherever whenever they dropped him.

Now, the second time he is a baby, his name is Matthew. Fat Man gets used to it after the first month. Sometimes he forgets the Little Boy baby's around. He starts talking to himself the way they did when Little Boy was a baby the first time, only now he can hear it with his ears, which are a part of his new shell—the little boy shell with its little boy ears. Fat Man will say things like, "God I'm tremendous," or, "I think I'm growing again." He stands in the middle of the room holding his flab out in front of him like pulling balls of dough from a loaf's worth. He looks at himself that way for a long time. After a while he puts his clothes back on and leaves to work. Little Boy won't move until Fat Man comes back. Or, if he does move, Little Boy will still move back into the same place before Fat Man comes back, so it's like he never moved. Fat Man comes back stinking from work, or with new books under his arms, borrowed from the widow's library, or with bread and milk for Little Boy, and wedges of melon, or a half-dozen eggs.

One day Fat Man puts a grape in Little Boy's mouth, but

Little Boy stops chewing halfway through. The chewing is too much to ask. Little Boy is so tired, all the time tired. He is sad about this girl, or maybe all the girls. So he's working his jaw and it feels like a rusty gate, about as heavy, and so halfway through he gives up. It goes partway down his throat, gets caught there, and at first Fat Man doesn't realize—he thinks Little Boy swallowed—so he puts another one inside. It rolls down Little Boy's tongue and sticks in his throat on top of the other.

Fat Man figures it out when Little Boy turns blue. Fat Man flails, shouts, "What in hell are you doing?" In his panic he squeezes Little Boy's throat, crushing the grapes so they go down.

The next day Little Boy has six bruises around his neck shaped like Fat Man's fingers. They feel tremendous. Fat Man resolves to mash up everything he feeds Little Boy or to cut it up small. He softens Little Boy's bread in milk or water. He works Little Boy's mouth to make him chew, and shoves the food down his throat with a finger if he has to. By the summer's end he has Little Boy on a mostly liquid diet consisting of water, milk, broth, and the things he can dissolve inside them.

Little Boy's favorite thing is to lie back on his chair, almost but not quite falling out, mouth open, and wait for Fat Man to pour his dinner down inside him, where it glows in his belly. Glows, and seems to grow.

Fat Man kisses him sometimes on his head after a meal, if he thinks Little Boy has tried to be less difficult. But Little Boy never tries. He doesn't want to make things easy. If his body falls into such a position as facilitates the meal, then he will let it stay there. If he won't make it better then he can't make it worse. This is one of the rules.

Another rule is he can't be a baby when Rosie's around. He doesn't have to talk or even think when she's near but he does have to clean. He has to do his job so he can earn his money, which goes directly to his brother, who can spend it however he wants. Little Boy never sees it.

Little Boy makes Fat Man clean him. The way he does this is he lets himself get more and more dirty until the widow asks Fat Man why he doesn't make Matthew bathe. That night Fat Man rolls up his shirt sleeves to his elbows, strips down Little Boy, and scrubs him raw. Pours buckets and buckets over Little Boy's head. He has to hold up his smaller brother with one arm under his armpits or Little Boy will slide under.

He pushes Little Boy beneath the water, ostensibly to clean him. He keeps Little Boy down there a while. Little Boy likes it, and anyway the rule is he cannot help himself.

Fat Man pulls up Little Boy by his hair, by the roots, and Little Boy's scalp burns, and he cries. He shouts, "WAAAAH."

"WAAAAAH."

Fat Man shouts back at him and splashes his face with buckets and buckets of water.

They continue in this way a while.

Fat Man takes to making Little Boy wear a big white cloth diaper, safety-pinned at the corners so Little Boy fouls nothing else when he fouls himself.

Some nights Little Boy gets hungry, or wets himself, and then he cries and cries, sometimes for hours on end. WAAAAH. WAAAAH. WAAAAH. He doesn't kick or thrash, doesn't roll around on the floor, is otherwise perfectly still. After a little while Fat Man will lose his patience, will get up in his face and start to scream back. He kneels over Little Boy, on all fours, and puts his face in Little Boy's, all his bulk hanging over all Little Boy's slight, and screams and screams. Little Boy cries, and Fat Man screams, WAAAAH, AAAAAH, WAAAAH, AAAAAH, and so on, all night, until their throats are raw and their faces are beaded with spit and tears.

The next day Fat Man gives Little Boy banana mash mixed with milk and sugar, which he thinks is Little Boy's favorite.

Little Boy does like it.

One night, while Fat Man and Little Boy sit at the table, Fat Man says, "You'll never believe what I found. Look. It's a little picture book." A small sheaf of papers with holes punched in the left margin, red yarn threaded through the holes.

"There's Mickey Mouse inside it. He comes to Camp Gurs."

Little Boy lets his head slump onto the book, pinning it to the table. Fat Man yanks up his brother's head by the hair and pulls the book loose.

"I found it in the playhouse. One of the Jews made it. See, in this cartoon, Mickey is a Jew. They tell him so. He didn't know about it until they told him, just as they told us who we really are."

Little Boy's nose-down on the table now, but Fat Man keeps turning the pages as if he were reading along.

"Things were very unfair for them. They had to ask the commandant of the prison for everything, the way we have to ask Rosie. It was worse for them, of course. I don't mean to compare. They had to be smart or people would take their food. They had eggs, but not many. They had bread. They had to make their own clothes. You can see how badly Mickey wants to be free." Fat Man turns another page. "Isn't the art wonderful? In the end, Mickey remembers he's a cartoon, and so he erases himself. Then he's free. He goes to America."

Fat Man tears up. It's on his voice the way whiskey stink is on a drunk, the way syrup smells on pancakes, the way cyanide smells of almonds. "I don't know why anyone would want to go to America."

He jerks up Little Boy's head. A string of drool dangles from his lips, the only thing that keeps Fat Man from shoving the book in Little Boy's face. "This is important," Fat Man snarls. "This is probably the most important thing that ever happened. You know what happened to the man who drew this? They loaded him up on a train, with all his friends, and they took him away to die. It was awful. It was the worst thing that ever happened and it started here. There's nothing to compare in all of human history."

He holds Little Boy's head by the chin and his hair so that they're facing one another. Little Boy's eyes are rolled down in his head, looking now at the open book on its last page, a picture of what seems to be New York, the lines wavy and childish, bustling against each other, elbowing for room. Fat Man looms at the top of his vision like a big fish bobbing for air. Little Boy sees that Fat Man has dressed himself in new clothing, and he understands that it was borrowed from the Jews that used to live here. Fat Man's stretching the fabric thin—Little Boy can see his flesh through his white cotton shirt, and his gut peeks out at the bottom like a pale orange wedge.

Fat Man says, "Do you want to know where you live or don't you? Do you care about anything but yourself? You can live and die inside your body, hard and cold and meaningless as a bomb that never went off, a yolk asleep inside a shell, or you can listen to me when I speak, hear what I'm saying, and live in other people, too, and feel for them and know them. Or you can live in ignorance. You can rest your head on the table and drool. You can be nobody if you want. You can be a vegetable."

But Little Boy isn't any of those things. He's a baby. He wants to know if people scream at babies for their lack of politics. Do they shout at a yolk to make it a chicken? Little Boy is runny and yellow inside.

"You're a coward! Lay about all day. Least I'm up and moving. You'll never see me stand still long. When you grow up you'll see you can't be a lump, not if you want to eat. You'll see you've got to work. You know how hard the Jews worked? Just for an egg?"

Fat Man wipes sweat from his brow with a dead Jew's sleeve. He leaves a stain like a caterpillar coiled on a leaf.

"I tell myself I won't hit you anymore. I tell you I won't, but you're so selfish. Living in a graveyard and you won't take time to look at the monuments, won't read the epitaphs. The prisoners carved them themselves. Maintained the grounds too. The way I do. It was part of their work."

He scoots back his chair from the table and scoops up his brother. Whenever Fat Man holds him, Little Boy knows that Fat Man knows he is a baby. Sometimes he even coos. Not tonight. Fat Man is going to hurt him, he knows it, and the goo goo ga ga shit will only make it worse—he might throw Little Boy in the creek.

He carries Little Boy to a faraway cabin. He brings him through the threshold like a bride or a cripple. There are one thousand pieces of junk: rulers, cups, shoes, coats, hats, folded laundry, bowls, spoons. There is a woman in the bed, surrounded by the baubles, certain watercolor paintings, and costume jewelry. She reminds Little Boy of things he's never seen, stories that he's never heard. A queen buried with her treasures.

The queen is very thin, her skin filthy. Her hair is stiff curls, sticking out at every angle, a wispy crown, colorless and many-colored—brown becoming gray, never really being brown, never really being gray, becoming blonde, not blonde, becoming white, not white, not black, nothing. Nothing becoming nothing, and becoming, and becoming nothing.

Then there are her eyes. She looks at the brothers, and Little Boy can only assume she sees.

"Look at her there, lying like a dead bird. Do you want to be like that?"

She closes her eyes.

"I feed her too. I feed her and then I come home and I feed you. I've been thinking, maybe I should leave you here. It would be more convenient. Do you want that? Do you want to lie here like a dead bird too?"

Fat Man sets down Little Boy on the floor, beside the bed, like an offering.

"When I come back tomorrow morning, maybe you'll have made a good decision."

He takes a hat from the rack on his way out. A black hat with a wide brim. He closes the door. Now Little Boy's alone with her. He hears her shifting in the sheets.

It turns cold. He stays still, feeling his soft shell all around him like a cathedral, echoing with him. As long as he's back on the floor when Fat Man returns it will be like he never moved.

He finds his feet and climbs up in the bed. His body is small again. He wraps himself in the blanket with the woman. In doing so he pulls a little from her, revealing naked arms and the drape of her shirt. The tops of her arms bristle with grass. There is a mass beneath her shirt as well, more grass. Out of her shirt's torn collar, a growing flower winds toward the ceiling. The blossom blooms. Red petals like ruby quartz. Her eyes are open. She's looking at the flower. He can only assume she sees. Leaves budding, and thorns. Not a rose. Clover on the collar bone.

Fat Man finds her that way the next morning. Still alive. He prunes the flower, trims the grass, and pulls loose the bloodied-red roots where he can. Little Boy's on the floor the way he was left. Still awake, becoming a cathedral.

What a little boy needs is a mother. What a fat man wants is a wife. What a homeless woman needs is a home. What this one needs is a warm place to die. What this one needs is a bath and a bed.

One night Fat Man bathes her.

One night she dies.

Does not become a mother or a wife.

No queen, but a body.

The brothers watch, transfixed, as her body becomes hair. Becomes mold. Becomes maggots. Becomes bones. Becomes spiders. Becomes flowers.

Becomes a seed.

See the brothers through the secret cabin's thick blue window like a square of still water. See the strange light she casts on the brothers. See the way they watch her. See the way their hair stands on end. See that Little Boy is sitting up: sitting like a little boy.

See how calm their bodies. The slow and steady of their breathing.

As if there is some weight, some heat, leaving them.

It goes dark.

In the dark they are whispering. The cabin's door opens.

Glints of motion. Sound of shoes on thin grass and bald mud.

The ease of digging in soft earth, even for such a large seed.

What a seed wants is a hole.

Little Boy helps his brother make the hole.

A seed wants a place to grow.

IKOTSU

THE SUBMARINE
BEHIND HIM

Wakahisa Masumi, the Oriental spirit medium, combs his hair. It hangs halfway down his back; the ends make him itch. He parts it down the center, a pink-white line dividing oil-slick tresses. The comb is jade, carved to look like it was made from tortoise shell, with little pearls set in the handle. They look soft but dig into the palm, leaving small red blisters with extended use. Using his fingernails, he plucks the short black curling hairs from his nose's prim cartilage and flicks them into the trash. Flutters his eyelashes: geisha, geisha. He gazes at the mirror, imagining a wife. Her lips and cheeks would be a little pinker, and her forehead would be smooth and calm as cream. She would feel like the underside of his wrist—the silk of the skin. Otherwise, there might be a strong resemblance. He was always a delicate boy, and quiet. Now he is beautiful too. He unwinds the loose hairs from the teeth of his comb, spooling them around his fingers. It feels cool. He lays down the comb and sets the coil beside it, among others in various stages of tangle and curl. He shaves the hints of mustache from his lip, using a straight razor and scented lather. His skin burns pleasantly.

There is a dead girl seated on the empty air beside him, plucking her eyebrows thinner and thinner. A bra hangs from her shoulders, unbuckled in the back, cups veiling only the tips of her nipples, the bruise-colored aureole setting suns above the lacy fringe. Her yellow high-heel shoes hang from up-curled toes, back ends bobbing. She watches herself in the mirror, checking her teeth and stroking her hair intermittently as she grooms. Her image is not in the mirror.

Masumi checks his teeth as well. He does up his hair in a tight ridge that climbs the crown of his skull like a centipede. When he puts on his hat he looks and feels a man again—feels his balls descend a little, feels his prick unfurl. The hat is white with a brown band, some kind of leather, perhaps calf skin—he doesn't remember. It has dimples on its sides. He flicks it askew. What a charmer. He drinks the lukewarm dregs of his flask, a peppermint schnapps, and sets it on the vanity. There is another half-finished bottle, whiskey, that he decants into the flask through a dented brass funnel he considers an old friend. The schnapps cost him too much, and the whiskey was worse. He'll have to win it all back.

As he stands up from the chair before the vanity, the dead girl slides horizontally into his place without seeming to notice, passing through the armrest, coming to rest in his chair. She plucks and plucks her eyebrows, bobs her heels, checks her dead girl teeth. The mirror does not see her, will not countenance her face.

Masumi sits on the bed to put on his shoes. There's a dead boy hiding underneath, peeking at his ankles. The dead boy doesn't wear a shirt and there's a dark pit in his throat where sound would leak if he really made any—that is, if he still used air for words. Masumi has not asked him where the hole came from or why he doesn't cover it. That's where his audience would go first. He prides himself on avoiding the obvious. In this case that doesn't leave a lot to discuss. The boy fingers the edges of his absences—the wound, the gums of his missing teeth—incessantly.

Masumi puts his head between his knees to see the dead boy, who grins up at him, gap-toothed.

"Hello Charlie."

"Hello," says the dead boy, sniggering. "Do you feel well today?"

"I'm hung over, and I've got an itch."

"What kinda itch?"

"The same kind I've had for months now," says Masumi. "The kind you can't reach. I'm going down to the casino. Don't wait up for me."

"If you see my parents," says the dead boy, and then he trails off. He wouldn't know what to do about it if he found them.

Masumi scratches the back of his head. He has, in fact, two itches. There is the ghost of a submarine that floats just above and just behind him. There is also the pull of the bombs, which manifests itself in his right temple. The submarine is silent. He has never seen it, only feels its judgment as it wavers pale and ominous, watching him. It follows as he buzzes the elevator and hovers behind him as he waits in the hall. The submarine has become a sort of comfort. The bombs are something different. He doesn't want to think about them.

There is a dead elevator boy in a hotel uniform. His black fingers pass through the door as he reaches to slide it open. The white, living elevator boy welcomes Masumi inside. "Hello sir," he says. Masumi nods. The dead elevator boy stands beside the living one, pulling an invisible crank as the living one pulls his. Masumi ignores the dead one. They want to be seen. They are prone to acting out.

Masumi lights a cigarette. Watches the smoke. Lets it build in his throat until it seeps out his nostrils. There must be a line in a poem somewhere about the way a pack can make you a dragon for a day. The living elevator boy coughs pointedly. The dead one doesn't mind at all.

Perhaps the best part of playing the casino is that no one pays Masumi any mind. He can sit at the slots unmolested, pulling the lever when he feels he wants to pull the lever and handling his coins when he doesn't want to do anything. He sucks on them as well, pressing the cool, greasy metal to the inside of his cheek. He can shoot craps, or he can play roulette. No one asks about dead relatives, or looks to him for guidance. Nobody meets his eyes, even. Perhaps they are afraid. Western wartime propaganda emphasized his culture's strange admixture of industry and savagery. They may be waiting for him to play a koto or eat from the end of a ritual knife. Or they may, to be more generous, only dislike the way he looks around a room, observing the death in all things: the ghosts among the crowd. He unscrews the cap on his flask, pours his boozy concoction in his half-full Coca-Cola. The remaining flecks of ice unsettle, pushed to the perimeter of the glass, and tilt from side to side. He stirs with his straw, takes a sip. Bittersweet.

Edith Piaf sings "Embrasse-moi" on all the casino's radios, which are distributed throughout the betting floor. Just now the song is getting to the really slow parts. Masumi, who never liked this one, loses five minutes trying to invent a trilingual pun that cuttingly describes the way her band handles their instruments— surely there must be a French word for performance that rhymes with a German word for strangling a sickly fowl, but he can't think of it now. It's been too long since he read.

When he gets serious, when he's lost enough money and had enough peace, Masumi goes to the blackjack table. He waits politely until he can sit, emptying his glass, drinking openly from the flask. Its concealment is an affectation. No one here cares. In fact the employees—the only ones with whom he will intentionally interact—prefer him drunk. He makes more mistakes that way.

There is a woman who waits for him most nights at the blackjack table, sitting legs crossed, martini in hand, watching the dealer, silently counting cards. She always dresses like a man— brown slacks, white shirt with open cuffs and collar, blue vest, brown fedora—and she keeps her hair tucked up and out of sight. There's no masking her breasts, however. There is no hiding her hips.

There she is now. Martini, olive floating like a life raft. A single chestnut thread has fallen from beneath her hat, bisecting her eye. A long, thin shadow follows, hooking the chin and climbing to her lower lip, where it meets its mother thread, split ends, clinging to the lip. Her eyes are green. She said her name was Lauren when he asked.

She won't acknowledge him until he sits down beside her. She'll stay when he leaves. These are the rules. Other men might object to her rigidity and coldness. Masumi prides himself on being unlike other men. When the seat beside her is vacated by a sweaty, red-faced man in a too-tight suit storming off, hat pushed down over the tops of his ears, Masumi takes it. He crosses his legs, remembers who he is tonight, uncrosses them.

"You're looking dandy," says Lauren.

"I was waiting for someone to notice." He puts his bet in the box.

The dealer lays down his cards. Masumi peeks at his own hand. It's a soft seventeen—ace hearts, six spades.

"Hit," says Lauren.

He knew that.

"Hit," he says. The dealer gives him a five. It's twelve, then. He hits again, seventeen, and again, twenty.

"Hit," says Lauren.

It's a stupid play, but she's usually right. He goes for it. The dealer tosses out the card eagerly. Diamond seven. Dealer takes Masumi's money.

"Look at it this way," Lauren says. "You just ate a lot of shit. Less shit to eat in the next hand."

The guy on Masumi's left wins. He tips back his drink and finishes it off all at once in celebration, apparently determined to never win again tonight. He looks like the kind of wealthy that comes here to purge a little. Masumi nods to acknowledge his neighbor's good fortune.

"I can't take it anymore, Lauren," says Masumi.

The dealer lays down two nines.

"Split them," says Lauren.

Masumi separates the cards, still face-down, and sets out another bet.

The dealer's top card is a ten. Masumi hits both his hands. Five and eight. He hits them again. Four and three. That's twenty, twenty-one. He feels good but he'd like to see the hole card.

"The brothers," hisses Masumi, beneath his breath. "I need to see them again. Just thinking about them makes my hands shake."

"You seem calm enough," says Lauren.

"I'm drunk." He unscrews the flask's lid, takes a swallow.

In a fit of triumphant laughter, the rich idiot next door elbows him in the side without seeming to notice he's done it. The dealer flips his hole card: nine of hearts. Masumi prides himself on his graciousness in victory—he collects his winnings with one hand, saluting the dealer in a short, jerky motion with his other.

Lauren smirks. "Where are these brothers?"

"Just a bit south, on the Spanish border, more or less. Not sure what they're doing there, but probably not hurting anybody."

"Hit," says Lauren. "If they're harmless, why do you get so worked up?"

The dealer adds a two to his seventeen. Lauren tells Masumi to hold, so he does. Dealer loses again, to him and half the table. Half the table cheers. Masumi maintains his reserve.

"If I go there," whispers Masumi, "if I see them again, I'll kill either them or myself. I won't know which until it happens."

"Collect your winnings," says Lauren.

Masumi chuckles and takes his money. He's ahead for the night. All it takes is to win a little more than he loses—if he can do that, he can afford another night in the hotel, another bottle of liquor, another rack of lamb, another chocolate ice cream with sliced, caramelized bananas and sprigs of mint on top. The casino's patience, its ability to come out just a little bit ahead each day, its constant impersonal hunger balanced by the way it contents itself with emptying the patron's wallet only a few hundred francs at a time, is an inspiration to Masumi. To attach oneself to the world and suck calmly and with care until the blood wells up beneath its skin and makes a bruise, and then to pierce the flesh, to let the blood thread through one's spit and down the throat. To nourish oneself on the trickle, this must be the goal of any person. Masumi may never be wealthy, but if he plays by the odds he can live well, and this can be a kind of happiness to replace the kind he used to feel. So far, tonight, he's ahead, which is just another way of saying he's winning.

"Hit," says Lauren.

He does, and goes bust. That's a good thing. Losing keeps him humble, keeps him mindful of the odds.

"You should go there. You should see them."

They don't talk about it anymore. Lauren thinks she's won. After several more hours, in which following her instructions most of the time leads to winning a small majority of hands, and in which Masumi empties his flask, lending a tearful, stinging bleariness to his eyes and a soft blur to all the world's edges, he decides she's right. Meanwhile, a beautiful Parisian with a bevy of bright scarves assumes Lauren's chair. Lauren effortlessly slides out of the way, orbiting the table so that she still faces the dealer, so that she can still see the cards. She's sitting on thin air now, like the dead girl upstairs. Most people feel an instinctive aversion to her seat. It can stay empty for hours in a packed house. The average Parisian is apparently, perhaps predictably, unimpressed by premonitions and haunts, or wholly numbed to them from ass to elbows.

Masumi approaches Lauren from behind. "I won't be seeing you again," he says, leaning forward to wrap his arms around her. Where they touch they do not touch—he passes through; it feels like nothing. Not even an active absence, but a passive one. He kisses where her ear would be if she had one, if she had anything. "I'm going to go down there. Maybe kill someone."

No one seems to mind his hugging the air. It doesn't matter. He'll never see any of them again.

"Have a good life," says Lauren, keeping her eyes on the cards.

In this last moment, the worst possible time, Masumi surrenders to the obvious. "I never asked you how you died."

She peels back the open cuffs of her sleeves, revealing trails of dried blood leading from inner elbows to wrists, delicate bones, firm muscles. He'd never noticed how strong she was.

He leaves her there.

When he gets upstairs, Charlie has gone missing. Masumi never finds him again. The dead girl, thank goodness, is still fussing in the mirror. She doesn't miss the dead boy because the dead can't see the dead. The dead can't see the dead, he thinks, because it would be too much comfort.

ROSIE DOES
THE MATH

John, dressed for work in a large gray shirt and leather suspenders, follows Matthew out of their cabin. Matthew's dressed for school: short pants, blue-collared shirt, brand new beret. There are more than three feet between them at all times—the length, roughly speaking, of the fat man's arms. This is an ominous radius.

Matthew mounts the bike. He puts one hand against the cabin wall and leans that way, raising his kickstand from the mud. He heels it back. Now he's upright, ignoring his dependence on the wall. John may offer Matthew help. From this distance it's impossible to hear. John grips the bike by its seat and sets it right. Matthew tries to pedal away. John holds him still and slips some cash into his pocket. He pushes Matthew along. The bike teeters, finds its balance. Matthew rings his bell three times.

Rosie likes to see them get along. The sun is rising. The air is cold with a bit of wind. She's still asleep. Rosie needs her coffee.

John waves at her and totters her way. He's getting larger.

Knock him on his side and you could roll him like a barrel. Someone could get squished.

He says, "Have you been to the museum yet today?"

"Not yet," says Rosie, rubbing her eyes beneath her glasses. The grease of her fingers is of course smeared on the lenses when they fall back into place. "I was going to have breakfast."

"Can I cook for you?" He thumbs his suspenders. "I swear I'll do better than last time."

Rosie is wiping her glasses clean on her blouse. "You better. I still can't get the taste of it out of my mouth."

"I told you what to do about that."

"And if I get sloshed, who's going to keep you and your little hellion from burning the place down?"

John looks genuinely hurt. "We would never do a thing like that."

She touches his arm, sliding her glasses back into place. "Just joshin'. I know you wouldn't. Although, you know, *he* might."

John makes her puffy pancakes. He puts fat cubes of butter on each stack and sprinkles a generous helping of powdered sugar over each plate, then the syrup. She makes her own coffee while he works the kitchen cabin's griddle. Her griddle, her pancakes, her butter, her sugar, her syrup. The fat man is liberal with her things. As the pancakes cool, he fries bacon. Grease flecks his shirt. The part of her that wants to sleep in peace tonight is at odds with the part of her that wants to calculate the meal's cost. An offer to cook is an offer to use her things, is an offer to further deplete her savings. He surely means to be kind. If he added up the money he might save by eating with her, if this is a shrewd money-saving strategy, then he is at least taking care in the cooking. He knows she has a weakness for butter, and that she likes her bacon soft and yellow.

If you don't have to pay electric, gas, or water, and if you bought the land outright, you can run a hotel on a war widow's government checks, assuming nobody comes there to stay. With several guests—and Rosie has only the newlyweds, Mr. Parcel, and Mrs. Dryden—one is required by decency and business sense to purchase more provisions than those guests will use: they expect options. No one wants to look at his neighbor and see an identical spread on the plate. They've got to feel special. So there's excess. Given time the unused eggs go rancid. You've got to throw those out. Sometimes Rosie gets antsy; she has a lot of egg dinners. The bread molds but you can trim it away if you catch it early, sometimes even if you don't. Then the rest is yours.

Rosie does resent living on her own scraps. The fact this bacon would go to rot if they didn't eat it, the fact the butter might otherwise sour, complicates her calculations. It might be saving them money in the long run. The long run is a lot to think about.

They don't say much while they eat. John drinks her orange juice. She knocks back two mugs of coffee before she's halfway through the pancakes. His silverware—her silverware, in his hands—is loud on her plates.

"We've got a new guest on the way," says Rosie. "He speaks *Japanese*."

"That puts us at five languages. My French and yours, our collective English, your burgeoning Spanish, Mrs. Dryden's Chinese, and now the newcomer."

"My Spanish does not burgeon. It putters at best," says Rosie, lowering her eyes. "It's too many guests. The budget will be very thin. If we can attract a few more, perhaps find another retired lodger—"

"Bless Mrs. Dryden," says John.

"—Then we might start to turn this ship around. There might even be a margin."

"A *profit* margin?"

"The same."

Budgetary concerns aside, it's nice to sit with him this way. She pours her third and final coffee. John has calmed in recent days. It shows especially in his eating. He used to be frantic, furtive—weird, frankly. He would hold things at a certain distance, on fork-end, until he was ready, and then he would take them in one bite. Chew, gulp, swallow. The next morsel, meanwhile, held again at that ominous distance. Now he's holding his rasher of bacon in his bare fingers as he speaks, waving it like a conductor's wand.

He washes the dishes. They will be used again in several hours, when their guests—the retired Mrs. Dryden, the lazing newlyweds, and the old man Parcel—wander from their cabins. Now they are curled in their blankets or loading coal into the fire, trying to squeeze a little more warmth from the stove and a little more sleep from the morning.

"Did you want to see the museum now?" says John. "If you have a moment. I know you're busy."

"I am busy," says Rosie. She doesn't want to think about it. "I'll have a look. The museum is a very important part of what we're here to do."

With his slow gait, he leads her there. He touches the back of his neck often and lets his head hang. From behind he looks like a lump. Already his armpits are deeply stained. She wonders how he does his laundry. There are whole days they don't see each other, though so few live or stay here. He never talks about himself.

They pass under what is, at first glance, an unremarkable tree. Brown bark, green leaves, standard. Rosie doesn't know about trees beyond a few species. Poplar. Oak. Redwood. Sequoia. Pine. Willow. She could not, with any confidence, assign those names to any actual existing trees. She might know a willow.

This one is like a willow, but with a thinner trunk, and fewer branches, though tightly packed. They are not as long as a willow's would be. They do droop in a certain way—they seem to weep. The green teardrop leaves flutter on the breeze. The breeze stops. With a sudden rustling they snap to one angle. As John passes, the tree reaches for him and follows. Or it seems.

Rosie asks, "Has this tree always been here?"

He stops and slowly turns. "It has."

All the tree's branches are still, quiet, strained for reaching. Its trunk bends very slightly toward him. A single leaf comes loose and falls on him, sticking to his face, just next to his mouth's corner.

Rosie walks beneath the tree. It does not reach for her.

They come to the museum cabin, once the prisoners' playhouse. He opens the door with such hesitance that she worries what he's done.

"It's wonderful," she says.

At the entrance the ground is empty but for signs of shoes: skid marks from old leather; mud crescents from heels; scuffs. As if just the day before several dozen people had been trudging, walking, pacing, running through. Rosie wonders how many were made by John himself. How many were intentional? Whose shoes did he wear while he did it?

The walls are covered with paintings and a sequence of cartoons featuring Mickey Mouse. No artists are credited beyond their signatures, if they left them, because so few can be identified. Here a portrait of a grave little girl with hair too thin. Here a watercolor of several bright, exotic birds perched together on a tree. Here a painting of a broke-down cabin of the sort this one used to be, the lines precisely accurate, the colors pointedly wrong, even ill.

The stage is where they found it. Empty, not counting the long shadow Rosie casts from the doorway, which mounts the stage and climbs the far wall. Before the stage, there are fifteen rows of chairs and stools, some improvised, some poorly repaired, some only moderately degraded by the passage of time. Several out and out broken—collapsed, legs splintered or half-gone, lopsided on the ground. On each seat, a token: a cup, a spoon, a shoe, a bracelet, several gold fillings, a toothbrush, a rubber spider, an empty can of corn, a pair of dice, shoelaces, tin jewelry, a sheriff's star, a dog bowl, a crushed hat, a knife, yarn, needles, twine, wire, crayon, comb, candle, card, cufflink, joy buzzer, jacks, pill bottle, pencil nub, underwear, watch face, thimble, pocket change, cigarette stub, half a belt, a pie tin, buttons, a shirt collar, a zipper, nylons, tongue depressor, false teeth. They all seem on the verge of a terrible collective rattle.

"Do you really love it?" John walks along the left wall, pretending to examine the paintings, the seating. He almost trips.

"It's depressing as hell," says Rosie. "But wonderful."

"It's supposed to feel bad, you know."

"I'm not an idiot, John."

After Rosie and John part ways, he sees the new guest, the Japanese gentleman, approaching in a hired car. John goes to meet the car, which stops halfway down the central road dividing the hotel grounds. It's slowed by the thick layer of mud that coats each tire. The gentleman climbs out, hopping several feet clear of the car so as to avoid the displaced muck. He's dressed in white top to bottom. John reaches to shake. As their hands touch, they share a gaze into each other's eyes. One of John's knees goes crooked, corrects itself. They hold hands too long. There is perhaps a jolt of recognition. The gentleman points to the trunk and John retrieves the luggage, sinking ankle-deep in the moat of mud surrounding the car. There are many bags. The Japanese gentleman pays the driver through the window. Once John has burdened himself like a mule he leads the gentleman away, making polite conversation Rosie can't quite hear from this distance. The gentleman does not offer to help with his bags.

She goes to her cabin. She goes to do the books, to find out how long they have left if things keep up this way.

Start at the beginning. Take the money her husband left. Reduce it by the cost of her journey, the paltry expense of the land, and the more serious cost of reconstruction. Subtract the cost of her multilingual peacetime library. Subtract her living expenses. Subtract the salaries of two employees. Subtract the cost of feeding the guests and providing them with certain niceties—complimentary chocolates, fresh towels, unlimited coal for the stoves. Subtract what she sends home to her mother to keep body and soul together. To be safe, assume two hundred dollars a year will unexpectedly catch fire and their ashes will blow away on the wind. Remember the tendency of things to become more expensive over time, and very rarely less. Add her government war widow checks. Repeat the annual deductions until the sum is zero. Three years is all they have. Two if she can bring herself to hire a real cook.

When the money runs out she'll still have the land, the cabins. She cannot imagine where John and Matthew would go—even John is strangely childish, dependent. They need a mother. If it comes to that she can sell the books to buy time and buy food. Some of the Jewish paintings in John's museum might be quite valuable. She could try to get a job in town.

She's been working in bed, cross-legged, the books spread out before her. Her mud-caked shoes are looking lonesome on the floor. She falls asleep sitting up, her back against the headboard.

When she wakes it's nearly time to practice languages. She

corrects her hair. She slides into her mud-caked shoes. The sun is high and the air a little warm. Warm enough. She goes to the library. The newlyweds are in the southeast corner, hidden behind as many shelves as they can put between them and the entrance. The young husband reads an English book to his pretty wife because it sounds exotic. His pronunciation is a molasses amalgam of British and southern American. He reads her *The Big Sleep*. It gradually becomes clear they're reading for the bad language, the punches, the booze, the guns, the sexual provocation—the only English words they really understand. Mrs. Dryden is asleep in a chair in the large, open reading area, a French history of the first great war fallen to the floor from her hand, open, pages down, pages bent. Rosie lifts the book, closes it, and puts it on the end table beside the old woman's chair, marking it where it fell open. It's unlikely that Mrs. Dryden has made it to this chapter on the war's origins. She is a very slow reader, except in Spanish, where she takes perverse pleasure in rattling off words through a tommy gun mouth, explosively trilling her R's, spitting consonants, rendering the lot incoherent. Not a language in her mouth: an attack.

Rosie sits down with a French dictionary and an early edition of *Les Miserables*. She feels the sleep coming on again. She blames Mrs. Dryden.

John's arrival is announced by his shadow on the carpet—it blots out the sunlight that comes through the library door. He's brought the Japanese gentleman with him.

"Mrs. Cummings," says John.

She smiles up at him, and then the gentleman, a beautiful man.

"This is Mr. Wakahisa Masumi, our newest guest."

"You can call me Masumi." He tips his hat very slightly without really lifting it from his head. "I was excited to learn that you encourage your guests to learn as many languages as possible."

He glances in the direction of the invisible, tittering newlyweds. Allows himself a brief smile.

"What languages do you speak, Mr. Masumi?" says Rosie.

"Ah, this is not quite right. In Japanese names the surname is first. I would be Mr. Wakahisa. I invite you to use my first name. Just Masumi." He goes to a bookshelf loaded with American novels. "I have English, Japanese, French, und ein bisschen Deutsch."

"Almost four then," says Rosie. "Congratulations, Masumi, you've nearly found peace."

"Have I, then?"

"If we all knew four foreign languages there no longer would be wars. You've got two and a half."

He smiles again, this time with a dark hint of irony Rosie isn't in on. She thinks how rude it is to make faces like that—faces that make people feel too acutely their own ignorance. His eyes are sharp and bright. He stands before her with his hands folded behind his back like a proud schoolboy. She can't begin to guess his age. It's hard for her with Japanese. Japanese are hard for her.

John is teetering nervously on his heels.

"Will you be willing to teach us some of your language while you are here?" asks Rosie.

"Which one?" says Masumi.

"All of them! But especially Japanese."

"It would be an honor to help you find your peace, Mrs. Cummings. Will I meet Mr. Cummings as well?"

John says, "He's dead."

They spend two hours together, their seats huddled in a small triangle, Masumi instructing them in the basics of Japanese pronunciation. He uses strange words as examples: murder, devil, ghost, destruction, wrath, victim, loneliness, tears. They must be important words in Japan, words frequently used in day-to-day conversation. John is unusually quiet. He doesn't make one joke. Masumi leaves without explanation. John soon follows.

Afterward Rosie falls asleep again in the library. When she wakes, Mrs. Dryden is still out cold. The newlyweds have left. Matthew is back from school—he rides his bike past her as she leaves the library. Then it's dinner. John cooked. Everyone eats together; the ideal time to practice languages. She wants to practice languages with them. They want to speak the words they already know. It's typical. Matthew looks sullen. She asks him, in French, how school is treating him. He stares at her blankly; he doesn't understand. Not so good, then. She will harangue his uncle later. The boy needs to practice his language. He doesn't speak enough.

Three more years of this. Two if she can find a proper cook.

COMPETITION
AMONG SAVAGES

Claire comes to school early. She comes to see the boys fight for her.

Peter sits at the back of the class every year. He always has and she suspects he always will. Strategically speaking, his harelip would be less noticeable were he to sit in the front row where only the teacher and the student to his right could see it. But Peter hasn't thought it through, or maybe he thought it through very thoroughly and realized he would still *feel* he was on display up at the front. So he sits in the back, and while he may get more stares in this way he can at least know he's done nothing to invite them. Claire would hate to look the way he does. She's always been pretty, just as her mother was always pretty, and they have discussed—in hushed, secret tones, when nobody could possibly hear their prideful confessions—the horror and the tragedy of life as an Ugly Person. "Everyone is beautiful inside," said her mother, "but most people don't take the time or the trouble to find out. I would hate to be the sort of person you had to know to love." No one ever needed to know Claire's mother to love her.

Matthew sits beside Peter and every morning he brings him a treat. Sometimes a cookie, sometimes a pastry, sometimes a chocolate from the factory. He also looks at Peter often, pointedly, as if to say, "I don't mind your disfigurement at all." By way of these two strategies he's forced Peter to treat him as a friend. The harelipped boy does not have the luxury of casually refusing kindness, no matter how contrived. His cheeks burn at every gift and he glares when little Matthew gazes, but there's nothing he can do about it. They are rapidly becoming best chums by the sheer force of Matthew's will. He passes notes in class—poorly scrawled, half-literate French, as Peter has shown her later. He has come to the harelipped boy's defense in one fight already, though he was neither needed nor wanted. He's drawn them together, on the same page, at arm's length, but smiling. The harelip did not translate to the stick figure. You could tell he was Peter because he was a little taller.

It's a strange way to woo a girl if that's what Matthew means by it. He has yet to speak to her except through the effects of his actions on Peter. Holding eye contact with Claire as he links his arm with the other boy's, glancing to see if she's glancing while Peter eats his treat. Smiling like a proud pup when he thinks he's done good. There is always the pause as he removes the latest pastry or cookie from his bag—Peter now watching, expectant— where he seems to consider giving it to *her* instead. She wouldn't accept it. She couldn't.

She might, if he guessed her favorite flavor.

Peter wipes his mouth, having finished a slice of chocolate cake. He licks his bottom lip. "Do you always have to watch me eat it?" he says. "It makes me feel all faggoty."

Matthew smiles, says, "I'm sorry." This is roughly one fifth of his French vocabulary. He collects the chocolate-smeared wax paper from Peter's desk, folds it into quarters, drops it into a paper bag, puts this paper bag inside his own bag. He unloads his school books, stacking them one by one on the desk. They look undisturbed—unused, even. Like many of the students here, Matthew has a job that keeps him busy after school, but Claire can't imagine what would keep him from trying even a smidgen. He should *learn the language*, at least.

"Hey," says Peter, glancing at Claire. "You know what we should do?"

"What?" says Matthew, in English. It's not clear if he's responding or merely asking what Peter means. *What* is sometimes his way of begging to hear it all again in English, a request the other students could sometimes honor but rarely choose to.

"We should arm-wrestle," says Peter. "Then we could finally know who is stronger."

They already know who's stronger. They've known it from the beginning, when Peter knocked Matthew off his bike. They've known it in the weeks since school began, for instance when Peter hoisted a bigger rock over his head in the rock-hoisting contest, and they knew it when Peter lifted Matthew and carried him on his back, and they knew it when Peter won their friendly boxing match by bloodying Matthew's friendly little nose, which took on a slight, permanent slant in the healing, its tip hooked just a little upward. Still, Peter scoots his desk up next to Matthew's, swivels so they're almost facing, and pulls Matthew's desk the rest of the way, their desks kissing. Claire pictures the boys themselves kissing and the thought is not disagreeable. Peter offers his hand, curled to half fist, elbow resting on his desk. Matthew looks to Claire for help. She'd rather see them fight.

Matthew takes Peter's hand. They each grip the opposite edges of their desks with their free hands, the sort of rule-breaking that suggests seriousness in much starker terms than mere passionless rule-following. Their pencil necks are already tensing in preparation, veins standing out like tripwires. Peter counts down from three. They push. They make grunts of frustration. Little Matthew is immediately at a disadvantage, pushed down several inches, but he holds it steady there a moment, cheeks going all red. Children filter into the room, some minding the competition in the back, others sensibly ignoring the rivalry, which will find another iteration tomorrow, and another the next day.

Claire opens her grammar and pretends to consult it. Insofar as Matthew has a chance in these contests, it's because he doesn't understand the goal is victory with dignity—without the skin inflaming, without the pores drooling, without depraved breathing, without losing one's cool. How he strained to lift that rock. How he flailed when Peter boxed him, at one point actually shoving a finger—by accident, she hoped—two knuckles deep in the other boy's nose, coming back with snot and blood. Now Matthew twists at the wrist, pulls the desk to stay steady, plants his feet wide. Does everything short of stand up and jump. Claire twists her hair around her finger and lets the coil hang.

Peter pushes Matthew's hand another increment. The strain is only visible in his neck. He doesn't huff or puff. He doesn't sweat. Doesn't crimson. Doesn't need to. He looks like he's waiting for something.

Matthew's hand is pressed lower, his arm nearly touching the desk, the hand itself hovering several inches past the little square of plywood. He groans, pulls his head in the opposite direction, drips, shuffles his feet, leaning with his whole body. All the other children have sat down in their seats. Most have pretended to forget the arm-wrestling entirely, perhaps because they are embarrassed for the combatants. Claire is deeply embarrassed. This is for her. Her gut's electric. The harelipped boy seems to leer. He always seems to leer. It may be real now, though—the corner of his mouth genuinely raised, the glinting teeth set hard.

Matthew's desk begins to rattle. The seat's hooves lift from the ground and clatter back, three always touching, but four never. Peter hisses from apparent pain. Matthew growls. He loses. His arm falls to the desk, his hand wrenched back at a ninety-degree angle from the wrist, something like elbow macaroni. He coughs like he's been socked in the gut. A strand of spit hangs from his lip.

"Good match," says Peter. He peels Matthew's good hand from the desk's edge and shakes it once, then scoots his own back into place. Just in time: the teacher has entered. He writes on the chalkboard. The children are to copy what he writes. Peter writes it all down. Matthew, still smarting, massages his wrist and looks at Claire as if it were her fault, as he always does when the contests are over. His face is twisted by resentment. His bottom lip envelops its better, revealing the stupid narrow knot of muscle in his chin, tugging the skin of his neck upward and partly onto his face, where it puffs and swells. He is like a wounded frog.

Claire turns away.

Claire means to leave school alone. She feels a little woozy, slightly off. Peter and Matthew follow her out. They walk on either side of her, elbow-lengths away. Either could, speaking purely in terms of distance and practicality, touch her skin, take her hand, hold her elbow, stroke the nape of her neck. Some days she might want them to, or at least one of them. Today she would like neither. It might have been their fight that made her feel so ill. Something left their warring bodies and entered hers. She might throw up.

"Your skin got really hot while we were arm-wrestling," says Peter.

"What?" says Matthew, in English.

"Your skin," says Peter. "It was incredibly hot. Are you okay?" He shows his palm. It's still a little red—irritated by the heat, apparently, or even burnt. It might be the beginnings of a rash.

Maybe what Claire has is catching. She rubs her tummy.

"Are you feeling okay?" says Peter.

"What?" says Matthew.

"Not you."

He gets that. Matthew hangs his head, kicks a rock hard enough to send it flying.

Claire says, "I'm fine. You two looked ridiculous, though. You're going to hurt each other someday."

"I doubt it," says Peter.

Matthew says, "Do you want to ride bikes? Claire can ride on my handlebars. We can take her home and that way she'll be safe."

It's been days since Claire has heard him say this much to anyone. She imagines Matthew working through a French phrasebook for an evening, underlining useful conjugations, building the invitation in a separate notebook. Has he explored the possible avenues of this conversation thoroughly? What else might he be prepared to say on the subjects of bicycles, security, and Claire? Does he know the word for *wheel* yet?

"I don't want to do that," says Claire. She waits for the what.

"We should go somewhere else then," says Peter.

"I question the handlebars as a conveyance," she says, wanting to go home but not with them. She waits for the what.

"You can ride my bike," says Peter. "I'll run beside you."

"I want to take her home so she'll be safe," says Matthew, getting in front of the other two and turning to face them.

"Safe from what?" says Claire.

Peter nods. This is the way the boys agree. She needs to be safe.

"Fuck that. I don't want to be safe. Put me on your handlebars, Matthew, but don't take me home."

Matthew says, "What?"

They go to Half Hill. Half Hill is a tall one, rising from the earth like a wave, flattening to a reasonable plateau, and then cresting harshly, falling inward, revealing its soil: the dirt, the rocks inside, and sometimes the worms. This open side is also partly mossed and grassed in horizontal gradations. Explanations for Half Hill vary considerably, being almost purely the subject of schoolyard speculation. No one their age can remember. Some kids say it was the Germans with one of their big guns—a rail gun, even. Others say it was a bomber—German or American. Some kids say there was going to be a building there, one in a weird style, integrated with the hill, and so the builders dynamited half the hill. It was going to be a haberdashery or something. No one agrees, and none of the stories are especially plausible. But there stands the hill nonetheless.

"The game is simple," says Peter, pacing before Claire and Matthew like a commanding officer, the flat side of Half Hill his backdrop. "You ride your bike up the hill as fast as you can. Then you ride as fast as you can over the flat part. That's where you get most of the speed. Then you launch off the edge. You dismount the bike as you fall, and take the fall as well as you can."

"What's the point?" asks Claire.

"You wanted something unsafe. This is it. Totally unsafe. We could all die."

"You'll wreck your bikes," says Claire.

Matthew says, "I will do it."

"Matthew, your bike is the only way you can get to school," says Claire. "We live close enough to walk. Peter, you love your bike. You don't want to hurt it, and Matthew can't afford to destroy his."

"What?" says Matthew, fuming. "I'll do it!"

"It's a calculated risk," says Peter. "Look, I'll go first and show you how." He walks his bike to the foot of the hill and mounts it. "People do this all the time," he insists. "It's no big deal."

He pedals hard. Climbing the hill is obviously not the part where you pick up speed. It's the part where you prove that you can bike uphill. The speed comes at the plateau—he hits an impressive pace, and, at the verge of the precipice, stands upright on the pedals. Claire's stomach twists up inside itself like a towel being wrung. From their perspective, the bike rolls off into empty air, aligning with the clouds. Peter tilts sideways until he and the bike are parallel with the ground, at which point he retracts his legs, tucking them up in his gut. He lands with a thud and coughs for a minute. The coughs become laughter. His bike lies three feet away, angled by its pedal, front wheel swiveled and spinning, back wheel still.

"I did it!" he shouts. He stumbles to his feet and checks the bike. "It's fine. Now Matthew can try."

"I'll do it," says Matthew. Someone must have told him girls like boys who plan to do things. He doesn't move from his spot at the foot of the hill, and it doesn't look like he's going to.

"I'll go with you," Claire says. "I'll ride on your handlebars."

Matthew stares at her blankly. It must be everything he wanted. They'll be flying off a little cliff, though. Did Matthew want that? It may be he doesn't know what she said. She boosts herself up onto the handlebars. He nearly falls, but Peter runs over, catches them, and holds them upright.

He asks Claire if she really wants to do this and she nods without thinking. "I thought you would go separately. I thought you could both use his bike, because it's more sturdy than mine."

She hates to see Peter crow when he's won. She hates to see Matthew sit and shake and crimson. This is also, in her life as their captive, a precious opportunity to be less than safe. That's enough in its own right.

So she shouts, "Go Matthew!" and Peter, in a too-rare moment of kindness, pushes the bike, helping Matthew climb the hill, running alongside across the plateau, and barking a reminder for the both of them to jump. Matthew stands on the pedals. He breathes on her neck. She pushes off the handlebars.

A long, sharp breath at the apex.

They land entangled—Matthew with one leg beneath the bike, Claire with her arm trapped under Matthew's torso, everyone crying. Peter comes down from the hill the long way. He tries to help them up. They hurt too much. Claire wrenches out her arm from beneath Matthew and rolls onto her side. Her mouth is bleeding. Her nose is bleeding. Her body hurts all over. Matthew is bleeding from his nose as well, and his leg has been scraped badly. The bike's right handlebar is bent to a weird angle. Peter is saying he's sorry. He's saying she shouldn't have done it.

She says, "It's okay."

Matthew curses in English.

She says, "I've got to pee. I'm going to go behind Half Hill. Peter, please don't let Matthew look."

Matthew rolls onto his back and lets his mouth hang open as if he's waiting for the sky to pour itself down his throat. He kicks once at the clouds. He says, "That was stupid."

Claire makes her way out of sight. She tastes her own copper, feels it running weirdly cold from her nose and down her cheeks, her neck. She draws up her skirts around her waist and pushes down her underwear. The grass tickles. She relieves herself. It soothes her stomach.

Wait. There is a cloud in her underwear. Rust among the

white. She puts her head between her knees to look a little closer. A smell she can't identify.

The boys are crying on the other side of the hill. Soon they will begin to fight again. Either ruckus will cover for her crying. Her guts are awful knots. Her stupid little womb is bleeding.

WHO THEY ARE

Fat Man and Little Boy sit together in the library cabin, their chairs catty-corner, their knees almost touching. It's the closest they've been in more than a month. Fat Man feels a charge passing between them. He does his best to ignore it. Little Boy kicks his feet as he pretends to read his grammar, lazily dragging a pencil across each line as if he is very slowly slitting someone's throat. He whispers to himself. His nose has been bent to a new angle, his bottom lip scabbed, his shin wrapped in gauze, blood-soaked and browned, sticky-bound to the long scab the shape of Africa. He ought to change the bandages. His brother has resolved not to tell him this, not to mother Little Boy anymore if he can avoid it. They get along better this way.

Presently Fat Man is consulting a book on the etymology of names. He says, "Why oh why did I name myself John?"

"What's wrong with John?" says Little Boy, closing the grammar without marking his place.

"It means 'Yahweh is gracious.'" says Fat Man, indicating his entry in the book. "Yahweh as in God."

"I don't see what's wrong with that. What does mine mean?"

"Let me see." Fat Man flips to the M's. "It means 'Gift of Yahweh.' Ugh. Yours is even worse."

"They're like the same thing."

"Yours states specifically that you were given to the world by God, but does not specify a reason or an end. It's the worst thing you could be called. It might equally describe the beginning of the future or the beginning of the end. In my case, I needn't necessarily be a gift from God and there's no ambiguity about who God is or what he's like. He's gracious. Kind."

"But isn't calling him gracious just another way of saying he likes to give gifts?" says Little Boy. He picks at his bandage, peeling it partly from his shin. He winces as the scab tears. A fresh trickle down his ankle and into his shoe stains his sock already fouled with sweat and mud. He dabs at the flow with his fingers.

"Jack, a diminutive of Jonathan, is a slang word for man."

"So what? Put the book down," says Little Boy, wiping his fingers clean on his short pants. "You're being weird."

"I'm not," says Fat Man. "I'm enriching myself. Learning about this world of ours."

"By looking up your own name?"

Fat Man hushes him. Though they are alone in the library apart from the newlyweds, who have proven resistant to learning any part of the English language that can't be swung as at least a little bawdy, caution's still in order.

"What are you really looking for?"

"Rosie."

Little Boy asks him if he's checked under "Rose." He hasn't. Rather than acknowledge his error, Fat Man turns to the proper page and reads aloud. Apparently the name originally comes from a German one meaning something like "famous kind." Kind as in "type" or "sort." Its similarity to the English word for the flower was a coincidence.

"So," says Little Boy, "Rose means a rose."

"What do you suppose Masumi means?"

"Japanese," Little Boy grunts. It is not clear if he means to indicate the language as a language, as the origin of the name, or for that matter the origin of the person.

"He makes me nervous. Does he make you nervous? I don't feel right around him. It prickles all over, the way he looks at you. At me, I mean. I itch the whole time we talk. Yesterday he sat beside me at lunch. We didn't talk but I could feel him watching."

"Everything makes you nervous." Little Boy rubs his nose at the tip, rotating the bulb at the end, attempting to reset it. The angle is all wrong.

"We can't all go flying off cliffs every time we get to feeling cagey," says Fat Man. "But listen. You can help me relax, if you're so concerned. In a couple days it'll come time for you to go clean his room. He may ask you not to do it. Be persistent. Get in there if you can. See everything you can see. When you're done, come directly to me and tell me what you've found."

"I may clean his room," says Little Boy, "but I won't spy."

Fat Man does not cuff his brother. Little Boy doesn't wince. They share a moment of silence that acknowledges what it could have been.

"Do you still feel the calm?" says Fat Man.

"I feel the calm she gave us."

"Do you feel it here?" Fat Man touches himself between his breasts.

"I feel it there," says Little Boy, touching himself the same. "I feel it here, too." He touches his gut.

"I don't feel it there." Fat Man looks down at himself. "One step at a time."

"I'm glad you don't hit me anymore," says Little Boy.

"I'm glad you stay out of my reach."

Little Boy leaves to clean the newlyweds' cabin.

Fat Man sits beneath the tree that's like a willow. He leans against the trunk. This seems to relax the branches—they wave about in the wind, only periodically reaching for him, stroking his face, his proffered hands. She makes him calm. She helps him breathe. He shuts his eyes. A coldness in his brain complements the thrumming warmth in his chest. The thrumming's like a candle burning in a drum. He massages the fat that hangs from his arms, slowly, one arm at a time, as if to worry it away. The cabins cast long, angular shadows on the ground, narrow as the light afforded by an open door. They twist and blur as the sun rolls back behind the hills. The tree like a willow has kept its shadow still, as it sometimes keeps its branches, focused on Fat Man, like a negative spotlight, changing with his breathing but otherwise still, stoking the cool in his brain, a cool rag loaded with ice, pressed to a reopened wound. He focuses on the top of his hat, a felt black wide-brimmed one that once belonged to a Jew, and which sits on the grass between his knees, stuck with grass seeds and dandelion puffs. The tree shades his hat blacker, so from above it's like an empty plate—a black, empty plate.

He lights a cigarette and holds it in his hand, knowing that his mouth can wait. He closes his eyes and thinks how nice some rain would be. He opens his eyes. Masumi is sitting beside him at a ninety-degree angle, facing outward. Their hands nearly touch.

"Hello Matthew," says Masumi.

"John," says Fat Man. "Matthew is my nephew."

"My apologies." He plucks a blade of grass and twists it. "You're smoking."

Fat Man considers his cigarette. "I was thinking about it."

"What were you thinking about it?"

"I was thinking how I like the way they look more than I like the way they taste." He puts it in his mouth.

"What are you thinking now?" Masumi pulls open his jacket, draws a flask out of its pocket. He cranes his neck to meet Fat Man's eye.

"I'm thinking I was right."

"You want a drink?" He uncaps the flask with a cheerful twist and pop.

"What's it taste like?"

"You tell me." He passes the flask.

Fat Man swigs. The air smells like sweet milk on the verge of curdle.

"Cigarettes. Everything tastes like cigarettes."

"This is a strange tree," says Masumi. "I've never seen one like it."

"Why don't you take off your hat? You can look at it the way I'm looking at mine."

"What do you expect me to see in my hat?" Masumi takes a pull from the plum brandy.

"The tree looks like a willow to me."

"It has a strange aura. Do you believe in auras?"

Fat Man sucks hard on his cigarette. "You want a smoke?"

Glug glug, says the flask. "No."

"I should go inside," says Fat Man. "It's getting cold."

"With all that blubber?" snorts Masumi. "You'll be fine. Tell me about the tree."

"It was here when we came."

"They let a pretty tree like this grow in a concentration camp?"

"We like to think of it as a hotel." Fat Man puts on his hat and curls up against the tree as if he means to go to sleep there, cigarette hanging from his lip, a small circle of spark bobbing in the dusk like a leaf on the water.

"It was a camp first."

"Have you been to our museum?"

"I have," says Masumi. "It was strange how little it was haunted."

"I feel very haunted there."

"Why did you take a dead Jew's hat?"

Fat Man rolls onto his other side, facing away from Masumi. He does not like this man with his white suits, his sweet liquors, his soft, buzzy voice like something left too long in a can. The tree cannot reach him down here, so low to the ground, nearly wrapped in her roots, which is fine by him, he does not want to be comforted right now, he wants to hate. The coolness in his mind becomes numbness.

"I asked you why you stole a dead Jew's hat."

The roots are rough against his face. "I didn't steal it."

Masumi keeps his tone breezy, even friendly, the excitement in his body manifesting as a series of rapid climbs and falls in key. "How do you even know it was a Jew's?" says Masumi.

"When did I say it was a Jew's hat?"

"There were French in this camp. They wore hats too. And shoelaces, and they used combs and razors, and they brushed their teeth, and they ate from bowls, with spoons, and they drank water from cups, sometimes cups with darling chips or dents in their rims, and they had broken toys and they made art, even, and they wore fancy dress as well—if not here, then at home." Masumi crawls around the roots, around the fat man, and kneels in front of him, taking a quick gulp of his brandy. Though crouched he looms, nose pulled back into a purple snout,

227

chin knitted up tight like a waffle. "The point is you might be wearing a Jew-killer's hat, not a Jew's, and then how would you feel? Or possibly you are wearing a hat stolen from a Jew by a killer, or possibly it was passed from one dead Jew to another in a series, as they died. You think you know who it belonged to but now it belongs only to you. The dead don't own anything."

"I don't know what you're talking about," says Fat Man. He rolls onto his other side, then totters back, back up on his ass to sit against the tree. "Why did you come here?"

"I came here to relax and practice languages. What else could I do here?"

"Do you know what your name means?"

"Submarine," says Masumi. "Submarine in deep water."

"I don't believe you."

"Suit yourself," says Masumi. He begins to walk distorted circles around the tree, placing his feet heels-first. "What do you think it's like to die?"

Fat Man twists out his cigarette in the grass and eats the butt. "I imagine it depends on how you go."

"Give me a for-instance."

"You're talking to a hotel employee, Mr. Wakahisa. I can tell you how to get a stain out of sheets. I can tell you how to make a room smell like new. I can tell you how to fry up bacon just the way you like it."

Masumi leans against the tree with one outstretched hand, crossing his legs at their ankles. He has very nice shoes that skin small feet; they smell of polish. The laces are neat, tight bows. "As a hotel employee, you are living on my money. So I'm not asking, I'm demanding. Tell me what you think it's like to die."

The tree like a willow trembles sympathetically.

"I imagine that for some it's like a long walk into a deep cave. For others, perhaps, like falling down a long ladder, the hands whipping the rungs as they pass, until they're all red and swollen, until they become the world, until they become the sun, until the burning hands wink out."

Masumi encourages the fat man to continue, rolling his hands one over the other as if a reel of a film.

"For some it must be like drowning in a shallow pool. For some like cooking on a spit. For some like a burst of white paint across the vision. For some, like an explosion, beginning in the bowels, tearing loose the limbs, blowing the head sky-high."

Masumi says, "I think for some it's like sinking to the bottom of the ocean in a tin can with just one window and no way out. As you go deeper the window turns dark, the deepest blue, your arms and legs go numb. You run out of air. You feel it in your feet first, your hands, and then your chest. Then you don't feel anything, or see anything, but it's not like you're smothering to death, it's just that the water's so deep, so dark, the deepest blue." Masumi smiles. "How do you think it's going to be for you?"

Fat Man isn't sure he'll ever die. "I think I'll be fine."

"I have a gun," says Masumi. He pats his side, where there may or may not be a certain bulge beneath his white coat. "I brought it here with me in case I needed to kill anybody."

"That's not allowed in this hotel," says Fat Man. His heart seems to repeat itself too perfectly, too crisply, several times—droplets falling from a sink faucet.

"Is that the widow's policy, or yours?"

"This hotel is about peace. It only follows there can be no guns."

"I know who you are."

"You can't even keep my name straight."

Masumi draws his fingers across the white brim of his hat, left to right, and opens his jacket to reveal holstered gun. "I know who you are."

"Who am I?"

Masumi says, "Who are you," and leaves Fat Man alone with the question.

The tree like a willow's shadow has faded into the general darkness of night—it is all dark, it is all shadow. The tree's weepy branches touch Fat Man as he stands. He runs a hand over one of them, accidentally pulling loose a leaf. It falls into the shadow. There is a lit window in the distance—Rosie's. It is a thick square of glass, yellowed. The tree seems illuminated because it is most of what he can see. The grass fades to black as it recedes from him. The cabins are still, empty, square blots of night. He is standing on an island built from what light his eyes can wring from the earth.

HE HAS A GUN

The *skritch skritch* of busy hands making notes. The jaw-clenching squeaks of new tin chairs on hardwood floors with too little varnish. The sun-bleached stripes that spill from windows across the aisles students crowd. Someone somewhere eating grapes on the sly. Claire chewing her pencil. The teacher's drone. The white chalk streaks on the thighs of his pants, the ass of his jacket. The white puffs accompanying any sudden movement.

A fly destined to live forever crawling on the ceiling, tasting things no one can see. They must be body oils, body salts, skin cells. Little Boy knows he's losing something every second of the day. He resents degrading here, in this too-small room, sloughing himself for the flies and mites and other creeping things. The children. It's their snot feeds the flies. That's why they creep under the desks, tickling young knees.

Little Boy's teacher calls him to the front of the class, one hand pressed to his tummy as if he were taking a pledge. He's written Matthew's name on the chalkboard.

"What? What do you want, exactly?" All English. He suspects the teacher understands him. The teacher is an educated man. He wears glasses. He has a fussy center part in his graying hair. He ought to know how to talk the way Little Boy talks.

"Matthew," says the teacher. "Matthew, please come to the front of the class and deliver your recitation."

Little Boy raises his hand. The teacher sighs.

"Yes Matthew?"

"Whadda you want?" says Little Boy, in English.

"Could you please come to the front of the class and deliver your recitation?"

Little Boy looks to Claire for help. She's mortified, nearly to the point of tears on his behalf. It must be pretty bad. Peter motions toward the front, walks his fingers down the aisle, mimes loud, obnoxious speech in what seems to be an imitation of their teacher: hand on gut, eyes half-squinted/quarter-crossed, finger twirling in the air.

Sometimes Little Boy can make the teacher forget him by force of will. He stares into the back of the next student's neck, seeing the strawberry beginnings of a pimple where it meets the shoulders, and a long, stray black hair. He imagines scratching off the cap of the zit—squeezing out the pus.

The teacher says, "Matthew?"

He goes to the front of the class. A room full of children, most taller than him, all more developed, gaze back perfectly blank. They scratch, boys and girls alike, at the hair that prickles from their arms. There's a boy in the back who's clearly touching himself with the sort of care and tenderness most commonly found between little old ladies and large, stupid dogs.

"What am I supposed to do up here?"

"Please share your work with the class. You may read from notes if you need to."

Little Boy looks to Claire. Looks to Peter. His friends, such as they are, have averted their eyes. Claire taps her foot on the floor, a metronome in skirts.

"Ah," says Little Boy. "I know. You'll like this!"

"In French, please."

Little Boy brushes past the bumbling teacher, goes to his desk, and slides out the wide middle drawer, where confiscated items are kept, as well as several candles the teacher uses to light his work after dark. The school building has not been furnished with electric lights, and the oil is expensive. Little Boy takes one of the fresh, unused candles. He walks to center stage, candle cupped in both hands. He turns the candle upside-down. He passes his hand under it, passes it over, as if to draw aside many small, silken curtains.

"What are you doing?"

Little Boy puts his fingers to his lips. "What I do next will astound you."

"Please sit down, Matthew."

"An American magic trick," says Little Boy. "Fire from the hands."

He presses his fingers to the wick, snaps them, lets go. The wick is cold and still. He does it again. Nothing. No flame. It ought to burn with a Japanese spirit. He tries again. His teacher tells him to sit down, he thinks. But he doesn't want to sit down. He wants to make a fire for his classmates.

"Wait," he says. He tries again.

The candle is a candle. It is a little yellow, only a little, the color of mucus. Cold and inert as a stone.

The teacher puts his hands on Little Boy's shoulders. The pressure of his chalky hands. White prints on Little Boy's shoulders. "Matthew," he says, and then some other words that probably mean Little Boy's in trouble.

233

"I've got it." Little Boy lifts the candle to his mouth, both-handed, like a goblet. He puts the wick in his mouth, suckles, and slowly pulls it free from his suck. His hands go orange. A small flame on the little candle. Several students clap with half their hearts. "There it is. See how pretty."

It warms his face from underneath. He imagines the light crawling up his neck, his chin, the sides of his face, highlighting everything sunken and all that protrudes.

The teacher snuffs it with his fingers. Little Boy's no longer lit up. His hands and face are cold. He sits down, taking the candle with him. The teacher may tell him to bring it back. If so, he doesn't listen, and the teacher doesn't press the issue.

Later, Claire passes him a note. "Learn the language," it says, though in French. He has an inkling what it means. He tries to lose the inkling.

Little Boy knocks on the door of Mr. Wakahisa Masumi's cabin. He has a bundle of cleaning supplies under his arm. A broom, a mop, a feather-duster, a small folding stepladder, all bound together with a thin white rope tied by Fat Man in a tight bow. Hanging from the other hand, a bucket with a garbage bag inside, several rags, sponges, soap, a water jug. It's heavy.

He sets down the bucket and leans the bundle against the cabin. Having waited what seems a reasonable length of time, he knocks again. He scratches at his shin with the heel of his shoe, careful not to open the scab from his fall, which has mostly healed, leaving an angry patch of skin. Mr. Wakahisa does not come to the door.

"Sir. Sir." He looks over his shoulder. "I've come to clean your room."

Nothing. But he saw the Japanese gentleman walk in. He had been waiting outside the cabin twenty minutes, saw Masumi come from the library—where he gave language lessons, no doubt—and watched in hiding as Masumi went inside. Little Boy had waited another ten minutes to let him settle in, and so he did not realize he had been waited for.

Masumi couldn't have fallen asleep in ten minutes. He must be sitting somewhere inside. There's a lot of room in there for one person. Several chairs, the bed, a couch. He could be standing. He is not pacing, or if he is it's in a pair of slippers; Little Boy can't hear him. He could be in bed reading. He could be feeding the fire. The sun is going down. Little Boy's shadow stretches sideways, long, like a banner. It seems awfully tall.

Little Boy knocks hard.

"Mr. Wakahisa?" says Little Boy. "Can I please come in? I need to finish this and do my school work."

As Little Boy attempts to gather his cleaning gear Masumi comes out of his cabin, locking the door behind him.

"John?" he says.

"No, it's Matthew."

Masumi speaks now in French. "John, how are you this evening?"

"Matthew," says Little Boy. "John's the big one."

"How are you this evening?"

Matthew shrugs. "Don't know French. Can I clean your cabin now?"

Masumi tries Japanese. "How are you this evening?"

"Don't know that either. Are you going to let me in or not? I can come back later."

And still in Japanese: "Why don't you learn the language?"

Little Boy lays down his burdens. He looks up at Masumi,

arms hanging limp at his sides but hands curled to fists; his lips are sneered. After a long while he says, "They told me you spoke English."

"I'm trying to teach you. I'm trying to know you."

"Still don't know French, sir."

"English then. You may come into my cabin only so long as you don't try to clean it. Leave your things there, in the grass."

"Can I bring them in, so no one sees them there? So I can say I did it? I wouldn't have to bother you again for days."

"Yes John," says Masumi. He takes the bucket himself. "That will be fine."

"It's Matthew," says Little Boy.

"Do you ever drink?" says Masumi. They sit on opposite sides of the table, a gallery of weird liquors between them. Every fruit is represented: cherry brandy, pineapple rum, lemon-lime martini, a globular bottle with clear brownish liquor, oranges floating inside. And other unexpected flavors: chocolate whiskey, toffee something, pine.

"I think I'm not allowed to," says Little Boy.

The room is very clean. There is a brown screen in the corner with cherry tree shadows painted in black on two of three panels; the center panel has a black sun in its high middle. The dresser has a white powder on its top but otherwise it's clean. The full-length mirror has several fingerprints across its middle point, oil streaks. The bed is neatly made. There are many trunks beneath the bed. The floor around the stove shows no charcoal specks or smudges. There are several variously sized glasses and flasks littering the various surfaces of the room, but the flasks are all closed and the glasses are dry.

"Why can't you drink? Perhaps in America such outdated

mores still stand, but in France, child, we all drink wine. If wine, then why not vodka? You see where I'm going with this." He pours Little Boy a glass of the chocolate whiskey. "I think you'll really like this."

"I thought Japanese liked sake."

"Drink up." Masumi pushes the chocolate drink across the table. Little Boy lets it touch his tongue enough to burn. Knowing now the flavor and the scorch he drinks of it deeply, holding the glass as before he held the candle. He wipes his mouth with the back of his hand.

Masumi says, "You can tell me anything."

Little Boy shakes his head.

"You don't like to talk?"

"Why don't you take off your hat?" says Little Boy. He gulps down more chocolate. "You're being rude."

"John, you're right. I'm sorry." He leaves the hat on. "Why don't you like to talk?"

Little Boy shrugs.

"Are you afraid of what you might say?"

Little Boy shakes his head.

"What might you say, John?"

"Matthew."

"What might you say, if you let yourself open your mouth? Would you scream? Would you weep? Would you confess?"

Little Boy finishes his drink and belches loudly. His eyes are bleary, swimming, he can feel them strain. He shakes his head. This looses the tears, makes them into several streams.

"You're not supposed to drink it so quickly," says Masumi.

A corner of blue shimmer fabric embroidered with needlepoint stars hangs out of the dresser's top drawer. Little Boy stumbles across the room to touch it. So soft.

"Does the mold still follow you?" says Masumi. "Do the

spores reach for your mouth? Do candles still spark when you touch them?"

Little Boy turns to glare at the Japanese gentleman. He says, "I've changed my mind. I want to clean your cabin."

"You think you've calmed but if you were calm then you could speak to me. You think you've changed but you haven't." He opens his jacket. The holstered revolver is polished and it glints and shines. "I've got a gun."

Little Boy pours himself another drink so later he can throw up. He says, "Who are you?"

"John, I will be your judge."

"Then I won't say any more. I'm going to take this glass. Leave my cleaning things outside your cabin for tomorrow. I'll come back."

"I'll shoot you if you go without defending yourself."

Little Boy tosses back half his second chocolate whiskey. "There's nothing to say, and nothing to defend. What do you think I did? I didn't do it. There's my defense."

Masumi draws his gun. He spins it on his finger like a fancy cowboy. Stops it aimed on Little Boy, grip tight, trigger half-squeezed. Lets it go and spins it more. His eyes climb and fall like a slot machine spinning as the butt of the gun replaces the nozzle replaces the ass replaces the muzzle.

"Goodnight," says Little Boy. He leaves the door open behind him.

The ground shifts under his feet like an ocean, or the flesh of some heaving beast. He wants to see the tree. He needs to touch her.

He pauses behind an empty cabin to pee. Some dots his bare shins and short pants. It strikes him that most of the cabins are empty. In the night they are like headstones, faceless as a movie screen without the projector. He hurls his glass against one.

He will wake up on the grass beneath the tree, in her gentle shadow, the branches reaching for him, swaying above him, reaching across each other in a tangle, like many schools of bait fish.

He will miss a day of school.

THE ACE

Little Boy tells Fat Man how Mr. Wakahisa Masumi asked Matthew into his room. He tells his brother all about the liquor, though he does not mention the second glass or how he broke it. When Fat Man repeats the story to Rosie, he does not mention the gun, though he knows it would surely lead to Masumi's ejection from the hotel. Fat Man can't explain to Little Boy why he did not tell about the gun; there was guilt in being on the wrong end of a weapon. Rosie, outraged, informs Masumi that he will be required to maintain his quarters on his own from now on, and that he cannot be alone with Little Boy, or any other children for that matter, until he proves himself trustworthy. He is welcome to provide and receive continuing daily language instruction. Masumi does so with apparent good will and earnest desire to teach and to learn. He behaves himself very well. He is even charming. Rosie comes to see the episode as an issue of cultural differences—if the French, a relatively civilized society, are fool enough to give children wine, she can only imagine what might be considered normal in a place like Japan.

The image of Masumi's table, legally Rosie's, laid out with such a wide array of liquors, stays with her. While she sacrifices everything for world peace and rebuilding, a person at least a little crazy is living it up in her hotel with decadence and style. It makes her ill. Makes her jealous. Makes her reckless. The next week she buys too much food. She bends her budget and then the next week breaks it, taking several dozen pounds of salmon. She teaches Fat Man how best to prepare fish, using lemons and butter and other things the hotel can't afford. The guests rave about the food. The newlyweds say they'll stay an extra month. They must be rich.

It feels inevitable when she finds herself taking John and Matthew to the movies. Call it the logical endpoint of a long, slow decline. She fends off fits of guilt by rubbing her temples with her thumbs and forefingers for ten seconds. It has to be ten seconds; it has to be those fingers; it has to be her temples; it only works on guilt. Not stress, not anger, not shame, only guilt. She has rebuffed three such attacks since deciding to come to the cinema. Once when she asked John and Matthew to come along, leaving the hotel in care of no one but the guests, who were not informed of their absence. Once in the car on the way over—the car that she rented at some moderate expense. She settled, during the ride, on buying a car for the hotel so as to pick up guests and bring them home when they were done (for a surcharge exceeding the gas and the price of her time, of course: another margin). This made the guilt acute. She rubbed her temples. Now, in the back of the cinema, she feels it again. A pressure in her sinuses combined with a heat in her lungs that makes it hurt to breathe. She rubs her temples for ten seconds, meanwhile surveying the audience, mostly the backs of their heads. John sits on her left, and

Matthew on her right. They gape at the blank screen, waiting for something to happen.

They're dressed in their finest. A suit with a jacket a little too small on John, unbuttoned because he can't button it. It used to fit him well; he's growing. Matthew wears his best pants, his old jacket with the elbows worn thin. The little boy has not grown at all. Rosie's father would have called Matthew a runt. She prefers the word "coltish." Still, she could lift him with one arm.

The boys are still gape-mouthed like tired mules.

Rosie says, "Is this your first film?"

"Yes," says Matthew.

"Yes," says John.

"Really?" she says, looking at John with disbelief. "You seem the type to love a picture."

"I guess I haven't had much chance."

"You'll like it. It's a lot of fun. Matthew, it's okay if you get scared. You can cover your eyes like this." Rosie veils hers with her hands, then parts her fingers to peek through. "It helps me sometimes during the battles. You know how I hate shooting."

"I don't like it either," says Matthew. "Will there be a lot of shooting?"

"Well," says Rosie, "it's called *The Ace*."

Matthew looks glum. "Will it be in French?"

"All English. You need to practice your French, though, so I wish it were otherwise. You've really hit a rut."

Matthew nods. "It's hard."

The lights come down. The audience quiets. Purses snap closed. Someone somewhere is chewing peanuts. The screen lights, gray sky and charcoal clouds, the dark underbelly of a bomber, like a whale, scratched and pockmarked by flak or bird bones. The hatch comes into view, through which the flyboys drop the bombs. The hatch is closing. A young boy leans over the edge, looking down on the audience with a mirror of John's stupid hanging jaw. The hatch is closed. The plane's tail floats past. Empty sky. Now three fighter planes in profile—one very close, only a nose and the rise of a cockpit, pilot a shadow; one further back, center-screen, partly obscured by the first, pilot a smudge; one still farther back, above the others on the flat plane of the screen though in fact it is level with them, very far, small, visible in its entirety. The title comes up on the screen. THE ACE: Roman letters cut from granite. The farthest plane begins to smoke, and falls, leaving a black trail. The nearest plane explodes without sound. All its little pieces. The camera jitters and calms like an animal. The title fades.

The opening credits introduce the cast. There's only one real star, an older man playing a colonel with a neck of steel. The rest are newcomers. The Ace comes last. There are two names by his credit. He was played by Able and Baker Hanway. The Ace smiles at the camera, his eyes lowered, and then they click into place. Even on black-and-white film you can tell that they're blue. So blue.

"Why are there two names?" whispers John.

"They're twin brothers playing the same role," says Rosie. "They're supposed to be very good."

"Which one are we seeing now?"

"Can't tell," says Rosie. "They're identical."

"Completely identical?"

"Shh." She touches his wrist.

The Hanway brothers look nothing like her dead husband. They are, or he is, whichever one now in this scene, like a corn-fed Gregory Peck fifteen years younger, the same painful-pretty face, cheekbones, but hidden underneath a thin layer of sugar fat, bunching up just slightly underneath the chin, like a fold of margarine; his skin (their skin) white like the light of the moon but not the moon itself, thick curly thatch of hair held this side of reason by a styling grease. They have wide, sloping shoulders, muscle-fatted thighs. She read they were from Indiana.

John says, "He's very handsome."

Rosie says, "They are. But we're not to talk during the film. It's rude."

She touches his hand. He turns it belly-up to welcome hers. His hand says, You can stay. Her hand says, It's a kind offer. She touches the middle of his palm and withdraws, slips her hand in her pocket. Seems that's where it belongs. She can feel her own pulse in her fingertips.

The movie proper begins with a mother receiving a letter. A soldier has brought it to her, his rank uncertain. She thanks him—the audience cannot hear this, but sees it by the inclination of her head—and takes the letter inside to read alone at the table. Where is her husband? Where are her sons? The house is empty. There's a clock shaped like Felix the Cat on the wall, smiling, wagging its tail. The hour chimes. She opens the letter.

The plot is easy to lose. Half an hour in Rosie comes to understand the mother has received notice her son, Danny Ericson, is a hero. This is news to the mother because—although she never quite comes out with it—she's always thought he was basically a loser. At home, word spreads about his heroism while his exploits continue in various theaters. Girls who never had an eye for him before suddenly take an interest; they follow him closely in the papers, which feature regular front-page articles on his many kills and daring maneuvers. They dub him The Ace. Some people speculate about the number of medals he'll get when he returns. Others speculate about his potential for politics, for film.

In one seemingly endless scene, a Hollywood director invites himself to dinner with Danny's parents, squirming visibly as he forces himself to choke down a full plate of green bean casserole.

Incredibly, all this takes place without dialogue. The scenes at home feature few sounds, usually drones or chimes of one sort or another, but no human speech at all. There is, however, a rising mechanical sound, at first a distant buzz that gradually grows louder, closer, more oppressive, becoming a chug and then a roar: the sound of a fighter plane's engines.

At war people can speak, though.

The Ace begins the movie with a number of friends of various ages and origins. There's the Texan pilot with the big chin, the half-Indian pilot who brings along on every flight a sharp little knife with an eagle feather hanging from the handle. There's the runty freckled kid whose engines keep stalling—the first to die, inevitably. There's the tall one with the dark hair and the soulful eyes, whose American name, Ed, does nothing to temper the impression that he is probably a Jew. Gradually The Ace's friends all die, shot down over the Pacific, exploded.

He takes it hard at first. Those Hanway twins can cry. When the first friend goes down The Ace threatens not to fly anymore. His handsome, no-nonsense commanding officer tells him it doesn't work that way. "You don't quit war," says the commanding officer. "It's not like working at the drugstore slinging milkshakes."

So The Ace goes back up and shoots down a few more Japanese. Then the Texan dies. The Ace weeps openly in the mess. His tears fall on his mashed potatoes and cornbread. Again, he threatens to quit. His commanding officer says, "You'll quit when you've killed every blasted Japanese in the rim, and not one second before, airman."

So The Ace goes back up and shoots down a few more Japanese. This time the maybe-Jew buys it. When they land The Ace can barely work up any tears at all. He eats his whole tray in the mess. The commanding officer comes by to touch his shoulder. He says, "Stay strong. We need you."

Finally it's just The Ace and the half-Indian with his knife up there. They don't ever talk to each other in the entire movie, but exchange stoic nods and one very intimate instance of eye contact, on leave, in a bar, where they both drink too much.

The strange thing about the movie is that though new pilots do seem to replace the ones who go down, they never show up in the lengthy, exhausting air combat sequences. The Ace is more and more alone. There are five American planes in the beginning, and in the end, after the half-Indian dies, it's just The Ace, fighting what seem to be dozens of Japanese planes, shooting down one after another. In the plane his eyes are steely blue. He is determined not only to live, but to kill.

Did Frank ever look like that? Did he knowingly decide to extend his life at the cost of another, or did it come as a surprise every time, right up to the end? Rosie can't stand to picture her husband wearing that expression. It might be—she hopes it is— that no one can wear that face except inside a plane, or some other military machine, which her husband never piloted, never drove.

The expressions and personalities of ace-pilot-Danny and mourning-grounded-Danny converge over the course of the film, until the hard expression is with him always, even while he eats and drinks. Now he flies missions alone. Soon he'll win the war, and then he can go home, and then there will be banquets in his honor, parades.

He never flies again. The next day comes the news of a bomb dropped on Hiroshima. Japan's surrender is inevitable. A few of the boys get some work, but never The Ace. He spends most of his time in his bunk reading cowboy paperbacks.

The movie shows footage of the mushroom clouds rising over Japan. Tendrils of smoke. Billow and bloom. Dust, and flaws in the film—the film's flaws are like a part of the bombs, another kind of explosion.

"So that's how it was," whispers Matthew, hoarsely. "I thought it was different."

The Ace goes home. He goes there in a plane, but someone else is flying. He's just miserable. But the audience knows what he doesn't know—how excited are his mother and father, all the girls at home, his chums, some also returning, but none so decorated as he.

At home he rides a bus a long time. When he gets off the bus he walks to a barn and waits there. His father picks him up in a car. They ride together in silence. His mother hugs him when he gets home, but it's somehow not like what Rosie imagined. The picture lingers with The Ace a while. He finds a job at a hardware store. Women depend on him to take down paint and other things from high shelves. The girls who were so hungry to see him back never materialize. He spends most of his time alone, the way he did before. There's a parade. It doesn't make him happy. Something about the bomb, thinks Rosie. He couldn't consummate his mission, did not in fact kill Every Blasted Japanese, did not conquer the Pacific. If they had dropped the bombs a year before, how much would it have changed things? Would his friends have had to die?

But it's more than that. Rosie wonders where the engine sound has gone that covered all the hometown dialogue, which can now be heard clearly. She realizes that there was never any letter about The Ace's heroism, that the newspaper articles were never written, that the girls never dreamed of his coming home.

These were his fantasies. Each vision was always preceded by a slow advance of the camera on Danny's face. This was the movie entering his mind.

The film ends with Danny Ericson watching a more handsome veteran dance with the girl of his dreams. Meanwhile Danny— now twenty-one—smokes a cigarette and drinks on what seems to be his usual stool at the bar. The credits scroll over a brassy, hopeful orchestral song that gives no quarter to the tragedy of the film's conclusion.

The part that will stick in her throat like a fish bone is the way they edited the film. It was all fades and wipes, or shots of similarly shaped things transposed on one another, so that an apple became a target, a pen became a plane, a cloud became a newspaper, a bullet a paint can, the sun a woman's eye, a woman's eye a firework, the firework an exploding American plane, the shrapnel confetti, peanut shells candle drippings, bunk bed dessert cart, whipped cream fire, the bombs became each other, became a tall building, the windows of the building became the eyes of the people who watched the parade, lining the streets. Everything was something else and nothing was itself. It made her teeth chatter.

They leave as soon as it's polite. John won't stop saying what a brilliant couple of actors they were. "You could tell them apart," he says, "or anyway I could tell them apart, absolutely, but still, what a couple of actors. Real movie stars." They get in the car. "Or maybe I couldn't tell them apart. Maybe I'm wrong about that. Imagine it though. Having a brother who looked and acted just like you. Wouldn't that be weird?"

"The bomb was different from what I pictured," says Matthew. "It looked really different."

"I think it would be strange," says John. "Picture another

man like me sitting here beside me, saying the things I'm saying, thinking what I'm thinking."

"Widows ought to get more for what we give up," says Rosie. "If he'd have lived after he hung from his parachute in that tree— if they'd shot him just enough times that he could still be saved— they would've had to spend probably thousands patching him up, keeping him in the hospital, attaching prosthesis. Then training him in the use of his new hands. They're lucky he died. They only have to pay me my allowance. They're better off if the wounded soldiers die. That's called a perverse incentive." She punches the steering wheel.

John touches her arm. She knocks his hand away.

THE MEDIUM AND
THE MEDIUM

The thing about the hotel—the thing about the prison—is there aren't many dead people walking the grounds. Some do lay around there, rolling from side to side, clutching their stomachs in hunger. Thin as pens. Sometimes Masumi sees a baby crying in his room, hid beneath the bed.

The thing about seeing the dead is objects don't leave ghosts. He would have thought they would. He didn't know he would have thought that, but he would have—after he could see, their absence struck him as strange. That you cannot find them with the dead might suggest that objects are still and always alive, however they degrade.

Masumi goes into Rosie's library. He finds her in the stacks, reading from the back of a book written in Italian.

He says, "You don't speak Italian."

"Maybe I should. It's a lot like Spanish."

"Which is a lot like French."

"So it should be easy."

"Some find it works that way," says Masumi. "Some find it confusing. You get a certain number of cognates commingling in the same cerebellum, it all starts to run together. Large in English is *grande* in Italian. Same thing in Spanish, same pronunciation. In French, it's the same but you say it a little different. *Largo*, though, sounds like large, but in Spanish it means long—it's a false cognate, in other words. In Italian it means wide, or broad, sometimes with connotations of liberalism, as in broad-minded. In French, of course, long is *long*. In Spanish, wide is *ancho*, unless we're talking about a gap, in which case it's *grande* again. In French, broad is *large*. A wide margin is *grand*. Of course, in English, a grand thing is sometimes very large and sometimes not. Sometimes it's a thousand. In German, wide is called *gross*. It's gross to be wide. In English, a gross is one hundred forty-four of the same thing. Not a thousand. Of course, if you're talking about width in terms of roundness, fatness, it's *dick*."

Rosie's face twitches at the left cheek. The twitch becomes a pained smile. "As in penis?"

"No, *dick* as in fat."

"Does it bring you peace knowing all that language?"

"I've always got a word for anything I feel, and there are lots of people I can talk to."

"Do you talk to them?"

"No. It's good to know I could, though."

"You don't seem at peace," says Rosie. "What you did to Matthew. You don't need to explain. I wouldn't be impressed. Just don't do it again. Find peace or get out of my hotel."

Masumi says, "There's something about this place. You know when I heard what you did with the camp I thought it was in quite poor taste. In fact, I still do. But something about that works for me. The crass American willingness to build on a graveyard, to erase history. But the cabins are beautiful. And, if

I am honest with myself, it is good to study language once more. That study used to be the center of my life."

Rosie listens with a stern, warning expression on her face, lips tucked in, eyes wide and unblinking.

"Don't worry," says Masumi, "I'll be good. I won't be any trouble. If I start to be trouble again, then I'll leave."

"See that you do," says Rosie. She can speak a cliché without the slightest indication she knows it as such. It sounds pure and cold and new. "I don't need your money."

"I don't think that's true."

They part on these terms. Rosie leaves the Italian book behind, unshelved. He slides it into place for her, running his hand over the spines to even them.

He finds a French history of flight and sits to read. It begins with the French contributions to the field, focusing on these at the expense of the Germans, Italians, Americans, and Japanese. One of the small pleasures of the languages of others is witnessing their petty nationalisms. He finds himself laughing at a paragraph lauding the craftsmanship, care, and elegance found in French plane designs as a way of downplaying the innovations of foreign engineers. He runs his hand over an illustration of a particularly tasteful aircraft, all soft curves and stylish bulges, tracing its wings and fuselage, imagining how each segment might look disembodied, exploded. The beauty of a machine's destruction is a ratio of its beauty intact.

The young, new wife sits down beside him. She says, her voice thick with sleep deprivation, "My father designed those, and helped to build them."

"Where's your handsome husband?" says Masumi.

"He's ill in the cabin. I've been caring for him but I needed a break. You should hear him going on about his stomach." Her own stomach burbles. The medium notices a pale, waxy quality to her skin. A zit crowns her nose, obviously much-molested, red and furious against her pallor. He watches the girl raise her thumb and rub it over the pus nub, which whitens and then crimsons again as she applies and releases the pressure, the way a thumbnail does when pressed.

"Are you sure that you aren't ill as well?"

"I mustn't be, the way he whines," she says, offering a lazy wink. "If I'm sick then he's dying, so I've decided I'm not sick."

"Very prudent."

She takes a handkerchief from the elastic waistband of her skirt and blows her nose, folds the fabric to cover her crime. She looks longingly at a portrait of an engineer—thick glasses fallen to the tip of his nose, wild lick of hair an island on an otherwise bare, long forehead, gentle eyes. With the ginger half-aggression of a young bride, she touches the page, bringing her soft elbow into soft contact with Masumi's gut, and in intimate proximity to the butt of his fancy little gun.

"Do you miss him?" says Masumi.

"I loved my mother more while he was alive. Now he's gone and we eat and sleep on his fortune, luxuriating in this quaint little hideaway, waiting for the letter demanding that we come home and stop wasting the money to which my mother feels she is entitled. But the truth is the rent here is very reasonable. We should have chosen, perhaps, a more frivolous hotel."

"So you do miss him, and you need to burn a little money."

She nods, taking the book from his hands.

"My wife can help you with that."

"You're married?" says the newlywed. "What does she look like? Is she very beautiful?"

"She's a Japanese woman," says Masumi, as if that is an answer. "She looks a bit like me, I'm told."

"How come I've never seen her here before?"

"She doesn't like to come out in the daytime. It would darken her skin, which is very fair, and concerning which she is also very vain. Also, she is uncomfortable in groups. She would be comfortable with you though. I can tell."

The newlyweds don't come to dinner. Matthew is sent to their cabin with a large platter of easily-digested foods: breads, jellies, fruit, steamed vegetables.

John raves, not for the first time, about the film they saw the week before. His enthusiasm fades to background noise, but certain themes and phrases assert themselves repeatedly—repetitions, no less, from other meals and conversations, wherein the fat man also touched his neighbors freely on their arms and wrists to emphasize his points and better capture their attention. "They're really brilliant kids," he says. "Handsome, of course, but both so talented and—and this is the really special part— both exactly *equal* in their talents. You understand? Neither one has anything over the other, or if he does, I couldn't spot it."

"Yes," says Rosie. "They were pretty good."

"Their genius lies in being identical, or alternately, in *appearing* to be identical," says John. "Now, it's possible this is only an illusion. Perhaps they've divided the emotional spectrum between them. Able, for example, might be responsible for sadness, disappointment, misery, loneliness, and the sort of joy that makes one weep. Baker would then be charged with savagery, anger, joy, laughter, humor, exuberance, and orgasm."

"You don't film orgasm," says Rosie. "People don't want to see that."

Masumi toys with his salmon. Lemon butter sauce drizzled over the pink meat, seasoned with crumbled herbs, fork tender. He sips the wine he brought to the table, the wine he is sharing;

the widow takes a sip as well, as does Mrs. Dryden. Matthew comes back from the newlyweds' cabin empty-handed, rubbing his stomach, ready to *chow*. He sits down across the table from the fat man, serves himself fish from the pile at the table's center, dripping citrus-laced dairy fat on the tablecloth in a trail of yellowed dots. There is still a little steam rising from his meal. Rosie covers the fish again and piles vegetables onto his plate as if she were his mother, neither making eye contact.

John drones on. "It might be that they've taken a more disorganized approach, with Baker doing all the scenes requiring tears, anger, giddiness, and jealousy, while Able claims hunger, fear, intimacy, and sadism, to name some possibilities. Or it might be that Able is responsible for the full range of emotion apart from those that require expelling fluids: weeping, spitting, ejaculation, bleeding, drooling, urination, and so on."

"People don't want to see those things," says Rosie, "or hear about them."

"They're artists ahead of their time. Someday people will film all of those things and more."

"Why should they want to do that, John?" says Masumi.

"People are curious about their bodies." He looks down at his plate: empty, eaten, in spite of all his rambling. "They want to know what it's like for other people."

"About the same, I imagine," says Rosie. She dabs at her cheek with a napkin.

"Imagine two men," says John, pushing through to his central point, "brothers, dividing the human experience between them, to make it manageable. Each masters his share of human feeling and leaves the rest to his twin. Together, their efforts make one man, perfect and round as an unbroken circle."

* * *

255

The young bride knocks at Masumi's door. He knows it is her because of how she knocks—her knuckles striking twice, firmly, and then nothing. The shifting of skirts outside as she sways, considering, imagining. These are the ways that she would do these things.

The medium welcomes her in.

"You *are* beautiful," says the bride, perhaps a little too surprised, touching the kimono, pinching the silk. "I love your robe."

"Thank you," says Masumi.

He's let his hair down. He wears a touch of makeup. He's left the peacock feather needles in their bundle, apart from the one that extends from his third eye. The rest seemed a bit much for close quarters.

"Where's your husband?" asks the bride.

The medium explains Masumi's gone out walking. This way they have their privacy. They discuss payment. The young bride passes the medium a fair chunk of her dead father's money—the high price of a personal consultation. They sit together at the medium's table, her simple wooden box between them, but closer to the medium's chair so it is clear the bride should not touch.

"I'm told you'd like to speak with your father."

"You can do that?"

"I can be a vessel. If you want me to."

"I would like that," says the girl, putting her fingers on his fingers.

"You might." He looks down at her hand touching his. "Please don't touch me."

The girl withdraws her hand. The medium gathers his brother's box to his breast, feeling the smooth, cool grain. He leans close enough to breathe its dusty, wooden scent. Like loaded dice rolling into place, his mind finds focus. It seeks a voice, a dead man's. The dead man is coming to him. They will meet in the middle. He will blank his mind and let it take a new shape, a new fire, burning through the fibers, and this will change the features of his face, drawing tight weak, neglected muscles, and slacking others favored by the medium, making the face feel as a pudding, shot through with stubborn strands or grains, entangled in a numbed mesh, a speaking slab joined to the skull.

The ghost enters the medium.

The ghost favors the eyebrows, the forehead, the muscle ridges of the cheeks. He lunges the head forward, close as he can to his daughter. "Adèle?"

"Daddy?"

"What have you done with my money?"

"It's still there, Daddy. We've only spent a little."

"It has to last you your whole life."

"I can work," says the young bride. "Gilbert will go into business."

"You married Gilbert?"

"He's a good boy. He takes care of me."

"I worry about you." The medium's face falls. His eyes water.

"Do you feel this?" She touches the medium's hand.

"No. I don't."

Masumi does.

"Do they still use my planes?" says the medium's face.

"Yes. Of course they do."

They talk about family things. She tells him of the aunt who died. The medium's mouth grows tired and dry. He needs a taste. How to tell the ghost? There is nothing to do for it but wait.

Later, when the ghost leaves Masumi, he feels his body tremor. The strange, other shape fades from his brain, his face. He is himself.

"Thank you," says the young bride. "It was strange. That was really him, wasn't it?"

"Next time I could be your grandmother." He pops the cork on a wine bottle and drinks from it, pulling the feather needle from his forehead. A drop of blood lands on the table, wet and heavy and still.

"I might be afraid to come again," she says.

"There's one other thing," says the medium. "You're pregnant."

"How can you know that? You see the dead."

"Sometimes the living are dead come back."

HIDE AND SEEK

Summer.

Claire rides her new bicycle behind Matthew's old one. He pumps his legs fast, pushing ahead, making her race. Her calves burn, thighs groan, lungs threaten collapse. Does he think girls only like the boys who race them? Boys who can kick up great spurts of mud with their wheels? The feeling of knowing they have a long way to go before they can ride the way you do? The stupid, careless teeter of your careening vehicle's rear end?

She does like it.

He's led her to his home, and now they weave between the cabins, around a tree like a willow, past bemused wives and relaxing husbands, some with lemonades in hand, some eating pastries, bananas, or wedges of orange. They are careful to avoid spraying dirt on the guests, but not too careful. The women love to see children at play. The men love to see their women love to see children at play.

A gust of wind, and Claire clutches her hat, pushing it down with the butt of her fist. The brim obscures the world. When she pushes it back into place, Matthew has swerved out of sight. She slows, braking almost too hard, and searches. He's on her left, at the entrance to a cabin like any other, jumping down from his bicycle's seat in an almost-graceful dismount designed to obscure the difference between the length of his legs and the height of his wheels. The dirt smears his bare ankles—his cuffs pulled up, it seems, for just such an occasion.

He motions her to follow. Her bike stalled, all momentum lost, she climbs off and walks it to the cabin. Matthew takes a brass key from his pocket and opens the door. To her surprise, he wheels the bike in with him, mud and all, tracking smears onto the floor.

She hesitates at the threshold. He comes back to the door and motions her in. "Come on," he says, in English, ducking back inside. She follows him. She dirties the floor with her bike as well and leans it against the wall beside his.

What a strange place. All the furniture has been pushed up against the walls, creating as much empty floor as possible. The chairs are upside-down on the table the way the staff puts them in restaurants come closing time. The empty floor is, apart from layered, aging bike tracks, scrupulously clean—but less clean than blank, really, because "clean" implies a sort of arrangement, and here there is nothing arranged, there is nothing to *be* arranged.

There is one pillow on the bed, center-mattress. There is one blanket. There is a sack of coal against the wall beside the furnace, only a little used. The furnace is neat, and the floor around it not smudged at all with black, as with other furnaces. There are no hangings on the walls, and the windows are covered with cloth shades, sky blue, to let in a little light. It is very dim.

Matthew sits cross-legged in the middle of the cabin, hands

at rest on his knees, breathing deeply. He opens one eye to check on Claire, closes it when he sees she's fine, she's calm too, she's still there.

"It's so quiet here," says Claire. "Peter would hate it."

She traces the sky-blue fabric's edges, picks off a fuzzball. She holds it in her fist, loathe to drop it on the pristine floor. "They let you have your own place?"

"No," he answers, in his slow, cotton-mouthed French, "but we don't have enough guests to fill up. There are a few secret cabins like this one."

"You speak well when you want to," says Claire. "You should do it more often."

"I don't like to," says Matthew, in English.

"Why not?" says Claire. She sits down with him, facing, their knees touching through her skirt, his pants. "Is it hard for you? I could help. I'm good at talking."

"This is a quiet place," says Matthew. "I like to be quiet."

"It's not a quiet place outside." Claire leans back, her hand flat on the floor.

"I am a quiet place."

Claire shrugs it off. If he's got to be quiet then she can love the quiet. She can be a quiet place too. She closes her eyes and imagines a meadow, seeds and spores afloat above the whorls of tall grass, the grass in shades of green, gray, brown, yellow, green. Framed by lovely trees, thin enough that you can see the way their shadows drape each other and make a network on the ground—branches interlocking branches like one thousand elbows, wavering as waver the strands of light that lick the bottom of a water dish laid out in the sun.

"Peter would hate this," she says. "This quiet. He couldn't stand it. He would have to challenge you, or sing a song, or draw on the walls, mess up the place. My mother says he won't be satisfied until he makes everything look the way he looks, which, according to my mother, is the way that he feels."

Matthew takes in a long breath. He lets it out on its own schedule. It makes her budding bosoms itch to see the flatness of his boy-bosom. She can spend what seems like an hour pinching and kneading her nipples if there's no one in the house. In the quiet her body is loud.

Matthew says, "What?"

"I was just saying how Peter doesn't like some things that we like. You don't like some of the things me and Peter like, too, but I was thinking how what he doesn't like, that you and I do like, is quiet, and being quiet together."

Matthew unfolds his legs and stands up. "This is no good." English again. "You're not quiet."

"I'm sorry," says Claire. "I'll do better."

"We'll go out and play," says Matthew, in French. "We'll play until you're tired and out of breath. Then we'll come back and try it again."

"I'm sorry. You know how I get." She doesn't know what this means, but Matthew nods, so apparently he does know how she gets; apparently, she gets some way.

He leads her back into the day. The sun is falling in increments, but the hotel people are still about, some of them playing horseshoes, lawn darts, and badminton, while others sleep or lounge. Gay colors, light dresses, low necklines, suit pants without jackets, slacks, comfortable shoes, slippers worn out-of-doors.

"Why are there so many now?" says Claire.

"Babies," says Matthew, in his clumsy French. "A young couple lives here. She got a baby even though they didn't think she could." He motions at the rest of them. "Their friends, and the friends' friends. They want to get babies too. But it takes a little while."

One of the wives sits in a cane chair, rubbing her small tummy through a baggy maternity dress, while her husband pours her a glass of slightly brown-tinged water from a bottle.

"How does it happen?" asks Claire.

The woman drinks the water, screwing up her eyes as she glugs. She shivers once in her neck and shoulders as the last drop disappears.

Matthew shrugs. "No one's sure. The water," pointing to the wife in the maternity dress. "The air. The mud. The food. The ghosts. Could be anything."

"Ghosts?"

"Dead Jews," says Matthew. "Come on. I want to do something."

"Something in particular?"

He shakes his head, waving his hands, offended by her misunderstanding or his own communication. "No, no. Just something."

"Maybe I could meet your uncle," says Claire. "I never got to yet."

Matthew takes tentative steps in what Claire immediately knows to be the opposite direction of where he might find his uncle. "I never met your mother."

Claire's mother is busy. She puts on the face that she wears when she says that her mother is busy. "My mother is busy," she says, and that's that.

"My uncle is busy."

"Busy with what?"

Matthew shrugs. He begins to walk again, snapping his fingers as if she is a pet that follows.

"Are you ashamed of me?" says Claire.

"What?" says Matthew. "Why should I be? Come on. Meet my uncle. You won't like him."

* * *

He takes her to the kitchen cabin. Claire feels the thirsty eyes of husbands and wives on their bodies like so many tongues. They aren't babies, but can pass given sufficient need. If they stopped someone would offer her a candy. They pass a young couple—newlyweds, perhaps—walking side by side under a similar collective gaze, arm in arm, their other hands cupping the young wife's swollen belly as if it is a tenuous thing and not the hard bubble, the bulgy sun, at the center of her body, at the center of their lives.

"She could burst any day now," whispers Claire to Matthew, though loud enough for the couple to hear—she has grasped their promenade and its purpose, the way it thrills them to hear the coming mother spoken of as if she was not there.

When they enter the kitchen, they find a monstrously fat man and a pretty-if-strange woman. Claire deduces that she is American because of her ankles; Americans' ankles are always red knobs sheathed in watery, bluish skin. Together they work a large collection of pots, some steaming, some rattling on the several stoves, some outright bubbling over. Some finished and waiting. The fat man—Matthew's uncle, apparently—and the woman—the widow, Claire guesses—work with few words, if not smoothly then at least directly, grunting cooking times at each other and reaching out with sauce-sodden spoons for a wipe clean from the other, using a towel held out backward, neither watching the operation, only trusting it to happen. They drip with sweat. It's sort of cute.

Matthew waits to be noticed.

"Hello," says Claire, offering a curtsy. "Are you Matthew's uncle? He doesn't seem to want to tell me for himself."

The fat man and the pretty-if-strange widow turn to her. Their aprons are identically stained, carbon streaks and old butter, crusted flour, tomato, and several grease burns.

"Hello," says the fat one. "My name is John. I am indeed his uncle. And who is the little lady?"

What lovely French, thinks Claire. "Claire Lambert." Another curtsy. "Matthew's friend."

"You're quite pretty, aren't you?" says the widow. "I'm Rosie."

"I wouldn't know," says Claire, covering her mouth and looking at the floor.

"Is she your little girlfriend?" says John.

Matthew twists up his face in anger, but does not answer. Claire only smiles, charming as she can.

"How cute," says Rosie. "How sweet." She turns to move something overheating from the range, placing it on one of several counters, where it bubbles, calming.

"Be careful," says John. "You know how it is here."

Matthew fumes.

"Are you taking her to your *secret* cabin? Have you shown it to her yet?" says John, grinning sidelong at Rosie, who suppresses her laughter.

"You don't know anything about it," shouts Matthew.

Everyone stares at everyone else for what seems like, but can't be, a long time. Matthew leaves, slamming the kitchen cabin's door behind him. Rosie guffaws, a throaty bark strange from her small-if-sturdy frame.

Claire hesitates to follow Matthew, looking to his uncle and the woman for help. She's blushing, too, and yes, a little furious, at what they knew, and how they said it now, in front of her, and all that it implies, as if they know—as if they know anything.

"Go on," says Rosie. "Follow him out. Give chase!"

* * *

He runs away from her for a long time. He hides at the corners of cabins, behind outhouses, leading her from the hotel's center and into its periphery, where there are fewer guests, some darting wild animals—small mice, black birds, crickets, chipmunks—unchecked weeds, unstable bushes with many yellow blossoms, clover, dandelions, a fuzzy purple plant with a poison-looking sheen, and already withering too-tall blades of grass budding with seeds at their brown, pointed crowns.

Matthew darts through a gap: a dark, small shape against the low sun. He runs behind another cabin. When she chases him around the corner, he's gone. She imagines him running with a full, jangling key ring, unlocking the doors of these outlying cabins, secreting himself in their shadows until she passes by a window, going the wrong way, and he runs out in the other direction, circling at some distance, so as to flit through her vision and be gone.

Just as her lungs are starting to really burn and she's lost herself completely in the identical rows of identical cabins, she hears Matthew yelp a short distance away. Rounding a final corner, she finds him, face-down, sprawled in the grass, and immediately decides he's only pretending. As she approaches, giving her heart a chance to settle and fortify, she prepares for his inevitable launch headlong down the alley, past the middle-aged couple playing cards on a table they brought for that purpose, and perhaps into the hotel's center to start it all again. He'll do it when she's four steps away. She walks softly. He'll do it when she's two steps away. He does not. She kneels and rolls him over; an easy thing, he is so light. His eyes come open. His chest rises and falls as hers rises and falls. They look at each other.

"I fell."

"Mhm," says Claire.

"You're breathless," says Matthew.

"You know the word breathless."

"Let's find a new cabin."

Perhaps emboldened by the chase, perhaps knowing how it would sting her lungs to find the air to object, he leads her by the hand. His hands are smaller than hers. She is taller than he. Once inside the cabin, Matthew pushes the table against the wall and stacks the chairs on its top as in the previous secret cabin, which still has their bikes. Claire pushes the sofa against the opposite wall, moving one end and then the other in several seesaw motions.

When they're done they sit in the center of the room, legs folded, and wait for their air to come back, really breathing for the first time in what might be an hour. Claire coughs harshly. Matthew closes his eyes and raises his arms almost parallel to his shoulders, feeling the air.

Feeling the quiet.

A long while later they can speak again.

"See how good it feels?" he asks her.

Claire's been tormented by every second of silence. She hated it. Couldn't he tell? Some of us may not have a lot to say but some of us have ideas. He kisses her. She laughs. He takes it all wrong. She shakes her head no and kisses him. It's fine. They touch each other. She rubs him through his shirt. He touches what there is of her breasts. He's terrifically hungry in his kissing, in his feeling. After every kiss she has the urge to ask him is this what he's wanted—is this why he's pushed her? His breath tastes like fried egg white. He's got gas inside him, waiting to push out, she can tell. Little belches between kisses, facing away. She doesn't mind so much. It can be that way for her too, though today she's almost calm, perhaps because she knows he'll do everything she wants and nothing she doesn't. He runs his hands over her sides. She feels her ribs resist his fingers. She reaches between his legs.

Squeezes, her fingers beneath, cupping, her thumb above, pressing.

Soft.

He's soft. Like a slug.

"Don't."

She curls her fingers more tightly.

"Don't," he shouts, and pushes her away. Too hard. She raises her hand to slap him. He cowers. She reaches out for him again. He scoots away, beginning to cry. "I can't. I never, ever can. Don't," he heaves. "I can't."

When she tries to ask him what he means he tells her to shut up.

She leaves him there. Walks home, in the dark, her bike trapped behind the door of one in a hundred anonymous, identical cabins. All the wives and husbands are indoors—she can feel them on the sticky air, working to conceive.

Days later, when Peter's flu has left him and his strength is back, he comes to see her at night, while her mother is out on one of her dates. He comes to her and they kiss. He is becoming a man. His back has grown broad, his arms muscled, and, when she touches it, when she grasps it in her hand, his prick is hard. They breathe into each other's mouths. His breath is like a heavy bread. They are both waiting until the day, the inevitable moment, where she will flick her tongue across the cleft of his upper lip.

He asks her what she is thinking. He kisses her earlobe, bumping foreheads painfully. They both ignore the impact. That happens sometimes, like the gas-bloat of a stressed stomach. She doesn't answer. She is thinking how Matthew doesn't like all the things they like. This, for instance. Matthew doesn't like this.

HOW MANY

Fat Man sees their car first. Short Mr. Bruce and thin Mr. Rousseau, the police from up north, investigators of the Blanc death, or, as they see it, murder by abortion. The car is a nice one, white, with shining wheels and a quiet little engine. It wears its roof like a hat. It isn't obviously a police car or not a police car. The other guests, the husbands and wives—some now mothers, bumping babies on their knees or feeding them with newly-swollen breasts—wave at Mr. Bruce and Mr. Rousseau as they approach, assuming them to be new guests, potential friends. Mr. Bruce smiles in the passenger seat. Mr. Rousseau scowls as he drives—the car does not come to him naturally.

Fat Man ducks into the kitchen. "They've come," he says to no one. The cabin is empty. There are many dirty pots and pans he has been meaning to wash. There is a boy who comes down to wash them in the evening, when he's freed from chores at home. He doesn't come long enough to do it all though, and he's all Rosie is willing to hire. She brought on a full-time maid, as Little Boy has failed to keep pace with the growing needs of the guests, but she didn't like doing it, and often mentions the new expense to Little Boy, though the hotel is thriving now thanks to the medium's cult.

Fat Man scrubs the pots and pans. He begins with a heavy black one. Its bottom has a scorched rind, a mottle of orange and carbon. He spoons it into the garbage can, scooping divots in the sauce. He turns the pan sideways and digs deeper, pushing more into the can. A mold is growing on the rind. He scrapes away the mold as well, cursing, wiping sweat from his eyes.

Meanwhile the other pots and pans grow differently colored molds, plants, and flowers. A little tree buds in a cup lined with cream; a lily in a pan littered with stale scraps of cornbread; a fat mushroom cap atop a thin, twisting stem in a bowl full of decomposing fruit. The growth ripples outward from Fat Man through the cabin, those things closest growing most quickly.

This, he thinks, is surely evidence against him. It explains everything. It reveals him. He empties all he can into the garbage, shaking scum, flower, weed, little tree, seed, fungus—all of which grow as he shakes them loose, and as he adds to the waste it becomes one solid mass, ingrown, a bin full of tumor, teeming, brimming. When they open the door he pushes the mass down with his hands. It writhes.

Mr. Bruce and Mr. Rousseau stand in the doorway.

"Chores?" says Mr. Bruce.

"I'm a cook," says Fat Man. "It happens. People make messes."

"People clean them up," says Mr. Bruce. He takes Fat Man's elbow. Mr. Rousseau takes the other.

"We'd like to rent a room a couple days," says Mr. Rousseau. "Use it as a home base."

"The widow handles all of that," says Fat Man.

"Why don't you go ahead and unlock one of them for us to start with, and we'll settle up with her later," says Mr. Rousseau, twisting the end of his mustache.

They lead the fat man out the door.

"We've got this thing sewn up," says Mr. Rousseau. They sit across the table in the cabin for which they promise they'll pay later. "Soon we'll lock you away for good."

Fat Man palms his face. "You still think I killed the Blanc woman?"

Mr. Bruce taps a fingernail repeatedly against his shirt's highest button. "Not just Mrs. Blanc. We think there are others. You've killed more girls than I've had. Does it make you feel like a big man to know you've killed more girls than I've had?"

"I already told you that I never even met Mrs. Blanc. I couldn't pick her out of a crowd."

"You said a lot of things," says Mr. Rousseau.

"You seemed *ambivalent*," says Mr. Bruce.

"I didn't do anything to those women."

"What about Adrienne Defoe?" asks Mr. Rousseau. "Paris, three years ago. Cut open with a long, serrated blade, perhaps a bread knife. Do you like bread?"

"Denise Desmarais? Paris, died two years back in a back-alley abortion. Bled out on the cobblestones."

"Danielle Morel," suggests Mr. Rousseau. "Strasbourg. Five years ago. At the time we thought she was a suicide. Slit wrists, found long dead in the bathtub. Blue skin, red water."

"White tub. She took a bottle of aspirin before she did it. We figured she didn't understand how painkillers work. Now we know it was you trying to poison her." Mr. Bruce turns a sharpened pencil over and over in his hand. "She was your first."

"I can't help but notice you're both wearing ordinary clothes," says Fat Man. "You don't look like police anymore. I don't think I have to listen to this."

"Very sharp," says Mr. Bruce, exchanging a smile with his partner. "We work for Mr. Blanc now. He pays us a modest salary so that we can focus our energies on solving his case, and his case alone. But you shouldn't leave your seat until you've heard us out."

He produces a typewritten list, some names crossed out, others underlined. But he reads them all, and he reads them all the same way. A flat delivery, pro forma, as if their meaning, such as it is, is already known, and in the rehearsal there is nothing new accomplished, but a recitation for its own sake, a list that exists to list and be listed, an index to itself. "Corinne Roux, Nantes. Caroline Fortescue, Nantes. Bernadette Boucher, Toulouse." Those should be Japanese names. "Christiane Bourque, Lyon. Alice Bessette, Bordeaux." A woman crouched melting all around her baby, back turned to the low sun of his explosion, the flash-bang, pika don. Their collective shadow stained onto the wall, a heavy smudge, the baby subsumed somewhere in the melting mother, perhaps identifiable in the bodies themselves— you would cut through the meat char, to the bones, to learn what was where—but the shadow lost in the shadow projected on the wall. "Dianne Chevalier, Paris. Florence David, Paris. Lorraine Girard, Paris." Meat rolling back from fine, delicate bones, in layers and peels, revealing the joint of a knee, revealing the cold, hollowed whiteness of a hip bone, rolling back, unveiling organs, which flow away as bright many-colored steam, revealing a spine, rolling back from the breasts, sponges sizzling, veins like fuses, revealing ribs, white smiles. A face becoming a skull, becoming a toothless, hollowed thing, the eyes boiling and then gone, all gone, revealing the brain, which hardens, raisin-esque, though the nose slowly collapses, though the ears drip away. "Alice Bernard, Paris. Lucie Michel, Marseille. Martha Grosvenor, Marseille." A city stripped the same. Trees aflame, revealing foliage, revealing grasses, revealing dirt, becoming mud, flowing away, pushed back all wiggle-pudding by the force of Fat Man's low sun, and layer, and layer, until the dinosaurs surface; their bones, the pterodactyl midflight midst the mud, the brontosaurus mourning its lost tail, the tyrannosaurus rex reaching up with stubby arms as if to finally crown itself king of the lizards; all floating out of gravity's grasp, into space, among the stars, revealing the core, the burning center, orange-yellow swirl, and underneath that red, a red light, pure as pure as pure as pure, *throb*—and him, Fat Man, exploding still, a white sphere opposite the red throb, singing, a single note, no sound now, nothing heard or felt in space, in vacuum, but still, the song, a single note, and all else gone but for the other's throb.

"All of them pregnant, or with a child recently born," says Mr. Bruce. "That's how we know you did them. It's a pattern."

"The pattern fits," says Mr. Rousseau, jabbing Fat Man's chest with his forefinger.

"Black palms," says Mr. Bruce. "Stained by sin. They used to think the body would show guilt. Then they decided against it. We'll show them they were right before."

Fat Man belches nervously, biting it back so the stench and the sound die in his mouth, becoming a burn in his throat. He wipes tears from his eyes.

"It's like fingerprint ink," says Mr. Rousseau.

Fat Man weeps openly. He blubbers, "You don't get it." Spit running down his chin.

"There, there," says Mr. Rousseau. He rubs the fat man's back in circles. "So we caught you. You had to know it would happen. Crack cops like us."

"All those dead girls," says Mr. Bruce. "You wanted to be caught."

Spit bubbles pop as Fat Man speaks, "No, no, no, no, no. It's not enough."

Mr. Bruce says, "Evidence? We're still building our case. Unless you are willing to turn yourself in. If you feel guilty, as you should. We brought the cuffs. You could try them on. See how you like their fit."

"No," says Fat Man, running at the nose, rubbing his palms in slow, vertical swipes across the tabletop, and then again, and again. "No, no, no. No, oh no. They're not enough."

"You mean you'll kill more?" says Mr. Rousseau. "We won't let you."

"I mean you need more names. Hundreds of times more names. Thousands of times more. There are scores of hundreds of women you haven't named, dead women, dead children."

"Is this a confession?" says Mr. Rousseau to Mr. Bruce, taking the pencil from his partner's hand—apparently, to write it down.

"Exaggeration does you no good," says Mr. Bruce. "If you want to be arrested, there can be no falsehoods in your acceptance of guilt. The scales of justice require you only take credit for what wrongs you have done with your own black hands— there can be no falsehood. Otherwise the scales will be lies, and the exercise moot. So if you tell me you killed hundreds of thousands, you'd better hope that you can name them all, if you want to be damned properly, and in proportion to your crimes."

"Let me write this down," says Mr. Rousseau, who takes the list of names from Mr. Bruce and lays it face-down on the table so he can use the blank side.

"What were their names?" says Mr. Bruce.

"I don't know their names," says Fat Man. He wipes his eyes

with his shirt, clears what he can from his mouth with his palms, wiping them to make a glistening shellac across the table.

"They were strangers?" says Mr. Bruce.

"Perfect strangers. I didn't know a one. I didn't see them, even."

"You're not being serious. Give back my pencil, Mr. Rousseau. He's trying to foul up our investigation. He wants to make it sprawl. He'll have us busy for years, hunting go-nowhere leads. If he really wanted to be punished, he would give us their names."

"Or at least descriptions, if he doesn't remember the names," says Mr. Rousseau.

"Precisely."

Fat Man closes his eyes and presses his temples. He thinks what'll happen to Little Boy if he goes to prison. He thinks also of the guilt his brother shares. He thinks how Little Boy would never come clean on his own. Fat Man will have to take the fall for both of them. He can be the guilty one. Little Boy can be the innocent. In this way they can live as they should, imprisoned and free. They can do both. Little matter if one should be responsible for one half and one for the other. It's easier that way—to share the guilt, share the prison, is impossible. Better that the heavy one should have to take the heavy load.

Innocence is the hardest thing. He wouldn't know where to start.

"I won't give myself up," says Fat Man. "That's not how it works. You're still something like police. Connect me to these women in a court of law, you can put me away. Find the others, you can put me away for them too. Keep me locked up for the rest of time. But I won't do your job. You find the evidence. You get the testimony."

"We'll talk to Matthew now, if you'll kindly call him to us," says Mr. Bruce. He takes a bar of chocolate from his pocket, peels the wrapping off one end, lays it down on the table.

"My nephew doesn't talk."

"You mean you've trained him to be afraid of police."

"I mean it's a miracle if anyone gets a full sentence out of him. You can try, though."

He goes to the door and shouts for Little Boy. "Matthew," he calls. "Matthew!"

They sit together, waiting. He says, "I'd like a little chocolate if you can spare it."

Mr. Bruce sneers. He has a piece himself, but does not share.

LITTLE BOY LISTENS

Upon Little Boy's sitting down, Mr. Bruce offers him the chocolate bar. If the missing piece concerns him Little Boy doesn't say so. He sucks his treat to make it last. The once-police ask him questions. He doesn't answer most.

"Matthew, do you know any of these women?" says Mr. Bruce. He reads a long list. Little Boy shakes his head. He really doesn't. A couple sound familiar. The rest are mysteries to him.

They describe the murders. How the girls were found. Some with necks snapped like flower stems. Some with guts cut out. Some merely disappeared. They might have run away, concedes the short one, but they fit the pattern: young, pregnant, pretty.

A feeling like a toothache grows in the center of Little Boy's brain.

In a wasteland you can look for food, water, or people. You can wait to die. You can assign the blame for what's been done, or you can accept it for what it is and survive. The food and the water can wait. The people can't. They can't wait to find the food and water. Some are screaming in a makeshift hospital bed. Others have glass in their feet. Ask yourself why you get nothing but hurt and bellyache. It's best to eat with other people if you have to eat. It's best to drink alone.

After the incident in Masumi's cabin, after vomiting outside, after falling asleep on the grass, Little Boy found a taste for wines and spirits. He sneaks them where he can. They make a feeling like the toothache, or the tooth itself, only numb, a calcium whiteness coating the nerves, a bone-brittle fog. He hid the bottles in the blankets of the bed in his secret cabin, then, under cover of night and moon glow, he moved them to his second secret cabin, in both cases leaving several glasses in the dresser, tipped over on their sides.

They roll and clink together when he opens the drawers. Then he has a taste. The taste is good. It makes him sleep. The sleep is good, and dreamless, apart from certain vivid flashes.

Mr. Bruce says, "I know you didn't mean to do anything you did."

This is true. Little Boy didn't mean it.

"It was all your uncle's fault. He'll be held responsible. All you have to do is help us. Cooperate, and we'll cooperate with you. You scratch our back, we'll scratch yours."

Fat Man looks at him and nods. Maybe he wants to be turned in. For what, though?

They ask him how he sleeps at night. Alone? With help? Does his uncle touch him? Does someone hurt him? Has he ever hurt someone? Or something? Maybe they're asking what he's done to other people. Maybe they're asking what other people have done to him. Maybe they don't recognize a distinction.

"Sometimes a little boy gets confused. He doesn't know who his friends are."

His hair is getting long. He lets it fall over his eyes. He sucks his teeth, prodding their backs with his tongue. He sometimes wonders if these are baby teeth or grownup teeth, and if the former, will he lose them, and if the latter, can he keep them? He sucks the chocolate.

The short one is rubbing his shoulders. He purrs into Little Boy's ear.

"If you tell us what you know . . . a very wealthy man . . . kind . . . he might adopt you . . . very grateful . . . tutors . . . fencing . . . horseback . . . imagine. All the chocolate you can eat . . . shares in the factory . . . a house like a palace . . . you never know, it never hurts to ask . . . he always wanted a son to call his own . . . only tell us what you've seen."

Little Boy shivers.

"You've got to gather your wits, now. Think carefully. Does your uncle ever do suspicious things? Does he disappear for days at a time? Does he bring home unfamiliar garments or bottles? Does he cry suddenly? Does he talk in his sleep?"

Sometimes Fat Man says things with his eyes closed. It might be sleep. He narrates the apocalypse. "Dogs dragging their bellies," he says, "over a junkyard." Bees falling from the air, wings stripped. Boot treads sculpt the sand. Water in strange places—in shoes, in overturned umbrellas, in cars, in bags, in egg cartons, in fish tins, in capitols—frozen, come winter, into eccentric ice cubes.

"Bodies twisted in half, their shoes going one way, their hats in the other." No more Jews, no more Japanese, all the blacks dead, white men perhaps an extra winter, warming themselves beneath the piled corpses of their enemies, blood igloos, all congealed, cat fur coats. "A smell you can't get out." The ocean swelling. Radio waves turned poison. Cups full with twitching ocular nerves. Piled teeth. "All manner of swarm." Fumes. Horror.

"What are you thinking?" asks Mr. Rousseau.

"What?" says Little Boy. He bites the chocolate bar through. It sticks on his teeth.

The short one cuffs his ear. Bright, brief stars.

"You can't beat a witness," shouts Fat Man, standing from his chair with some effort, stomping his left hoof.

"You can discipline a child." Mr. Bruce slaps the back of Little Boy's head. "Come on. Tell us what you've seen."

Little Boy puts his face on the table. "I don't understand what we're doing."

Mr. Bruce screams, "WE ARE RIGHTING THE GOD-DAMNED SCALES OF JUSTICE." He rips the chocolate from Little Boy's hands—an audible snap as the string of drool connecting his chin to the bar breaks, spattering his cheek.

Now Rosie bursts through the door. "What in hell is going on here?"

She says it in English, in Spanish, in French, in Japanese.

Four languages for inner and outer peace.

In a barren field you can plant seeds or you can leave things as they are. You can break the silence or keep it. The widow chases the police out of the cabin. They say she can't do that. She says get off her land. They say it is French land. She says the French sold it. She harps on French surrender. The once-police defend their country. Fat Man makes a farting sound with his mouth and hands. Rosie invokes the image of her husband hanging from a parachute, shot to pieces in a tree. This was for their freedom. Little Boy pretends to be asleep on the table. When everyone is dead you can try to bring them back, you can bury the bodies, or you can step over them.

Fat Man says he will bodily carry out the intruders and throw them at the wheels of their car. They say they will be back. They will find all the victims. They'll name them. When all names are all collected they'll come back, and then he'll see what justice is. The short one knocks over a mirror. Rosie demands he pay for its replacement. He says he will not pay. She demands he pay for the mirror's replacement. He pays.

Little Boy enjoys the silence—the quiet shiftings and huffs of the short one searching for his wallet, lost among the many pockets, the shuffles and puffs as he takes the paper money from its folds.

"Now go," says Fat Man.

Seeing Little Boy is asleep, Rosie lifts him and lays him on the bed. In a minute he will shift and wrap himself in the blankets. His chocolate lips will smear the pillow case, leaving a brown sideways smile.

"Why are you crying?" says Rosie.

Little Boy can't see it without opening his eyes. He can't hear it either; instead the slow, pacing shuffle of his brother's shoes on the floor.

"I hate to see a man cry."

Some time later Little Boy hears a kiss.

"I am not a handsome man," says Fat Man.

He says, "I am a fat man."

He says, "Your husband was a handsome man."

"He was," says Rosie. "He was very handsome. So I've tried that already. It didn't make me happy."

More shifting sounds. None clear. Could be anything.

"Do you think that I can make you happy?" says Fat Man.

"No. But I could make you so."

Little Boy regulates his breathing.

"Don't worry," says the widow. "I'm barren. I can do whatever I want."

There is a whisper. There is a whisper.

There is a whisper.

Peace and peace and peace.

There is a sound that could be a wooden chair shifting beneath the weight of two bodies. All its pieces snapping into the sweetest position of their most perfect strain, their maximum capacity, the tremor of bearing all that can be borne.

Or it is the sound of a door slowly latching?

What do you do in a quiet room?

What can you? Alone.

The objects are innocent. They can stay that way. The knife did not mean to cut. The gun does not weep. So why should the bomb?

If you are alone, then no one is hurt. If no one is hurt, you are pure: beautiful and small.

THE BABIES

Another summer, after breakfast. Fat Man tickles the newborn baby underneath her chin. She coos and grasps his finger, hers sinking into the fat of his. Fat Man says, "What's the little beauty's name?"

"You don't remember?" asks the mother, feigning hurt. He begins to apologize. "That's all right," she says. "I know we all keep you busy. We're calling her Rose."

"After the widow?"

The new mother nods.

The baby is a blonde. Ghostly strands spiral in a crown, shining all around her head, half invisible against it. He smells her head. The sweet baby potato smell. He rubs her little tummy.

"What a good little tummy," he says. "What a good little girl. No crying." He kisses her head.

"She never cries when you've got her," says the father. "You've got a way with the little ones, don't you?"

Fat Man lowers his head, shielding his eyes with the wide brim of his hat. "They seem to like me. Who knows why?"

The father rubs Fat Man's back without recoiling from the pool of sweat between his shoulder blades. "Don't be so modest. You've made us feel at home this whole year. What's for dinner tonight?"

"Swordfish," says Fat Man, tickling the undersides of the baby's feet. She kicks and kicks. Her eyes lock with his. Lovely blue. "Ice cream for dessert. American-style sundaes, actually—banana splits, chocolate sauce drizzle, salted peanuts, sprinkles, lots of whipped cream, and a cherry on top. A chocolaty stout is recommended."

Now come the former newlyweds, now the hotel elders—patriarch and matriarch—a wailing baby in each of Daddy's arms: the twins. Their firstborn toddles behind, tugged by a long red ribbon tied around her wrist by doting mother. "Can we borrow John a moment?" asks the panic-stricken patriarch. "They won't stop."

"Of course," says the first father. Fat Man passes off little Rose and takes the twins, who immediately quiet. Baby Rose looks over her father's shoulder to watch as Fat Man rocks the babies to peace. He cups their rumps and blows on their bare bellies. They laugh and laugh.

"Pretty babies," says Fat Man. "Good little boys. You be good brothers to each other, okay?"

Now Little Boy comes by. He sets down his cleaning things and asks for a baby. Fat Man gives him one of the twins. Little Boy makes faces at his share of the brothers. They show the babies to each other, holding them beneath their arms, bobbing them up and down. The baby brothers touch their feet. Everyone laughs. But then there are more babies crying. Everyone is having such a rough day! Fat Man laughs and laughs, like a baby. So does Little Boy. They laugh and laugh together. Everyone laughs with them. Someone loads each brother with another baby. The matriarch's ribbon-bound toddler latches on to Fat Man's knee with her free hand, the other extended as far as possible so she can reach, pulled taut by the red ribbon clutched absently by her mother. Soft, sweet skin presses on the brothers from all directions. Fat Man can't keep track of all the good little babies.

Soon Rosie comes upon the happy gathering. "Now what have we here?" She touches John's back, as the father did, between the shoulder blades, in a pool of damp and stick. "Are my boys being good?"

"He's so good with babies," exclaims the matriarch.

"Come along John," says Rosie, very nearly flirtatious. "We're going to a movie."

"I want to come," says Little Boy.

The young matriarch says, "You need to stay here and help us with all these babies."

Fat Man and the widow leave them in this way: mobbing Little Boy, bringing children peace by proximity. They take the widow's car. When he is a driver Fat Man keeps his eyes on the road, searching for obstacles, mindful of every possibility, every physical necessity. He drives as if a crash is imminent. As a passenger, he is more laconic, gazing a long way down the road. The widow touches his knee, once, lightly, only a little. He says, without looking away from the rural blur where the land meets the sky, "Do you ever miss your husband?"

"It's a damn fool who parachutes into a foreign country when they've got machine guns aimed up his rear."

"Do you ever miss me?"

"I haven't had the chance."

The Oriental spirit medium is passed out underneath the tree that's like a willow. The branches pull away from her as best they can, rising up on end. The effect is that of a large, powerless animal raising its hackles, as much to beg for mercy as to press a threat. The shadow avoids the medium as well, falling against the sun, out in the open, diametrically opposite the direction of every other shadow cast by every other thing. The medium's legs are splayed within her red, silken robe, which is parted too far up, a sliver of pale skin, smooth and smooth, and the inner silk, a darker shade of red. There are loose threads at the fringes. Her forearm lies across her eyes to shield them from the light. There is a vodka bottle flat on its side, among the roots, empty of all but the dregs. Little Boy takes the bottle. He tilts it in circles, sloshing the liquor.

Fat Man says, "This is just like in the movie."

"How is this just like in the movie?"

"They found a beautiful woman on the ground in a park."

"Who did?"

"Able Hanway. Or Baker. They were playing the same man again." He kneels, touches the silk, and sniffs his fingers. "I think it was Baker. Anyway, they carry her back to their apartment. She wakes up in their bed and screams. It turns out she has amnesia. That's the premise of the film."

"Did the beautiful amnesiac turn out to be a fraud who made the brothers foul themselves on stage in front of an audience of hundreds?"

"No," says Fat Man. "She turned out to be an angel. The main character helped her remember who she was, but the more she remembered the more distant she grew, until finally she had this sort of mile-long gaze, and a strange, almost creepy smile. Finally she had to leave and go to heaven. She said she would see them again someday. But of course it wasn't 'them,' it was him, because there was only one of them on camera, weeping. I think it was Able. I think he's the one who cries for them. He's good at it."

"Maybe we should get Masumi," says Little Boy.

"Let's take her home to him," says Fat Man. "Maybe she'll be grateful and decide not to hate us anymore, and she'll convince him of the same."

It's strange to see the Oriental spirit medium outside, especially in daylight. Little Boy claimed to have made sightings in the night, when the medium was said to walk among the cabins and the trees, always alone. When pressed, however, Little Boy had to admit the figure he had seen was only that: a figure. It had always been possible that this medium, though Japanese, was not *that* medium. Many must have left Japan, Fat Man figured— there would be too many ghosts. Masumi still walked and ate and studied language among the hotel's guests and staff, though he often left on trips for weeks at a time, under cover of darkness, when no one could see him go—and indeed, none did. He, unlike his wife, known only as "the medium," did not like speaking with the other guests outside the library and the occasional comment during meals. He had come to quite like Fat Man's cooking. He had not threatened anyone in some time, though Fat Man caught him, at least once a week, boring holes into Fat Man's skull with his eyes: a steady, focused glare. His wife's leadership was essential to the health of the hotel, both as a community and in terms of finance, which led Rosie to accept the Oriental spirit medium, as well as the unstable, alcoholic Masumi.

Fat Man gathers the medium in his arms. She is light, but not as light as she looks. Very slack. Warm. She shifts in his arms, going taut for just a second, long enough to curl against his body, warming his gut. He wants to kiss her cheek.

"Here," says Little Boy, and he takes several of her peacock feather-needles from among the grass and roots. He pricks his finger. He says it doesn't hurt very much, though as a drop of blood squeezes through his skin and out, he notes that he can feel his own heart beating.

"How does it feel?" says Fat Man.

"Slow," says Little Boy. "Like tides."

Masumi is not home. The brothers knock and knock and knock until they are sure. Little Boy takes out his key and lets them in. Fat Man goes first, and drops the medium on the bed, where her hair fans out beautiful and black, and her feet tangle themselves at once in the sheets. She pulls the sheets up over her breasts, though not her midsection or hips. Her eyes flutter open and closed. She resolves to sleep a little longer.

Masumi's clothes are scattered on the floor in the shape of a flattened man. The white suit jacket, the white slacks, the socks laid out beneath the cuffs, one balled up, the other in the shape of a hockey stick—the shoes, laces still tied. A shirt, an undershirt, in two wads side by side on top of the jacket, like weird linen breasts. Little Boy prods one with his toe.

Masumi's gun is on the dresser. Fat Man toys with it. He runs his hand over the barrel, feels the back end of the handle, all its fancy inlays. The gun is very cold. It makes his skin rise up in goose bumps. He scrapes his arm gently with his left hand's nails, feeling them catch and stutter like phonograph needles on the scabby, gummy little caps that dot his skin.

Fat Man aims the gun at the door and squeezes the trigger. To his horror, it fires. The sound is nothing like he imagined. The bullet lodges in the door, which puckers all around it, a black quarter in a wooden kiss. The medium sits up like a mousetrap sprung, lifting bodily from the bed, hovering a second, hair rising like the tree's weeping, lifted branches.

She falls into place, her hair collapses, clapping. "What the hell did you do? Get the fuck out of my cabin!"

"I didn't know it was loaded."

"Then why did you pull the trigger?"

"I assumed it wasn't loaded."

"Why would you *ever* assume that?"

Fat Man flails with the gun, now pointing it at the medium, not quite recognizing what he's doing, not quite understanding that he means it as a threat. He means shut up. The medium growls and throws herself down on the pillow. She says to get out. She says, "Let me sleep."

"Public drunkenness is a crime," says Fat Man. "We're here to keep you in until you're sober. What would your husband think if he saw you this way?"

"He'd probably join her," says Little Boy, who is meanwhile prying the squashed bullet from the door with one of his keys. His thumb touches it briefly. "Still hot," he hisses.

Fat Man sits down at the table. He makes himself a drink, mixing lemon juice, sugar, and whiskey. The lemon is a little dry but it still squeezes nicely. He says, "Where is your husband anyway?"

"He's on a trip. Go away. I don't like you."

"Your husband says he knows who we are."

"He hates you too. He's a proud Japanese."

"I want to know who you are."

She says, "My name is Masumi."

"Like your husband?"

Little Boy says, "I got the bullet loose." It lies steaming on the floor. He crouches over it, hands out as if he is trying to warm them.

The medium says, "It's a neuter name. Both men and women have it. So my name is also Wakahisa Masumi. You should leave. Things are much easier for everyone when we don't see each other."

"What's your problem?" says Little Boy. "What do you have against us?" He nudges the bullet with the toe of his shoe.

"He forgot?" says Masumi.

Fat Man shrugs, sipping his drink. "I can't tell what he knows."

"I know your names," says the medium. "You're Little Boy. You're Fat Man. Why do you call yourself Matthew?"

"Other people call me Matthew," says Little Boy. "That's how a name works." He looks from one face to the other, awaiting explanation. His eyes are fogged. "Quit staring at me."

Masumi comes to the table. She invites Little Boy up as well, patting the third seat. She makes herself a drink and pours him one too.

"I'm not allowed," says Little Boy.

Fat Man says it's okay.

Masumi says, "My husband and I came here with plans to kill you both. We found, though, that you'd changed. You were calmed. The vortex of spirits centered on your bodies has become a much more contemplative swirl. We did not know what it meant. I still don't know what it means. You still glow inside with Japanese, your body swollen with their love and need. It is a measure of your selfishness the way you bloat with them. He tried to kill you both. He didn't try very hard, I guess. He couldn't do it. You've grown." She holds up her hands parallel and then extends her arms to spread them, illustrating growth. "He has come to see you both as Japanese."

"Japan is not our home. We were born there," says Fat Man, "but that's all."

"That's usually all it takes," says Masumi. "But it's more than that. You define us."

Little Boy looks down at the still-steaming bullet.

"We define America," says Fat Man.

"I've never been," says Masumi. "I can't say what defines them. The hamburger?" She lights a cigarette and offers one to Fat Man, who takes it happily, trading the gun without a second thought. She gives Little Boy one as well—at Fat Man's insistence, he smokes it.

"As long as you're here and you stay calm, I can guide more ghosts into the world in human bodies, fully formed, good as the ones you took from them before, if perhaps a little whiter. Think of it as an underground railroad. In return, you get to stay in your hotel, with your widow, and enjoy this strange peace that you've made. You get to hold the babies."

"The babies frighten me," says Fat Man.

"Because you know what they are?" asks the medium.

"Their love."

Little Boy says, "I'm getting sleepy."

He takes a short drag, coughs harshly. His smoke bleeds into their smoke. Tendrils and teeth in a haze.

"Tell me," says Masumi, "who was the tree before? It reaches out for you. It knows you, as the children do. But it isn't Japanese. It will not speak to me." Masumi cocks the gun. "Tell me where the tree comes from."

"Little Boy will tell you," says Fat Man. "Point your gun at him. I'm tired of being the target."

THE SEED

"She was a tramp that Fat Man found by the well. She said her name was Anne once, but she never answered to it after. She stayed in his secret cabin all the time, where he keeps all the Jew stuff. Not the museum but the secret museum. She was very thin. She was dying. When I was being a baby he would lay me down beside her bed. She would sprout things. Molds, blades of grass, flowers. Fat Man fed her what he could get her to swallow. He was very kind to her.

"She smelled terrible. We couldn't bathe her. One time Fat Man tried. He wrapped towels around his arms to protect her from his closeness, and tried to carry her to a big bucket full of soapy water. He had a sponge and wash cloth as well. He was saying he would take care of her. He was saying he would make the itching stop. She would scratch herself when she could find the strength, opening sores. The blood would mold if he was anywhere nearby."

"If Little Boy was near," says Fat Man, "it would become a

stream of marching fire ants as it left her body. They would walk down the blankets, off the bed, and out the door."

"We understood she wasn't going to get better," says Little Boy. "I didn't ask—I still wasn't talking—but Fat Man said he wouldn't take her to a doctor because he couldn't afford to pay for the treatment. When she spent more of the day asleep than awake, when she stopped shivering, when she stopped scratching, when she no longer took any notice of the things that grew on her, we knew she would die soon. We gave her so many blankets and pillows. Well, he did. I watched him do it. I still wasn't moving.

"There was a dim spark left in her when it started. We couldn't get far enough away to stop the growth. At first it was mold. It covered her all over like a cocoon, green and white and black, the air around her thick with spores. We could see her moving a little inside it. Fat Man tried to peel it away from her, he tried to tear it open. It grew around his hands. He tore them out. It stuck to him, and grew, and grew. He scraped it off himself and backed away. It changed colors and the surface roiled with familiar shapes. They changed quickly. I thought I saw faces. So did Fat Man.

"We saw each other. We saw the police. We saw Rosie. We saw you. We saw my nurse. We sat to watch. It shed warmth on our faces."

"She struggled then," says Fat Man.

"As much as she could. For a moment one of her hands pierced the growth, grasping at the air, and it cast a talon shadow on the ceiling and another, paler shadow on the wall. Then it grew over. Her elbow collapsed inside the mold and her arm fell back in."

"Her body tightened, curling inward," says Fat Man. "A sound like a cicada, but more musical, came from inside as the body in there trembled and shook."

"The mold gave way to maggots. She was beaded with the maggots, the same as the Japanese soldier's body, and others. They squirmed out, and writhed on her, and then there were more, and then there were more, and as their bodies piled up they tried to eat more but already there were others eating through where they had eaten, emerging underneath them, and beneath those more, so the pile rose.

"Soon the maggots were like a fire and because the maggots were alive they could not eat each other or themselves. They did though begin to wilt as they heaped up near the ceiling, turning ashen and then shriveling inward, blackening, like cigarette ends, and crumbling into themselves.

"They would crumble, and come apart, and the ashes fell on the floor and the Jew things. When they burst they made a sound like fire spitting sparks. Their ashes fell and turned around the pile, revolving. At the base of the pile, where more were always coming out, pink and white and gray, becoming grayer, there was what was left of the tramp, some skin and muscle, a lot of bones. The maggots slowed as her flesh dwindled. The pile became a small, wavering flame, and then it was nothing. The air was hung with ash. My face was very warm. We were sweating. I took off my clothes. So did Fat Man. Our sweat dripped on the floor. The drops made big, shiny circles, at first separate, and then overlapping, growing a puddle.

"The light came from in the bones, or between them, a glow, which was rich and thick inside, and thinned as it bled out on us."

"The bones grew flowers," says Fat Man.

"White ones, red ones, yellow, budding from the bones themselves—no stems, at first. Lilies and daisies, roses, even dandelions, only the blooms, opening all over the bones, spitting pollen up among the ashes. Then stems grew from between the blooms, and these came to flowers, and stems grew from among them, and these became flowers, and grass grew out between the blooms, and clover grew. These too took a shape like a fire, and as they rose and swelled they seemed to burn, and the warmth grew warmer. The light from inside it grew brighter.

"A smell like wet grass clippings wafted. It was also like a dog's breath. It was a hot smell as much as it was a green one. It was alive as it was dead. With everything that grew from the body we felt more calm, and as each one extinguished, calmer still. The weight came off me. My heart cooled," says Little Boy.

"All the flowers, grass and clover, everything, twisted into one fat stem, thick as a torso, stained with all the colors of the flowers in green shapes like burns through paper. As its center twisted tightest the stem's top twisted outward, loose, and this made the bed of a very large red rose with some orange petals and some blue swirled inside it, growing and growing until it crushed the stem."

"Thousands of little baby spiders crawled out," says Fat Man.

"They crawled out and down the bed and over the Jew things, growing as they walked, and when they came to us they were large and bristling with hairs, which grew to inches long. They walked up on us and became fat, then died and fell away. The flowers wilted and turned brown, like a kernel or a shell. The spiders stopped coming and the shell wrinkled and closed in all around her."

Fat Man said, "She's becoming a seed."

Little Boy said, "We should take her outside."

"What do you think she'll become?"

They didn't know. They decided to plant her. They laid her on the ground. The seed had a knot at its center that looked like a person. A person curled up.

Fat Man said, "You did this to her!"

"No I didn't."

"Yes you did, you did this, you killed her."

Little Boy punched Fat Man in his knee. Fat Man fell on him on purpose. Little Boy bit Fat Man's cheek. Fat Man barked and punched Little Boy's head. They kicked and kneed one another. Fat Man was smothering Little Boy with his bulk. Little Boy couldn't breathe. Little Boy passed out.

When Little Boy woke, the fat man was lifting him up on his shoulders. Little Boy sat still; he didn't want to hurt his brother anymore. He wanted to be good. They watched the tree grow. It came up from the ground very fast. Fat Man apologized.

He said, "Not just for this. For everything."

Little Boy said, "I love you so much."

Fat Man said, "I love you too."

HIDEKI AND MASUMI

"I told you you could be a good speaker," says Fat Man. He twists out his cigarette in an ashtray surrounded by empty liquor bottles. There are a dozen butts, some very old, lining the edge of the tray, their ash ends collapsed into a pile. The orange bits of his own cigarette burn out quickly.

Little Boy shrugs. "Throat hurts."

"You exhausted the ghosts," says Masumi. "I see how it was now. They were molds, then maggots, then flowers, then spiders, and so on. Most gave up on following you after that. Many of the rest helped make a tree. There are only a few left."

"What do you think it's like being a tree?" asks Fat Man.

"I don't think it's like much of anything," says Masumi. "Which makes it very close to nirvana."

"They still come to us, if we wait long enough. If I touch the wick of a candle and wait, there will be fire. If I am careless in my eating, the food will rot. When I'm agitated, it can be as bad as it ever was. I want them to leave me alone," says Fat Man. "You

297

could still kill me. I wouldn't mind very much as long as you don't hurt Little Boy."

Little Boy yawns and pours himself another drink. His eyes are red from the late hour, the cigarettes and booze. "Can we go home soon?"

"I would sooner kill him than you," says Masumi. "At least you know what you've done. You've got to live with it. What's he got to live with?"

"Self-imposed stupidity," says Fat Man.

"What?"

"Shoot me," says Fat Man. "Right between the eyes. Make me look like that door."

"If I kill you you'll probably come back. Somewhere, some way. You're not ready to leave yet. You'll make a body from more Japanese. Perhaps a very ugly one."

"Uglier than this?" says Fat Man, hefting his tits. "Uglier than this?" tugging at the mounds of his cheeks and his jowls. "And this?" holding out his arm and batting at the dough that hangs from his bones.

"You never know. You might become a brand new thing. You've been one before. Imagine the monster you could build for a body."

Little Boy yawns loudly.

"If you won't kill me, then I'll kill you."

"That would be okay," says Masumi. "That would be fine."

"Who are you?" says Fat Man. "Tell me or I'll kill you."

"You're forgetting I have the gun." She puts it to her own head, up against the ear.

Fat Man imagines the bullet going in one side and out the other unscathed, the medium grinning stupidly as it passes through her.

"Tell them your story," says the medium, "or I'll kill you."

"When is your husband due home?"

"Masumi was a student," says Masumi.

Masumi was a student.

Masumi studied English and French, with some necessary excursions into German, the three being so closely related. He was also capable of reading simple Spanish texts with the help of a dictionary.

Like most students at his school he read at least one book each day. Not simple books either. Wittgenstein, Kierkegaard, Bentham, Kant, Heidegger, Darwin, Nietzsche, and so on, all in their original languages. He kept a journal on every book he read and all the thoughts that came while he read them.

His older brother Hideki was a student as well, who focused on German and English, with some excursions to French. Because Hideki was in the next year, he and Masumi did not see each other often, and did not speak extensively. Hideki would sometimes give Masumi an envelope of the sort you might use to deliver a personal message. Inside there would be a typed partial list of books Hideki had recently read, and that Masumi must therefore read as well. There might be a brief note after the author's name, a single word or a short phrase—"Spirit"; "Patriotism"; "Fear & Agony"; "The individual's loneliness"; "The necessity of injustice"; "Horror"; "Need." More often there was nothing.

Sometimes there were poems, haiku or other traditional forms, in which Hideki compared himself to the cherry blossom, the hummingbird, or the crane. There were frequent errors and unnecessary spaces in his typing. He crossed out the things he didn't mean to write but they were still plainly visible.

Hideki was handsome. Hideki had large, broad hands and

a strong face. He kept his hair cropped close to his head. He was popular and athletic. Masumi loved him and hated him as younger brothers do. He was aloof to Masumi. Masumi respected the distance he maintained.

Then there was the war. As soon as it began all the young men and the older boys knew they would die by American guns. The question was when. The emperor reminded the people of the cherry blossom. They reminded each other of the cherry blossom, and they reminded themselves.

One night Masumi went to Hideki's room and knocked on the door very loudly. Hideki let Masumi in without question, closing his books and stacking them neatly. Masumi shouted how wonderful it would be to die in service of their country. Hideki said, "We should not have to die. We are the future of Japan. The nature of war is that it allows the fathers to wash their hands of their sons, and therefore the future."

Masumi said it was the nature of war that it should lead to the Japanese future. Only once the Americans were humbled would history advance.

Hideki argued, with reference to Kant, that war was wrong.

Masumi said he would be proud to die for his country and become a cherry blossom.

"Even dignity," Hideki said, "evades the strongest man in death."

Masumi said a blazing death in war is not like a slow death in one's bed.

Hideki agreed with this. He said, "It's true that there are far fewer opportunities for pleasure in a gunfight. Our grandfather could still read as he was dying."

Masumi argued reading was not the sole purpose of life, with reference to Nietzsche. Hideki interrupted him and said, "Why did you learn three languages and much of a fourth?"

"It allows me to better understand the ideas of others."

"It doesn't help you fire a gun?"

"It doesn't."

Hideki said, "Then why did you bother? You should quit the study of language and begin the study of guns. Then you can die more quickly, and therefore, more gloriously, with reference to the idiotic argument you are trying to advance."

Masumi said he would leave the study of languages, then.

Hideki said he was a fool. He struck Masumi on his cheek. Masumi's vision flared. Soon they were on the floor. Hideki's knee was crushing the air from Masumi. Masumi pulled his brother's hair. It went on like this for a long time. The fight ended when Hideki took a letter opener from his desk and pressed down Masumi's head on the floor as if holding down a chicken for butchering. His eyes were narrow and cruel, his hand was very strong. The letter opener was textured on its surface by his fingerprints and palm prints, dots and ridges of human oils, and this made it seem heavy.

Hideki breathed in deeply. He considered the letter opener. He considered the neck of his brother, who flailed and pushed ineffectually at Hideki's jaw and chest, trying to shove him off.

"No," Hideki said. "I will let you do it your way." He laid down the letter opener. He climbed off Masumi and pulled him up with both hands. Masumi never considered that he might want to kill Hideki for what he had almost done. He only loved Hideki in that moment, the hatred was gone from him, and he knew that there would be much to learn from this moment in future reflection.

He did not, however, apologize for what he'd said. Neither did Hideki.

After the fight they were cold to each other. They were not only aloof, but cruel, making themselves absent from each other's lives whenever possible. When Masumi went home to visit their parents, Hideki refused, deciding instead to stay at school and study. He was reading the complete written works of Marx. It was, he said, more important than family.

Masumi's father drank sake with him late into the night, and they talked of war, of when it would be Masumi's turn to fight. Masumi did not tell his father how his brother felt because he knew that it would bring his father shame. Instead he agreed that it was good there were two sons in the family, as it increased the chances that one would survive. Masumi said, "I hope it is Hideki. He will make a good father."

His father agreed. "You, though, might make a better husband."

Hideki and Masumi were allowed to continue their studies for a longer time than they expected. They were being preserved, Masumi thought, because the military agreed with Hideki that the educated sons of Japan would be her future. They would be civic leaders, city planners, engineers, philosophers, and writers.

Hideki was making plans for a literary magazine. He was writing letters to a girl. No one knew her name, though some claimed to. He was, in short, beginning his life, rather than preparing to end it.

The other students behaved and thought very differently. Some took up risky behaviors, fighting with knives, espousing illicit or practically-illicit belief systems, or, in one case, beginning an affair. It was only a rumor that two boys were sleeping together but the rumor didn't die until one left for the war, where later he did die. Others settled for cigarettes and alcohol.

It was common to study the aircraft and other military assets of Japanese and foreign armies alike. Masumi read descriptions of the sounds the planes made as they flew overhead. He was especially interested in the "screamers," German fighters with noisemakers in their noses that shrilled, striking horror in their victims. He was also fascinated by missiles, and the German super-guns, the former exceedingly practical, the latter gaudy and terrifying, wasteful in a way that made them seem somehow more immoral than other weapons.

Firebombing held no mystery for him. It was a stupid way to kill another person. No risk, no romance, only a city become an oven.

Masumi was taught it was shameful to surrender. It was beyond the pale. One of the first things the military taught him was how to shoot himself with his own rifle, planting its butt in the earth, putting the barrel in his mouth, and pulling the trigger with his foot. It was preferable to charge the enemy in a way that gave them no choice but to kill you. If they could not be persuaded to kill you, then you would have to do it yourself. Under no circumstances could a Japanese soldier be taken prisoner. There was nothing worse. When soldiers questioned these rules, they were savagely beaten. Most did not question the rules.

When it was becoming clear the U.S. would win, the Japanese began the kamikaze.

Masumi's class was given a presentation on the necessity of victory and the power of the Japanese spirit. A plan was laid out before them, without euphemism but somehow still indirect, circular. The words were true but their tone was not true. It held hope. The plan was to take planes and fly them into American ships. This would make the pilots heroes. It would also, it was hoped, inflame the Japanese spirit, bringing courage to the surviving soldiers and fear into the Americans.

It would be strictly on a volunteer basis.

The students were lined up side to side, single-file, and blindfolded, so no one would be ashamed to raise his hand if he did not want to die or if he was afraid. Of course they could hear

their fellows raise their hands when the call to service came. Masumi raised his hand not out of cowardice but because it was
what he believed.

They took him to an air base and they trained him in flight.
No one pilot got his own plane; they shared, swapping freely. It
was therefore inaccurate to say Masumi was learning to fly his
own coffin. This was, however, how he felt. It took the thrill
out. And there was always the possibility he would die prema-
turely, whether from his superior officers' regular beatings, or
from crashing his plane during training. Some students did that.

Masumi lost weight. He took an interest in Communism, not
as a movement but as an explanation of what had already gone
wrong. From this high moral vantage he could see that history
moved in its chosen direction at its own speed, and that there
was little one could do about it one way or the other, with the
possible exception of those lucky few who sped its progress. If
he was very lucky then he might be one of those. It was his hope
that his death would not only benefit Japan but hasten its becoming a Socialist state. Otherwise, if it did no good, then at least
he knew his death could do very little harm. A superior officer
found one of his Communist books among his things and put a
knife to his throat. Masumi was prepared for this experience by
his fight with Hideki, and also by the beatings, and also by his
belief that he no longer cared if he lived or died. When the officer
saw surrender in his eyes he spat on Masumi, saying he should
put the knife into his own body if he loved his country.

Masumi did not see the point in dying if he could not kill an
American or sink an American ship. The army had invested time
and food and other resources in preparing him to do these things.
It would be a waste to kill himself otherwise. He explained this
in a calm, even tone. The officer let him live. He took the book,

however, cutting out the pages with his knife, stomping them, and emptying his canteen on their ruins.

He came back to Masumi and broke several of his fingers.

Masumi's parents wrote to him. They said they had learned where he was. They said they wished they had heard it from him. They asked had he heard from his brother. There were rules meant to keep a family from losing all its sons but sometimes the rules might not be followed closely, or there might be a mistake, especially as the military grew desperate. They asked him was he eating well. They asked him was he beaten often.

He wrote back to say he was fine. He was proud to die for their safety. He was not beaten excessively. He did not know where Hideki was.

The kamikaze were mostly ineffective. Many were shot down before they could reach their targets. Others hit their targets but did little damage. Some did sink their ships. There were announcements. The Americans were disturbed. That was something. Although sometimes it seemed they were laughing. Not frightened so much as amused.

Still there was a craze for kamikaze in the military. Every general felt pressured to create his own. The navy made speed boats loaded with explosives for the purpose, and frogmen who would swim to plant explosives on the undersides of ships. There was also the one-man submarine. It was about the size of a torpedo. You could barely fit one person inside it. He didn't have a lot of air because he didn't need a lot of air. He didn't have a lot of fuel because he didn't need a lot of fuel. The idea was you launched the submarine out of the torpedo tube. Then the pilot would ride it into the side of a ship.

There are a hundred ways to make a man into a bomb.

Masumi got a letter from his brother with a list of readings.

There was a technical manual on a machine Masumi didn't recognize. There was a history of Buddhism. Beside the technical manual's name Hideki wrote, "A Son's Resignation."

Beside the Buddhist history, a word or short phrase crossed out so many times it was illegible. No poems.

It was time for Masumi to crash his plane. They gave him little fuel. He flew with a picture of his mother. His parents had sent it for that purpose. They had also enclosed a picture of a girl Masumi never met—one they said he would have liked. She was holding a paper fan over her mouth, peeking out above it. The paper fan was painted with pink blossoms. They said he could think of her as his reason. He left that picture in the barracks.

He meant to die.

He flew out until half his meager share of fuel was gone. There was nothing on the water to crash into. He returned to the base. They broke his arm and made his eyes swell shut.

Two weeks later, when he had healed enough, they sent Masumi up again. Again, he meant to die. He imagined his death as the one that would turn the tide. He would sink a destroyer or perhaps a carrier. As the water rushed into the hull's breach, so would the Japanese empire rush into American soil, leveling the movie theaters, the malt shops, the liquor stores, the pornography rackets. They would destroy all obscene art and low culture. As a result, two hundred years from now, the people's revolution would be made real. The happy offspring of a Japanese-American union would parade golden and wise. They would spin noisemakers and play rustic arrangements of "Ode to Joy" and other fine humanist works. They would never know who made it possible—which diving plane, which sinking ship.

There were no ships. No targets. Masumi returned home and threw himself on the ground. His chin scraped the pavement, and he bled as they kicked him on his legs and stomach, careful this time to avoid the arms. He bruised and tendered. His skin was marked up a spectrum of yellow, red, blue, purple, black. They said they would send escorts next time in spite of the expense. This was becoming necessary more and more often. He wondered if they would shoot him down if he turned back. Wouldn't it make more sense to kill him once he'd landed the plane, so someone else could use it? The Americans were already taking down enough Japanese planes.

Masumi never flew again. Before he got the chance, there was a raid on his base. American planes strafed their hangars, destroying everything. Many died.

After Hiroshima, after Nagasaki, after the surrender, after the emperor's voice went out over the radio announcing the surrender, Masumi was allowed to go home to his family. He found his father drinking sake, staring at the wall. His mother read poetry in bed.

She said she was glad Masumi was home.

She said she had missed him while he was at school.

She said, "Hideki is dead."

The army had sent them a box a month before. Inside the box was a bag of money, a notice of Hideki's posthumous promotion, and a written description of his death. There was also another box, smaller, wooden.

"I can't look inside the smaller box," said his mother.

"How did he die?" asked Masumi.

"Your father has the letter."

Masumi asked again how Hideki died.

"He was piloting one of those baby submarines," said his mother. "Apparently it was a test run. They put it in the water. It never came back up. They say it sank very quickly. They say he must have drowned or, if he was lucky, simply run out of air, passing out before the water breached."

Imagine your brother in a submarine. He cannot move his arms or legs. He sees through a sort of bubble on top of the tube. He is sinking deep into the blue until the blue becomes black. His lungs fill with water or they empty of air. He cannot feel his limbs. He only sees the blue so blue it's black, and then the insides of his eyelids, and then the black. Wonder how and when he knew he was dead, that he had really crossed the threshold, that he was done. Wonder if he ever knew.

"We got more money because he died the way he did, because they promoted him," said Masumi's mother. It would have been the same for Masumi. He would have been promoted too. "Your father took the money and bought sake. He hasn't gone to work. Yesterday someone came to check on him. Your father threw a bottle at his head."

Masumi went and sat with his father. After a long time, his father seemed to notice him. "You're home."

"I am."

"Hideki is dead."

"I know."

"He was my favorite."

"I know that too."

His father fell asleep drinking sake.

The next day Masumi found the small wooden box.

He reached to open it and see what was inside.

His skin touched the soft, almost-smooth grain of the wood.

He had a vision.

He saw their grandfather as if he was alive again. He saw his grandfather's father, and his wife, and her sister. He saw all the dead.

Masumi never opened the box.

Soon he ran away from home.

It's different for women. There is no shame in survival. No

one wanted you dead in the first place. You don't have to think of your brother. If you do, a small drink helps, or sometimes a big one. You can be pretty. You can wear a nice robe.

I'm sorry you found me out there under the tree.

The medium puts the gun on the table and pours himself another drink. He says, "You can still kill me if you want to. That was my other plan, if I didn't kill you. Maybe shoot me in the back of the head."

Fat Man says, "I wouldn't do that, Masumi. I'm guilty of much worse."

"Pour me another drink while I down this one." He takes what he's got in a swallow while Fat Man obliges him with another. He wipes his mouth with his sleeve. Hisses like a happy snake. Hisses for the sting. He downs the second glass.

Fat Man pours him another. "Easy there. I only know the one hangover cure." He indicates the gun.

Little Boy says, "So you're your own husband?"

Fat Man elbows him to be quiet.

"He was me, yes," says the medium, in his man's voice, "and I was him," in his woman's.

Little Boy mulls it over. "You never opened the box?"

Masumi shakes his head.

"So you don't know what's inside?"

"No, I don't."

"Are you ever going to open the box?" says Little Boy.

"No."

"So you'll never know what's inside it, even though your life revolves around it entirely now," says Little Boy.

"That's right."

Little Boy takes the box.

"Wait!" shouts Masumi.

"No!" shouts Fat Man.

They both go for the gun. Fat Man gets it first. He gestures with the business end.

"Put it down," says Masumi.

"I'm doing you a favor." Little Boy shakes the box. There is no rattle inside. Perhaps a flutter. "Sounds empty to me."

Masumi advances on Little Boy, making his hands talons. "You slow, stupid, dull-witted boy."

Little Boy turns his back on them. He squats, setting the box on the ground, shielding it from their view with his hunched body. He opens the box. The sound of a machine's parts falling into place. The sound of a pendulum at its lowest point. The sound of a box being opened.

Masumi groans—grabs Little Boy by his hair and his ear. As he's dragged away, Little Boy says, "I don't understand."

Fat Man peers into the box while the medium screws his eyes shut and thrashes the boy.

Inside there is a small piece of white paper, curled inward on itself like a lock of hair.

"Stop, Masumi," says Fat Man. "It's too late. He's already done it."

Masumi lets the boy go and approaches the box. He sets it on the table, knocking over several bottles, which pour out on the floor, *dook dook dook.*

Masumi takes the curl of paper from the box. "I wish I never saw this."

Two Japanese characters, stacked in a squat column.

Little Boy gets up and goes around to see it over his shoulder. Fat Man, slipping the gun into his pocket, does the same.

"What does it say?" asks Fat Man.

The medium closes his eyes. He waits until the air inside him feels like it's enough.

"The first character means leave behind. It almost always refers to death. The second character is bone. Together in this way, it means remains."

"Remains," echoes Fat Man. "Like a body?"

Masumi nods.

Little Boy is crying. "They look like brothers."

遺骨

REMAINS

THEY LIVE

A week later Fat Man and Little Boy find the tree like a willow destroyed. The tree is collapsed into a heap of large charcoal segments, recognizable as former limbs, as quarters of the trunk, and knots. The tree will issue ash for days. The fire chars the grass around the roots but does not spread. Masumi is there, dressed as a man, though his long hair is let down, hanging in wild black streams over his face and pushed behind his ears under the white rim of his hat. As they approach, he gestures at what he's done and jumps on the pile, stomping with both feet, kicking up wild flurries of black powder. It looks as if he's crushing grapes for wine. The ground is littered with bottle necks and bottle ends, which refract and flare the light at many points, sharp ugly scatter shine.

"You've blinded me," he screams, blowing his hair out of his face. "You've taken my second sight." He indicates his eyes with fingers one and two, then jabs himself in the forehead where the third eye would go. "How am I to see my brother now?"

He says, "You never should have opened my brother's box!"

He says, "I'll kill you!"

But Fat Man has the gun.

He describes for them the joy of burning down their tree. He poured his alcohol on her, threw bottles up against her until they broke and stained the bark, until the air was thick with it, and his eyes, ears, and nostrils stung, so that he was drunk on the air, and he felt its bitter tingle on his skin. The air was drunk on him, he boasts. He soaked a rag in alcohol. He fed the rag to his last lovely brown bottle of bourbon. He lit the rag and threw it at their tree.

"Did she suffer?" Masumi asks the brothers. "I don't know anymore. I can't see. But now she's free, and so are all the rest you trapped in there. They're all free to haunt you."

Before stumbling back to his cabin, Masumi screams that he'll kill the brothers. He says he'll tell the world who they are. He says he'll reveal them. He says he'll get his gun back from the fat man. He says all the hotel babies will grow up to know Fat Man and Little Boy, and that they will continue to recognize them, and be drawn to them, and look at them with so much love, and someday the brothers will have to admit and explain what they are, what they were, what they always will be.

The next morning, Rosie leaves a note in an envelope wedged under the door of Mr. Wakahisa Masumi and Mrs. Wakahisa Masumi. The letter demands that they leave. It threatens the full force of the law. It advises them a car has been hired to drive them wherever they wish the next morning. It offers the widow's condolences for Masumi's brother, included at Fat Man's insistence. It thanks them for their contributions to the hotel community, especially in languages, where Mr. Wakahisa Masumi's skills are commendable. His drinking, however, gives the widow cause for concern. Mrs. Wakahisa Masumi would be wise to make him see an expert next time he has a spell.

Mr. and Mrs. Wakahisa Masumi take the car. No one sees them go; it is dark when they leave. Their cabin is pristine. There is some concern in the community at their passage, that this might affect the influx of souls into bodies—into babies, that is: and babies into mothers.

Fat Man and Little Boy mourn the tree for several days, loading its wood into a wheelbarrow, rolling it out of the hotel grounds, and dumping it into the river, which carries it away, out of sight. They see a turtle's head bobbing in the river. See water bugs on the surface.

Little Boy says, "Why was he always so mad at us?"

Fat Man says, "You should know."

For a long time, Fat Man lives in fear of Mr. Bruce and Mr. Rousseau's return. It seems impossible to him that they should really try to track down a hundred thousand dead women, all of them pregnant, all of them pretty. The definitions of both words would have to be stretched beyond all recognition. Still, they don't come after one year, and they don't come after two, and he begins to think they never will. He begins to think he's safe.

It makes him feel ill to be safe.

Rosie asks him, a few months after the once-police have gone, what made them take an interest in the first place. "Are you guilty?"

"Yes. But not of what they say I am."

"What have you done?"

"My life is built on the destroyed lives of others. It's built on death."

"That's all of us," says Rosie.

* * *

And the sun rises yellow, and the sky is clear. The grass tilts in the breeze, and people forget the war, or they remember everything else. There are no more secret cabins. Fat Man and Little Boy still share one. Rosie has her own, where she spends most nights alone. The excess Jew things are kept in the museum cabin, or they are sent to relatives who write to ask for them, or they are sent with relatives who visit. Some—the really worthless things, the broken cups and frayed shoelaces—are simply thrown away. They no longer bring Fat Man comfort.

Ivy finds the cabins and begins to climb. Fat Man offers to scrape it away. Rosie says the land is making them welcome. She says to let it be.

And the guests summer in Gurs with their children, and the children grow. They love the fat man and his nephew, but also other things: their mothers, their fathers, dessert, games, and some of them the library. Rosie buys picture books.

They are not like the piggies or knots of piggy-flesh. They are strong, they are quick, they are some of them beautiful, they are some of them plain, they are some of them quite ugly, but all of them complete.

And cicadas hide in the trees, and gnats swarm wherever there is damp. Fireflies in the summer. The children jar them as their parents did before. The jars glow. Some forget the air holes. Their fireflies die. Others remember; theirs live a little longer. They rinse the bodies and the grass out of the jars into the river. When it rains Gurs smells of chocolate. When it's dry the hotel smells of grass. There are wild strains of it among the rest. Blue-tinted blades, and red. Fat Man wonders sometimes how they came to be here. The ivy climbs the walls very slowly. Sometimes it seems you can hear it.

* * *

Fat Man ages, or seems to. He fattens, slowly. Lines crease his face. They might be only fat folds. His body slumps around him, he is surrounded by it. His arms hang heavy, his wrists' fat threatening to consume his hands, which remain their same size, his fingers at some theoretical horizon of their swelling. His palms remain black. His thighs rub together when he walks. He powders them to limit chafe.

When he and the widow make love she mounts him. He lays back and pulls his stomach out of her way like a curtain.

She had to tell him seven times—in her straining, whispering way—that he was "so big" before he understood it was a compliment.

Sometimes she faces away when she mounts him, nightgown gathered up around her waist like a sash. He doesn't know if she closes her eyes. If not, then what does she look at? If so, then what does she look at?

Little Boy does not grow. He does not grow older. They have a fifteenth birthday party for him; he blows out the candles. He blushes. He says, "You didn't have to." They have a sixteenth birthday party for him. He blows out the candles. He blushes. He says, "Haha. I guess I'm a runt." None of his friends from school attend because he doesn't have them anymore. He runs and plays with the children of guests afterward—children three, children four. He seems happy this way.

Rosie says they need to take him to a doctor.

"He's just a late bloomer," says Fat Man.

"He looks like he's nine. When did he last grow even an inch? He's been exactly the same since the day I met you."

"So he's a little stunted. There's nothing wrong with that."

"Maybe he's a dwarf."

"Dwarfs don't look like he does. They're squat, and their arms

319

don't work right. I promise he's fine. If he doesn't grow soon I promise I'll take him to a doctor."

There is a whole week where Fat Man forgets he was ever a bomb. It comes back to him in the night. He is looking at the other side of the door's frame while he smokes a midnight ciga-rette in the cabin's open doorway, his back propped up against the side with the hinges. It occurs to him he hasn't been thinking of himself as a bomb. It occurs to him he was one.

It occurs to him you can never be consciously innocent. You only really know what you've done wrong. This is partly because there is so much you haven't done there is a boundary on how much and how often you can think of it. He is innocent of rape. He is innocent of gossip. He is innocent of kidnapping. He is in-nocent of child molestation.

To recite one's innocence, he thinks, degrades it. A list of what he hasn't done becomes a list of things he could do. The rest, the things he hasn't considered or even imagined, are an abstraction. This is innocence. This is the look in Little Boy's eyes, as he does not grow, but grows apart from Fat Man—the milky white, the perfect fog of innocence. Little Boy doesn't know what he could do. He doesn't see how he could hurt all the people around him.

There is a day a year later when Fat Man forgets—for that day, he is only John.

Another month, there are two weeks.

One day, there is an hour.

It always ends the same way. The chill, the ache, the lurch of remembering, of coming up short, of realizing he hasn't been thinking of himself as himself. He wonders, after the fact: While I didn't know, was I happy? Was I any happier at all?

He can't remember. The guilt is beyond him when he forgets

who he is. When he remembers, it's the forgetting that escapes him.

The chocolate factory smells the same in both states. He knows that much for sure.

Fat Man finds Rosie in the library, in tears. She is searching a German dictionary. Fat Man rubs her back. He gently touches his knuckles to her cheek. He asks her what's wrong.

"Nothing."

"Then why are you crying?"

"I can't find the words." She breathes shallow.

He puts his hand on her stomach, trying to slow her. He says, "What words do you need?"

"The words I need to tell you what's happened. I talk each day about the importance of knowing several languages and when it counts I only have the one."

"What do you need to tell me?"

"You're going to be a father," says Rosie, closing the dictionary. "Ein papa."

Fat Man leaves the library. He walks faster than he knew he could, his thighs swishing with each step. After a moment's hesitation, Rosie follows him out. She catches up quickly.

"You said you were barren," says Fat Man.

"These things happen. You should comfort me. I'm the mama."

"You should comfort me," shouts Fat Man. "You've had how long to adjust? Days? You just told me. I've never seen myself as a father."

"You're practically a father to Matthew."

"He's always been more of a brother to me."

"What a strange thing to say."

"Rosie, are you sure?"

"The doctor is quite sure."

They hold each other.

Rosie says, "I don't believe in abortion."

"Of course not," says Fat Man. "Of course not."

They marry. Fat Man asks her often before, during, and after the ceremony if she's sure she wants to be with a lout like him. "It's the risk I took," she says one time, "sleeping with you like a child." Another time she says, "I can put up with you if you can put up with me." Another time she says, "Just don't go off to any wars." Another time she says, "You're not so bad." And another time, "You make me laugh." And another time, "You're beautiful." And another time, "Okay, you're ugly, but in a way I find beautiful." And another time, "Not if you keep asking me." And another time, "For God's sake yes, you dumb son of a bitch, I love you more than anything. This is really, honestly, truly, and actually, exactly what I want."

He moves out of the cabin he shares with Little Boy. Little Boy sleeps alone. He lives alone, though they often take their meals together, along with the rest of the hotel community. Little Boy keeps his cabin clean. He is so well-behaved now it makes his brother nervous. He is supposed to be seventeen. He looks the same as ever. Younger, even. More innocent. More rosy in the cheeks. Actually and truly happier, perhaps, though he never speaks unless he has to.

At night, Fat Man dreams of his child to come. Nightmares, all of them. In one his son is born with a black iron shell. The son can't move, but stands a statue in the shape of a boy, arms raised to flex biceps. In another, Rosie births a bomb like Fat Man, a little one, along with several gallons of a black sludge like crude oil. The bomb rolls over several times, each time with a heavy clank. It does not explode, but lies smoking, quiet and still, an evil egg. In another dream, Rosie births rot. It comes out of her in colored smoke, or a gas lit from inside, red and yellow, green and blue, and the warmth between her legs collapses, becoming a space, and it spreads to her inner thighs, her pubis, her stomach, and she slowly collapses, the flesh rippling, dimpling, and staining with the rot colors, becoming a void.

He asks Little Boy what it would be to be a half-boy, half-bomb.

Little Boy says, "What?"

Marshal Philippe Pétain dies on an island somewhere. He was so old. They say that by the end his memory had left him so he didn't even know what Vichy was. He might have thought that he was on vacation. He might have thought he'd always lived on that island.

Rosie comes home with a bust. She walks into their cabin with it balanced on her big baby gut, between her breasts. For a moment Fat Man thinks he's gained what Little Boy took from Masumi—he thinks he sees a ghost, a victim of the guillotine. The white of the bust's skin seems to glow in the night. The blank eyes accept his stare.

Rosie says, "I thought we should have one. Everybody else does."

"We'll have to paint his face," says Fat Man.

"I thought we might leave him like this."

"I don't know how I feel about the old man."

"I think he meant well, apart from what he did to the Jews."

"That's some exception," says Fat Man.

"Everybody had camps," says Rosie. "He was old and afraid."

"Keep him off our baby at least. He's a bad influence. And keep him away from me as well. He was a very bad father."

They go to bed.

A nightmare wakes him. He sits at the table, arms folded underneath his chin, eyes level with the bust's. "They're coming for me next," says Fat Man. "Thank God. I hope they put me on an island."

The bust is like the moon.

The moon is outside. He can only see the rim.

The rim is like a zero. A zero's something like a number, but it's not—not really.

Like Fat Man is no kind of man, no kind of father.

LITTLE BOY ALONE

Fat Man takes Little Boy for a ride in the car. He says they're going to the doctor. Little Boy says he doesn't want to. He says he'll run away if Fat Man tries to take him to the doctor. Fat Man lifts Little Boy on his shoulder like a bale of hay. He throws him in the backseat of the car. They drive away.

Once they've left the hotel grounds, Fat Man says, "I'm not taking you to the doctor."

"What?" says Little Boy.

"But when we get back, we have to say you went."

"Fine."

The car bumps along. Little Boy says, "Then where are we going?"

"The movies," says Fat Man. "There's a new Able and Baker picture I want to see."

"Then what'll we do?"

"We'll go back home," says Fat Man. "We'll tell Rosie she was right. The doctor diagnosed you with a rare form of dwarfism.

He says it's not hereditary, though. That way she won't worry anymore if there's something I'm passing on to the baby."

"Is there something you're passing on to the baby?"

"Damned if I know. But you're a dwarf now. Got it?"

"But I'm just a little boy. That's all."

"I know it," says Fat Man. "But you really should be growing. That's what little boys do."

Little Boy sulks.

They see the Able and Baker film. This one is a romantic comedy. The filmmakers play with the twins' reputation by making them portray two characters, two men who compete for the same woman's love: two identical twins separated at birth, adopted by very different families, living very different lives, in total ignorance of each other's existence. The woman they're competing over is a secretary. One of them is her boss. The other's a tough, sleazy mobster. The roles are credited to the brothers collectively, so that it's impossible to say which is which, or if perhaps they trade between scenes. The boss is cool, calm, collected, and responsible, but perhaps a little too stern. He never smiles, though his eyes do sparkle, and when he tilts his head a certain way— well, he must be something like happy. The mobster is a hothead, constantly angry, ready to explode. But he's passionate as well. He and the secretary share some kind of kiss. He lets her see him cry, and he's beautiful when he cries, really gorgeous. So the secretary has to choose, and it's difficult because each man speaks to a different side of her. She begins to diverge as a character in the movie's second act, becoming two women. The boss's loyal helpmate and the gangster's partner in crime. In a dress appropriate to the office and a fine scarf, she helps the boss navigate a meeting in a client's home, with all its social complications. In a too-short skirt and half-open blouse, she helps the tough steal several tins of caviar for a dinner at home. But eventually she's got to choose.

The strange part is the way they shot the movie. It would have been big news to get the Hanway brothers on screen together, and the plot seems to beg for it, but the film is made as if they really only had one actor to play both roles, avoiding at all costs of contrivance and implausibility the meeting of the two characters. Their final confrontation takes place over the phone. The results are awkward and undramatic. Fat Man, their single biggest fan, is still captivated. Little Boy, meanwhile, is bored; he only likes it when he gets to see the main lady's knees or a hint of her breasts.

"This all but proves my theory," raves Fat Man on the way home. "They've divided the emotional spectrum between them. They did it by hot and cool, it seems. One of them—Able, I think—is responsible for reserve, calm, care, gentle things and gentle feelings. The other is in charge of passions. Anger, fear, hatred, love, pity, and the like. That must be how they do it. That must be how they manage."

Little Boy rolls his eyes. "How do you manage?"

"I don't. Misery, joy, pride, guilt. I've got to do everything around here."

"I don't want to be a dwarf," says Little Boy. "I want to be me. I don't see why we can't do it that way. Tell them I'm just still little and young."

"You want me to tell her you've got a mental disorder too?"

"No," says Little Boy, and he crosses his arms.

Rosie takes the news well. "You poor thing," she says, hugging Little Boy to her breast, rubbing his back. "Will you be okay? You poor thing. You tell us if you need anything."

He will soon be done with school. Then he can work at the hotel full time. What a lucky little dwarf is he.

* * *

Sometimes Little Boy sees Claire at school because he makes the mistake of turning around and looking where she's sitting. She keeps her eyes on her books. She chews her pencil. It makes a crunchy pulpy sound like it might break, or she might bite through. She blows the hair from her face. He never accidentally looks where Peter sits because Peter sits right behind him. Sometimes Claire walks past Little Boy to get where she's going. She seems like twice his height. He can barely see her face past her breasts, looking up at her as he does.

One day, he follows Peter and Claire all the way home, walking quiet as a mouse, hiding behind other people, brick corners, mailboxes, lampposts, and road signs. It's easy to hide when you're small.

They go to a bridge overlooking the river and sit on the railing together. When no one's too close to them they kiss. Little Boy climbs a nearby tree for a good view. He can't hear what they're saying. They hunch, leaning inward, cheek to cheek, and seem to whisper, holding hands. She nods often. He talks much more than she does. Little Boy thinks what an idiot Peter is to talk more than he listens, especially with Claire, who always said such lovely things, though Little Boy could rarely understand them.

He misses Peter's friendship, if that's what they had. He misses Claire's hand between his legs, pressing—searching for signs of life. She could have searched a little longer. She might have found him there.

When the baby comes due, Fat Man uses Rosie's money to rent a hotel room by the hospital in the city. He tells her at dinner. Because he does not mean to bring his brother, he does not tell Little Boy, though Little Boy is also there.

Little Boy pretends to misunderstand. "Will I have my own bed?"

Fat Man looks to Rosie.

Rosie says, "We thought you could stay here and look after the hotel for us while I have the baby."

Fat Man says, "We think you're ready."

"I thought the staff would look after the hotel," says Little Boy, motioning at the recently hired groundskeeper and the repairman, who eat tonight with the family and the guests.

Rosie says, "You are the staff."

Little Boy looks down at his plate. Greasy, buttered carrot coins, bits of cabbage, baked chicken with a lemon glaze, sawed to pieces, bacon. He works to summon tears, screwing up his face, tightening the hinges and the cords. "I never got to stay in anybody else's hotel," he says, when the tears fail to come. "Why are you leaving me alone? Is it because of my condition? Is it because you like the new baby better than me?"

Fat Man thumps the table with his fist at the word "condition."

Rosie puts her hand on his hand. "He can have his own room," she says. "Next door."

When Fat Man goes to town to see about a second room it turns out the hotel has none free on that floor. If he considers renting one on another floor he doesn't do it, perhaps because he understands Little Boy would never accept it. They all go together. They all share the one room. Little Boy chats up Rosie as Fat Man checks them in. He asks her is she looking forward to the baby. She says yes she is looking forward to meeting him. He asks her is she afraid of giving birth. She says that women rarely die now if they have a hospital bed, which she will.

"I didn't know it could kill you. Now that scares me too," he says, touching her stomach. "This little thing. He could do that much damage?"

"It's very rare," says Rosie, removing his hand.

Fat Man carries all their luggage, refusing the porter. Little Boy squeezes Rosie's hand as they ride the elevator up. She doesn't squeeze back, but she doesn't take it away.

Little Boy will have to sleep on the floor. He elects to sleep at the foot of the bed, explaining that otherwise "somebody" might step on him when they get out of bed. "Someone big and fat."

Little Boy wakes as Fat Man tries to sneak out the hotel room door. He whispers, "If you let me come along I won't wake Rosie."

Fat Man watches Little Boy pull on his socks and shoes, his big coat, his furry hat and knit gloves. He keeps his long underwear on as it was. They sneak together, keeping quiet all the way down the hall, all the way down the stairs, all the way out the hotel. They walk hand in hand, hands in gloves, huddled, chins tucked in their collars.

"It's like old times," says Little Boy.

"I guess," says Fat Man.

"You and me, walking together like brothers. You want to get something to eat?"

"Everywhere's closed."

"We could break in somewhere."

"You don't do that if you've got the money to pay." Fat Man pats his back pocket, indicating his wallet.

"I'd like a raise," says Little Boy.

"I'll ask the widow."

"You should call her Rosie." Little Boy kicks a frozen chunk of snow. It skitters down the block. "Or your wife."

"I don't like to," says Fat Man. "I don't deserve her."

"What'd she ever do that was so great?"

"You'll understand someday."

"Are you scared about the baby?"

"I'm worried that he'll be like us."

"How do you mean?"

"I mean a bad person. Or no person at all. I wish I could see what he looks like in there. I have dreams. Dreams where he comes out diseased, or he kills us, or there isn't anything in there at all—only a kind of force. A pain."

"You're not a bad person," says Little Boy.

"Yes I am."

"You were always kind to me."

"I beat you."

"Sometimes a child needs it," says Little Boy. He blows a stream of vapor into the air.

Fat Man lights a cigarette.

Little Boy says, "Can I have one?"

"No," says Fat Man. "They'll stunt your growth."

Little Boy stays in the hotel four days alone. With Rosie's permission, he orders in food. He tips too generously because he thinks he deserves to spend the money, and because the staff are peons like him. They have his sympathy.

He eats as much as he can because he wants to, because he still can, because he is so thin, and because he still needs to grow. Protein. Sugar. Carbohydrates. No fiber—he needs to keep it *in*.

He rolls around in bed.

He watches out the window.

He writes a letter to Claire.

He destroys the letter.

He sits at the hotel desk for six hours, drawing on the complimentary hotel stationery, anything he can remember.

He draws the nurse who carried him to the theatre.

He draws her kissing the man, her friend.

He draws a mask that watched them.

He draws a pig.

He draws a Japanese soldier using his foot to trigger his rifle.

He draws Mickey Mouse erasing himself.

He draws Fat Man scowling.

He draws Claire.

He draws Peter.

He draws naked breasts. Several pairs of different sizes.

He tears up his drawings and throws them out the window, where they fall like the snow.

He tries to masturbate and fails, looking out the window at the girls that pass, all bundled up for warmth. The eroticism of a scarf. The sexiness of thick socks.

Fat Man comes home with his exhausted wife in a wheelchair—they will be moved to a suite on the ground floor. He also has a baby. The baby is normal. She is wrapped in many layers of blankets, wearing a yellow hat. She has big eyes like marbles. Fat Man insists she is beautiful.

Fat Man says, "I have a daughter! A healthy, lovely daughter!"

Fat Man says, "You have a cousin!"

He offers Little Boy the baby. Little Boy will not hold the baby.

Instead Little Boy dotes on Rosie, who glows from lack of sleep and the layer of sweat and grime that builds on her as she goes days without bathing. He brings her glasses of water.

He watches her breastfeed. He sits and pretends to draw, or read one of the books Fat Man got him, facing perpendicular to her wheelchair or the bed, so that he can keep her in the corner of his eye. She is too tired for modesty.

Every morning Little Boy asks what is the baby's name.

Fat Man says, "I don't know."

"What about Rosie Jr.?" asks Little Boy.

"That's stupid," says Rosie, breastfeeding.

Little Boy looks at her a little too long.

She says, "Keep your eyes to yourself."

They drive home together. The baby has been named. It was Little Boy's idea. He was looking down on her in Rosie's arms.

Rosie said, "Would you like to hold the baby?"

This had been offered many times, and each time Little Boy said no.

Today he said yes.

The baby weighed six pounds. Little Boy never asked, but they told him. She felt lighter than that. He was surprised by how thin she was, by the way he could feel her bones through her baby fat.

He said, "She looks like a flower."

"What kind?" said Rosie.

Little Boy brushed a hair from her forehead. "A magnolia."

"Magnolia," said Fat Man. "We'll call her Maggie for short."

Her name is Magnolia. Fat Man and Rosie let Little Boy hold her all the way home, in the back seat. He kisses her head. He lets her clutch his fingers in her little hands. When she messes herself he doesn't complain, but breathes it in.

THE BIG KID

Maggie brings her picture to Cousin Matthew. It's a picture of them playing with a dog. She wants to have a dog of her own.

Maggie says to Cousin Matthew, "I drew it!"

He takes the picture. "Why thank you. It's just what I always wanted. Did you draw this?"

"I told you that," says Maggie, rolling up her shirt in the front, showing her belly.

"It's very beautiful. What's this here?"

"A doggy," says Maggie.

"Who's this?"

"That's you, Cousin Matthew."

"I can tell by the hat. I look good. So who's this pretty little girl in the yellow triangle?"

"Me!" She puts a curl in her mouth to suck the end and chew it.

"I guess you want a dog pretty bad." Matthew knocks his hat skewed. "I bet we can get you one if you're good."

He touches her tummy. She pushes it against his finger the

way it makes him laugh. He laughs for her the way she wants him to, squinting his eyes all squinty. She laughs back the way he likes her to. They go back and forth like that for a while, getting louder and louder, until she squats down and balls up the laugh in her tummy. Then she jumps straight up, rattling her knees, and laughs as big as a pirate.

"Jeez, you win, as always."

"As always," repeats Maggie. "As always, as always."

"As always, as always," she sings. "AS ALWAYS AS ALWAYS."

As always there's somebody new coming down the road to stay at their hotel. As always, nobody told Maggie new guests were coming. As always, they assume she'll be okay to share the grass and the houses. There won't be any kids or if there are then she won't like them. If they have to fight it will be her fault, especially if she wins, AS ALWAYS.

The car stops close to the middle of the hotel grounds, near the kitchen. A big family piles out, which is not as always, but different. There's a mom and a dad, and four kids get out of the back. The kids run around all over the place like little hellions. The dad has to threaten them a lot to make them line up single file. It's not clear why they've got to line up that way. The dad takes a fifth kid out of the front seat. The fifth kid wiggles his legs a little like he wants to be let down. His dad holds him up though, rubbing his back, and the kid has his arms wrapped around the dad's neck like a tight scarf. The kid looks wrong. Maggie can't see why but she can tell she doesn't like that kid. The other four seem okay. They watch their dad march the fifth kid into the cabin, where the mom is waiting with the door open. It's like they're the fifth kid's audience. After the dad goes into the cabin the four kids in the line follow him, each getting a kiss from their mom as they go through the door. It all seems like a lot of work.

Maggie goes to the kitchen cabin. Her dad is making pancakes for lunch because she asked him to. She asks him if he knows what.

He says, "No, what?"

"There's a new family."

"Did we leave the door unlocked for them?"

She says they did. She asks, "What's wrong with the fifth kid?"

"I don't know, Maggie. I'll find out if you promise not to be a rude little creature and ask." He thinks a moment. "The fifth kid, did it look like he was the oldest?"

"Don't think so," says Maggie. "His dad carried him in. He was kind of big though."

Maggie's dad tells her to play outside until lunch time. She does. Cousin Matthew finds her and they play together; hide and seek. He always likes to be the hider, so, as always, she is the seeker, which is okay because she likes to seek. She is good at finding her cousin. He always leaves a clue for her. He'll hide everything except his hat and let it peek out over the well, or whatever he's hiding behind, like if he's inside the car he'll let his hat show through the car window, but it's not always his hat. Sometimes he'll cough or sneeze. It has to be a realistic clue— something that really might happen—or she'll refuse to find him and he'll have to stay hidden all day.

She finds him hiding in an outhouse. This time the clue is that he leaves his shoes hanging by their laces on the doorknob. "Found me. Just like a bloodhound."

The lunch bell rings. Cousin Matthew says he'll eat them all if he gets there first. Maggie hits him and laughs when he pouts like she hurt his feelings. She pretends not to believe him about his feelings. One time she made him cry and her mom wouldn't let her have dinner. Her dad kept saying he was fine, he needed to toughen up, it wasn't her fault Cousin Matthew took everything so damn serious. Her mom said she had to learn sensitivity. So it makes her mad when Cousin Matthew acts hurt because she knows it could put her in trouble. Cousin Matthew says, "You shouldn't hit your cousin." She wants to tell him not to take it so damn serious.

Everybody eats together.

Cousin Matthew says, "Magnolia has to sit with her mother today."

Her mom asks was she mean to Cousin Matthew. Maggie says they played hide and seek. She says, "Cousin Matthew is tired, and sore I found him hiding in the outhouse."

"Gross, Cousin Matthew," says Rosie. She wrinkles up her face and sticks out her tongue. He fakes a smile the same way he fakes being upset. The only problem with Cousin Matthew is he's such a faker.

Rosie puts blueberries and strawberry circles and raspberries on Maggie's pancakes, with a little powdered sugar. The berry juices together make a kind of light syrup.

The new family's mom says it's nice to see Maggie's dad again, and her mom. She says, "This hotel has turned out very well. You would never know it used to be a prison."

"Thank you Francine," says Maggie's mom, who says she doesn't like to think about the prison anymore—"not since I had Maggie."

The new dad says, "What a pretty little girl you've got, too."

"Thank you," says Maggie, the way that she's been taught. She does a big smile.

The grownups say about how pretty the hotel is and how the cabins don't seem like what they were, and they say about how hard it was to deal with the mud, and her mom recommends the museum her dad keeps. They ask what kind of museum. "In honor of the prisoners," says Rosie.

Maggie's mother also says about the international library. She says about knowing four languages and how it can bring anyone peace, and the world. Her voice lights up the way it does when she says about these things.

"How many languages do you know?" asks her mom.

"Rather less than four," says the new mom. "I know French and English. Albert only speaks the one."

"People learn very quickly here. We can improve your English, Francine, and Albert can learn his first words. Unless you'd rather expand into German."

"They might not want to at all," says Maggie's dad. "Not everybody wants to."

"I know French, English, German, Spanish, and Italian," says Maggie.

Her dad says, "You know French and English, darling. You only know zoo animals and numbers in the other three."

Her mom says, "Her generation will be the first to keep the peace."

Her dad says, "I heard from our little scout here you had five children. Where's the fifth? Not that these four aren't cute enough."

Maggie doesn't think they're very cute, but nobody asked her. She pulls something out of her nose. It's green, but with a little blood. She rolls it between her fingers until the stickiness dries up and what's left is hard, a duller green, sort of gray, like a rock.

"We have six, actually," says Francine.

"Our two eldest like to eat alone," says Albert. He shrugs as if to say, What can I do?

Francine tells the rest to introduce themselves. Rosie catches Maggie pinching her snot and stretching her fingers apart, making the little snot rock stretch to fill the gap. Her mom takes it roughly with a napkin. She balls up the napkin tight and slaps Maggie's hand. "None of your nonsense. Not tonight. I don't have the energy."

Maggie says she never has the energy. She says to please let her eat her pancakes in peace for once. Her dad stares her down. She eats her pancakes in silence, which is like peace, but not as good.

After the meal Maggie is watching her dad and Cousin Matthew do the dishes. Albert, the new dad, comes up and murmurs, "Did those two police come to see you?"

"Years ago," says her dad, after a long pause. "Did they come to you too?"

"A month back," says Albert. "I thought they were done with us."

"Mm," says her dad. He wipes his forehead, leaving a puff of soap bubbles.

What if her dad's hair was all bubbles? That would be wild.

At night her dad likes to sit outside with Albert and drink beers once it gets late and the crickets are practicing choir. Cousin Matthew sits with them too, though he doesn't talk much and they don't seem to want him. He drinks milk, because it makes your bones strong and it makes a body grow. Sometimes he holds Maggie on his lap. Sometimes she sits on her dad's lap. They barely seem to notice when she climbs up. She plays with her dad's neck fat, slapping it so it wiggles while he talks, and his voice wiggles too, like a jump rope if you wave one end around but not the other.

One night her dad asks Albert what he's doing there if they've already got six kids. Albert leans back and pats his gut. "We're trying for a seventh. Seven dwarfs for my princess, or something like that."

"Seven," says Maggie's dad. "Wow. Just these two have kept me busy."

Cousin Matthew laughs weird.

Albert says, "You know I couldn't stand the thought of kids. I did everything I could to avoid them. Once I got started, though, I couldn't stop. Francine kept popping them out. It was terrifying, but by the time she was starting to deflate from the last one I wanted another. It was like I was hungry. She wanted another one too. It's destroyed her body, of course. Mine too. I look awful with this beard, I know, but I feel obligated. It hides a little of the bloat. Have you ever grown one?"

"I'm not sure I can," says Maggie's dad.

She slaps his neck fat. It wiggles.

"We're both worn out but she wants one more. To my horror, so do I. We know this place has a reputation. Something in the water, right?"

Another night, late, Maggie counts the beer bottles on the grass. Some are fallen over, some are standing up, it gets confusing. She thinks it has to be eleven or twenty. There's a caterpillar inching up the side of one, a little green guy. She wants to squish him but it makes her dad upset when she hurts a bug. She kicks over the bottle with her foot as if it was an accident.

"I still haven't met your oldest two," says her dad. His talking is a little slurred, which, according to her mom, means he's had enough. "The twins."

"They like to stay inside," says Albert. His talking's slurred too. "They're shy."

"I'm a nice boy," says Maggie's dad. Cousin Matthew snorts. Her dad insists, "I am!"

"They've had it rough," says Albert. "If I bring them out, you have to prepare yourself for it now. You can't laugh at them or get scared. They like meeting new people but they hate when they scare new people."

"Why should I be scared?" says her dad. "Why should a couple kids scare me? Is there something wrong with them?"

"They're beautiful," says Albert, and off he goes.

He comes back with the fifth kid in his arms, waving its legs, arms wrapped around his neck like a scarf.

Francine is following him. "Not now, Albert. Tomorrow. Please, Albert, tomorrow when you're sober and they're more awake."

"If we refuse him we're denying them," says Albert. "I will not deny my sons."

He sets the fifth kid down on his seat. Maggie's dad squeezes her close and puts a hand over her mouth—not for the first time; it means he doesn't trust her not to say something unbelievably rude.

"This is Dorian," says Albert, "and this is Pierrot." He's pointing at the same kid.

Maggie crosses and un-crosses her eyes. The fifth kid blurs and comes clear, splits and recombines. He has two heads joined at their backs just behind their inward-facing ears. These ears look like clay. They are too smooth, only half formed. The heads are turned one quarter away from each other, the faces facing opposite directions. One head's jaw hangs open. The other head keeps its mouth closed. The necks beneath the heads arch away from each other and then back inward, nearly meeting in a long, wide clavicle with two parallel horseshoe-shaped indentations in two open collars—collars raised as if to make a wall between their necks, to keep them from joining as their heads have. There is an egg of open space between their necks, through which Maggie can see part of the moon.

Maggie understands she is looking at two kids.

Their shirt is wide, aqua-green, with uneven shapes hidden beneath it. Down the center of the trunk, a ridge like the leading end of a wedge. An arm comes out on each side. They wear shorts with three legs, their outward facing legs very far from each other. Their middle leg has a gap above its knee where two thinner legs seem to separate like a cleft in the roots of a tree. Further down the leg, a second, smaller shoe hangs off the ankle at an angle, a baby boot, like a white rosebud or a hanging bell, resting limply on the larger, leather shoe. The other feet kick a little, like Maggie when she tries to swim, though more slowly, in coordinated circles.

"They share a little bit of brain," explains Francine, speaking in English, "and some other organs. The doctors wanted to separate them, though the odds weren't good they would live. They said it wasn't worth living like this. I told them all to go to hell."

Maggie nips her father's hand because she wants to talk. He squeezes harder.

"These are the ones you were pregnant with when we left?" he says.

"They developed too quickly. They were born only a little after you left. The doctors were bewildered, though they said there had been a few cases that year. There haven't been any since. They think maybe the Germans," she trails off. "I don't know. But we love them, don't we?" She repeats it in French.

Albert says, "Of course."

Dorian and Pierrot struggle to angle their eyes so they can see Maggie. They each have to gaze sidelong to look dead ahead. It makes her think of lizards. The one on the right closes his mouth. The one on the left says, "Hello."

"Hello," says Maggie's dad. "I'm very pleased to meet you."

"This is Uncle John," says Francine.

"Hello," says the one on the left. He reaches across himself to offer his hand. Maggie's dad leans forward to shake it, finally releasing her mouth.

"Hello," says her dad.

Dorian and Pierrot smile, closing their eyes in a way that says they feel happy. Then the one on the right—is he Pierrot?—begins to cry.

"They never feel the same thing at the same time," says Francine. "Something about the brain parts they share. Only one of them ever gets to be happy. More and more often it's Dorian. Pierrot is getting used to it."

Cousin Matthew stands up. He goes for Pierrot's hand. "It's good to meet you," he says. "You remind me of me. Maybe I can be *your* uncle."

"Sure," says Albert. "Uncle Matthew."

Pierrot, holding Cousin Uncle Matthew's hand, rolls his eyes up to look at his face, while Maggie's dad continues to shake Dorian's hand, and Dorian stares back at Maggie's dad. Pierrot smiles. Dorian begins to weep.

"Good for Pierrot," says Cousin Matthew.

"Too bad for Dorian," says Maggie's dad.

Soon the fifth kid is put back to bed. Maggie sees him three more times before the new family leaves. Pierrot never smiles again. Once, he looks very angry. Dorian is delighted.

CHILDREN OF THE ATOM

Picture Hollywood, summer 1956. The spindle palm trees with their leaves all shiver-shivering. All the highway tangles. Here are the beggars and the street performers—guitar, harmonica, kettle drum, saxophone, tap shoes—hats upside-down, weighed down with change and petty cash, sidewalks littered with cardboard fried chicken buckets, popsicle sticks or tongue depressors, chewing gum wrappers, cigarette butts with ash trail smears punctuated by dirt imprints of half a boot's tread, tough guy toothpicks, and a part of somebody's tire. Here's the idling cop car parked up against the curb, right next to that fire hydrant. Maybe he's getting his hair cut at the barber. Here are men and women, young and old, coming out of the barber's, most of them sporting the same seven haircuts, and half the guys with Hawaiian shirts unbuttoned down the top third, curls of chest hair. If someone smokes a marijuana cigarette in an alley, leaning up against a dumpster, what they're saying is leave me alone. If someone stands in that same alley though, just at the edge of the shadows, fluffing her bleached-blonde hair and waving a purple boa, wearing a pink polka-dot skirt with the hemline raised well past the point of modesty, clicking her heels on the pavement—if someone's dressed like this and she blows a bubble of Double-mint, and she lets it pop so it hits her nose, and she sucks that back up in—then what she's saying is don't let me spend the night alone. Here's the newcomer who has to learn to tell the dif-ference, standing center-sidewalk, one hand on his gut, the other checking the umpteenth time for his wallet. His wife is at a shop window looking at exotic belts. His brother, his nephew, his son, Little Boy, is standing beside him, his daughter's hand—Mag-gie's—squeezed tight.

Little Boy says, "Don't you dare leave my sight, Magnolia. Don't you dare leave my sight."

Fat Man says, "We should find somewhere to eat."

Rosie says she isn't hungry yet. She says they can wait to find somewhere nice.

"Do you know how long it's been since I had a real American burger?" says Fat Man. Which is, implicitly, a lie—fact is he's never had one. He adjusts his shirt.

Rosie says, "You like them?"

"What's not to like?"

"Where do you want to go then?" says Rosie.

"What about there?" He points down another street, the word "BURGER" glowing red, though the rest of the sign is obscured. "Something-Burger," he says. "Sounds great. It's always the little places that blow your socks off with a sandwich." He totters in the Something-Burger's direction. "Come on," he says. "I'm starved."

A streetcar rolls by briskly. It is in fine condition. Everyone in-side is alive. He remembers the ones that he saw in Japan, rolled over on their sides, warped and impacted, full of the dead. This one makes a cheerful chiming. A boy hangs off the back.

It's been a month since Francine and Albert came to Hotel Gurs. Two weeks after they left for home, Francine called a near-by restaurant, offering the waiter who answered a small fortune if he would have Fat Man on the line the same time the next day. The hotel itself does not, of course, have phone service. Fat Man dreaded the call until it came. It was almost a relief to hear Francine's voice, even as she delivered terrible news.

"The fake cops, Bruce and Rousseau, came with real cops," she said. "They arrested Albert. Took him away. I've got no idea what the charges are, they wouldn't explain it. They said they'd been watching us—that coming to see us again when they did, before we came down to the hotel, was a feint. They wanted to see what we'd do. They said we went running to you. They called you the mastermind. I don't understand. They said it wasn't about the Blanc woman anymore, it's much more than that now. I think they'll come for you next. They want to bring you in, I think. I think they'll come very soon." She cried into the phone. It made the line crackle. "He'll probably look guilty if you run but at least I know he's been a scum. You were always kind to me. I think you should leave the country for a while, until we can figure out what's happening."

"Shh," said Fat Man. "Shh-shh-sh. Thank you for calling me. We'll set all this right, I'm sure of it. We'll do as you say. We'll run. I won't tell you where. That would just make things look worse than they already do." He calmed and soothed her while the waiter, hoping to receive his money from the gentleman rather than through the post, listened with wide eyes and prying ears. Fat Man shot him several contemptuous glances, to which the waiter was either oblivious or inured.

He drove home planning to let himself be arrested. This was, after all, what he had wanted, even planned. They would put him away for as long as the law said he deserved for as close as they could come to the number of killings he had in some sense committed. But now that the ax was falling he feared for his neck. When he came in the door of his cabin and saw Rosie playing marbles with their daughter he said, "We're going to Hollywood!" big and happy as he could, waving his arms in wild circles.

When she asked him why he said they deserved it. When she asked him why again he said he wanted to see where magic was made. He had grown to love the cinema more than almost anything. His interests had expanded from films featuring the Hanway twins to a series of noirs, detective films, and gangster flicks. Rosie called them his tough-guy pictures. There was something to it. Fat Man had skipped adolescence for a cushy adulthood. He had never set a proper goal, never known for sure what he wanted, had always been soft, and was now at his softest: grotesquely overweight, a doting father, and an exceedingly grateful husband. Some nights he would sit up late thanking Rosie for loving him, wrapping himself around her, spooning her insistently. She found it alternately adorable and infuriating.

After dinner, Rosie asked him if it was the police that made him want to go to Hollywood. He asked her what made her think that. She told him a letter had come for him while he was gone. The envelope was a large brown one of the sort used to mail documents. It was heavy. There must have been a lot of paper inside. There was no return address.

"Open it," she said.

He made to leave with the letter.

"Open it in front of me."

Inside, a thick sheaf of papers bound by a straining yellow rubber band. He broke the rubber band with a yank of his hooked fingers. The papers were typewritten, the words crowding each other, not even single-spaced but overlapping slightly, so that p's, y's, and g's intersected uppercase letters, so that l's impaled what was above them. He understood, after some study, that these were names: the names of women. He flipped through the pages. There were so many, all with dates appended, going back and back, from now to several years before Fat Man and Little Boy even came to France.

"You never talk about your life before meeting me," said Rosie.

"There's nothing worth saying," said Fat Man.

"You never told me why they won't leave you alone."

"They're confused."

"Who are all these women?"

"Dead women."

"We'll go to California. Whatever you've done, I want you safe."

Tickets were bought. They stayed in a Paris hotel under false names while they waited for their flight. They told the staff they would be visiting Rosie's family. Maggie was promised she would see where the movies were made, and Little Boy understood without being told that they would be fugitives for a while. Fat Man took Rosie out for dinner. They had the duck.

She asked him, "Did you do what they say you did?"

"No, not what they say."

She asked him why he looked so guilty all the time.

He said he didn't look guilty. He said he looked afraid.

"What are you afraid of?"

"Losing you."

Now the rest of the Something-Burger sign comes into view. It reads ATOMIC BURGER, the glowing red text emblazoned on a neon-green rocket, launching from the joint at an angle. The windows are painted with cartoon mushroom clouds rising from cartoon burgers and shakes, low prices markered in yellow at landfall. Outside the door there's a brightly-colored toy plane the kids can ride in for a quarter. A little girl sits in the cockpit, pretending to machine-gun her brother.

"Christ," says Fat Man. He turns to Little Boy, still holding Maggie's hand, and Rosie, who adjusts her hat to better block the sun.

"What?" she says. "You don't want to go anymore?"

"Well it's in pretty bad taste, don't you think?"

"What is?"

He waves at the sign. "Atomic Burger. Why not just call it 'We killed several hundred thousand innocent Japanese Burger'?"

"I guess," says Rosie, still adjusting the brim of her hat. "I mean, I can tell you exactly why you wouldn't do that, but I see your point. But I don't think they mean it that way. It's about the future."

"The future," says Fat Man, shaking his head.

She sighs. "Look, we can go somewhere else, you're the one who said he's starving."

But Fat Man feels a pull. He turns to Little Boy for help. Little Boy looks back blankly. "No, no, it's okay. Come on. I'm over-reacting. You know how sensitive I get."

"I suppose," says his wife.

They go to Atomic Burger. The little girl in the toy plane machine-guns them as they go through the double doors. A bell rings; Fat Man jumps. A waitress tells them to sit anywhere they like. Her paper hat is shaped and painted like a boat—a destroyer. She wears a sort of futuristic stewardess uniform, a long blue skirt and short-sleeved jacket with neon green fringe, the rocket logo replicated on her right breast—a name tag: Charlene. All that and a pair of yellow vinyl cowboy boots. Rosie tugs him gently by his elbow to a booth. Little Boy and Maggie sit on one side, the grown-ups on the other. The kids kick their feet. Fat Man passes out the menus. The cover is a drawing of a droopy-faced dog piloting the plane outside, wearing flight goggles and a helmet. A small pink paper advertisement disguised as a coupon but offering no discount falls out of the menus when they open, inviting the reader to a used car lot five miles away, where the deals are wild and crazy and the cars all look new.

Fat Man presses his hand to his gut and adjusts it. "Smells good in here," he says.

Grease and salt, fried potatoes, grill sizzle. The place is full of brat kids picking their noses, shouting at their parents, speaking over each other, ordering the chicken tenders, chewing gum long past the point of its flavor's exhaustion, tugging at the waitresses' skirts, demanding attention. They wipe their snot off underneath the tables in full view of their parents, who are too harried to stop them, or alternately do not care. One bounces a little blue ball off the ground, or the window, or the table, and back into his hand. Two of them, brother and sister, run through the joint laughing like fools, taking turns chasing. A waitress asks them to go to their parents. They say they haven't got any. The brother, meanwhile, puts his gum in sister's blonde frizz.

There is a pretty half-Asian waitress with a sullen expression clearing a table with a ketchup handprint on it. There is a dark birthmark on her calf the shape of an amoeba. She wipes away the red handprint. She drops the sodden towel on her cart. She rights the fallen salt shaker. She scrapes the salt off the edge of the table into a cupped hand, and shakes this onto a plate on the cart. She licks her thumb's end. She goes into the kitchen, walking in this closed-off way, knees rubbing together under the skirt. She does not feel Fat Man's eyes. Little Boy doesn't notice.

Rosie asks the kids what they're having. Little Boy wants the Double Nuclear Burger with Cheese. He says Maggie would like the Nuked Cheese Sammich best, please. Maggie nods—that sounds pretty good. Fat Man can't decide between the Atom

Burger (basic model, bacon optional) and The Burger of the Future (onion rings, peppercorn mayo). There is also the one with the mushrooms. Fat Man can't remember how he feels about mushrooms. Rosie rarely buys them, but that only suggests that *she* doesn't like them.

The air conditioning unit runs loud, seeming to beat against itself. But it's still so damned hot. The waitress Charlene comes and asks them for their order, chewing on her pen's cap. Fat Man decides on The Burger of the Future. Rosie asks for a salad. She's told there aren't any salads. She asks for the chicken; she's told there aren't any chickens, unless she wants the chicken tenders, but those are more for kids—very small, shaped like airplanes, sort of silly. The breading has a lot of sugar in it. Okay she'll have the burger then.

"Which one?"

"The basic one."

"You want cheese, ma'am?"

"Why not?"

Little Boy orders for himself and Maggie. The waitress gives them crayons from a crayon box she carries. They draw on the blank white undersides of their paper placemats. She does a picture of Dorian and Pierrot, which is all she's drawn since she met them. Rosie says it's just a way of processing her feelings. She says Maggie is a deeply feeling girl. The brothers always look like they're in pain the way she draws them. They seem to try to push each other away, their heads tilted as if pulling, and one of them is always crying, though it changes which is which. The only detail that ever looks quite right is the egg-shaped gap between their necks, inside which gap she always draws a little moon, just as she saw it then. The rest is sort of a mess.

Fat Man watches the salt and pepper shakers like it's the only way he can keep them from talking.

Someone else comes in. A couple teenagers. The girl is pretty. The bell rings again. Charlene tells them to sit where they like. She'll be with them shortly.

There's a pain in Fat Man's gut that won't go away, though he knows what he can do about it. There's a gun there, Masumi's— empty, cold, and hard. He's been wearing it taped up in his own folds to hide it from his family, who use his pockets freely, who wipe their snot on his pants, who make him carry things for them, but who don't touch him otherwise now. He used medical tape—the kind that sticks to skin, secreted in the line that bisects his stomach like a sideways ass, wrapping bandages around the point of division. It makes him walk a little funny but discomfort suits a man of his girth. It seems right that he should waddle, that he should rest a hand on his gut as if to hold something in place, seeming now to suffer an ulcer, seeming now to adjust a hopeless girdle. When Fat Man left the country he couldn't bear to leave the gun. While he taped and bandaged it up inside himself, Rosie knocked on the bathroom door, asked him what in hell he was doing that was taking so long. He said it was a number two. She said to hurry it up then. He said, "You can't hurry genius."

Now the kids are asking for more paper. Rosie takes some from the notebook she keeps in her purse for this purpose, tearing out three sheets each for Little Boy and Maggie. The kids snatch them from her hands.

Fat Man asks Rosie how it feels being back in the USA. She says she doesn't feel like she's back. "It all seems so new. Some of that is I've never been to the west coast. Some of that is I haven't been back since the war. Some of it is they're a bunch of brats here and I'd like to wail on them a while."

"I could go for some wailing," says Fat Man.

"Or whaling!" shouts Little Boy, making a big fat gut on

himself in the air with his hands. Maggie giggles. Fat Man kicks him underneath the table.

"That was uncalled for," says Little Boy.

"What did you do?" says Rosie.

"Nothing," says Fat Man.

"Nothing," says Little Boy.

Little Boy salts his fries basket. He pours ketchup. He asks Maggie would she like anything on hers. She shakes her head nuh-uh. They knock their feet together sideways underneath the table. The soles of his shoes make a nice cloppy sound against the soles of hers.

He cuts her grilled cheese in half down the diagonal because the kitchen didn't bother and because that's what she likes. He asks her if she wants her crusts. She says yes. Rosie has been teaching her to clean her plate so she can get big and tall. Little Boy doesn't see the urgency in that. All the pretty girls are short.

Maggie scrapes off the scabbed cheese goo where it dripped from the sandwich onto her plate and sucks it off her finger. Little Boy eats his fries. He asks where they'll go for the rest of the day. He asks if they'll see a movie. Rosie says they can see the people who make the movies instead. Fat Man says that they can see a movie if they want. They'll be here for weeks, after all. Little Boy says can they go to the beach. Fat Man says that can wait until tomorrow. Little Boy says can they tour the homes of the stars. Fat Man says they can do that in a few days.

Little Boy says he promised Maggie a tour of the homes of the stars first thing.

Fat Man says he shouldn't promise things he can't deliver.

Maggie is still picking the cheese from her plate.

Little Boy nudges her with his elbow. "I bet you can't eat your sandwich before I eat my hamburger."

She wolfs it down, finishes before everybody, gets cheese on her cheek.

Little Boy napkins it off.

She says, "Can I ride in the plane?"

"I haven't got any quarters," says Fat Man. "It's not so fun anyway."

"I'll get some change if you give me a dollar," says Little Boy. "I can take her outside."

Rosie opens her purse.

Fat Man closes it and says, "I don't want her playing with that kind of toy. They warp young minds. Look at these kids."

He motions at the Hollywood children. One of them has climbed up on a table. The kid wears a cowboy hat and a T-shirt with a sewn-on picture of a bucking bronco. He pretends to shoot with gun-fingers. "Pow pow! Pow! Pow pow pow!" His mother tries to pull him down by the cuff of his pants. She begs him to behave. He stomps on her fingers.

"You want her acting like that?" says Fat Man.

Little Boy says, "You wouldn't be a brat, would you Magnolia."

Maggie shakes her head.

Little Boy says, "Come on, we'll play in it without the quarter. The best part is sitting in the cockpit anyway." He leads her out by the hand. He hoists her up into the cockpit. When he looks in the window he sees Fat Man is looking out at them, watching so closely. Like he doesn't trust Little Boy with his daughter. He ought to. Little Boy knows her best. Little Boy takes care of her all the time. Little Boy knows how to make her laugh.

Little Boy named her, for God's sake. He loves her more than anybody.

He stands behind the plane, hands planted on each wing. There are four fat springs underneath the plane, attaching it to the base, and in their center a hydraulic mechanism to make the plane bounce for a paying customer. Little Boy can tilt and jostle it a little if he puts his back into it. "Now you're shooting them down," says Little Boy. "Fire the machine guns, Magnolia."

"Budda budda budda!" she shouts.

He bounces the plane. "Now they hang left. Swoop with them."

"Eeeeaaaauuurrrrrrhh."

He tilts it left as hard as he can, lifting the right wing, pushing on the left one's end.

"There's so many of them, coming at you from all directions." He pokes her all over with his fingers, makes her giggle, pokes her under her arms, between her ribs, in her tummy, belly button, back of her neck, behind her ears, saying pow pow pow, pow pow pow.

"No, nooo, no, I dodge them."

"You can't dodge them all. Your engines are failing."

"I fix the engines," says Maggie. "I'm a mechanic."

"Japan comes into view!"

"Japan?"

He turns the plane left, twists it to the right, pushes hard to quake it, she's laughing and scared all at once.

"Budda budda budda budda!" she shrieks.

"You only have a short window of opportunity to drop the bomb and win the war."

"Drop the bomb?" says Maggie.

"No, no, not yet. You've got to wait till you're over the target."

Maggie hunkers down. She squeezes the wheel. "I'm ready."

"Not yet," says Little Boy, husky, low in his throat. He wipes sweat from his forehead. "Not yet."

"I'm ready!"

"Give it another second. Be patient. Calm. You only get one chance." His body hums inside. His guts clench and loosen. Stomach burns. The feeling of free fall. Weightless. Turning mid-air like a pinwheel. The moment before impact. Heat. Light. Thunder. White-out. White.

"Now," shouts Little Boy. He sticks his fingers in his mouth and whistles, starting high, then falling by gradations as the bomb falls away. He shouts, "KABLAM!" and simulates a rumbling in his throat and in the wings, jumping with both feet as high as he can and stomping, shaking the plane hard, making Maggie's teeth chatter. She laughs and laughs and laughs. "Now fly away. Go, go, go, before they catch you. Don't let them see your face."

"They'll never catch me."

"You're free!" he says. "You're free!"

He looks back inside and his eyes catch his brother's. Fat Man is pale. He sweats. He turns and says something to Rosie, who quickly scoots out of the booth. Fat Man climbs out and walks, stiff, a little crooked, toward the back, hand sliding along the wall as if for guidance.

A man in an apron exits the restaurant. The bell rings inside. He has a mole on his chin with a long black hair, and his nose is raw and red. He puts his hand on the plane's nose. "You're supposed to pay for that," he says. "You see the quarter slot? That's where you put your money."

"I haven't got any money," says Little Boy.

"Then I'm taking her out." The man in the apron lifts her from the cockpit by her arms. "Go find your parents and ask 'em for quarters if you wanna play."

"Take your fucking hands off my cousin," says Little Boy, "or I'll tear your balls out with my teeth."

The guy sets down Maggie, who bites her lip and grinds the toe of her shoe into the pavement. She might cry. Rosie comes out the door. She says, "Is there a reason you're man-handling my daughter?"

The galoot says he works at the restaurant. That's all he's got. He goes back inside. Rosie lifts up her little girl. Little Boy rubs Maggie's back.

"We'll leave as soon as Daddy comes out of the bathroom," says Rosie.

They jaywalk across the street when traffic slows. A homeless man sits on the nearest bench, at the very edge, inviting anybody who wants to sit with him to go ahead. Rosie prefers to stand.

Little Boy says he'll get Fat Man.

The galoot glares at him from the kitchen as he passes.

He knocks on the bathroom door. "Are you okay in there?"

Fat Man says he's fine. "I'll come out soon."

"Rosie wants to go to the hotel."

"My bowels appreciate the update. Why can't you people ever let me use the bathroom in peace?"

Little Boy leaves Atomic Burger. He crosses the street back. Rosie has persuaded the homeless man to leave the bench. She sits there with Maggie, the little girl now very tired, yawning, blinking often, one eyelid lagging the other in a sort of drunken wink. Little Boy asks to hold her. Rosie lets him do it. She adjusts her hat to better block the sun, and looks at her watch, and waits for her husband.

"He'll be along soon," says Little Boy.

"You can't rush genius," she says.

There is a billboard advertising the services of a Madame Masumi, "Consultant to the Stars." Pictured thereon, a beautiful Oriental spirit medium, but without a wooden box or peacock feathers: instead many necklaces of beads in various sizes and colors, many gold and silver bracelets, hair entwined with crow feathers, a small sort of purple turban, someone's idea of a Japanese sorcerer's robe. The faintest suggestion of cleavage. There is a number you can call. Little Boy asks Rosie does she see the billboard.

"It doesn't look like her at all," says Rosie.

Little Boy agrees it can't be her.

Fat Man sits on the toilet, unwrapping the bandage that holds in the gun. It was, he realizes, unnecessary to hide the gun. No one has put a hand in his pocket. Maggie has not wiped snot on his pant leg. Nobody would have felt it. No one's gotten close enough to have the chance. They are farther from his body than he thinks.

The gun has been hurting him. He peels off the medical tape and rolls it into a ball, which he drops in the waste basket. He extracts the gun from his folds. Somehow it's still cool to the touch. He checks the chambers: still empty. He groans as he squeezes his insides, as he cradles the gun in his sticky, pulsing fingers. If someone tries to hurt his family he can scare them away. If someone tries to come for him he can scare them away. If the police come because they've heard who he is, he can scare them away. It's only if he has to fire the gun that he's in trouble. He should be in prison. He should have stayed and let them take him away.

He stands up, rests the gun on the back of the john, peels toilet paper and wraps it all around his hand. He looks in the bowl to see what he's done.

There is a thick, black shit in the shape of a bomb shell. It looks too round and perfect to have come from inside his body. The ends taper smoothly. When he flushes it spins on one end for a long time, like a lazy top, refusing to sink.

He thinks, "There I am."

He thinks, "There I go."

He thinks, "That's me."

He tucks the gun under his belt, the handle sticking out at an angle but invisible beneath his untucked shirt, the hammer like a silver tooth digging into his hip.

Seeing a movie in Hollywood is like going to church. Everyone dresses up. The ushers guide you to a place where you'll feel welcome or at least out of the way. The room swells with talk until the show starts, and then everybody shuts up. The audience's eyes fill up with hope and need while the music blares and then, when the talking starts, they settle in. This one will be like the others. But you've got to respect it. The ritual of the movie is more important than the movie.

It's another Hanway brothers film. This one about a detective looking for a man who killed three girls. It unfolds like a slow-motion chase scene. The audience sees the killer shoot someone who is sobbing off screen. That somebody shrieks and abruptly stops crying. The killer handles several pieces of evidence that will give him away. Detective Jack Miller—the Hanway brothers, Able and Baker—comes onto the scene a moment later, handles the same evidence, deduces the location of the killer, and follows him to a casino, where the crook is gambling, until he leaves for the hotel bar, and then the detective comes to the casino, and asks after the crook, and deduces the crook is headed for the hotel bar, where the crook drinks a martini. The crook drinks a little while and then leaves out the back way, leaving several clues, which the detective draws together so that he finds out where the crook lives, and he goes there, only to find the crook has already emptied the place, and just left for the coast. The detective follows, meeting a beautiful woman on the way. The beautiful woman gets kidnapped by the crook just as the detective is catching up to him. Then there's an actual chase scene through town, the crook in a taxi, the detective in a borrowed police car, over a bridge, across a river, into the back streets, the crook wiping sweat from his brow, the dame taunting him. He'll never make it, Detective Jack Miller is hot on his tail. He should turn himself in. What did he kill those girls for anyway, didn't he know he'd be caught? He has to be caught, justice demands it. Just as the detective is pulling up right behind him, bumper to bumper, the crook swerves the wrong way and wraps his car around a tree. The detective cries as he pulls the dame's limp body from the back of the car, her hair blowing in the wind, the car burning behind them, the fire climbing the tree, making the whole thing burn, palm leaves and all. But it turns out the dame is fine. She's alive. Everything is fine. They kiss. Which brother is she kissing? Is it Able? Is it Baker?

Fat Man holds his wife's hand. Rosie rests her head on his shoulder. Maggie and Little Boy whisper all the way through, Maggie struggling with the plot, Little Boy pretending similar confusion.

The house lights come up, star-shaped glowing glows. Everyone leaves, families holding hands to keep from getting separated in the crowd. Fat Man realizes when they are all gone that he is still there, with his family, who are waiting for him to let go of the arm rests and breathe again.

His wife whispers in his ear. He doesn't know what. Little Boy and Maggie stand at a distance, holding hands.

In the hotel, Fat Man hides the gun behind their toilet. He'll get it back next morning.

He dreams of handcuffs squeezing off his hands.

He dreams of the electric chair.

He dreams of wrapping his car around a tree.

He dreams of what it's like to explode.

They go shopping. The store is three stories high. Escalators. Rosie directs Fat Man and the children to the third floor. Sunglasses for everyone. A pair shaped like stars for Maggie. Cheap-looking, costly, plastic yellow frames. A blocky pair of squares for Little Boy, green frames, almost too big for his head, though they do veil the weird bulge of his eyes. Blue and pink for Fat Man and Rosie, in that order, normal shapes. They need Coppertone sunscreen, the very newest in skin-protecting technology. They are a fair-skinned family. The little girl on the bottle looks coyly over her shoulder as the dog pulls down her swimsuit bottoms.

Fat Man notices the children have disappeared.

"They're playing hide and seek again," says Rosie. "Go find them before they get kidnapped."

Fat Man stumbles through the store, feeling drunk. There's so much merchandise. He turns a corner, confronts a wall of bags and luggage: umbrella bags, buffalo-bound luggage, fitted bags with clasped lips, luggage like upholstery, tobacco pouches, bags for athletic equipment, purses. He careens right, only to be confronted by a rack of shoes and slippers, laces in various states of undress, tongues hanging out, soft shoes with fur around their mouths and little red bows, shoes with nonfunctioning buckles, and at the aisle's end emerging to a display of lighters, lighters endorsed by various brands and baseball teams, matches too, and tins of lighter fluid, to see them is to plan a barbecue, feel the pieces sliding into place, wonder where they keep the meat.

Down the escalator. Walking against the stairs, going the

wrong way. He's so wide people have to back down and let him exit before they can get back on, rolling their eyes. He nearly collides with a rack of children's scuba gear, and avoiding that finds the lamp aisle: lamps shaped like dogs, lamps shaped like cats, lamps shaped like rearing horses, lamps shaped like bouquets of flowers with a lampshade held above them on an incidental metal rod, lamps with pipe racks for bases, pipe racks loaded with demonstrative pipes and pipe supplies.

He looks for Little Boy and Maggie in cosmetics, gathering uncomfortable glances like flies to flypaper, tucking in his chin, hands in his pockets, no harm meant here. Women can dye anything. They can pencil their eyes. They can paint their skin, and powder, to cover, obscure. He walks out into nylons. They don't like him here any better. Goes to menswear. Finds ties piled like bodies. Finds a thousand argyle shirts, sweaters, vests, socks: dress socks and casual. Crosses the store, into sporting goods. A pile of boxed basketballs, laced or laceless. A pyramid of free weights. Racquets. Fishing rods and tackle. Fisherman hats. Those vests. Those rubber pants. Weird hooks with many snares. They could catch six fish at once. Vast spools of line. And here dog toys. It's enough to make you weep. Chew toys you can't imagine. Jerky for the animals. Biscuits, special cookies, bags of different-pastel-colored tennis balls. For playing catch.

In toys trains, electric or push. Toy guns. Solid metal model planes. Wooden horses. Horse heads on sticks. Plaster mammy pushing baby in stroller. X-ray glasses. Candy cigarettes. Spy decoder rings.

He finds them with the swimwear. Rosie too. She holds shorts like a circus tent up against him to test if they'll fit.

He scolds the children. "Don't you ever run away from me. Don't you ever dare. You could get lost in here. Don't you see you could get lost?"

"We'll need nose plugs," says Rosie. "Do you think that you can find us a four-pack?"

They leave the chiming row of registers loaded down with one full bag of stuff they meant to buy and several more filled with things they never planned on. As they approach the exit Fat Man feels the eyes of two security guards settle on his bulk. One guard fat, one guard small. One guard with a soup-catcher mustache. One guard clean-shaven. One guard with his shirt's buttons aligned in a perfect column. One guard with his buttons all askew. One guard with mirrored sunglasses. A second guard with mirrored sunglasses. As they turn slightly inward to watch the Fat Man's body, as they realign their shoes to point at his shoes, do their faces harden? Do they shift behind the sunglasses? Do their eyes narrow? Do their lips curl in contempt? As did those of the soldiers, as did the police, as did the once police? Do they reach for guns? Do they *have* guns? As Fat Man draws nearer the door, the small guard pulls his sunglasses down the bridge of his nose. He seems to have two pairs of eyes. One pair outraged and the other opaque.

Fat Man says, "Is there something the matter?"

"We've got to search you, sir," says the fat guard. "Men of your girth often hide store items in their clothing, thinking we won't notice. Frankly, sir, you look suspicious."

"Now wait just a minute," says Rosie.

Fat Man hides behind her. He holds up their bags in front of himself. Maggie pulls her mother's skirt.

"My husband hasn't stolen anything. I was with him the whole time we were in there," Rosie says, though this is not true.

"With all due respect, ma'am," says the small guard, "who are you supposed to be that you think we give a damn?"

"Is she somebody famous?" asks the fat one.

The small one shakes his head. He circles Rosie. Fat Man wonders what they'll do with him if they find the gun. What Rosie would think. He's straining to breathe. The artificial coolness of the air is stifling now in a way he never noticed before. He circles Rosie too, careful to keep the thin one on her other side.

"Sir," says the fat one, approaching Fat Man from behind, "it looks suspicious when you try to avoid us. You're upsetting your daughter. Don't make her cry."

Rosie says, "John, maybe you should let them do it so we can go. When they find you're not a thief we can go to their supervisor."

"Don't let them touch me," says Fat Man. He wheezes. "They hate me."

Both guards reach for him from either side of Rosie. He drops the bags, spilling their contents, and pushes out his hands to stop them, to keep them at arm's length.

"How'd your hands get like that?" says the fat guard, taking Fat Man's left hand.

"Is it ink?" says the small guard, who takes the right hand.

Some crackle between all their fingers, which the guards do not seem to feel. The fat one's eyes are still hidden. The small one's eyes are wet and pink as if he's been rubbing them too often.

"It's just how they are," Fat Man says. "Please don't search me. Please let me go. I can't stand to be touched."

If they find his gun they'll arrest him. They'll ask him for ID. He'll only have his passport. They'll track him back to France, make some calls, learn he's a fugitive. They'll extradite him or lock him up here. The gun's surface has warmed, is the same temperature as his body. It is harder than his body, though. If they pat him down they'll feel it. He wants to take it back inside himself, to secret the gun in his folds.

He looks to Little Boy for help. Little Boy, however, is waiting by the door, as if none of this is happening, as if it will quite soon be settled.

Rosie says, "My husband is a good man. He doesn't need to steal anything because he has everything he could want in life. He would never do that. If you search him, I'll assault you both, and pull you down by your ears, and stomp on your heads, and make fools of us all until one of you manages to arrest me." She smiles at them. "Do you want to do that, boys? To fight me and to lock me up? A woman? Here and now?"

They are still holding Fat Man's hands.

She says, "Is that what you want?"

They are squeezing Fat Man's hands. Can't they feel the spark? They long to beat him down, he knows it. But do they know the cause? His crime? No one knows his crime. Not even Little Boy, who still waits at the door. Other customers are leaving the store, walking around this strange confusion of bodies, averting their eyes.

The guards release Fat Man's hands. They look at their own hands—checking for ink stains, for signs of what they've touched.

"That's what I thought," says Rosie. She puts their purchases back in the bags, loads them onto Fat Man, and leads him out by his sleeve.

As his family rounds the corner, as Rosie mutters and smooths their daughter's hair, Fat Man looks over his shoulder. He sees that the fat guard has followed.

The guard had to run to catch up. He is all out of breath; his shirt is coming untucked. His right hand is a fist but there is nothing of his former anger in him. His sunglasses fell off while he was running. His eyes are not unkind.

"I'm sorry," he says. "You dropped this." He opens his fist. There is a small rubber ball, orange, a toy for Little Boy, resting on his pink palm like a pearl in a clam.

Fat Man takes the ball and flings it into the street. It bounces off a taxi's hood into the sun's glare. "That's not mine," he lies. "You've wasted both your time and mine."

Little Boy pours sand over Fat Man, asleep. "Come on Magnolia," he coaxes, whispering. "Help me bury him good."

Rosie, reading, says, "Make sure to leave him air holes."

Little Boy pats a layer down on Fat Man's chest. Maggie practices writing her name in the layer. Little Boy does Fat Man's gut. Maggie starts to build a castle on it, dumping her plastic bucket on the soft apex. The tower crumbles as he exhales a snore.

There are children running on the beach, kicking up jets of sand behind them. There are mothers holding sobbing babies.

Little Boy wants to lie down with his brother. They don't do that anymore. He buries him instead.

There are waves licking the shore. There is driftwood. There are women laying out to tan. There are men rubbing them down with sun lotion. There is the sun. It's quiet here.

Maggie stands with arms hanging limp at her sides, fists dangling at their ends, squinting up into the sky.

"Don't do that," says Little Boy, waving for her attention. "You'll kill your eyes."

The next day, the same beach. Rosie rubs down Fat Man with sun lotion, his skin like sheets beneath her hands. Folds and swirl, give and sway. The beach is mostly empty today. People don't look at the fat man. They don't want to see her rub the oil into him. The children are off playing.

Fat Man says, "It's been a long time since I asked you if I was really what you wanted."

"You always ask me this."

"I'm not always on the lam when I ask you."

Rosie sighs. "Are you my dream boat? The man I always hoped I'd be with someday? No. That was my first husband. He was my soul mate. It didn't make me happy. I've told you all this. I've told you how I begged him not to go to war. I've told you how, when I heard that he was dead, I was as relieved as I was miserable. Sometimes the perfect thing is the wrong thing."

"But do I make you happy?"

"You don't make me happy," says Rosie. "Nobody makes anybody happy. That's not how it works."

"What makes people happy then?"

"Nothing does. They feel about the same from the beginning to the end, regardless of what happens to them and who they meet. We only cause little fluctuations in each other, I think. I have always been mostly unhappy and afraid. Sometimes you give me happy fluctuations. Sometimes sad ones. I'm grateful for both." She squirts a blob of sunscreen on his chest and he rubs it in. "I wouldn't have married you if I hadn't gotten pregnant, I guess. I never thought I could get pregnant, or we wouldn't have done what we did. But I don't regret it either. We have a wonderful daughter."

"I'm going to go float on the water a while," says Fat Man.

"Stand up first," says Rosie. "Let me do your legs."

Fat Man floating on the ocean.

Fat Man in his red-and-white striped circus tent shorts, nose plug, goggles, skin shiny from sunscreen. Arms floating limp beside him. Legs kicking lazy, just enough.

Fat Man staring at the sun. The clear sky seems to waver.

Only the motion of his body on the surface of the water. He bobs and sways.

Were his gun here, if he could bring it along to the beach, he would load it however he could. He would put rocks in the chambers, or snail shells, or pearls.

It's warm here.

He weeps inside his goggles.

It's very warm.

Little Boy sees a Japanese girl in a checkered swimsuit. She lays out on her towel, soaking up sun.

He goes to her.

She is flanked by handsome white men reclining in folding chairs, under matching umbrellas, one in sunglasses, the other without. The one without has his eyes closed. The other one might. Little Boy squats by the girl.

Little Boy says, "Hello, my name is Matthew. Did you know that you're beautiful?"

"Thank you."

"Do people tell you so often? They should."

"They do."

"So you don't care when I say it, because you've gotten used to it already and it doesn't mean anything now."

"I guess so," says the Japanese woman in the checkered swimsuit.

"So what if I said you were amazingly beautiful?" says Little Boy. "What if I said you were the most stunning woman I'd ever seen?"

"Thank you again."

"What if I told you you look like a nurse?"

"I don't know. I'm trying to relax here. How about you go play?"

"Don't you want to kiss him on the cheek?" says one of the handsome men—the one on the left. He pushes his sunglasses down his nose so Little Boy can see how blue his eyes are.

"He's been really nice to you," says the other handsome man, whose eyes are also very blue.

The Japanese girl sighs. "Okay, kid. C'mere."

She sits upright. Her wet breast touches to his stomach. Her lips graze his cheek.

Little Boy blushes deeply. "That was nice."

"Uh oh," says the handsome man on the right.

Fat Man's hand jerks Little Boy's shoulder. "Where is Maggie? Where is your cousin?"

Little Boy cowers. He scans the beach and begins to weep. "I don't know."

"You have one job," says Fat Man. He slaps Little Boy across his cheek. "You have *one* job. You watch your cousin."

"We'll find her, I promise. I'm always the hider. She's no good at hiding."

"She's with your aunt," says Fat Man. "We already found her. You were lucky."

The handsome men say, at the same time, in the same voice, "I don't believe we've had the pleasure."

The Japanese girl in the bathing suit lies down and closes her eyes. Both handsome men extend their hands.

"Able?" says Fat Man. "Baker?"

"Don't leave us hanging," they say, together.

He shakes their hands in both of his. "I may be your biggest fan."

"I've been wondering who it would be," says the one.

"It's so good to finally meet you," says the other.

* * *

"You see what I mean?" says Rosie as they ride in a cab to the Hanway brothers' mansion. "This is a happy fluctuation. It's nice. Your favorite actors, and they're having you over for dinner. It almost makes this whole mess worth it."

Fat Man nods, adjusting the gun he's hidden in his jacket pocket.

The palm trees are ghosts in the street lights, their trunks only partly lit, the weird bushy leaves up top set aglow from beneath, becoming like strange faces. Picture the highways at night, the few cars, their turn signals leaving red ribbon trails of light as they swerve, quiet but for the rush of air around them, the empty exhalation that accompanies the passage of a bridge, a truck, another car speeding—like a low, giant hiss or the sound of the world turning.

"Do I look nice?" says Little Boy. "Do you think the girl in the swimsuit will be there?"

"I wouldn't count on it," says Fat Man. "They must know a lot of girls."

But Little Boy is counting on it.

Squares of light from buildings just off the highway, offices working late, planning the future. Old folks' homes where no one sleeps. Department stores just shutting down.

They come to the gate. Someone buzzes them in. They roll through corridors of vegetation, berry bushes nobody has bothered to harvest—rotted blueberries and raspberries somebody ought to pick, blackened and bloated, ready to burst. A sweet smell of rot comes into the car with the air conditioning. Thick underbrush leering down at the cab from above. Tropical flowers, all cast in different shades of blue by night, cooled, therefore, seeming to whisper to each other, to the passengers as they brush the windows with their petals.

373

One of the brothers—Able or Baker—comes out to meet them, pays for the cab in cash. Class act. He punches in a pass code to unlock the door. "You have to have security these days," he says, "for the freaks." He leads them inside. "There are two floors, both with very high, echo-y ceilings. Our rooms are upstairs. There's a pool out back, and our chef's quarters as well. He was just laying out dinner."

The entryway is lined with trendy art and coatracks, the coatracks hung with other people's hats and jackets. A dog wanders by as they enter the greeting room, a hound, sniffing at the ground as if following some trail.

"What's the doggy's name?" asks Maggie.

"Magnolia's wild for dogs," says Little Boy.

"That one?" says Able, or Baker. "I'm not sure, sweetie. What do you want to call him?"

"Puppy," says Maggie. "Wait. Snuffles."

"Snuffles is good," says Able or Baker.

"Wait! *Rocket*."

"Rocket's good too."

The smell of fish fills the home. There are big, soft chairs, and cigar butts in the ashtrays on the end tables, and lamps shaped like parts of women's bodies. Table lamps like hourglass torsos, tall lamps like long, graceful arms bent to gentle angles, standing on their fingers. Not pornographic—more classical in their impression, refined. Though one alone might be otherwise, collectively they are lovely.

Their guide leads them in following the fish smell down a long hallway with mirror walls and hanging lights overhead. They follow the smell through what seems to be a living room, where there are six full-sized wax statues of the Hanway brothers in various lifelike poses. One pair sitting on a couch together, one of them telling a joke, the other slapping his knee, eyes squeezed shut and mouth opened wide to let out laughter. One pair standing, eyeing each other suspiciously across several feet of empty floor. They are all dressed in fashionable clothes. One of these is dressed like a gangster, the other like a businessman—the difference being largely one of posture and expression, the gangster having also perhaps a certain oily sheen to his skin. They stroke their chins. One pair is dressed like police officers, holding hands.

They seem to study Fat Man, who feels a shiver in his spine, who feels the coldness of the gun tucked in his belt.

"We didn't commission those," says their guide, "but we did accept them. How do you say no to yourself? It wouldn't be healthy, we figured. Bad for the old self-esteem."

"They look very real," says Rosie.

"Well," says their guide, "so do we. Come on—there's someone here tonight that you've just got to meet."

He leads them to the dining room, really more of a hall. At its center a long table draped in white with maybe two dozen chairs around it. There are full place settings at the chairs with silverware and glasses and red cloth napkins and little crystalline dessert bowls, but no plates. Beyond that table there's another, smaller round one that seats eight. It has no tablecloth but does have plates, silverware, long-stemmed wine glasses, water glasses, and three bottles of red wine, two still corked, and two bottles of cola for the children. The plates hold fish filets drowned in an orange cream sauce and surrounded by wedges of lemon and lime.

Masumi's seated at the table, dressed as in the billboard—jewelry and little turban. So are the other Hanway brother and Keiko, the young Japanese girl who Little Boy said looked like a nurse. Keiko is systematically squeezing the juice from every citrus wedge onto her fish, where it pools, a yellow-green watery swirl in the orange sauce. Masumi glances up and if she recognizes tonight's guests she doesn't show it. Maybe her eyes dilate a little. Maybe not. Fat Man looks to Rosie, who shrugs, and to Little Boy, who finds nothing amiss. They sit at the table. Little Boy beside Keiko, Maggie beside Little Boy, Rosie beside Maggie, Fat Man by Rosie, by Able or Baker, by Baker or Able, by Masumi. One of the brothers pours the adults wine, though not for Masumi, who covers her wineglass with her hand when it comes her turn, smiling coyly. Keiko immediately sips hers without allowing her eyes to stray one moment from her work with the wedges of lemon and lime. Little Boy asks her will she open his bottle of Coke.

"You're an adult," says Rosie, who's pouring Maggie's bottle. "You can open your own Coke."

"Actually you can have wine if you want it," says Fat Man.

"He has a condition," explains Rosie.

"Right," says Little Boy, still holding out the Coke for Keiko. "My condition. Can you open it?"

Keiko lays a pulped lime down on a heap of the same on the rim of her plate and takes the Coke from Little Boy. With some effort she opens the bottle, hands it back. He pours it in the glass for himself. A big head foams up to the rim.

"You should tilt the glass," says Baker or Able, helpfully reaching across the table to demonstrate.

"Fish is very good for you," says Able or Baker.

Fat Man says, to Keiko and maybe Masumi, "It's good to meet you. My name's John."

"Keiko," says Keiko.

"Masumi," says Masumi. "We've met."

"Have we?" says Rosie.

"Madame Wakahisa Masumi, consultant to the stars. I'm a changed woman. Sober five years." She indicates the emptiness of the wineglass. Her slightest movement sets off a series of jingles, jangles, and rattles from her jewelry.

"She's a miracle-worker," says Able or Baker. "Beautiful, too."

"She does readings for most of Hollywood," says Baker or Able. "Palmistry, tarot, coffee grounds, astrology, you name it."

"Maybe you should have a reading with her, John," says Able or Baker, elbowing him gently in his side, just missing the gun tucked in his belt, beneath his shirt and jacket. "She'll do you a world of good, I'll tell you what."

"Did you all know each other in a past life?" says Baker or Able.

"I used to live at their hotel," explains Masumi.

"How is your husband?" ventures Rosie.

"He left me," says Masumi.

"Do you still practice your languages?"

"No. Everyone in Hollywood speaks English, more or less."

Fat Man concentrates on his fish.

He imagines for a moment there is a mold growing on the cream sauce, as in the old days. But there is no mold. The fish is very good. He finishes his while the other diners are only getting started. He eats what sauce remains from his plate with a spoon. He eats the citrus fruit as well, right up to their skins. He drinks his wine and pours himself another glass. He drinks this too.

"Whoa there big fella," says Able or Baker. "We can get you more fish." He rings a silver bell. The chef brings more. Fat Man begins to sweat, devouring the food as soon as it's in front of him. Rosie touches his arm. He doesn't look up from the plate.

"Good to see that John still has his healthy appetite," says Masumi, without apparent judgment. "Do you mind if I use your phone?"

"Not at all," says Able or Baker.

"Go right ahead," says Baker, or Able.

She leaves the table, brushing the back of Fat Man's neck with her hip as she goes. It feels like an accident.

"Gone to call a client no doubt," says Able or Baker.

Fat Man thinks otherwise: she's calling the police. He asks Maggie not to pick at her food. Every time she does it makes a scraping sound that he can't bear.

"It's good you like the fish," says Baker or Able, "but save room for dessert."

"It's pie," says Able or Baker. "Chocolate, I think."

Rosie asks what Keiko does for a living. Keiko says at the moment she's a mooch. The Hanway brothers explain they met her in a Japanese restaurant and they're trying to get her discovered. For now they bring her to every meal they have with anybody else and wait for someone to ask if she's an actor, at which point they'll say yes and she'll be discovered. Little Boy asks her is she really Japanese. She says her parents were. He tells her he thinks Japanese women are the most beautiful women in the world.

"What am I supposed to say to that?"

"You don't have to say anything."

Rosie tells him that's rude. The Hanway twins are laughing.

When Masumi comes back to the table she won't meet Fat Man's eyes, which he takes as confirmation that she's called the cops. It would have to take more time than that for tarot, astrology, coffee grounds, or whatever. The United States has extradition with France. He knows because he's checked.

He eats three slices of the chocolate pie though everybody else has only one. Rosie wipes it off his nose, his cheek. She asks him does he feel all right. He says everything will be fine. She asks him does he want to go home. He says it would be rude.

Afterward Able or Baker asks the women if the men might be excused for a brief conversation. Keiko says she wants to go to bed. Masumi says she's got another consultation very shortly.

"Don't worry about us," says Rosie, taking Maggie in her lap. "We can entertain ourselves."

The Hanway brothers lead them back to the room with the wax figurines. They sit down on the couch beside the sitting, laughing wax. Fat Man watches the wax police out the corner of his eye, fidgeting with the gun through his suit jacket's pocket. Little Boy sits cross-legged on the floor.

"So," says Able or Baker.

"Can we ask you something?" says Baker or Able. "Both of you."

"We were wondering, where do your names come from?"

"Matthew?" says Little Boy. "The Bible."

"Mine's the same, I assume," says Fat Man.

"They mean the same thing, more or less," says Little Boy. "Gift of God. Something like that."

Fat Man nods.

"Ours came from bombs," says one of the twins. "I was named after Test Able."

"And me, Test Baker."

"Those were demonstration bombs dropped in the ocean to show reporters what an atom bomb looks like when it explodes," says Able.

"They were us," says Baker.

"I read about you," says Fat Man. "I saw the pictures. I never thought that there could be others like us."

"You're Fat Man," says Able.

"You're Little Boy," says Baker. "We knew the moment we saw you. We felt it."

"Did you feel it?" says Able.

Little Boy says, "What?"

"What was it like?" says Fat Man.

"It was pretty okay," says Baker.

379

"Dandy," says Able. "I was born a little before he was. I knew somehow that there was going to be another one, so I waited through all that, just sort of floating in the water, and then once he was with me we went swimming."

"It took us a little while getting to Hollywood, but boy it was worth it," says Baker. "We just had to get back in the limelight. We couldn't stand the idea of being thought of as just a flash in the pan, as they say."

"I mean how was exploding."

"How *was* it?" says Able. "How *is* it?"

"It's grand," says Baker.

"If you don't mind my French, sir, I'd call it fan-goshdarn-tastic," says Able. "How do you find it?"

Fat Man reels. He wipes the sweat from his head with a sleeve. "You're telling me you've done it since?"

"Done what?" says Little Boy.

"Sure thing," says Baker. "Like clockwork. Every two months."

"Right now we're equidistant, temporally speaking, between two explosions," says Able. "The glow is just starting to fade from our last one, and over the next few weeks the urge will build in us again until it gets to be unbearable."

Little Boy says, "Can I have another Coke?"

"What?" says Able, says Baker, says Fat Man.

"Sure you can, kid," says Able. "You want it now?"

"I can get it for myself," says Little Boy.

"No trouble at all," says Baker. "I'll get it. You want one, Fat Man? Of course you do. I'll make it two."

He leaves the room.

Able says, "How often do you manage? It must be tricky with a family. Where do you do it? We bought a little island. We have a guy who flies us out and leaves us there a couple days. It's in our contract. Contracts. All of 'em."

Fat Man says, "I can't explode."

Little Boy says, "I'm thirsty."

Able laughs and slaps his knee. He looks exactly like the laughing wax beside him. "But you're a bomb. Why, there could be nothing more natural. Have you been trying to explode? Do you feel shy about it or something?"

"No," says Fat Man. "No, no. I never tried to explode. I very specifically try not to."

Able's face starts to look very mildly concerned, which Fat Man can tell is in Able's case really an expression of extreme worry. Able gets up from the couch and goes to Fat Man with his hands outstretched, resembling in posture and attitude the mildly concerned wax police over Fat Man's shoulder. He puts the back of his hand to Fat Man's head. "Oh my, you're burning up. And no wonder."

"Is John sick?"

"You can call him Fat Man with me, Little Boy, and yes, I'm afraid he's quite ill."

Now Test Baker comes back with the Cokes, and this leads to a reiteration of the state of play as Test Able understands it, and the further information that Little Boy doesn't explode either. The entire time, Test Baker is slowly rolling a cold, perspiring Coke bottle back and forth across Fat Man's forehead.

Rosie is searching for Maggie. Little Boy has long insisted that she is a poor hider, which made Rosie confident that if Maggie chose to hide in the twins' labyrinthine mansion then she would be able to find her. So far she has. But with each iteration of the game, her daughter becomes incrementally more adventurous, and Rosie suffers a slightly longer period of mounting panic wherein she believes she will never see her daughter again. Each time she finds her daughter, however, she recognizes the feeling as stupid and sends the girl to hide once more.

The first time Maggie hid beneath the table. Rosie couldn't help saying that it was a stupid place to hide. Maggie looked as if she might cry until Rosie covered her own eyes and started counting again, this time to fifteen instead of ten. Maggie used the extra five Mississippis to hide on the opposite end of the long table. This time Rosie congratulated her on hiding in "Just about the last place I thought of looking." Maggie thrust out her tummy with pride and Rosie started counting again. This next time produced the first instant of mounting terror because Maggie left the room. She was only standing on her toes against the wall beside the frame of the door that led to that room, however, and when Rosie went into the room beginning to think she might cry at having lost her daughter forever, there was Maggie, tickling her mother's butt and shouting "BOO!"

Next Maggie found a bathroom and hid between the tub and pristine toilet. On the wall inside the shower, opposite the shower-head, was a water-damaged painting, once a watercolor, now a blur of gold and purple, red and green, the thick paper wrinkled and flaking. Rosie thought that it was maybe once a sunset.

Next Maggie found a library down the hall. This time Rosie went the wrong way, ending up first in a room containing seven empty birdcages of various sizes, each one's door hanging open. A large white birdcage empty. A small green birdcage empty. A hanging birdcage empty. Water dishes half-full or plain empty, newspapers sodden or fresh, some cages coated with dust, some perhaps freshly abandoned. There was a small white bird with red eyes perched atop the largest cage. It was very much still there. After a full minute of slowly mounting panic, Rosie found her little girl among the books of the twins' library.

Now Rosie doesn't know where Maggie's hiding. She genuinely does not know. She has found what she believes to be the master bedroom. She checks underneath the beds and in the adjoined bathroom, not because she believes Maggie is here—she can't hear her daughter's telltale breathing—but because she wants to see the way the brothers choose to sleep. There are two beds here a dozen feet apart. There is a heavy curtain between them, on runners as in a hospital, which is presently folded, but which might extend so as to divide the room. There are two matching dressers on opposite ends of the room. There is a refrigerator in the bathroom, stocked with beer and cola. There are newspaper clippings taped to the mirror. Some review the brothers' films, though none of their recent work is represented. Some of the clippings are about bombs. Test Able and Test Baker. These clips are faded. Their ink gone gray, paper yellowed.

Above their matching beds, one picture each. The pictures very large, say ten feet by ten. At first she mistakes them for murals. Rather they are photos inflated far beyond their natural dimensions. Savage in their grain and blur and fuzz. In each photo, a mushroom cloud billows. Gray and black in shadow. Brilliant white where light.

One of these above each bed.

Not matching. There are two.

A different one above each bed.

Rosie has never before felt what she would call a premonition. Now there is something in her knees. Her daughter is still missing.

Fat Man paces the room with all the wax statues, trying his damnedest to explain why it's wrong to explode, gesturing wildly with the still-closed soda bottle they were just rolling around on his face. The Hanway twins listen intently. The wax policemen are behind him, holding hands on either side.

"People die," says Fat Man. "Sometimes hundreds of thousands. The land and air are poisoned. People's skin burns. They are reduced to shadows cast on cement walls. You can't control who dies. Anyone dies. Everyone dies. You can't stop it once it's started. You can't explode *enough*. You can only explode."

"That's why you do it where there aren't any people," says Able.

"Really it's no trouble, you can both use our island," says Baker.

"We like to be alone when we do it," says Able.

"But you can go when we're not there," says Baker.

"You're not getting it," says Fat Man. "I don't *want* to explode. I *hate* exploding. Little Boy here won't acknowledge that it's ever even happened once, he hated it so much."

"You can't deny who you are," says Able.

"Deep thought," says Baker.

"Any more than you can deny your skin," says Able.

"Not possible," says Baker.

"You're a bomb," says Able.

"I was a bomb," says Fat Man. "Now I'm a father. I'm a husband. I'm a brother."

"You're a father," says Able. "That's true."

"The kid's cute," says Baker.

"We know it was different for you," says Able.

"There were," Baker pauses, "circumstances."

"A war on," says Able. "People got hurt."

"So did you," says Baker.

"We've got it easy," says Able. "We know that."

"What?" says Little Boy.

Fat Man leers at him with awful violence in his eye.

"But this not-exploding experiment, Fat Man. This thing you're trying," says Able. "Has it made you happy?"

Fat Man contemplates the bottle in his hand. Its contents are warming. Its sweat mingles with his. "Nothing makes anyone happy."

"Who told you that?" says Able.

"You know what makes me happy?" says Baker. "Expressing myself, listening to my body, and giving it whatever it needs."

"Nothing makes anyone happy," says Fat Man. He looks to Little Boy. Asks him, "Isn't that right?"

Little Boy says, "I don't want to talk about it."

Little Boy says, "I don't understand what any of you are talking about."

Little Boy says, "I'm going to go somewhere else."

Fat Man says to Little Boy, "Don't leave me here with them."

But Little Boy is going to leave.

Fat Man slaps Little Boy's face as he's leaving. Little Boy walks right through it, though the impact's awful loud.

The twins look to each other. They approach Fat Man from both sides and rub his shoulders, so there are their wax cop selves behind him and their twin flesh selves before him, the wax selves stern, the flesh selves kind, eyes overflowing with love, misting now with sympathetic tears.

"Hitting him won't make you feel any better," says Able.

"He's your brother," says Baker.

"The only one you've got," says Able.

"He's no brother of mine."

"You know how we learned to be actors?" says Baker.

"You'll laugh," says Able.

They tell him the story of when they first swam to that island shaped like a kidney bean. They tell him how they looked each other in the face and saw nothing. One of them asked the other why he was looking at him that way. The other said he didn't know what he meant. So what was his face all about, then? Well what about *his* face? One brother shoved the other. One brother shouted at him to stop it. One brother shouted back. Fat Man asks them don't they know which one was which. They say that they don't. One brother punched the other. The other brother pushed him to the ground. They were naked. Their knees beat against each other's knees. They slapped each other's faces, and screamed, and wailed, and wept, and rolled around in this way, beating one another. Until they realized their expressions were no longer empty.

"We were emoting," says Able.

"Quite convincingly," says Baker.

"As far as we could tell, we were feeling things about each other," says Able.

Fat Man asks them what in fuck this has to do with him and Little Boy, who feels nothing for him, who doesn't care enough even to hit him back anymore.

Baker says, "I think you need a consultation."

"Madame Masumi?" says Fat Man, incredulous. "She's a hack. She's a *man*, for God's sake. She hasn't had her powers for years."

"Don't worry," says Able. "We'll cover her fee."

Little Boy finds Keiko drinking wine alone in her room. There is a bed, a desk, a small bookshelf. Keiko's dress is draped over the chair that sits at the desk. She's wearing a plush gray robe. She lays on her stomach on the bed, looking at but not reading an open book, the wine glass set down on the floor when it is not in use. She kicks her feet behind her slowly, as if swimming. Little Boy watches her a little while. He appreciates her quiet.

"Hello Matthew," she says, without looking up. "I guess I should have known to lock my door."

"You don't have to worry about me. I'm just a little boy."

"What about your condition?"

"That is my condition." He closes the door behind him. "Have I told you that you're pretty?"

She takes a swallow of the wine. Stops kicking her feet.

Little Boy says, approaching the bed, "Have I told you how you look like a nurse?"

"Will you leave me alone?"

"I'm afraid. My brother slapped me," he says, showing her the red palm mark on his face. "Sometimes he just explodes. Will you hold me?"

"I thought he was your uncle."

"Sometimes I get confused."

They set up in the dining room. Madame Masumi lays down three tarot cards. The first is the tower. The second is justice. The third is the hanged man.

The tower is a tall white tower, more an obelisk, struck by lightning, a golden dome or crown knocked from its top. Its windows lit with flame. A man and woman fall to the crags below the tower.

Justice is a blond man with a golden crown sitting on a golden throne enrobed in golden robes, framed by two stone pillars with a golden shroud hung between them. A golden scale in his left hand. A sword with golden hilt in his right.

The hanged man is a man hanged by his right foot. He has a golden shine around his head. He is hanged from a cross made of two trees. His hands are bound behind his back or held there. He is calm or he is dead.

Fat Man's eyes boggle at the clear message of the cards. "Doom, doom, doom. No great surprise there. How soon will they be here for me? Did you call them?" Whether he believes she called the cops or only wishes, he would like it over. It feels very late. His body's exhausted. His eyes are all bleary. Masumi's long, purple candles are producing an excess of smoke, though little light.

"John, the news is not so grim. This is why it takes training to read the cards. The death card, for instance, means change. The tower card represents the end of a false belief or institution. Your relationship will be tested. Something you believe about yourself or your loved one will be revealed as false."

"Why are we talking about my marriage?" asks Fat Man. "My marriage is fine. What we're supposed to be talking about, what you used to *always* want to talk about, is the fact I'm a bomb."

Madame Masumi places her index finger on the justice card. The long nail is painted eggshell white. "This card tells us that your life and priorities are out of balance. You need to see your loved one for who she is, anew, as if for the first time, and approach her with a fair mind and a cool heart."

"Look," says Fat Man. "I've got your gun." He pulls it out from underneath his shirt and jacket. Its weight is like a small rock in his hand. He nudges it toward Masumi, across the table-top. "Go on. Threaten me like the old days."

"Calm down," says Able.

"Be cool," says Baker.

They both say, "Breathe."

"The hanged man," says Masumi, "is amplifying the justice card. It means you need to meditate, to look at life from a new perspective, a state of calm and contemplation. Only then can you know the right approach to your romantic conundrum."

"I'm giving you permission to shoot me before the cops come," says Fat Man. "You can tell them I gave you permission."

He reaches for Masumi, who flinches. Fat Man lifts her face by the chin; he looks her in the eyes. She's wearing eyelash extensions. Her eyebrows are plucked to arch wisps. Her makeup applied so thickly as to smooth her face away to nothing. She has no lines, no pores. He studies her eyes.

"Go on. For your brother," says Fat Man. "Don't let me explode."

Masumi pushes the gun back across the table.

"This is yours, not mine," she says. "I am a new person. So are you."

She lowers her face and kisses his hand, leaving a red blossom on his knuckle.

She snuffs the candles with her fingers and shuffles all her cards together.

The brothers pay her fee.

She leaves.

The gun is in Fat Man's hands.

"We forgive you," says Able.

"We forgive you," says Baker.

"She forgives you," says Able.

"Forgive yourself," says Baker.

"We'll go to our island tomorrow," says Able.

"You can explode," says Baker.

"Imagine that weight coming up off your chest."

Fat Man tucks the gun in his waistband. His shirttails are out now, the shirt itself rumpled, the suit's pits stained through. His soda is empty.

He says, "There's nothing else to me but weight. No joy or beauty. No real feeling. Only weight."

He says, "I'm taking my family. We're leaving. Thank you for dinner."

Rosie's been searching for Maggie twenty minutes now. There have been no clues. No snorts, no giggles, no breathing, no scurries of small feet. The mounting terror is now only terror. All the hallways look the same. Either she's walking in circles or there are several copies of the same painting hung on several different walls. She calls for Maggie. "It's not a game. I'm not playing!"

Instead John finds Rosie. He looks an awful mess, like some stumbling drunk. She asks him what's happened.

"We're leaving."

"Did they upset you?"

He won't answer.

"Were they strange? I think they're very strange. I think their home is strange."

"Where's Maggie?"

"She's hiding. We were playing. But now I can't find her."

Rosie sees Masumi's lipstick on his hand. He sees her see the lipstick. He wipes it on his shirt. This only leaves a vivid mark like a trail of blood down the left side of his gut.

"Please help me," she says.

They look for Maggie. They open every door. Sometimes finding a room, sometimes a closet, sometimes a bathroom. Always one where there should be another. Where common sense demands an office there is a coat closet hung thickly with coats, but no little girl between them. Some of the coats belong to women. Some belong to very small people, or children.

"Where's Maggie?" says Rosie. "Where's Maggie?"

They come back to the master bedroom. There is a large window overlooking the backyard, which has a swimming pool in the shape of a star. Rosie looks out the window to see if Maggie's crouching somewhere out there, among the flowers and the palm trees and everything else overgrown. She hears the nearest bed sigh behind her as John sits down on it.

"Get back up. Help me find our daughter."

"Rosie? When I ask if you're happy?"

"Our daughter," she reminds him, still searching the yard.

"Why don't you ever ask me if I'm happy?"

She turns to look at him. As he slumps on the bed's end, which sags deeply beneath him, he seems to project the mushroom cloud on the wall from his back as if he were its source.

"Everyone knows you're unhappy, John."

He fidgets with his shirt. Attempts to wipe away Masumi's stain.

"I don't have to ask because I know."

"Is it my looks?"

"Get down on your knees and check beneath the bed for our daughter before I kill you with my bare goddamn hands."

Fat Man slides down from the bed like a deluge of mud and mud. He rocks forward onto his hands and knees and lifts the sheet from the bed. Seeing nothing, he waddles forward, while Rosie watches coolly, from some painful remove: the fat man crawling, the fat man's wife watching the fat man crawling. The trail of crushed carpet he leaves in his wake like parted water now forever parted. He leans forward to peek beneath the bed.

Gasps.

The gun falls from his body like an egg.

As Rosie watches she feels herself leaving her body to watch her body watch the fat man and his gun, and the small white hand that darts out from beneath the bed, and takes the gun, and pulls it underneath.

"Maggie," shouts Rosie, pulled back inside her body with a painful rubber force. "Put it down!"

She drops to her knees, burning them on the carpet, and crawls to look beneath the bed, where she can barely make out anything, but knows as if by feel and smell and sound as well as sight the shape of a sleeping dog and her daughter, who is looking down the barrel of her husband's pretty gun, who is thumbing the trigger. Who is thumbing the trigger.

John says, "It's not loaded."

Maggie, as if to confirm, pushes the trigger back so that it clicks. The dry, hollow, toy-like snap of the gun's silver hammer.

Rosie—thinking, Too late Rosie, your daughter should be dead—takes the gun from Maggie and hurls it at her husband's face. It hits his nose, and maybe breaks it, which makes him bleed. She pulls out her daughter from underneath the bed. She lifts Maggie in her arms, and Maggie's asking what's happened to Daddy. Daddy who is still on all fours, who is bleeding down his face and jowls onto someone else's carpet. Who is looking up with pleading eyes. The sleeping dog under the bed whines.

"If there's one thing I can't abide, it's a weapon," says Rosie. "You know enough languages you ought to be past that."

John sits back on his feet. They'll go numb like that, she thinks.

Rosie says, "Why do you have that?"

"It wasn't loaded." He says, "I am a weapon."

"Did you kill those girls?"

"Not the ones they say. But some others."

"What were you going to do with the gun?"

"I don't know yet what I'll do."

"I'm going back to France. If you can make it back without getting arrested, we can talk through everything there."

Fat Man's tears are diluting his blood, which is creeping down his shirt.

"I'm a bomb."

Maggie's hiding her face in Rosie's neck.

"I don't know what that means, but I don't like it."

"I'm trying to tell you."

"No," says Rosie, pointing at the picture over Able's bed, or Baker's. "That is a bomb. You're a father. Not a very good one."

She heads for the door, begins to close it behind her, and turns to look at him through the crack. He can see Maggie's arm around her mother's neck, but not Maggie. Rosie knows this. She is maybe being cruel. She is waiting for her husband to tell her to wait. She is waiting to find out what she'll do when he begs her. But he doesn't beg. Only weeps and bleeds, though he's losing energy for both. His face is settling into its half-dead, half-miserable default.

"I hate to see you unhappy," she says. So she closes the door.

Fat Man can track her passage through the home, her growing distance, by the sounds of closing doors. As she grows farther away, the sounds grow louder. She may spend the rest of her life slamming doors. She may spend the rest of her life, he thinks, more or less as unhappy as she is now, and maybe always has been. This, this moment now, this feeling, is a fluctuation.

To slither up the bed behind his nurse. To breathe the scent of her neck, of her hair. To wrap his arms around her waist. Or better yet, to slither up the bed and curl and rest against her stomach, to breathe the scent between her breasts, and from her neck and hair. To let his body shiver. Let it tremble. Let the tremble wrack his body. To push the book away. As he now does.

Little Boy asks her if she will hold him like his nurse did. Little Boy asks her does she love him. Little Boy asks her does she know how beautiful she is. Little Boy breathes. Her scent.

Keiko pushes him far enough away, on the bed, so he's at arm's length. He actually rolls over once completely, she pushes him so hard. As she pushes him and as he rolls he catches a glimpse of her bare breast beneath her robe. Keiko slaps his face. "You're not a little boy!" she says. "You're a creep!"

She slaps him again, exactly where Fat Man slapped him, so that he can feel his face begin to bruise, two overlapping bruises, a hand within a hand. She pushes him off the bed. He falls on the floor. Stares up at the ceiling. Keiko peeks over the bed's edge, a tendril of her hair hanging down half the distance between them. Her head recedes.

"Go on," she says. "Fuck off."

He runs.

There is no water in the swimming pool shaped like a star, apart from a small bucket that holds a mop, propped up in the corner of one of the star's points. Fat Man lies on his back at the bottom of the star. He stumbled here through the mansion. He did not see the Hanway twins in his passing, unless they were hiding among their wax doubles in the wax double room. He bled on everything he passed.

His eyes are closed or he is looking at an empty sky.

His body is a shell.

Where is Little Boy's body?

Where is his daughter's body going now?

Where will it be tomorrow?

The Hanway twins are asking him to get out of their pool, please, or their backyard's greenery is rustling in the wind.

Where is Little Boy's body?

His body is a shell.

It was like rubbing your hands together to make them warm.

It was like breathing in and in.

It was like drowning in an empty pool.

It was peaceful.

It was deafening.

It was blinding.

It was being a moon.

It was coming back from the dead.

It was forgetting.

It was perfect, awful memory.

It was like having no brother, and being nobody.

His eyes are closed or he is looking at an empty sky.

It was like being born.

Fat Man is born.

and his body splits beneath his arms, new hands emerging, climbing on new arms beneath the old ones, while new legs thrash out from his hips, and new arms beneath the new arms, and new legs beneath the new legs, climbing

his body jerks with each new growth, pulled this way and that by the force of his force, and his jaw cracks from his screaming, and from his open jaws an arm, and with every inch of that arm's passage it widens, so that the jaws are more and more divided, ripped asunder,

and the arm burns,
and the fire

burns

as his body aching swells, as the fat grows up around his head,
rolls up over his chin and his ears, rolls up over his nose, rolls up
over his eyes, blacking

all he sees,

and closes, his fat, over his head, sealing at the crown, puckered
around the arm that split his jaws,

as there grow new arms between the new arms and new legs, he
is a wad, he is and he is and he is arms and legs and arms and legs
projecting from a swarming trunk of flesh,

like say a tree,

fingers growing from palms, fingers growing from knuckles, fin-
gers growing from fingertips, fingers growing from elbows, fin-
gers growing from knees, fingers growing from armpits, fingers
growing from groin, from ass, from between toes, growing out,
extending hands, hands becoming arms, growing fingers, growing hands, growing arms, thrusting out,

reaching up

in a stream
twisting
together
and from this twisting
spreading,

new arms growing from new arms, hands reaching out, trembling, and new hands reaching out, trembling,

grasping at the air,

and new hands, and new feet lashing, bare feet, how they prickle and they tingle in the wind

until his body is a flower, a disc of arms up on a stem, of arms, the disc reaching all directions, tearing the air, like a skyscraper, like a capsizing ship, like a spotlight

feet for roots, in the star pool, circled feet, toes out-facing

two largest arms at the top, outspread, like antlers, as if to welcome or to warn, and from these two arms many more hanging, and from these many hang many more, and from all these wrists hands, and from all these hands so many fingers, and all these fingers needing

this is what it's like to explode

* * *

The flesh flower sways. It must be one thousand feet tall. It is also like a mushroom cloud. Its stem built from braided arms. The mushroom cap at the top the bloom of the arms—their uncoiling. At the base of the flower, the bloat of Fat Man's greatly expanded torso, dotted with nipples, toenails, and massive, spongy moles, from which sprout huge feet like stone sculptures. These stabilize the structure, though not very well—it leans as if it might fall. It groans as it sways.

Ash falls from it like dander.

Little Boy begins to cry.

Little Boy witnessed the explosion, was searching for his brother when it happened. He now stands at the pool's edge, between Test Able and Test Baker, who also maybe weep behind their hands.

"He was right," says Test Able.

"He shouldn't explode," says Test Baker.

They stumble backward, parting their fingers slowly, and as they better see they leave more quickly—shouting, "Don't you explode either!"

They are back in their house and they've locked the back door. They turn off all the lights, running through the rooms, random windows blinking out, until their house is a silent giant towering over Little Boy just as does his brother, but empty, a jumble of dark stone and dark glass, whereas his brother is full. His brother. Somewhere in that. There must be something left of him.

They have to leave. They will be found. There was a moment where Little Boy didn't know what he would do. This now is the moment he knows what he'll do.

Little Boy goes down into the pool by way of the staircase, following his brother's blood. He is among the roots of his brother, or a root-like tangle, and it writhes against his ankles, pulsing. They are only skin. Though blackened as if charred, the char flexes; there is flesh beneath it. He mounts one of his brother's giant feet. Its char skin is fever hot; burns him through his shoes. The blood flows underneath. He crawls up to the ankle, which is stood on by another massive foot. He hoists himself up on his brother's toe.

Little Boy looks up. There is an opening in the stem of giant braided arms a dozen yards beneath the swell. He'll have to get up there. He comes to the trunk. These arms wide as redwoods are grown with many grasping hands, each one black-palmed, not merely char but really truly black. Each one his brother's. He takes his brother's hands. The hands take hold of Little Boy's feet to support him. They take hold of his calves, his shoulders, beneath his arms. They touch his cheeks. They help him climb.

The wind batters him. A tiny figure up so high. Sweaty hands pulling him by his hair, pushing up from under his feet. Full arms of normal size, but oddly shaped, as if taffy, as if boneless, extend from the trunk, lifting the hands, helping him.

When the wind blows hard, and it whistles like a coming train, and the trunk leans, and he hangs from the side, sick with fear of falling, the hands hold him so tight. The arms wrap around him. They keep him there, tucked against the trunk's unbearable heat, until the wind softens and the explosion rights itself.

Little Boy climbs.

There are hands of all sizes. They grow larger as he nears the top, the bloom, the cap, the unwinding—hands like sofas, hands like Mt. Rushmore. Small ones as well, like baby fists, like strawberries.

* * *

He walks along a finger like a bridge. The tip shaking beneath him, mere feet away from the fingers beneath. He has to leap.

He leaps. The world swirls.

The fingers curl upward to catch him. They squeeze him crushingly tight, and for a moment he is smothered, rolled up in their grip. There is a long instant he thinks they will crush him. Where he thinks that if he's crushed then he deserves it. They don't crush him. They unfurl. He finds himself at their edge; he could roll over one more time and fall to his death.

Instead he crawls along the fingers, down, into the breach.

Where it is black and red. Where the underside of skin is raw. Muscles like curtains. Growths of bone. Here the hands are skeleton claws, cruel bones, their palms as black as ever. The heat is incredible. Little Boy takes off his clothing. He leaves it at the threshold.

He descends into his brother.

Into hot breath. Total darkness.

The bone hands helping him down.

He crawls blind through a narrow, pressing tunnel.

Body caverns.

"Brother!" he calls. Echoes and echoes.

"Brother!"

There is a pulsing sound somewhere beneath.

There is a faint light.

Here the walls trickle blood.

It paints Little Boy red. Paints him sticky. Paints him hot. He pushes his way through a curtain of nerves. They light up where he touches. They sting. Shadows of hands like shadows of a jungle canopy crawl across his body. They warp and waver with his curves and divots. There is a chamber with a thousand lungs hanging from the ceiling, pumping air. Turning blue blood into red. Or some are iron lungs—black, largely inert, humming darkly. The light grows.

He sees, just beneath the flesh, hints of wire: ridges, protrusions, blinking lights, blue.

Now, past a loose internal sphincter, there is a chamber full of flesh sculptures, which resemble a painter on a ladder, but the painter's missing half his body, the half that held the can of paint, and which resemble a man lying on the ground, and the man's skewered with nerves and bone and other, and which resemble bodies flying backward from a force, arms and legs trailing, these suspended by wires, arms and legs dissolving, cold black spheres hanging also amid the bodies, only black spheres, only hanging, and there are bodies resembling a herd of pigs of increasing deformity, and resembling a family at a low dinner table, but the family's all bone, and resembling some hundred pairs of men holding hands, or fused there, which men are grown more thickly from the walls and floor and ceiling as the chamber becomes a passage, and Little Boy must crawl through them, between their legs or arms, and he is slicked with the gore that they seep at their surfaces, and there are more and more of these so that he has to climb through them, and they press on his body.

Until he is in a tight tunnel lined with large, sharp filaments of hair as wide around as his fingers. These make him bleed. His blood mingles with his brother's blood. The light grows more intense though it is narrowed to a distant, blinding point, circumference of a peephole, intensity of the sun. He feels its pinprick heat on his forehead.

"Fat Man!" he shouts. "It's Little Boy!"

"It's your big brother!"

His voice echoes as a voice might in a drum.

He shouts, "I'm coming for you!"

"We have to go!"

The sharp hairs retract into the flesh tunnel almost completely, so they are little studs, and do not pierce him too badly.

He comes to the tight pucker at the tunnel's end. Reaches through, both arms pushing to spread it open. To leverage against the flesh wall on the other side. To push his head through, and his shoulders.

He slides gore-slick through the hole, down the wall's gentle slope, onto the warm floor and into the light, which is cast by some soft blue harsh-glowing crystal, like a heart become quartz. The walls of the cavern—massive, more an amphitheater—are thickly bejeweled with some million open hands, blue in the blue crystal's light, with black palms made bruise-blue by selfsame light. They are here and there shelled with metal—black metal, silver metal—and it hangs from the ceiling, rotating slowly, reflecting the blue crystal's light. Pieces of bomb shell. There, in the far wall, a large hole in the shape of a mouth. Through the hole, Fat Man's face, speckled blue and red and yellow as if with some child's paints.

On closer examination, the hole is not a hole but a cell. The cell is set low in the wall, its floor several feet beneath the floor. Little Boy kneels to better see inside. Though lined with small white teeth, the cell's opening is barred by long arms, which extend from above and below, where lips should be, and clasp each other's hands. Fat Man is pushing his face through the bars. He puts his arm out through another gap. He reaches for his brother. Little Boy reaches for his brother's hand. There is no room for the fat man between the bars. Little Boy is looking for a weapon—a way to break the arms. He takes his brother's hand. The skin is soft like putty.

"I'm here," says Little Boy.

The skin hangs loosely from his brother's arm like lichen. Little Boy perceives, beneath the skin, his brother's bones. His knuckles, wrist, and elbow. Inside the cell, Fat Man is huddled. Though the skin remains, the fat is gone. His stomach skin hangs around his hips like a skirt. The skin of his legs pools at his feet. The fat is gone. The hollows of his face are deep and darkest blue. The hollow lines between his ribs. The dimples in his knees. Only the excess skin suggests what he has been.

Fat Man no more.

Acknowledgments

I wrote this book's first draft as an MFA candidate at New Mexico State University. Tracy Rae Bowling and I were newly married when I started. She was and is my first reader; her love and support make my life and writing possible.

I owe the best parts of this book to my thesis workshop: Tracy, Erin Reardon, Daniel Cameron, Laura Walker, and Craig Holden, who led us.

Thank you to my other writing teachers at NMSU and Butler University: Evan Lavender-Smith, Mark Medoff, Dan Barden, Robert Stapleton, Susan Neville, and Patrick Clauss.

I first had the idea while researching an assignment for Sarah Hagelin's class. That was lucky. Thank you, Dr. Hagelin.

Thank you to everyone who ever taught me anything, beginning with my mother. Thank you to my father and my brothers.

The characters of Masumi and Hideki owe a great deal to Emiko Ohnuki-Tierny's *Kamikaze Diaries: Reflections of Japanese Student Soldiers* and Bernard Millot's *Divine Thunder: The*

Life and Death of Kamikazes. The portion set in France owes much of its tone and color to Rod Kedward's *France and the French*. Horst Rosenthal wrote and drew the Mickey Mouse comic described in "Cathedral." Roxane Gay and Kyle Minor helped me with several little bits of French. Charlie Tangora gave me the Japanese characters for "remains," which was another very lucky thing.

If this book seems polished, professional, or concise, it has everything to do with the efforts of my editor, Buzz Poole, and my copy editor, Lori Shine, who makes the trains run on time. Thank you to them and to the Black Balloon team, including Janna Rademacher, David Bukszpan, Jennifer Abel Kovitz, Arvind Dilawar, Barbara Cleveland Bourland, and those I don't yet know.

Thank you Matt Bell, Patrick deWitt, Robert Lopez, Lindsay Hunter, Blake Butler, Amber Sparks, and again Evan Lavender-Smith, for your good hearts and kind words.

Finally, thank you to the community of readers and writers that has made me feel welcome and wanted over the past five years. If you are reading this now, then you're part of that community, and I'm so glad.

Fat Man and Little Boy is the inaugural recipient of The Horatio Nelson Fiction Prize, an annual award given to a previously-completed manuscript that comes with $5,000 and a Black Balloon Publishing book deal.

This contest has no reading fee and is open to anyone who has previously completed an unpublished original work of fiction of over 50,000 words.

We dedicate this prize to Admiral Lord Horatio Nelson, a man who defied convention at every turn. A one-eyed, one armed lunatic genius who never gave up, he began his military career fully intact, but eventually lost his right eye (Corsica, 1793) and his right arm (the Canary Islands, 1797) in battle. He refused to wear an eye patch over the wound and used it to deliberately ignore a direct order from a superior officer during the Battle of Copenhagen in 1801, coining the phrase "turning a blind eye." When egomaniac and noted short stack Napoleon attempted to use our beloved balloons for evil during the 1798 Battle of Aboukir with a "military balloon corps," Nelson immediately destroyed the approaching objects, putting a permanent stop to the short-lived European militarization of these symbols of wonder. Our hero.

Like Nelson, we believe in relentless creativity and perseverance against all odds.

Are you the next literary Horatio Nelson we're looking for?

Check blackballoonpublishing.com for your chance to enter.